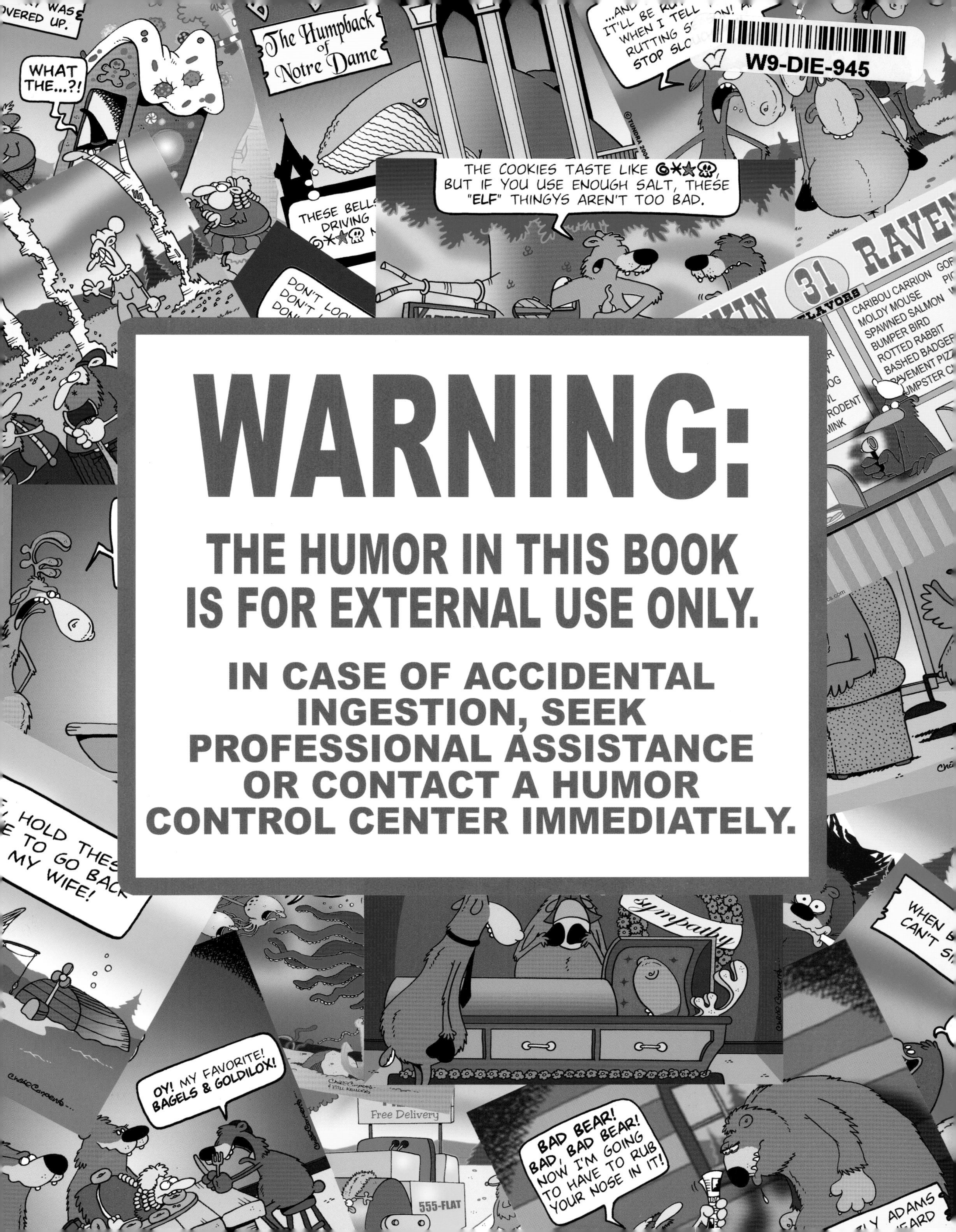
WHAT THE...?!
The Humpback of Notre Dame
THE COOKIES TASTE LIKE @*☆☠, BUT IF YOU USE ENOUGH SALT, THESE "ELF" THINGYS AREN'T TOO BAD.
31 FLAVORS
CARIBOU CARRION
MOLDY MOUSE
SPAWNED SALMON
BUMPER BIRD
ROTTED RABBIT
sympathy
OY! MY FAVORITE! BAGELS & GOLDILOX!
Free Delivery
BAD BEAR! BAD, BAD BEAR! NOW I'M GOING TO HAVE TO RUB YOUR NOSE IN IT!
555-FLAT

WARNING:

THE HUMOR IN THIS BOOK IS FOR EXTERNAL USE ONLY.

IN CASE OF ACCIDENTAL INGESTION, SEEK PROFESSIONAL ASSISTANCE OR CONTACT A HUMOR CONTROL CENTER IMMEDIATELY.

NOTE: **This page left intentionally blank to lessen printing cost.**

CHAD CARPENTER'S

TUNDRA

100% NATURALLY FLAVORED COMICS

OH BOY! I CAN'T WAIT TO GET OUT THERE AND GRAB MYSELF A COUPLE SEALS FOR BREAKFAST! AND **THEN** I'LL...
...ON SECOND THOUGHT, I THINK I'LL JUST LAY IN BED ALL DAY.
BIPOLAR BEAR

HELLO MICHAEL!

MERRY CHRISTMAS!

Chad Carpenter... 2007

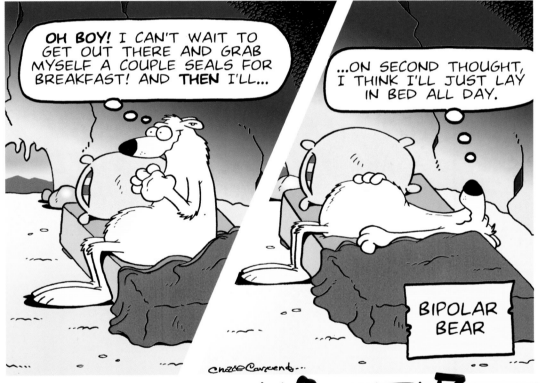

TUNDRA

100% NATURALLY FLAVORED COMICS

PUBLISHED BY

TUNDRA & ASSOCIATES, INC.
PO BOX 871354
WASILLA, ALASKA 99687
TUNDRA@ARCTIC.NET

FOR ADDITIONAL COPIES OF THIS OR OTHER
FINE TUNDRA MERCHANDISE PLEASE VISIT
THE OFFICIAL TUNDRA WEBSITE AT:

www.tundracomics.com

LIBRARY OF CONGRESS CATALOG NUMBER: 2007902420
FIRST PRINTING MAY 2007
ISBN: 978-1-57833-370-7
PRINTED BY EVERBEST PRINTING CO., LTD., CHINA

DEDICATED TO MY BIG BROTHER
DARIN

NOT ONLY FOR THE MANY CARTOON IDEAS
HE HAS PROVIDED FOR THIS VERY BOOK,
BUT ALSO FOR THE HUNDREDS OF OTHERS
HE HAS GIVEN ME OVER THE YEARS.

MOM WAS WRONG.
WE _DO_ HAVE HALF A BRAIN BETWEEN US

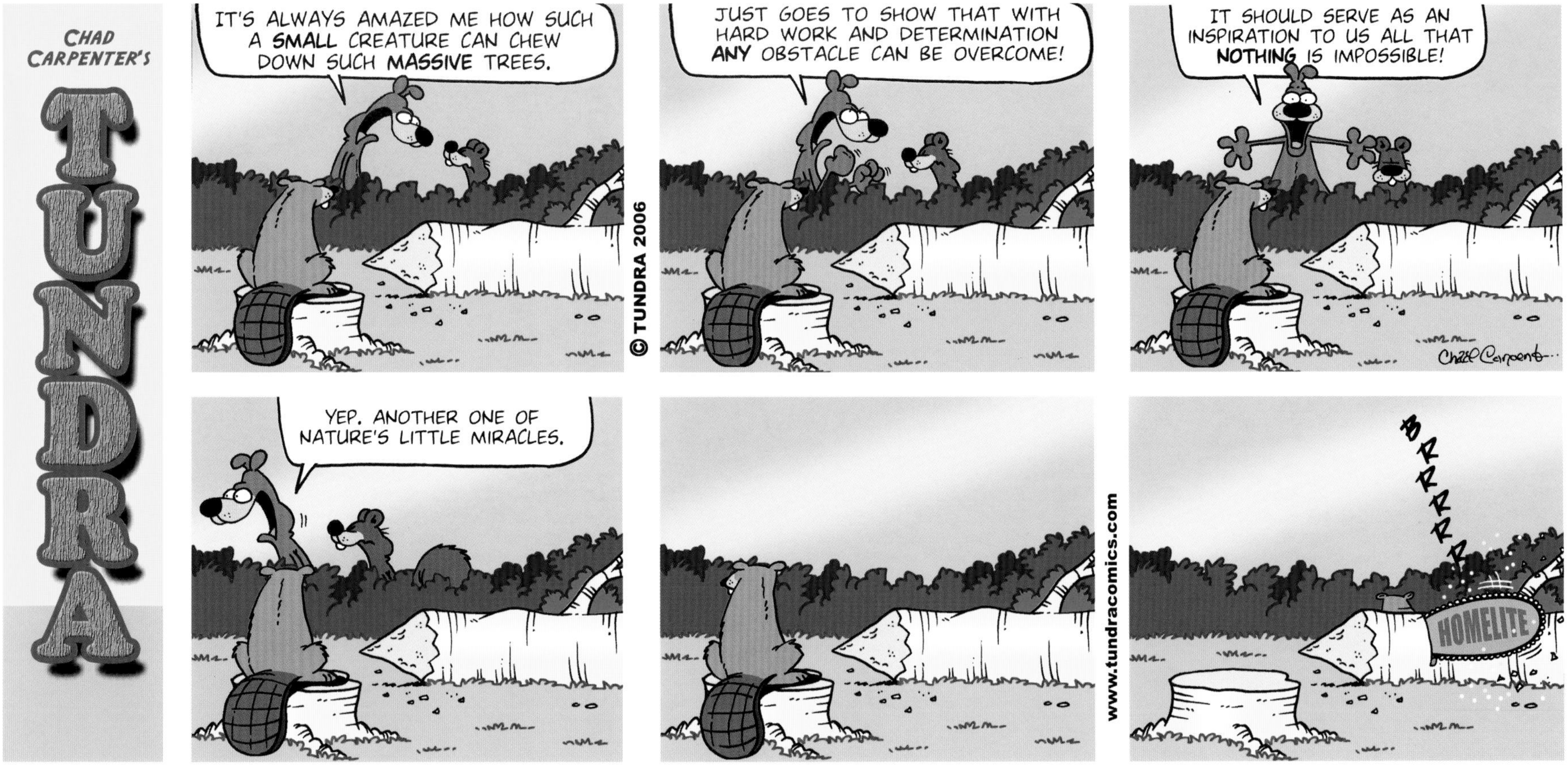
CHAD CARPENTER'S
TUNDRA
IT'S ALWAYS AMAZED ME HOW SUCH A SMALL CREATURE CAN CHEW DOWN SUCH MASSIVE TREES.
JUST GOES TO SHOW THAT WITH HARD WORK AND DETERMINATION ANY OBSTACLE CAN BE OVERCOME!
IT SHOULD SERVE AS AN INSPIRATION TO US ALL THAT NOTHING IS IMPOSSIBLE!
YEP. ANOTHER ONE OF NATURE'S LITTLE MIRACLES.
BRRRRR
HOMELITE
© TUNDRA 2006
www.tundracomics.com

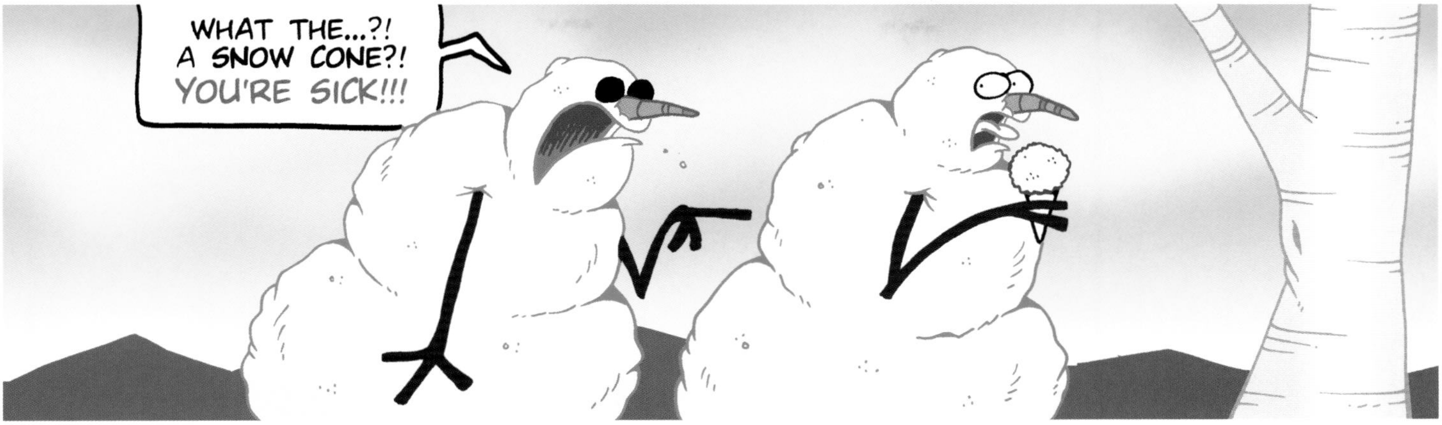
WHAT THE...?! A SNOW CONE?! YOU'RE SICK!!!

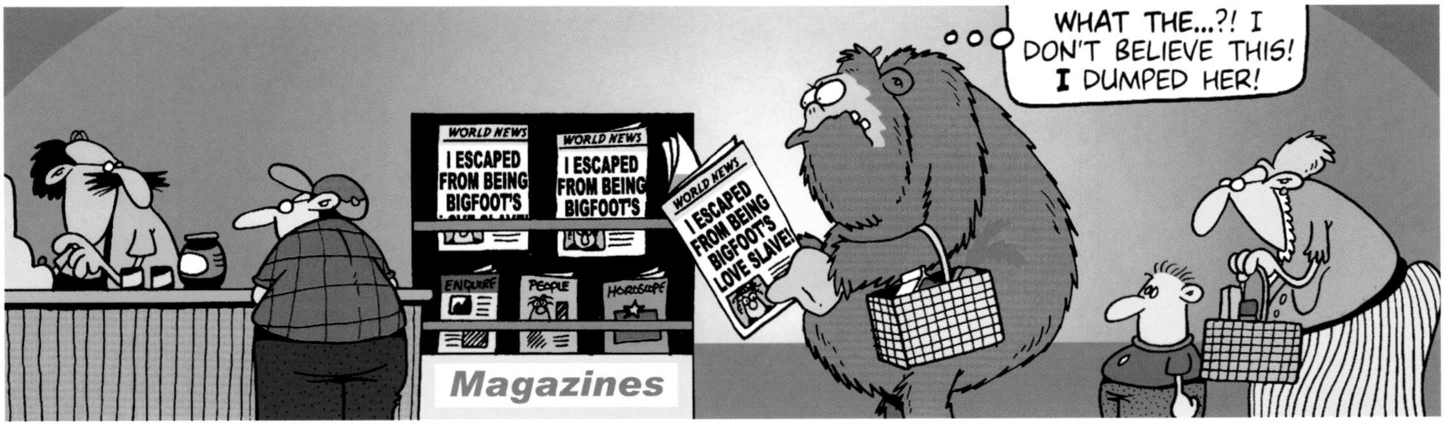
WHAT THE...?! I DON'T BELIEVE THIS! I DUMPED HER!
WORLD NEWS
I ESCAPED FROM BEING BIGFOOT'S LOVE SLAVE!
ENQUIRE
PEOPLE
HOROSCOPE
Magazines

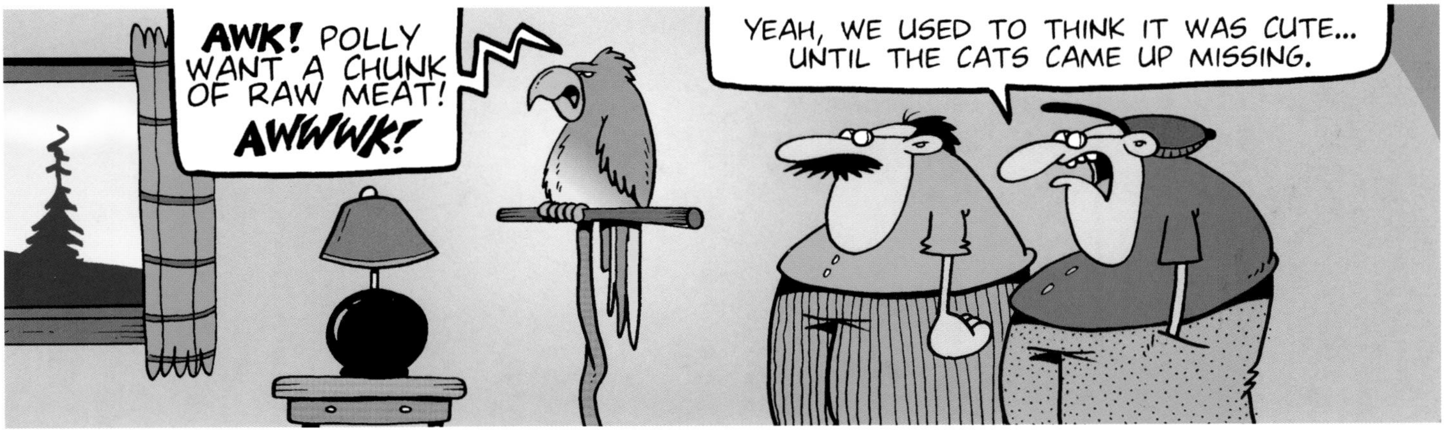
AWK! POLLY WANT A CHUNK OF RAW MEAT! AWWWK!
YEAH, WE USED TO THINK IT WAS CUTE... UNTIL THE CATS CAME UP MISSING.

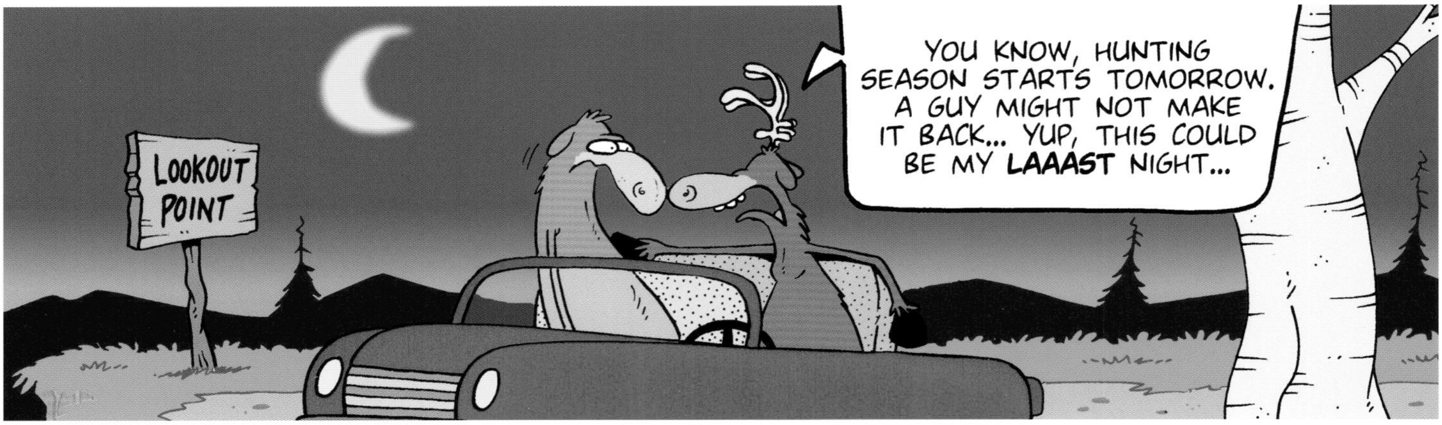
LOOKOUT POINT
YOU KNOW, HUNTING SEASON STARTS TOMORROW. A GUY MIGHT NOT MAKE IT BACK... YUP, THIS COULD BE MY **LAAAST** NIGHT...

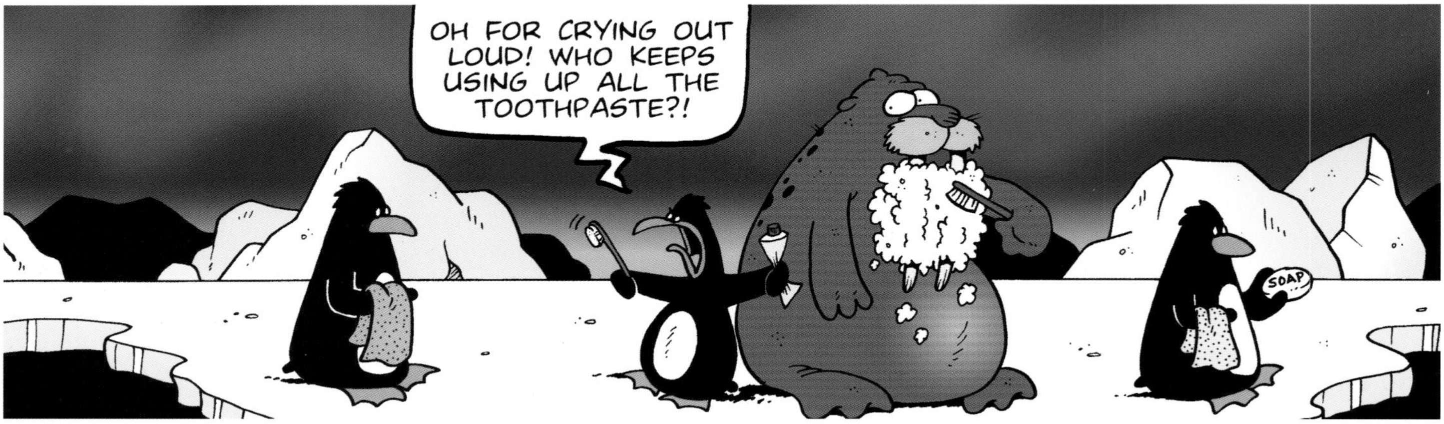
OH FOR CRYING OUT LOUD! WHO KEEPS USING UP ALL THE TOOTHPASTE?!
SOAP

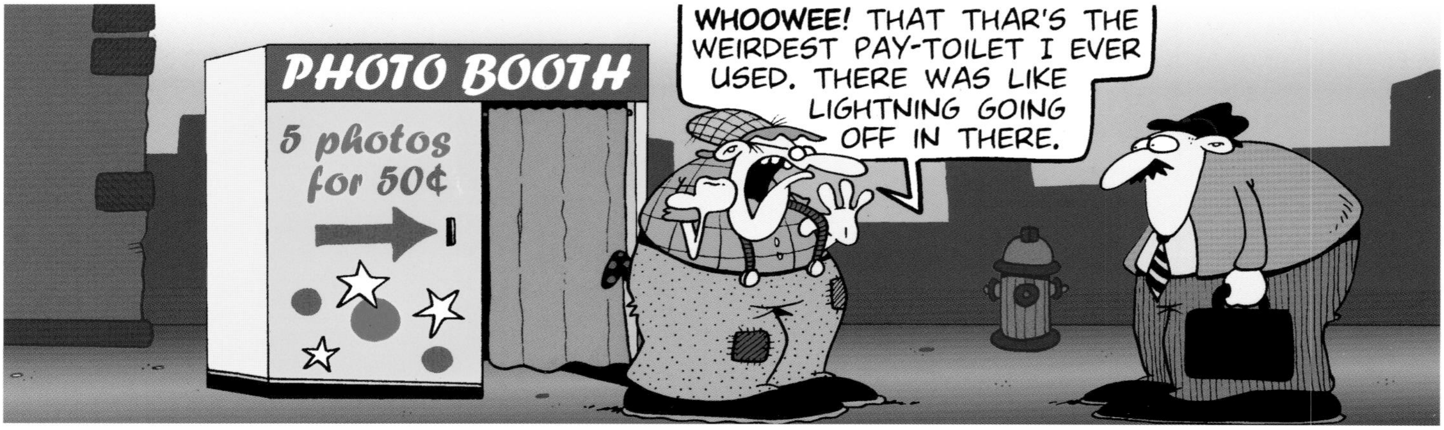
PHOTO BOOTH
5 photos for 50¢
WHOOWEE! THAT THAR'S THE WEIRDEST PAY-TOILET I EVER USED. THERE WAS LIKE LIGHTNING GOING OFF IN THERE.

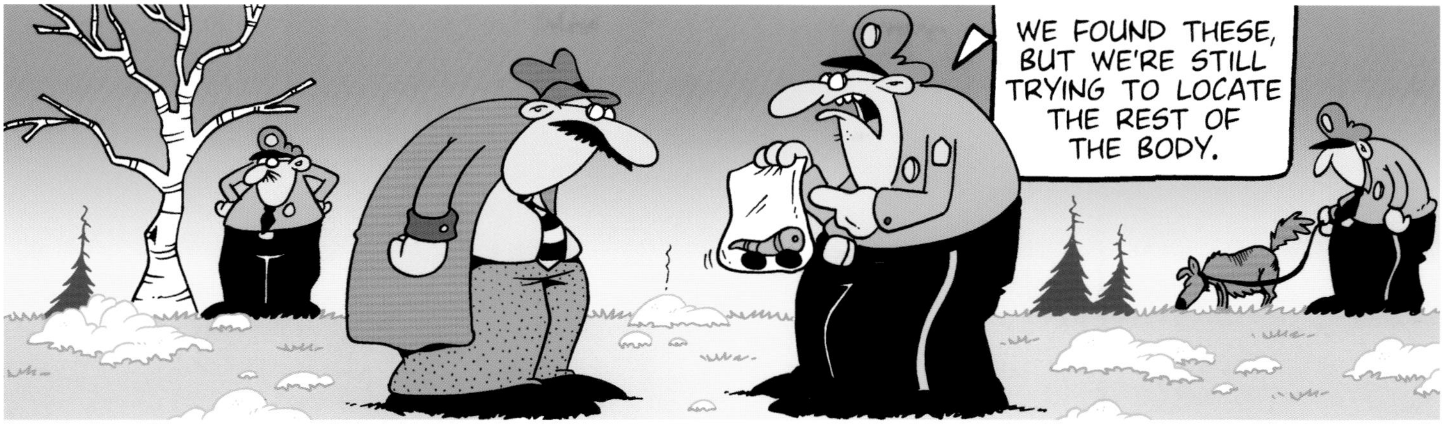
WE FOUND THESE, BUT WE'RE STILL TRYING TO LOCATE THE REST OF THE BODY.

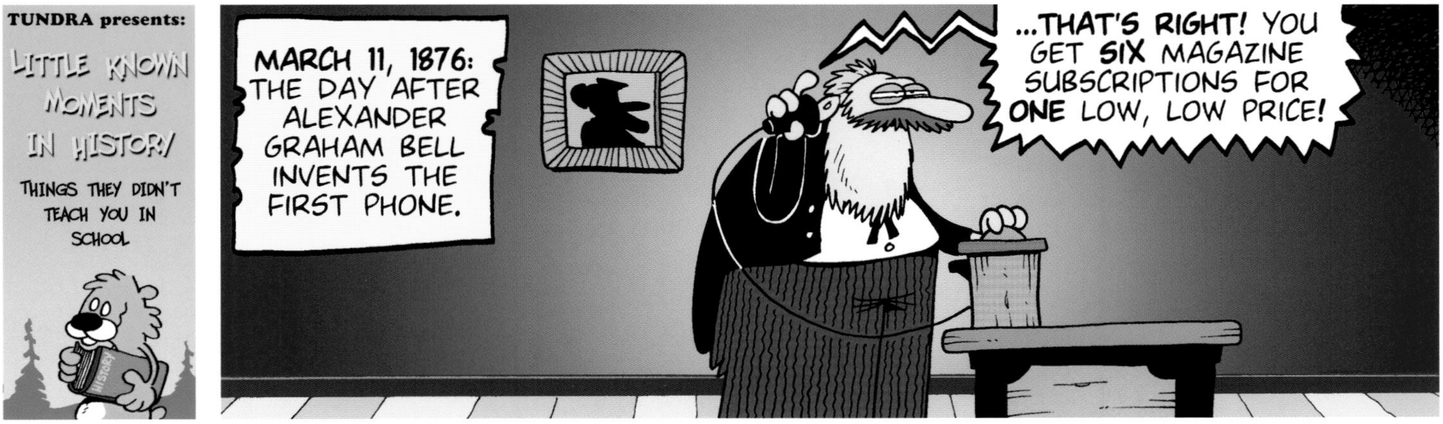
TUNDRA presents:
LITTLE KNOWN MOMENTS IN HISTORY
THINGS THEY DIDN'T TEACH YOU IN SCHOOL
HISTORY
MARCH 11, 1876: THE DAY AFTER ALEXANDER GRAHAM BELL INVENTS THE FIRST PHONE.
...THAT'S RIGHT! YOU GET SIX MAGAZINE SUBSCRIPTIONS FOR ONE LOW, LOW PRICE!

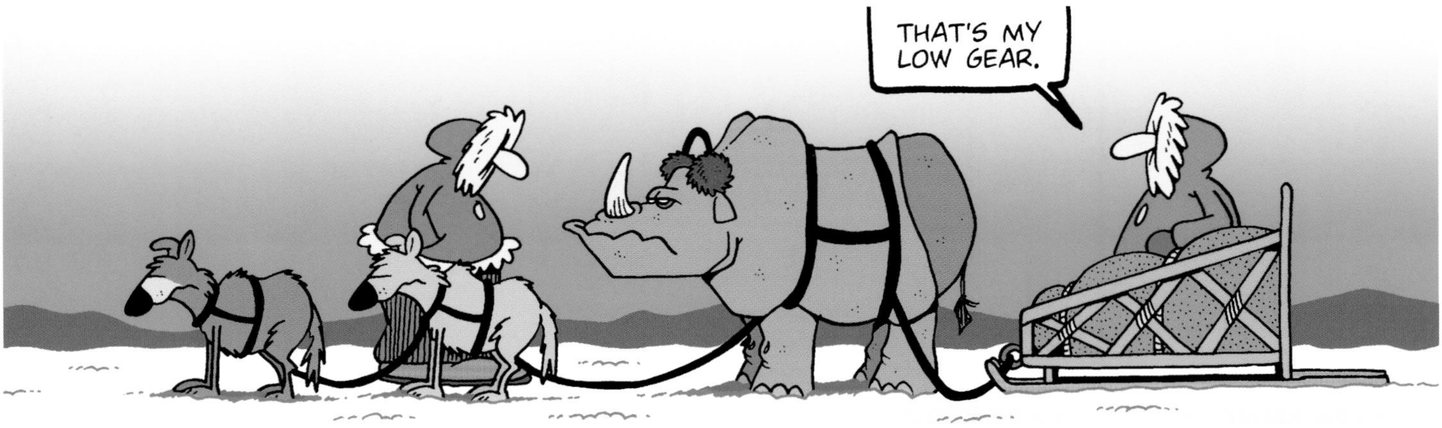
THAT'S MY LOW GEAR.

Chad Carpenter's
TUNDRA
THIS IS RIDICULOUS! I'VE BEEN PUSHING THAT SNOWBLOWER AROUND ALL DAY AND IT SEEMS LIKE THERE'S STILL JUST AS MUCH SNOW IN THE DRIVEWAY!
I'VE NOTICED.
© TUNDRA 2005
I KNOW WHAT THAT SNOW IS THINKING! IT THINKS I'VE GIVEN UP! BUT I'VE GOT NEWS FOR IT...!
DO TELL.
www.tundracomics.com
I'M GONNA SNOWBLOW THAT DRIVEWAY UNTIL EVERY LAST FLAKE IS GONE! GONE I TELL YOU!
I ADMIRE YOUR WORK ETHIC.
THAT'S RIGHT! I'LL HAVE THE LAST LAUGH! I'M NOT GOING TO LET IT BEAT ME!
THAT'S THE SPIRIT BUDDY!
I'LL CLEAR THAT DRIVEWAY IF IT TAKES ME ALL NIGHT!
GO GET 'EM TIGER!
WHY IS DUDLEY PUSHING THE LAWNMOWER THROUGH THE SNOW?
SHHH. YOU'LL RUIN MY FUN.

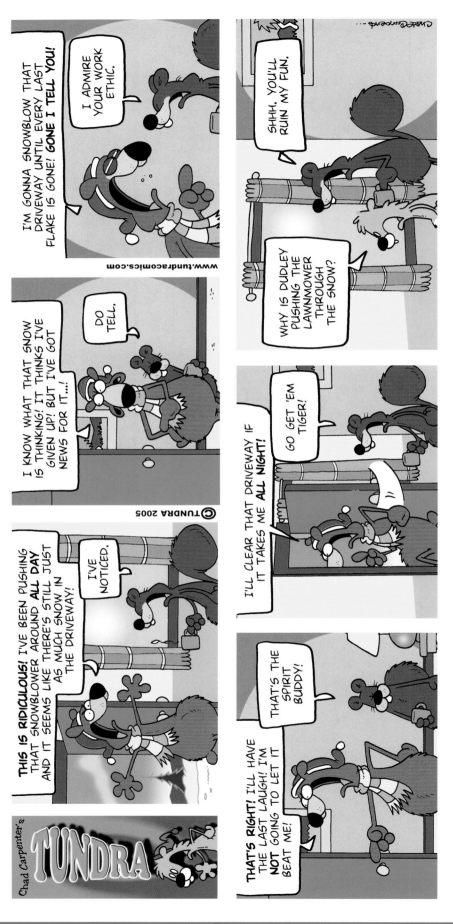

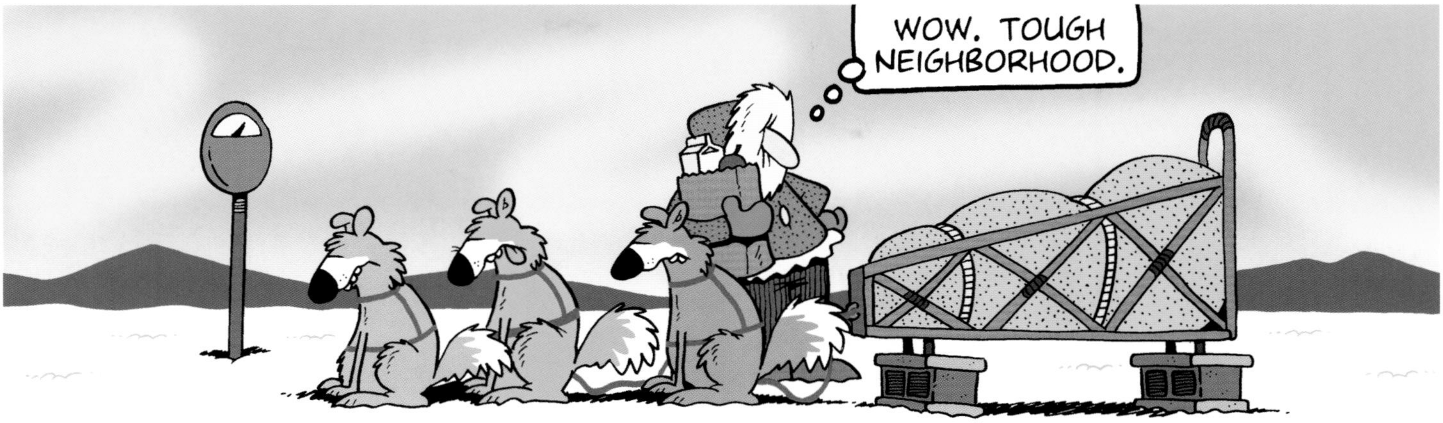
WOW. TOUGH NEIGHBORHOOD.

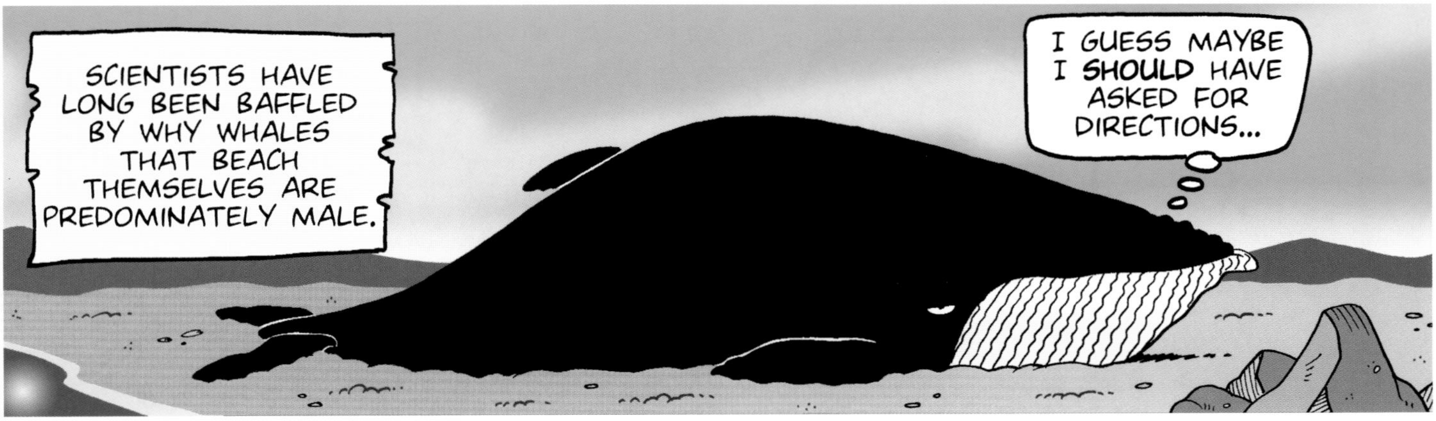
SCIENTISTS HAVE LONG BEEN BAFFLED BY WHY WHALES THAT BEACH THEMSELVES ARE PREDOMINATELY MALE.
I GUESS MAYBE I **SHOULD** HAVE ASKED FOR DIRECTIONS...

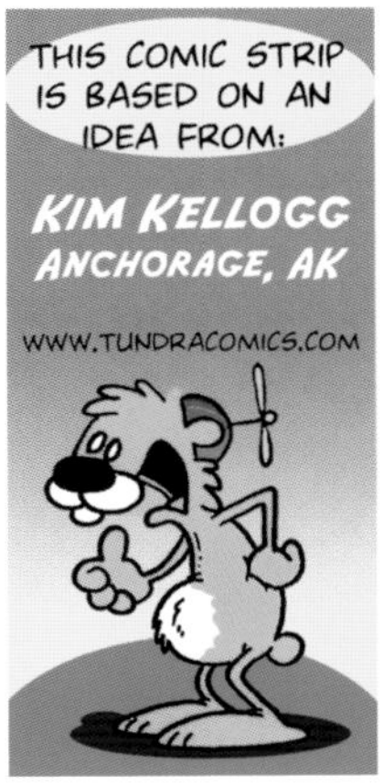
THIS COMIC STRIP IS BASED ON AN IDEA FROM:
KIM KELLOGG
ANCHORAGE, AK
WWW.TUNDRACOMICS.COM

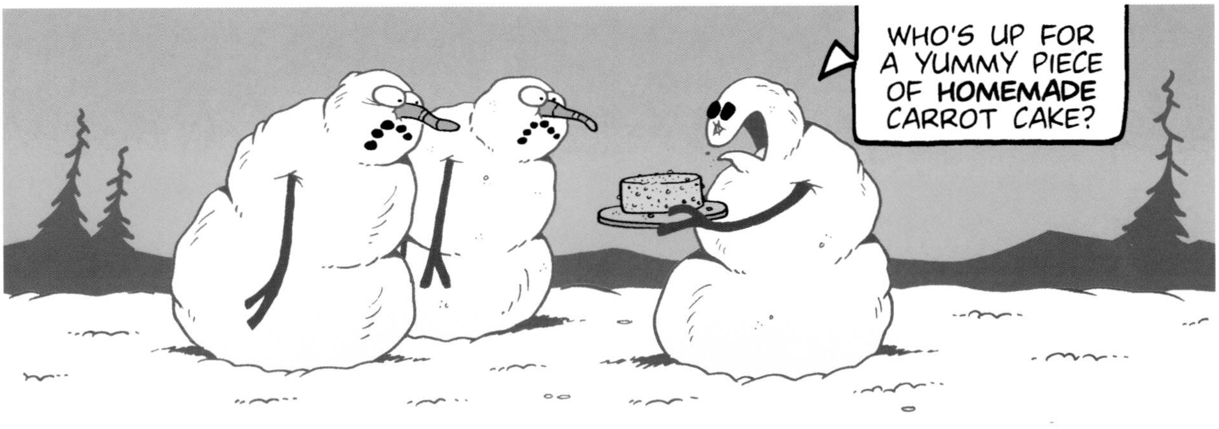
WHO'S UP FOR A YUMMY PIECE OF **HOMEMADE** CARROT CAKE?

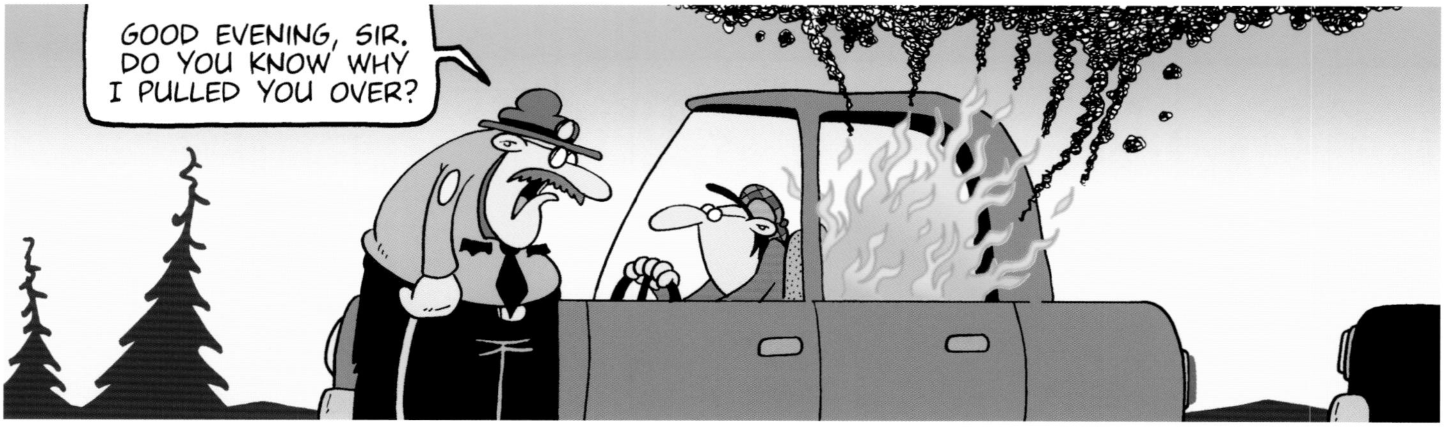
GOOD EVENING, SIR. DO YOU KNOW WHY I PULLED YOU OVER?

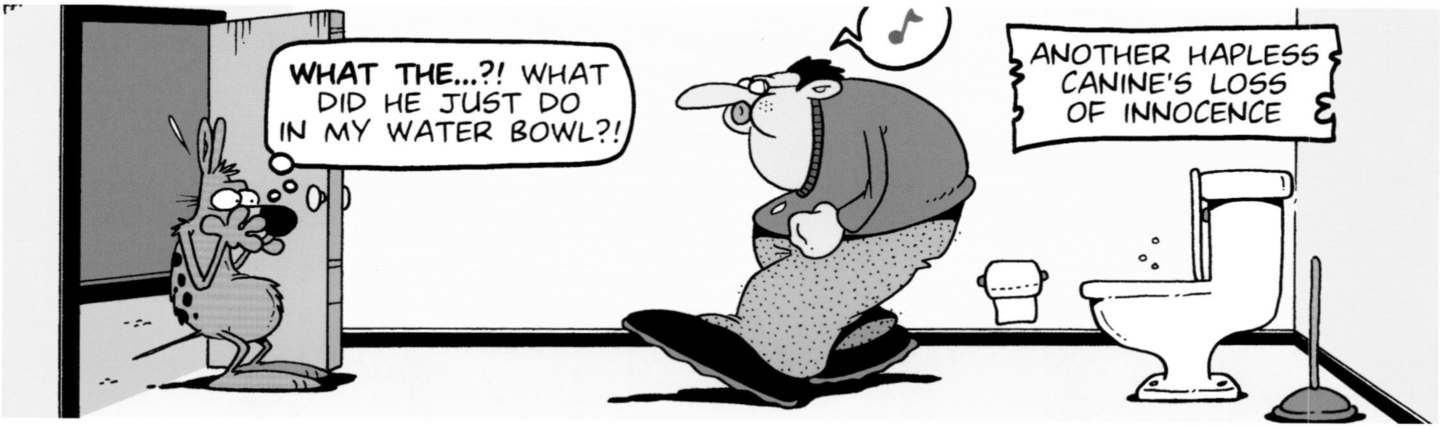
WHAT THE...?! WHAT DID HE JUST DO IN MY WATER BOWL?!
ANOTHER HAPLESS CANINE'S LOSS OF INNOCENCE

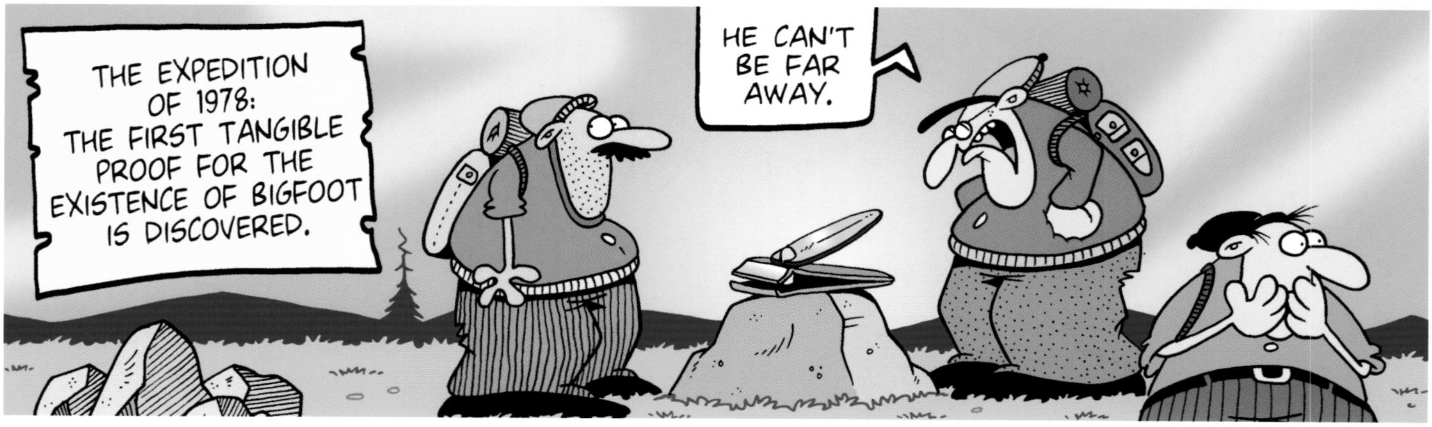
THE EXPEDITION OF 1978: THE FIRST TANGIBLE PROOF FOR THE EXISTENCE OF BIGFOOT IS DISCOVERED.
HE CAN'T BE FAR AWAY.

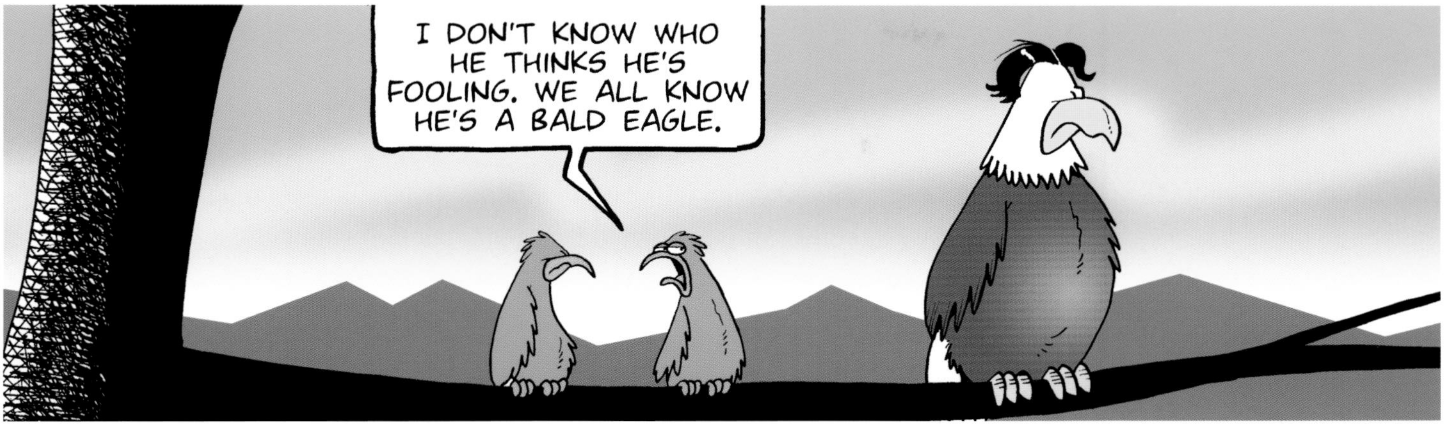
I DON'T KNOW WHO HE THINKS HE'S FOOLING. WE ALL KNOW HE'S A BALD EAGLE.

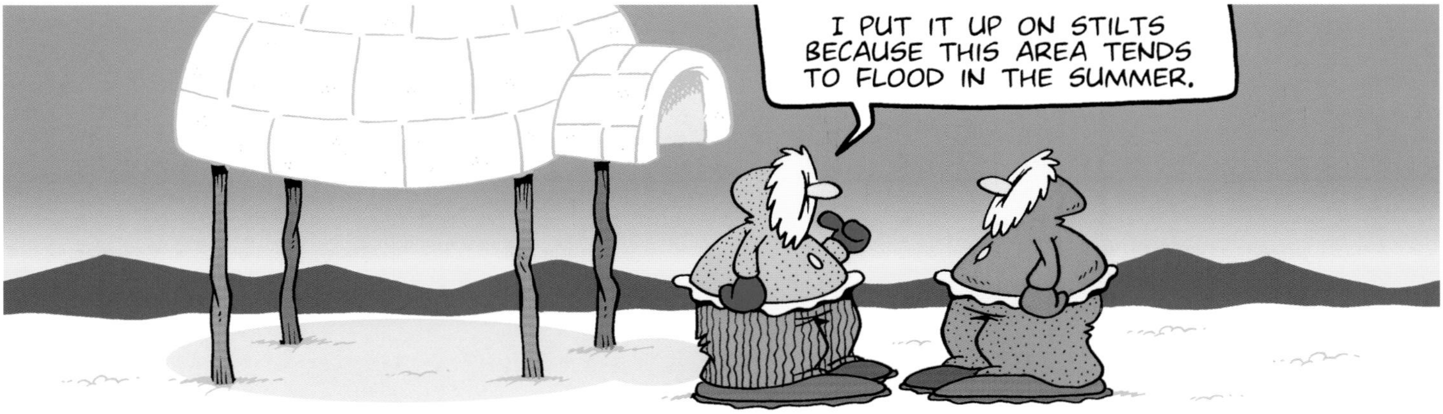
I PUT IT UP ON STILTS BECAUSE THIS AREA TENDS TO FLOOD IN THE SUMMER.

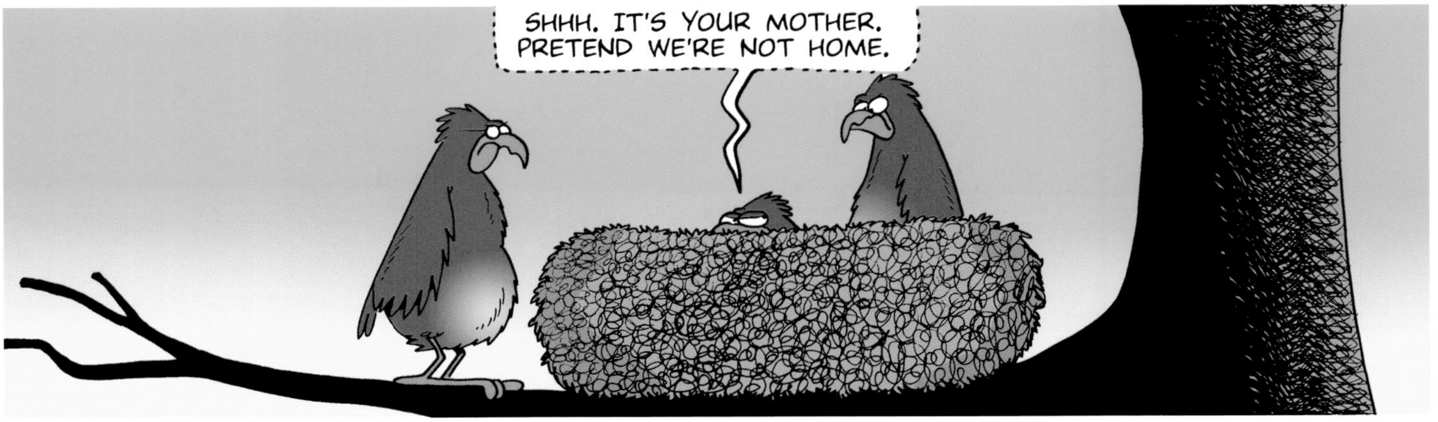
SHHH. IT'S YOUR MOTHER. PRETEND WE'RE NOT HOME.

Chad Carpenter's
TUNDRA
OKEY-DOKE!
HELLO AND WELCOME TO THIS WEEK'S SUNDAY TUNDRA COMIC STRIP!
OR AS WE CALL IT IN THE BUSINESS, THIS WEEK'S SUNDAY TUNDRA COMIC STRIP.
IT'S HARD TO BELIEVE THAT THE VERY FIRST TUNDRA STRIP APPEARED A WHOLE SIXTEEN YEARS AGO!
AND A LOT HAS CERTAINLY CHANGED OVER THOSE YEARS!
C'MON... C'MON...
©Tundra 1991
FOR EXAMPLE, WHEN DUDLEY WAS FIRST SEEN IN THE STRIP, HE LOOKED LIKE SOME SORT OF STRANGE, MUTATED BLOB.
WHEREAS NOW, HE LOOKS LIKE A TOTALLY DIFFERENT SORT OF STRANGE, MUTATED BLOB.
ANDY AND I HAVE ALSO GONE THROUGH SOME RADICAL CHANGES OF OUR OWN.
BETTER LOOKING EVERY DAY!
SADLY THOUGH, NOT ALL OF US HAVE AGED SO GRACEFULLY.
IT IS THE UNFORTUNATE TRUTH.
IT SEEMS THE STRESS OF CREATING A DAILY COMIC STRIP FOR SO MANY YEARS HAS TAKEN ITS TOLL ON OUR BELOVED CARTOONIST, CHAD.
THEN
NOW
OH THE HUMANITY.
www.tundracomics.com
WE WOULD JUST LIKE TO TAKE THIS TIME TO SAY THANK YOU FOR YOUR YEARS OF SUPPORT.
YEAH. WHERE ELSE ARE A COUPLE OF SIXTEEN-YEAR-OLD RODENTS GOING TO FIND WORK?

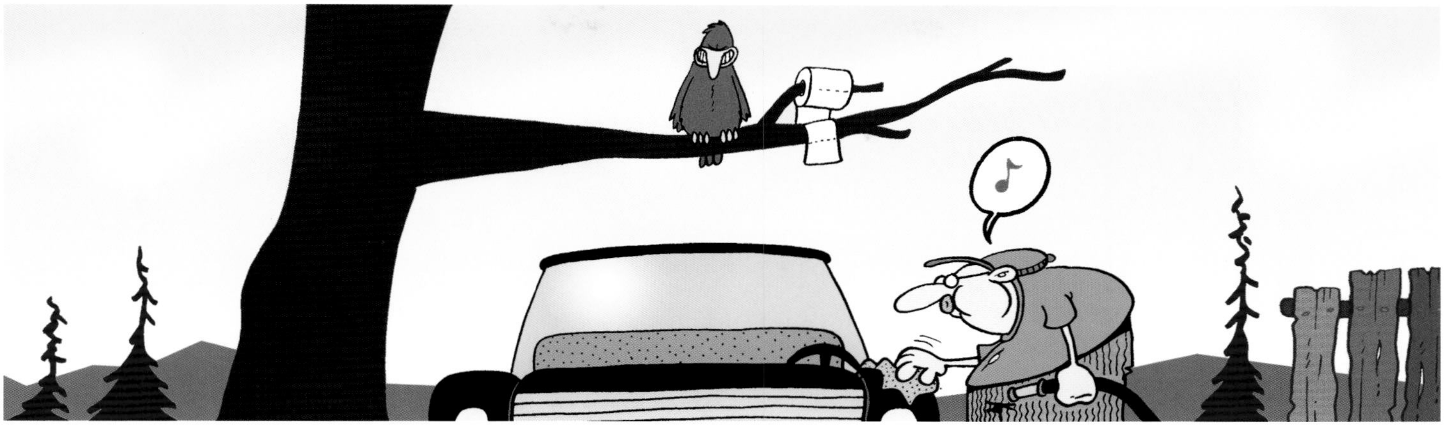

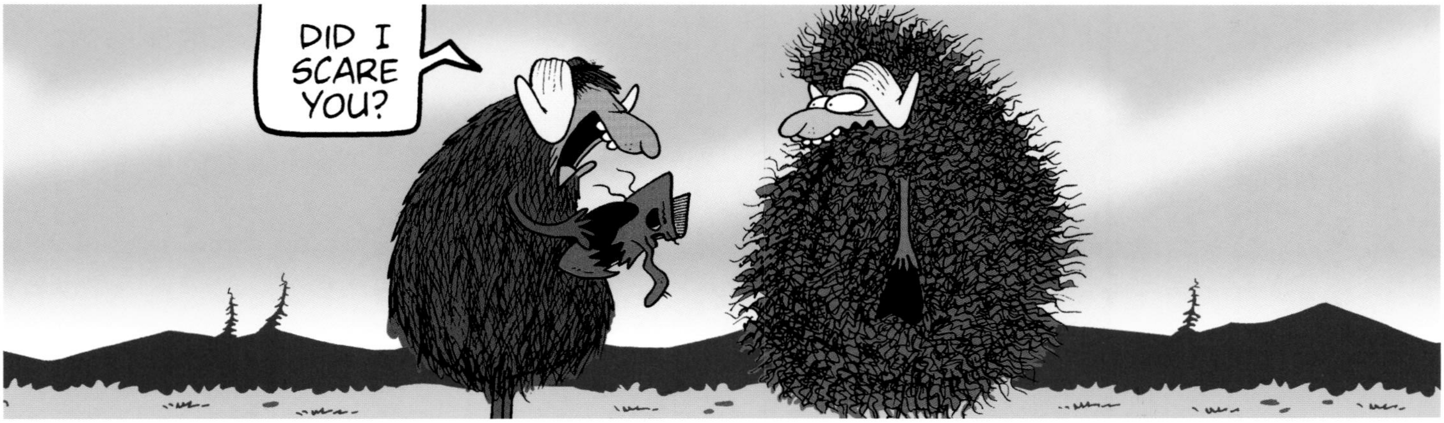
DID I SCARE YOU?

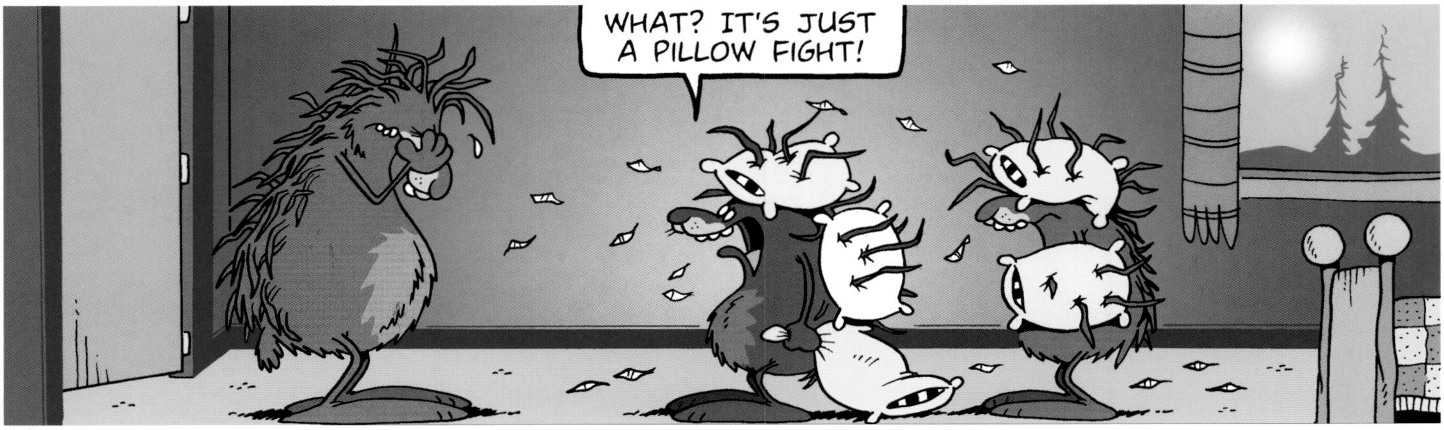
WHAT? IT'S JUST A PILLOW FIGHT!

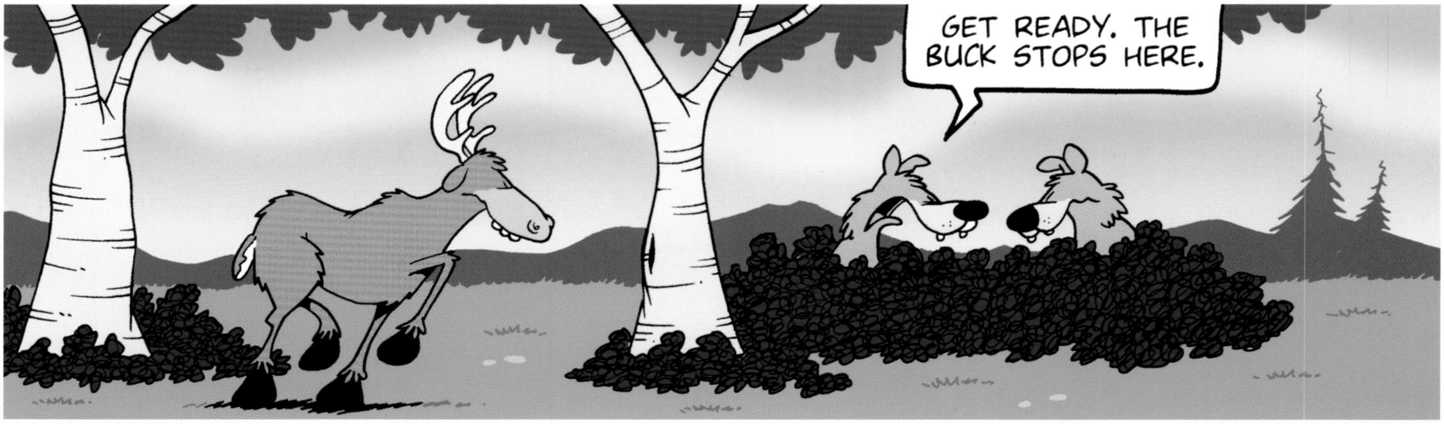
GET READY. THE BUCK STOPS HERE.

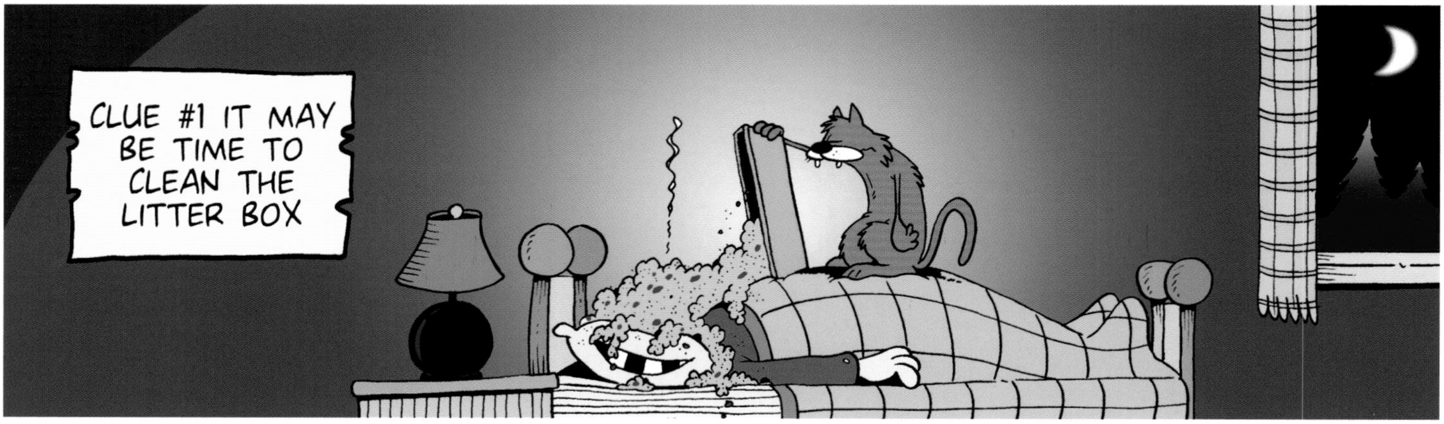
CLUE #1 IT MAY BE TIME TO CLEAN THE LITTER BOX

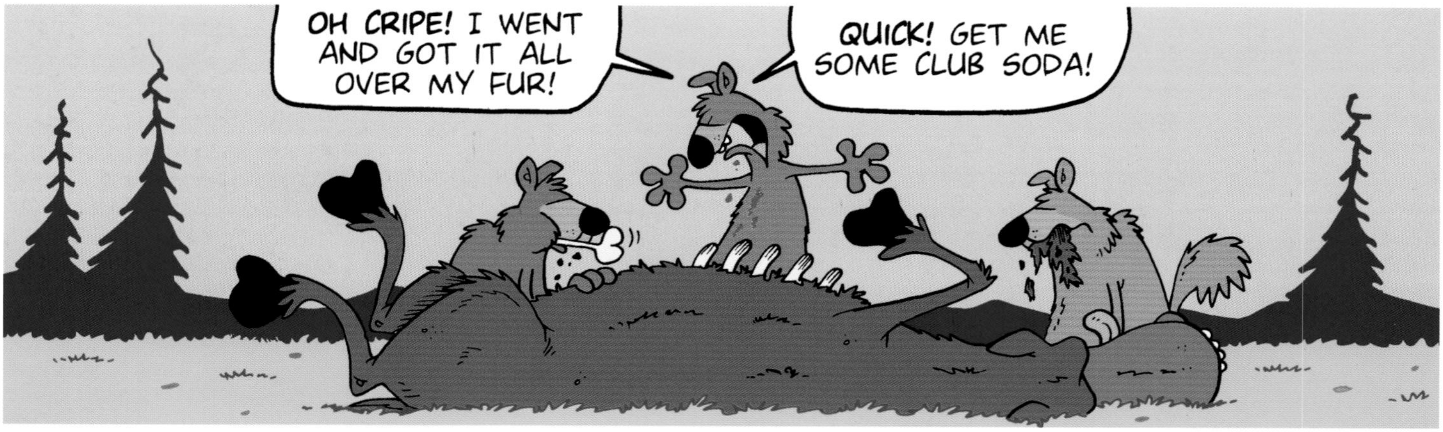
OH CRIPE! I WENT AND GOT IT ALL OVER MY FUR!
QUICK! GET ME SOME CLUB SODA!

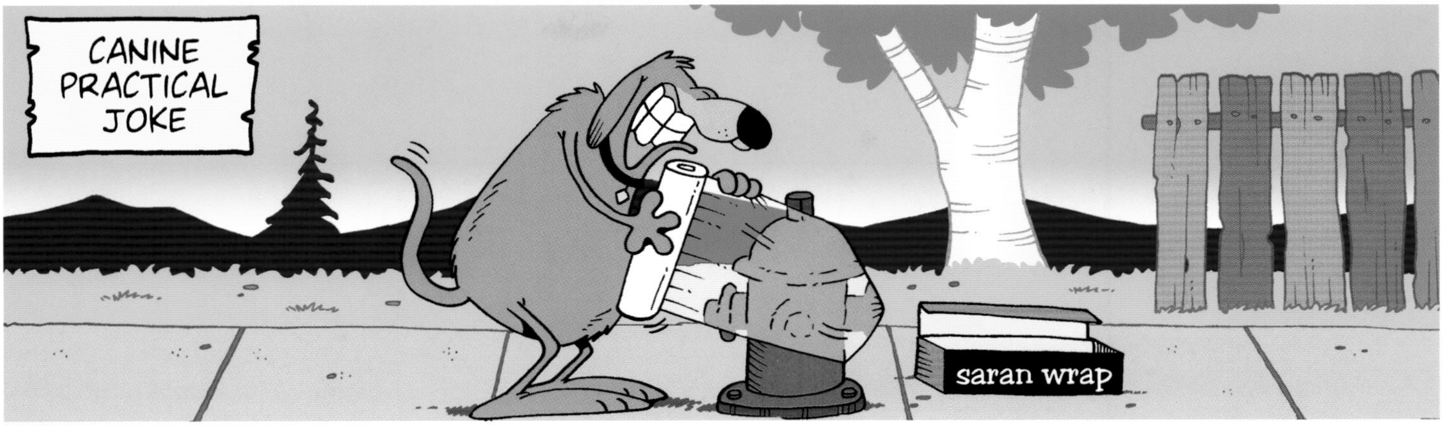
CANINE PRACTICAL JOKE
saran wrap

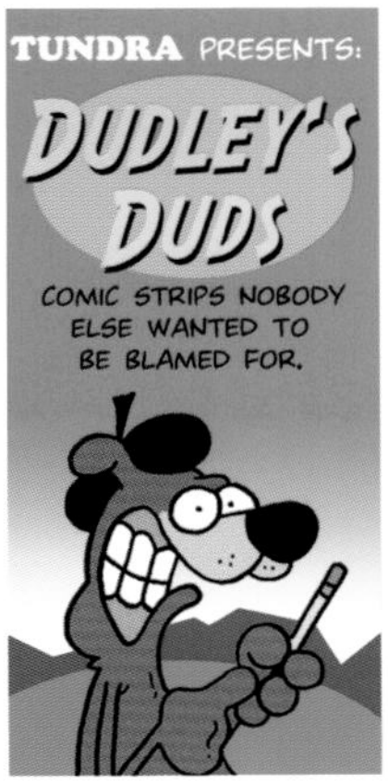
TUNDRA PRESENTS:
DUDLEY'S DUDS
COMIC STRIPS NOBODY ELSE WANTED TO BE BLAMED FOR.

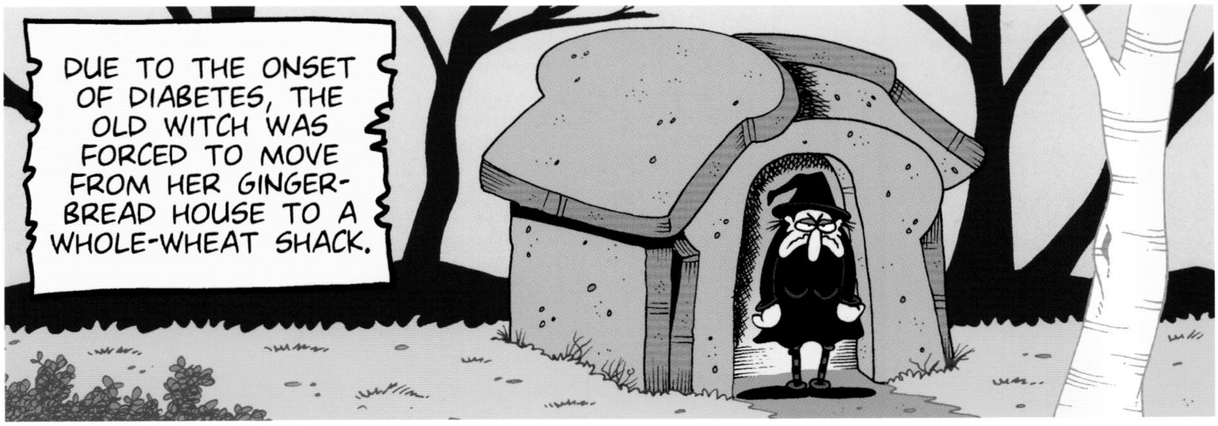
DUE TO THE ONSET OF DIABETES, THE OLD WITCH WAS FORCED TO MOVE FROM HER GINGER-BREAD HOUSE TO A WHOLE-WHEAT SHACK.

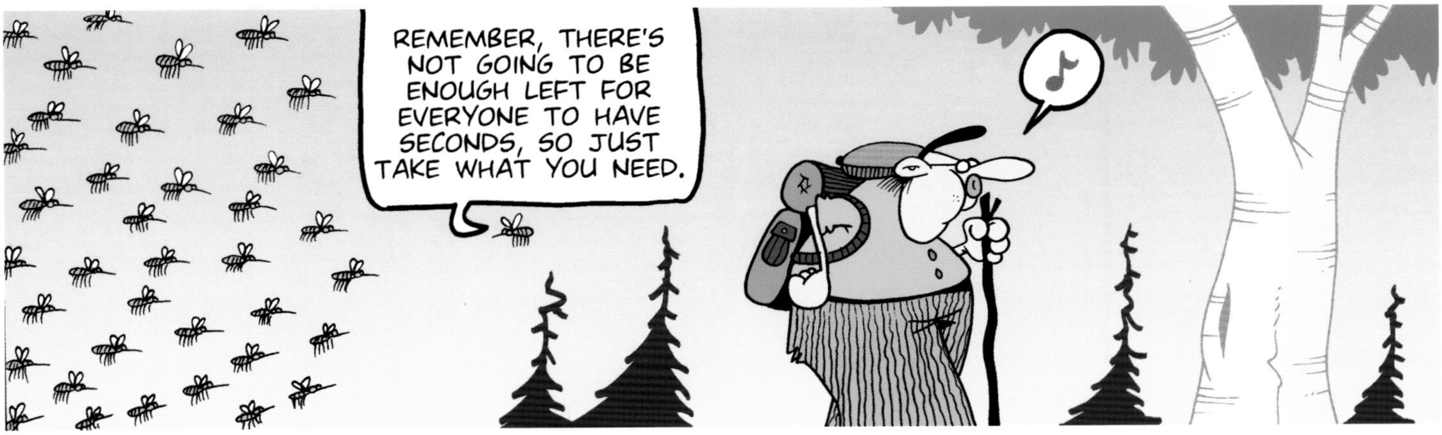
REMEMBER, THERE'S NOT GOING TO BE ENOUGH LEFT FOR EVERYONE TO HAVE SECONDS, SO JUST TAKE WHAT YOU NEED.

Chad Carpenter's
TUNDRA
YIP YIP YIP YIP YIP YIP YIP YIP YIP YIP YIP
YIP YIP YIP YIP YIP YIP YIP YIP YIP YIP YIP YIP YIP YIP YIP
YIP YIP YIP YIP YIP YIP YIP YIP YIP YIP YIP YIP YIP YIP YIP YIP YIP YIP
www.tundracomics.com
©TUNDRA 2005

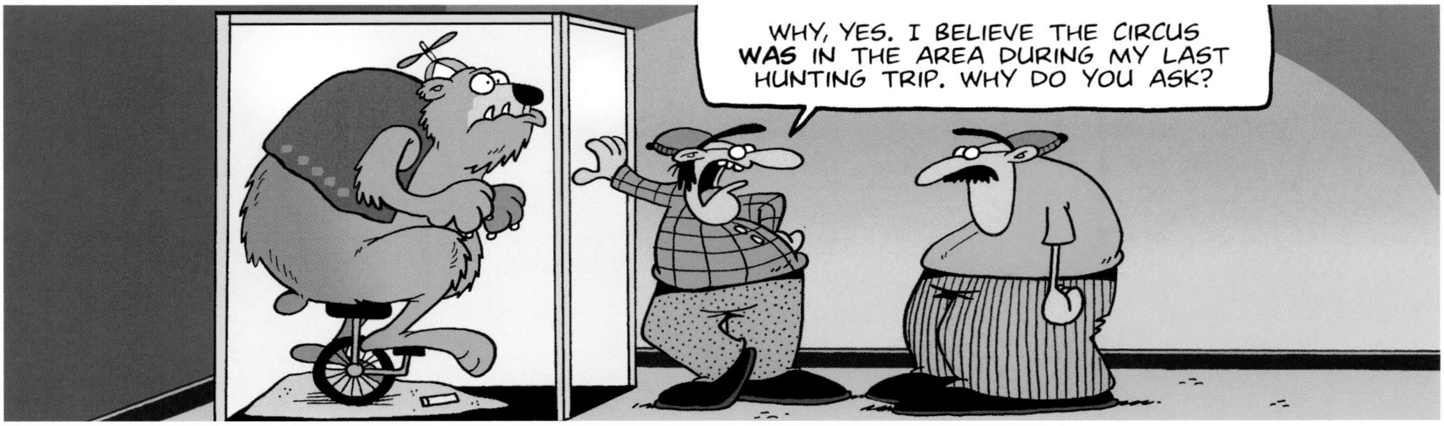
WHY, YES. I BELIEVE THE CIRCUS **WAS** IN THE AREA DURING MY LAST HUNTING TRIP. WHY DO YOU ASK?

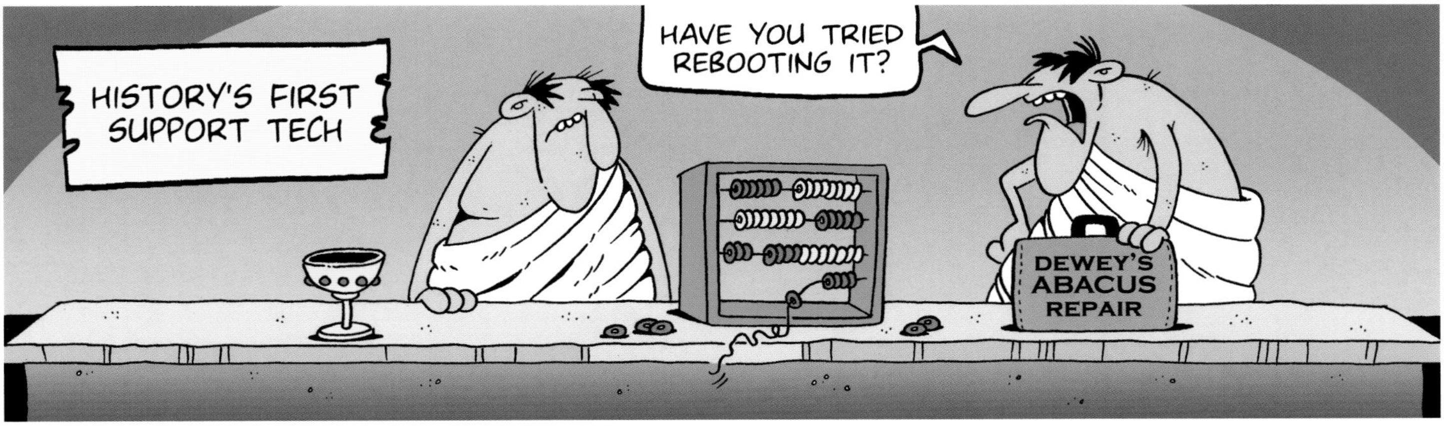
HISTORY'S FIRST SUPPORT TECH
HAVE YOU TRIED REBOOTING IT?
DEWEY'S ABACUS REPAIR

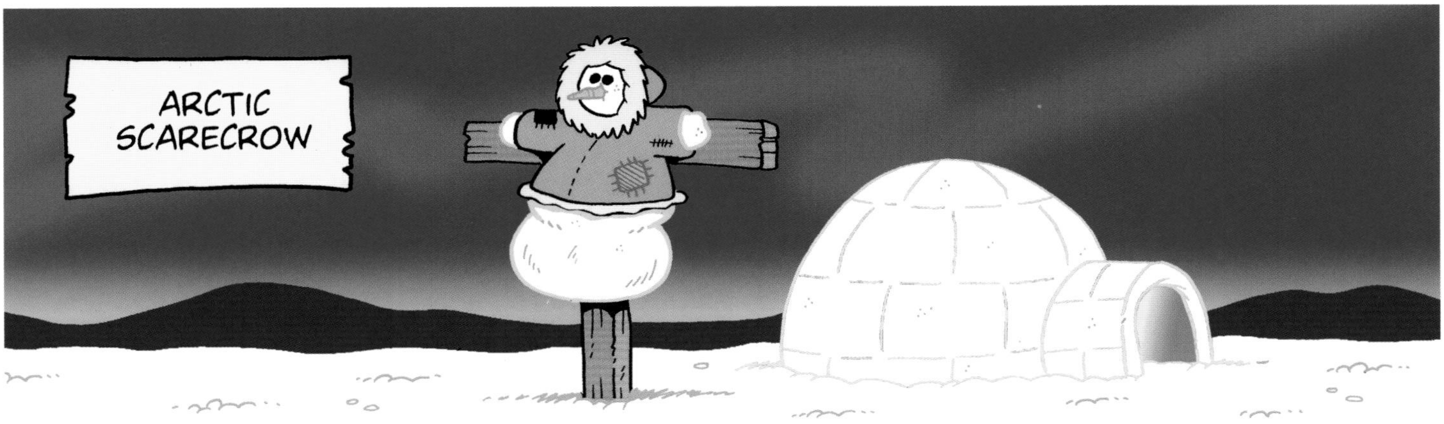
ARCTIC SCARECROW

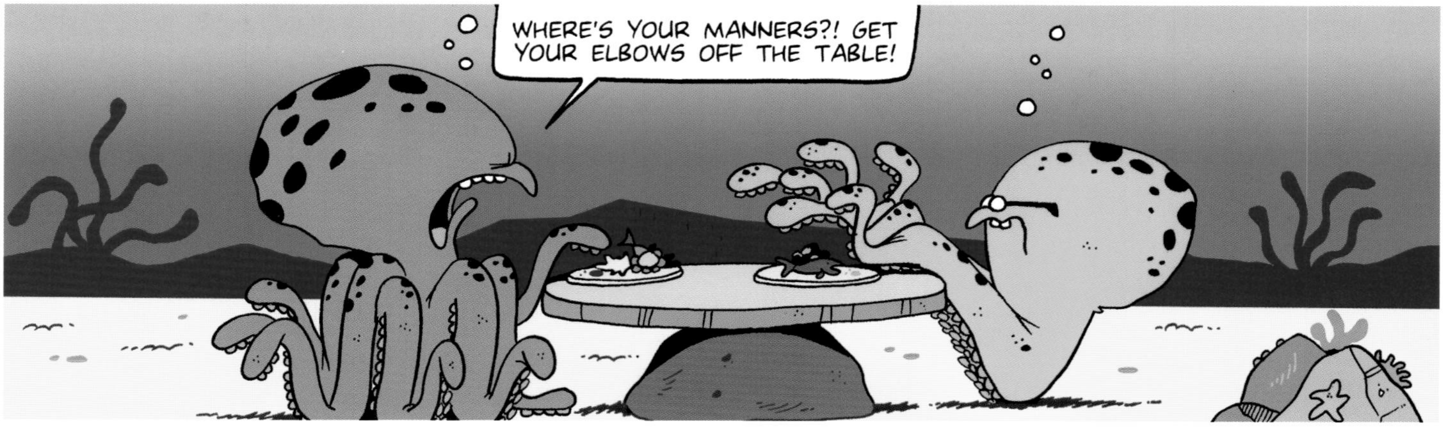
WHERE'S YOUR MANNERS?! GET YOUR ELBOWS OFF THE TABLE!

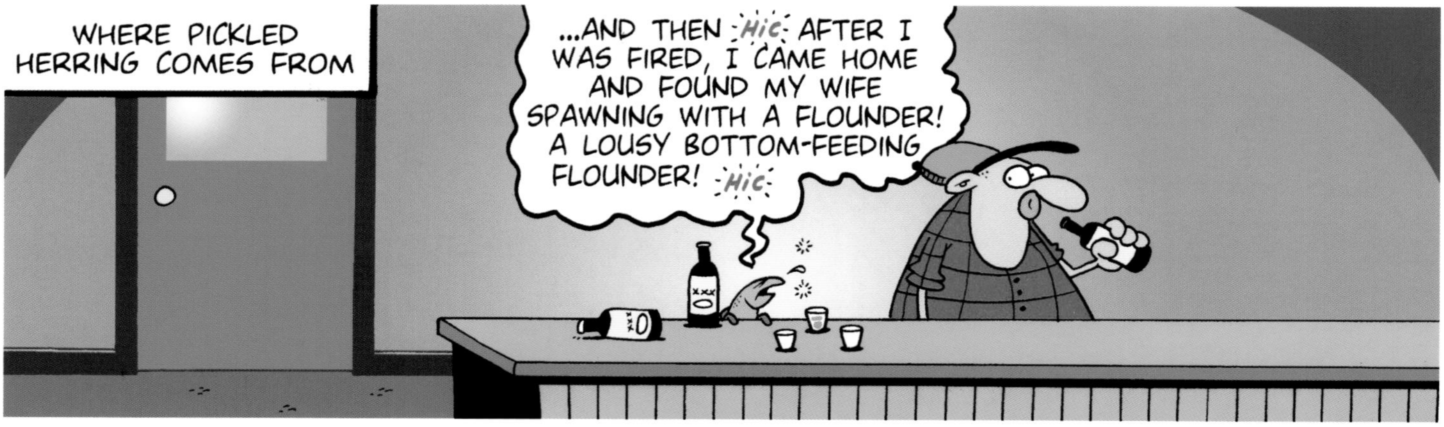
WHERE PICKLED HERRING COMES FROM
...AND THEN HIC AFTER I WAS FIRED, I CAME HOME AND FOUND MY WIFE SPAWNING WITH A FLOUNDER! A LOUSY BOTTOM-FEEDING FLOUNDER! HIC
XXX
BLUE PRINT

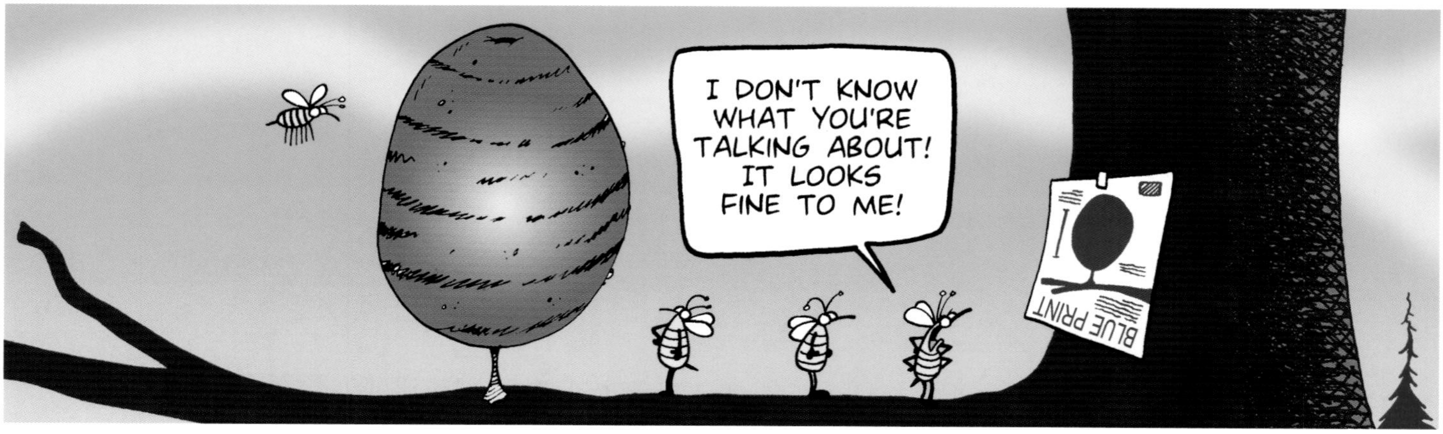
I DON'T KNOW WHAT YOU'RE TALKING ABOUT! IT LOOKS FINE TO ME!
BLUE PRINT

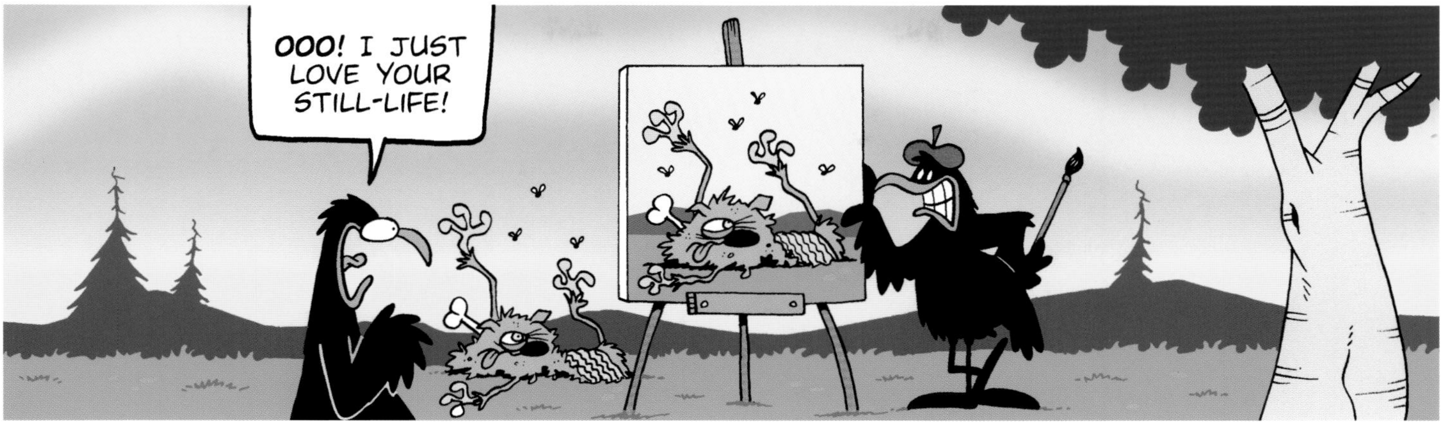
OOO! I JUST LOVE YOUR STILL-LIFE!

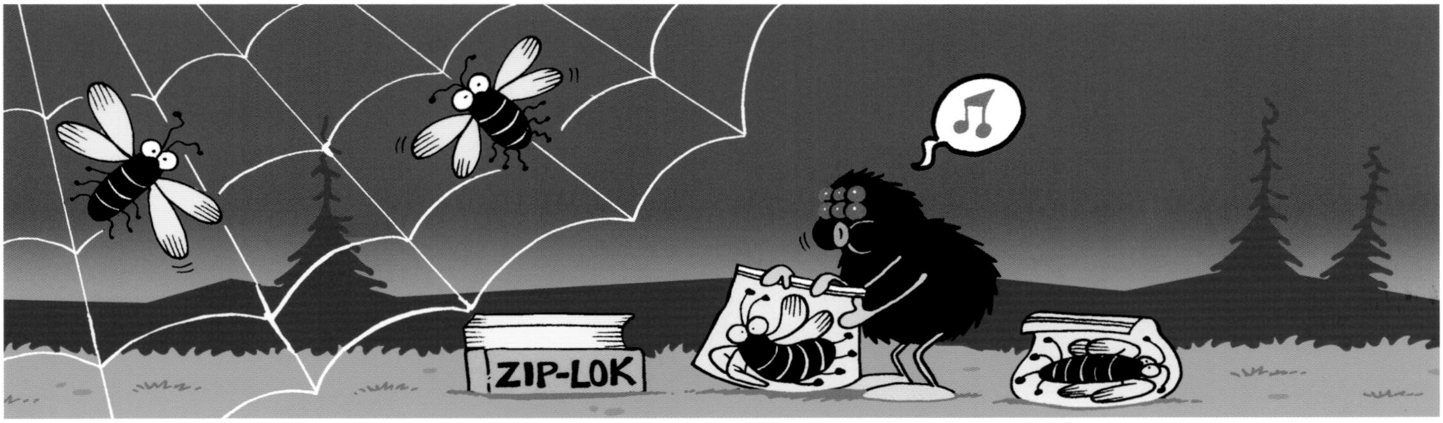
ZIP-LOK

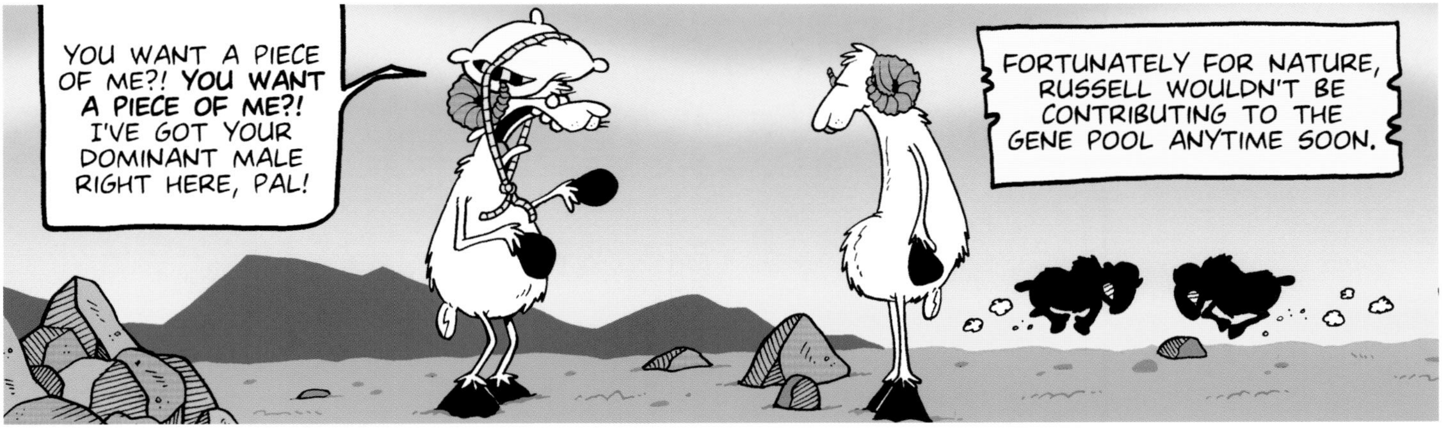
YOU WANT A PIECE OF ME?! YOU WANT A PIECE OF ME?! I'VE GOT YOUR DOMINANT MALE RIGHT HERE, PAL!
FORTUNATELY FOR NATURE, RUSSELL WOULDN'T BE CONTRIBUTING TO THE GENE POOL ANYTIME SOON.

Chad Carpenter's
TUNDRA
TUNDRA SEAL OF APPROVAL
OKEY-DOKE!
OOO! I JUST LOVE MAKING SNOW ANGELS! I ONLY WISH I COULD MAKE ONE THAT WOULD STAY HERE ALL WINTER LONG!
OH REALLY? STAY RIGHT HERE, DUDLEY. I'LL BE RIGHT BACK!
©TUNDRA 2005
HERE YOU GO, PAL. A LITTLE SPRITZ OF WATER AND YOU'LL HAVE A NICE LITTLE ICE ANGEL IN NO TIME!
...UG... HAVING... A...HARD... TIME...UG... MOVING...
SEE YA' IN THE SPRING, CHUMP!
R-R-REALLY K-K-KINDA' N-N-NIPPY...
DID YOU JUST FREEZE DUDLEY TO THE DRIVEWAY?
EVERYBODY NEEDS A HOBBY.
YOU GUYS WON'T BELIEVE THIS, BUT SOMEONE PUT A BIG LOG RIGHT IN THE MIDDLE OF OUR DRIVEWAY.
GOSH. MAYBE YOU SHOULD MOVE IT.
HEE HEE
www.tundracomics.com
YEAH BUT I'M GONNA' NEED DUDLEY'S HELP. I HIGH-CENTERED ON IT WHILE BACKING OUT OF THE GARAGE.
SHERM WILL HELP. I'VE GOT A FEELING HE'S GOING TO NEED A RIDE TO THE AIRPORT ANYWAY.

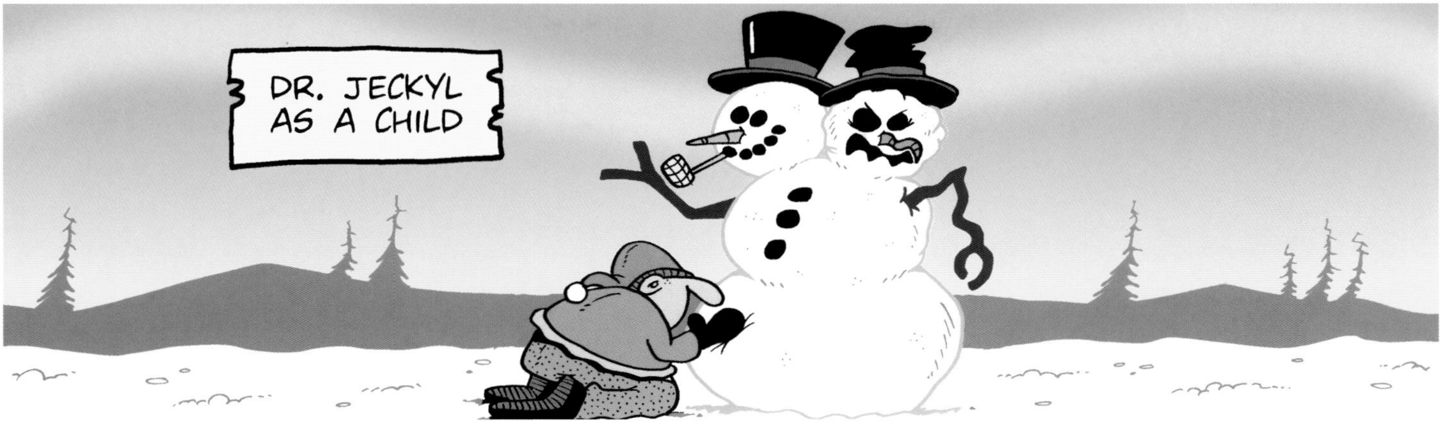
DR. JECKYL AS A CHILD

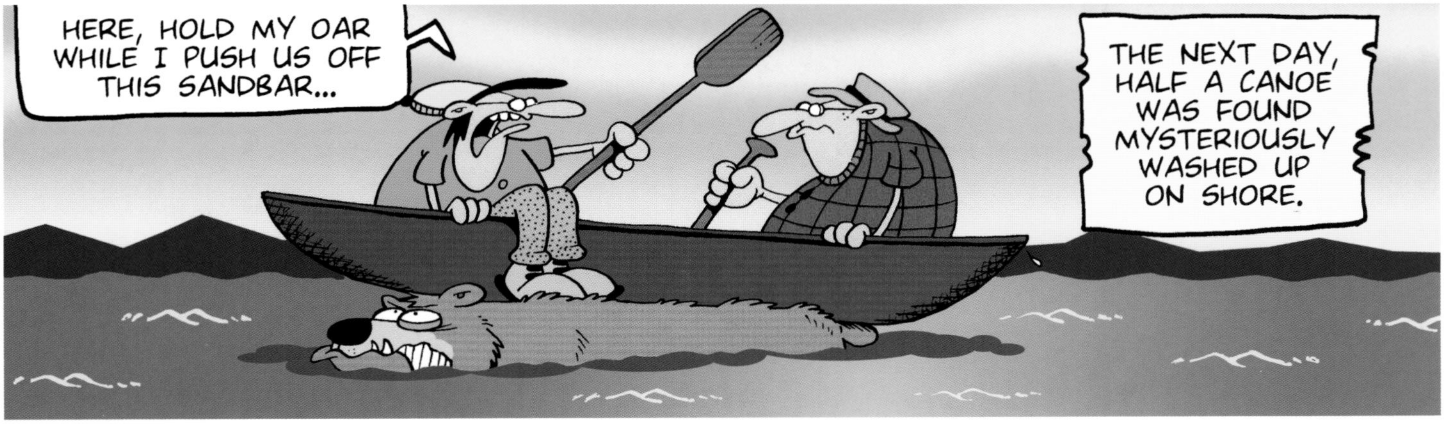
HERE, HOLD MY OAR WHILE I PUSH US OFF THIS SANDBAR...
THE NEXT DAY, HALF A CANOE WAS FOUND MYSTERIOUSLY WASHED UP ON SHORE.

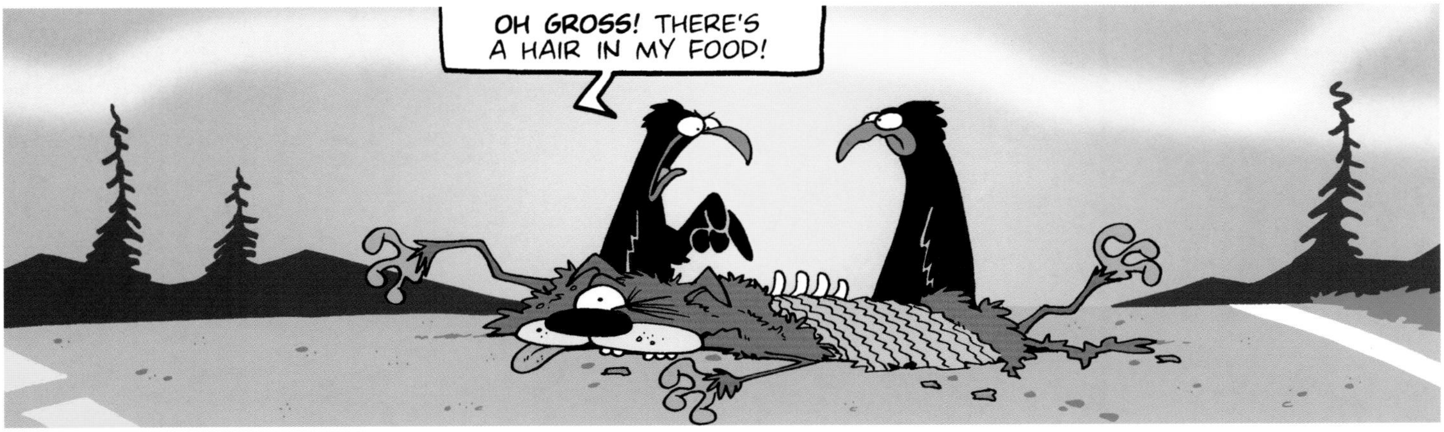
OH GROSS! THERE'S A HAIR IN MY FOOD!

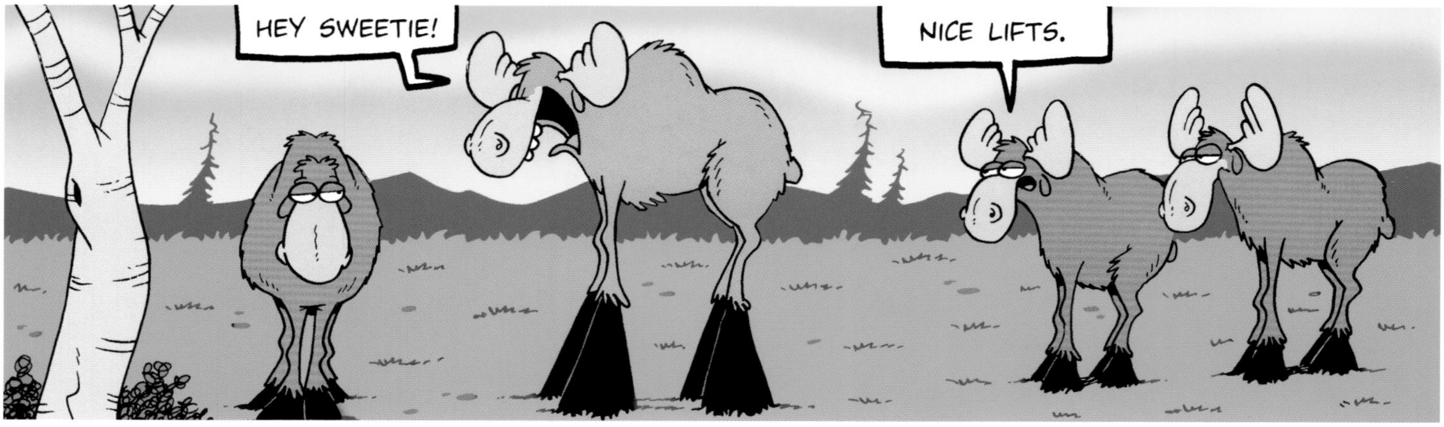
HEY SWEETIE!
NICE LIFTS.

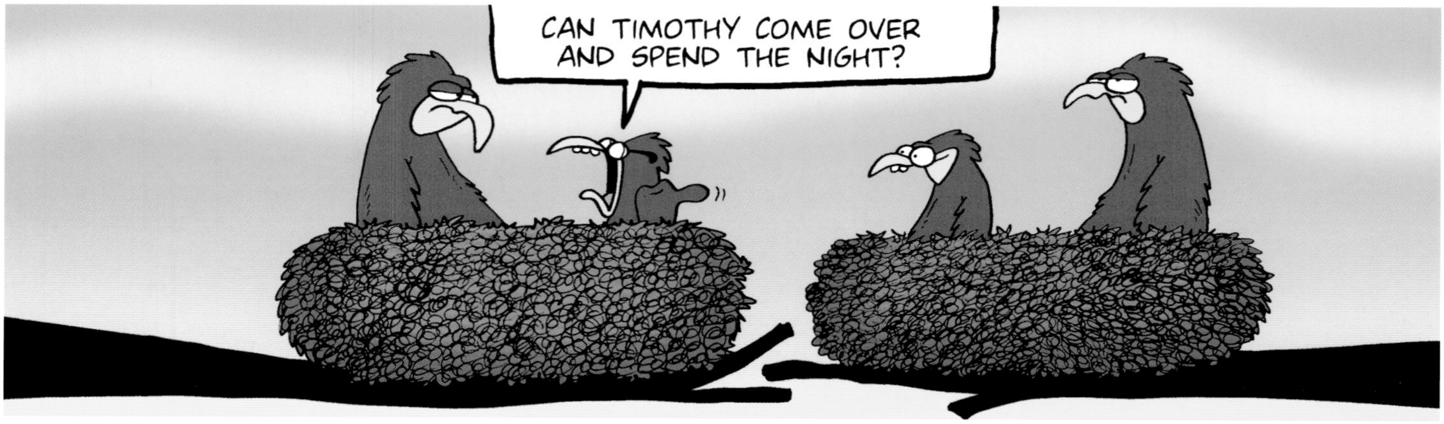
CAN TIMOTHY COME OVER AND SPEND THE NIGHT?

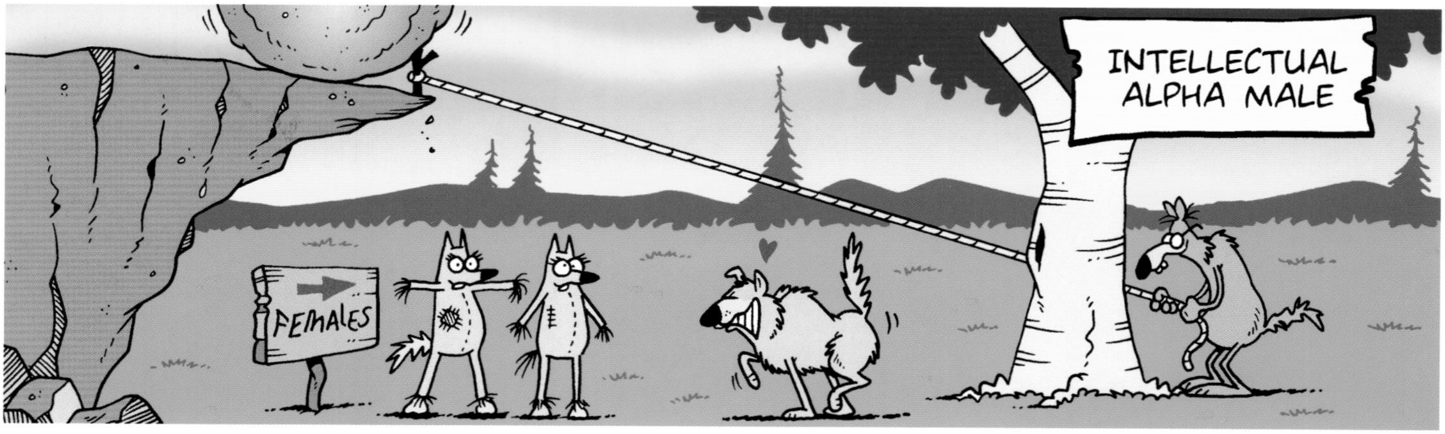
INTELLECTUAL ALPHA MALE
FEMALES

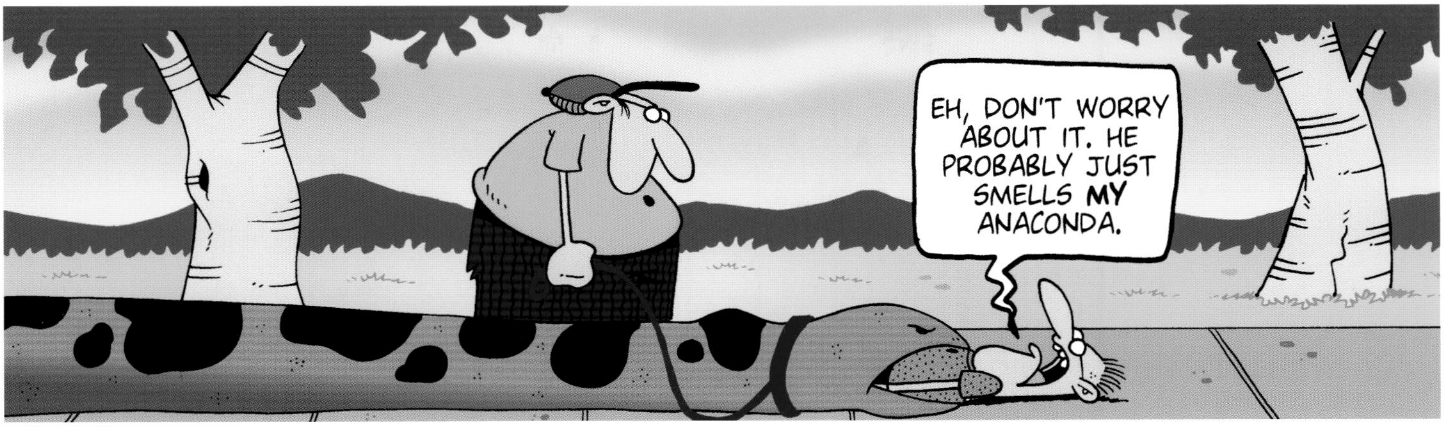
EH, DON'T WORRY ABOUT IT. HE PROBABLY JUST SMELLS MY ANACONDA.

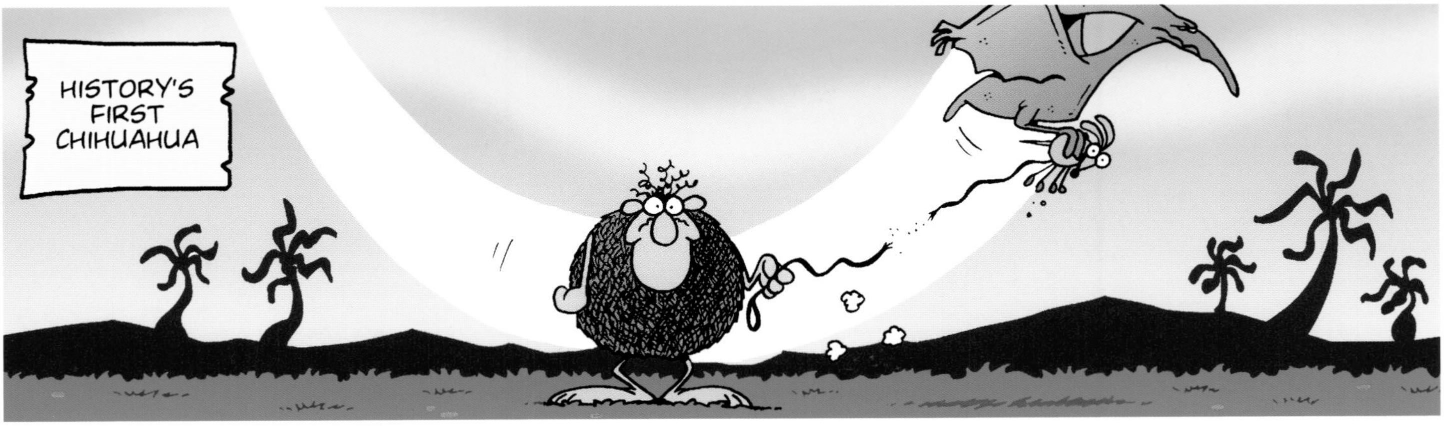
HISTORY'S FIRST CHIHUAHUA

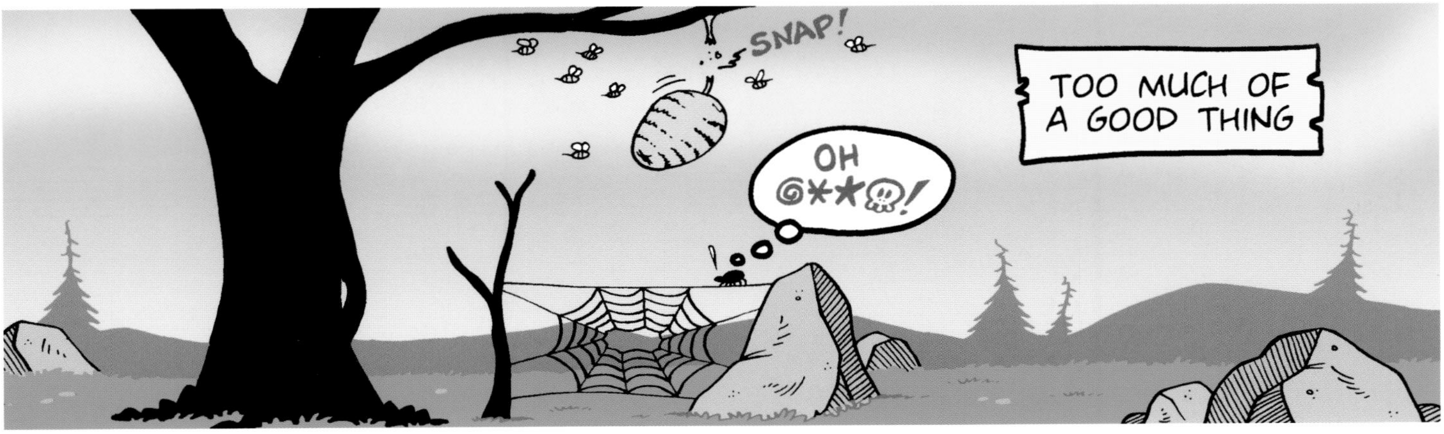
SNAP!
TOO MUCH OF A GOOD THING
OH

Chad Carpenter's TUNDRA

JUST THINK! NO MORE COLD WINTER NIGHTS! NO MORE FROST-BITTEN TOES! NO MORE SHOVELING SNOW!!

OH YEAH. NOW IT'S JUST RAIN, MUD & MOSQUITOES. I CAN'T WAIT.

AH, YES! THE SWEET, SWEET SMELL OF SPRING!

NOTHING THAT A BILLION GALLONS OF FEBREZE WOULDN'T TAKE CARE OF.

© TUNDRA 2005

OH ISN'T IT LOVELY! BIRDS ARE SINGING! FLOWERS ARE GROWING! GRASS IS TURNING GREEN! SPRING IS IN THE AIR!

THE ONLY THING I NOTICED IN THE AIR IS A WINTER'S WORTH OF MELTING DOG BOMBS.

WAKE ME IN JULY. I'LL BE HIBERNATING.

MAYBE WE CAN SUE HER FOR BEING AN UNFIT MOTHER!

SNOW?

www.tundracomics.com

MOTHER NATURE PROVIDES US WITH EVERYTHING WE NEED! FOOD, WATER, AIR, SUNSHINE, DOUGHNUTS...!

YOU'VE GOT THE WRONG ATTITUDE! YOU NEED TO EMBRACE MOTHER NATURE!

26

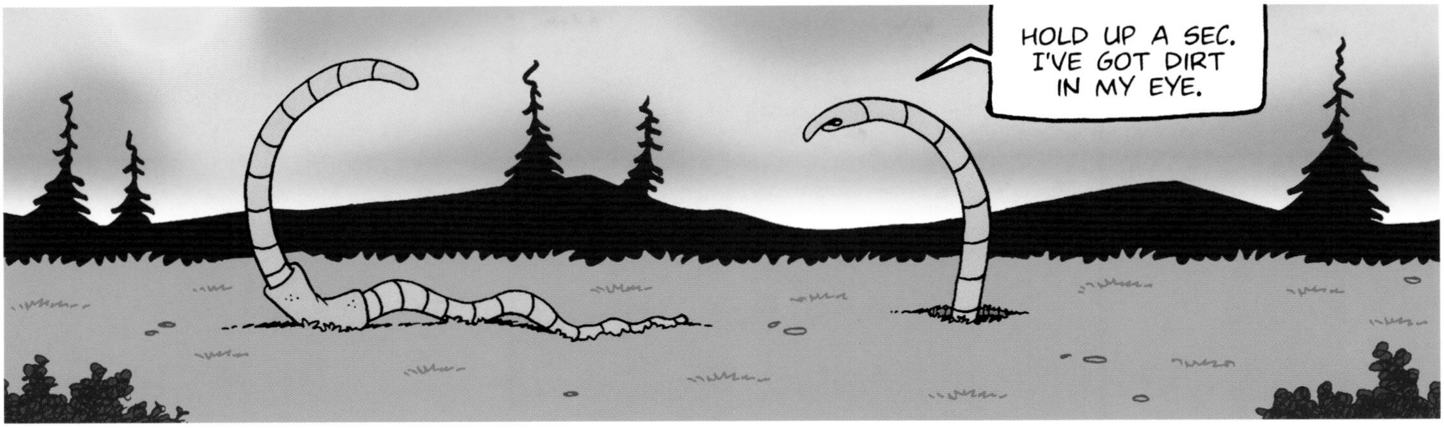
HOLD UP A SEC. I'VE GOT DIRT IN MY EYE.

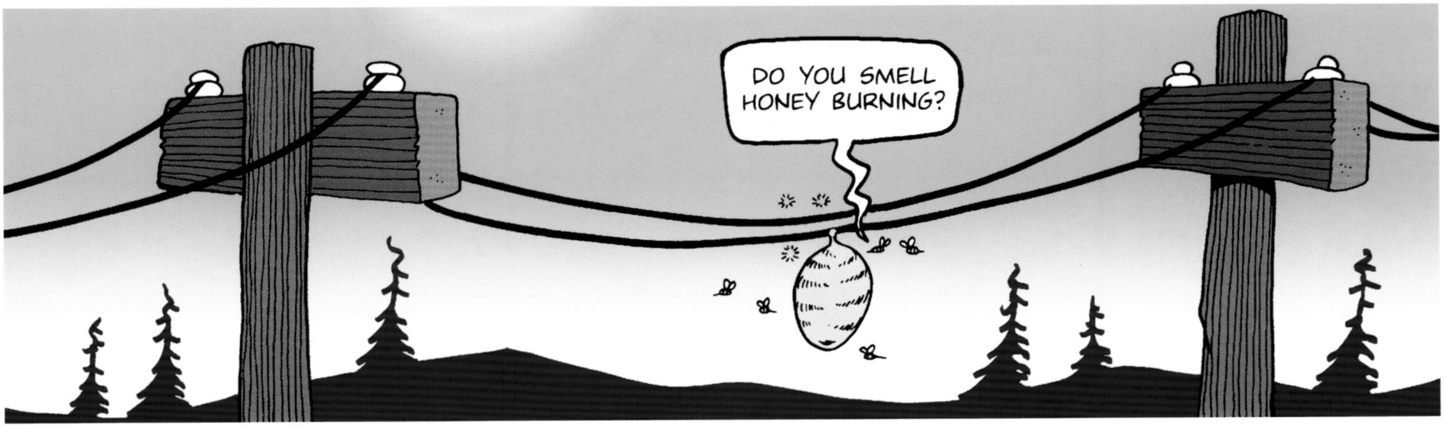
DO YOU SMELL HONEY BURNING?

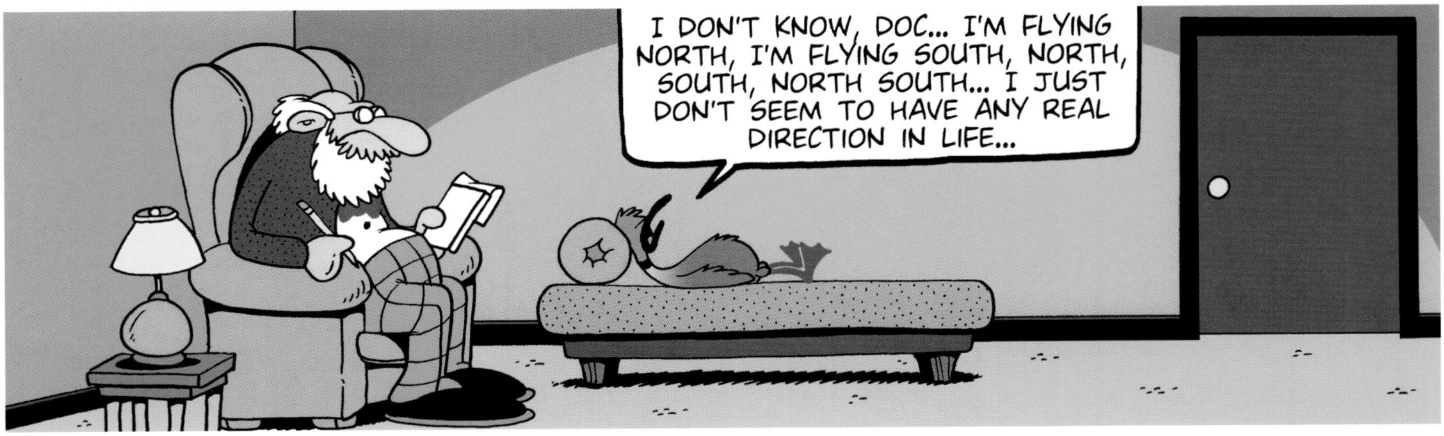
I DON'T KNOW, DOC... I'M FLYING NORTH, I'M FLYING SOUTH, NORTH, SOUTH, NORTH SOUTH... I JUST DON'T SEEM TO HAVE ANY REAL DIRECTION IN LIFE...

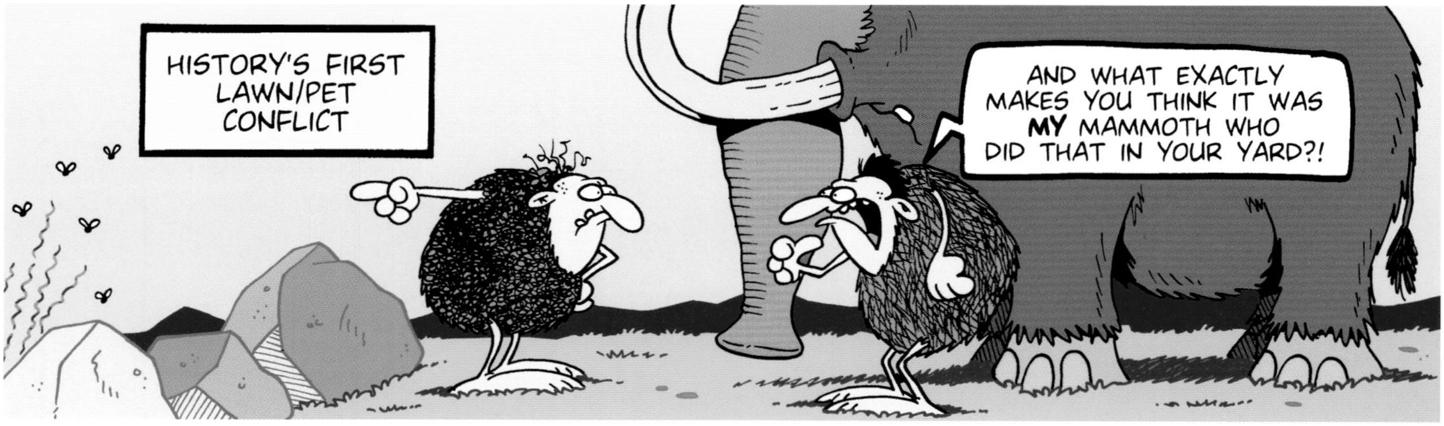
HISTORY'S FIRST LAWN/PET CONFLICT
AND WHAT EXACTLY MAKES YOU THINK IT WAS **MY** MAMMOTH WHO DID THAT IN YOUR YARD?!

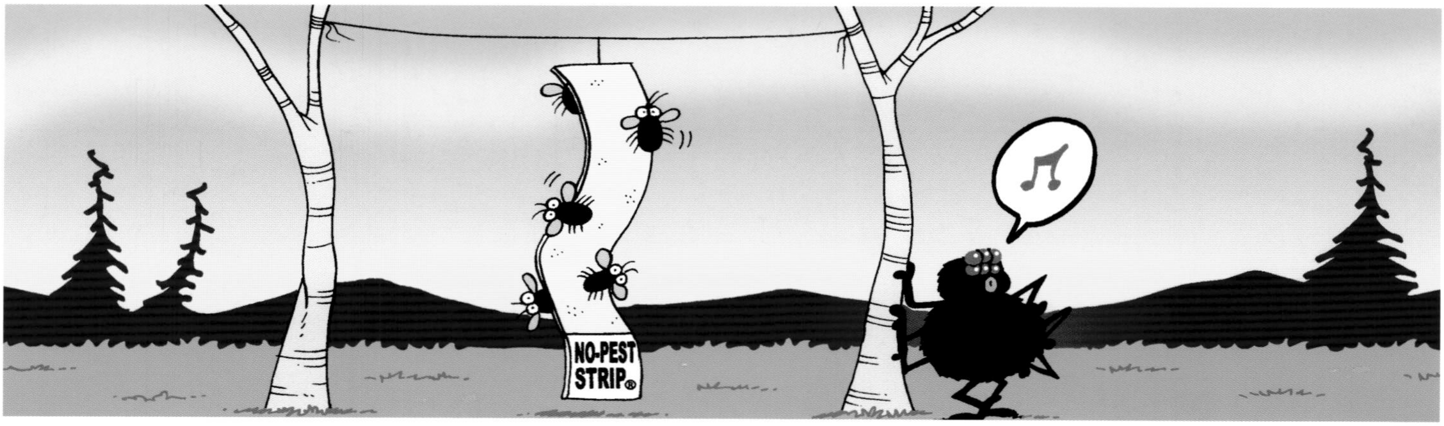
NO-PEST STRIP®

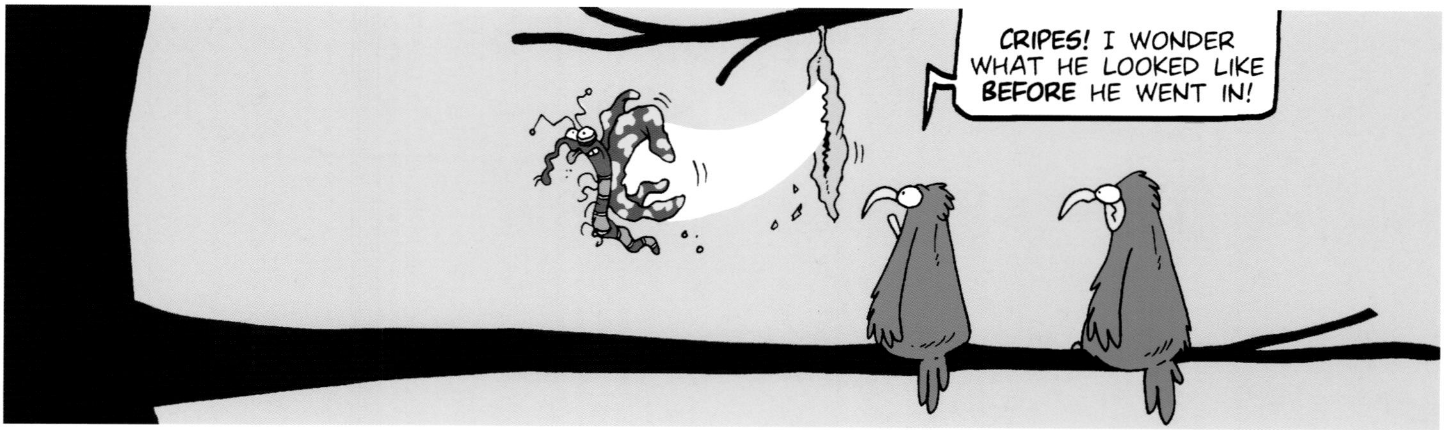
CRIPES! I WONDER WHAT HE LOOKED LIKE **BEFORE** HE WENT IN!

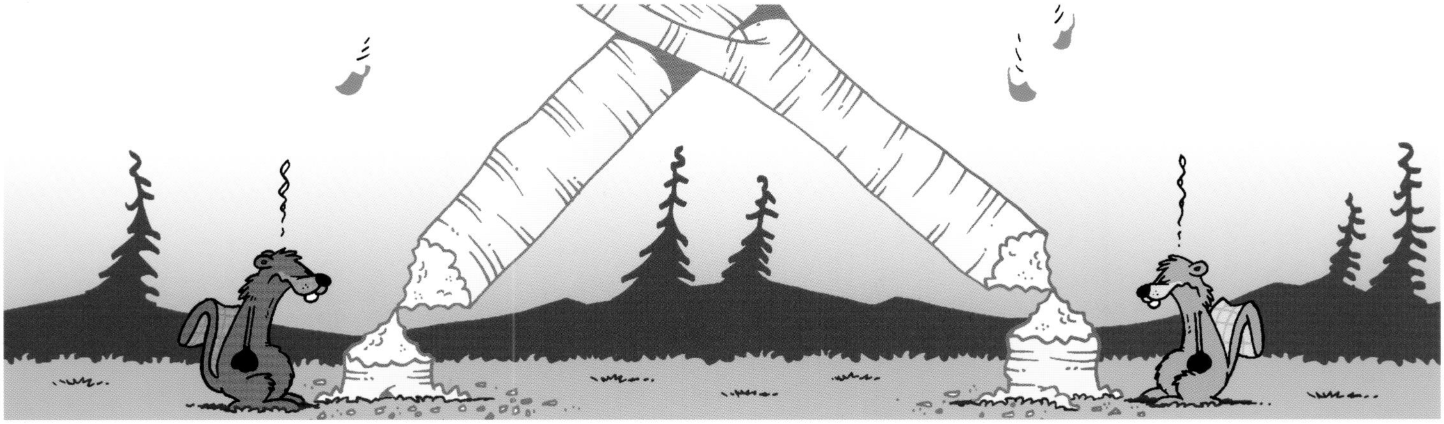

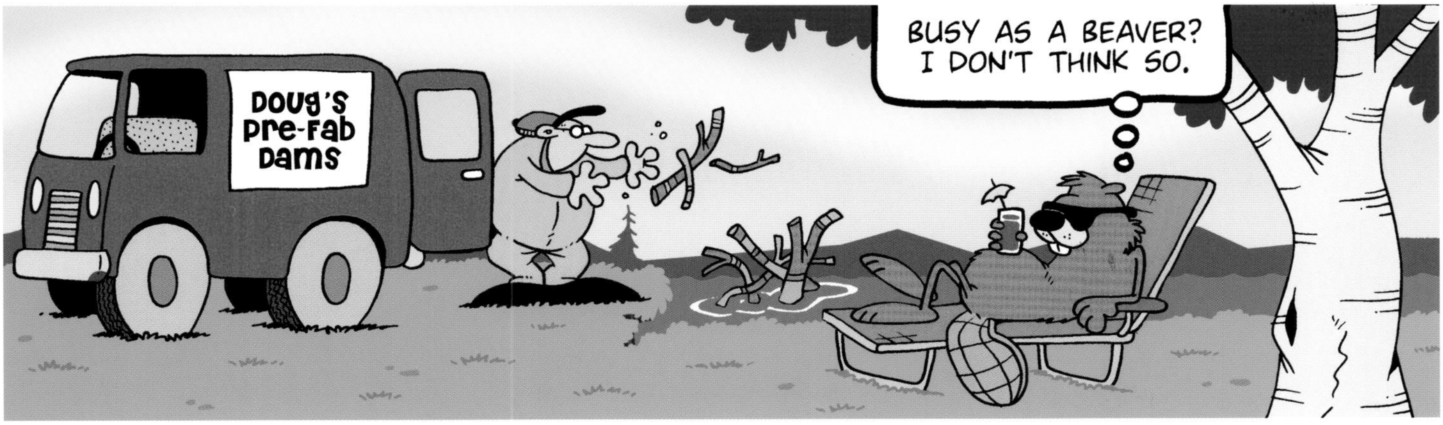
DOUG'S PRE-FAB DAMS
BUSY AS A BEAVER? I DON'T THINK SO.

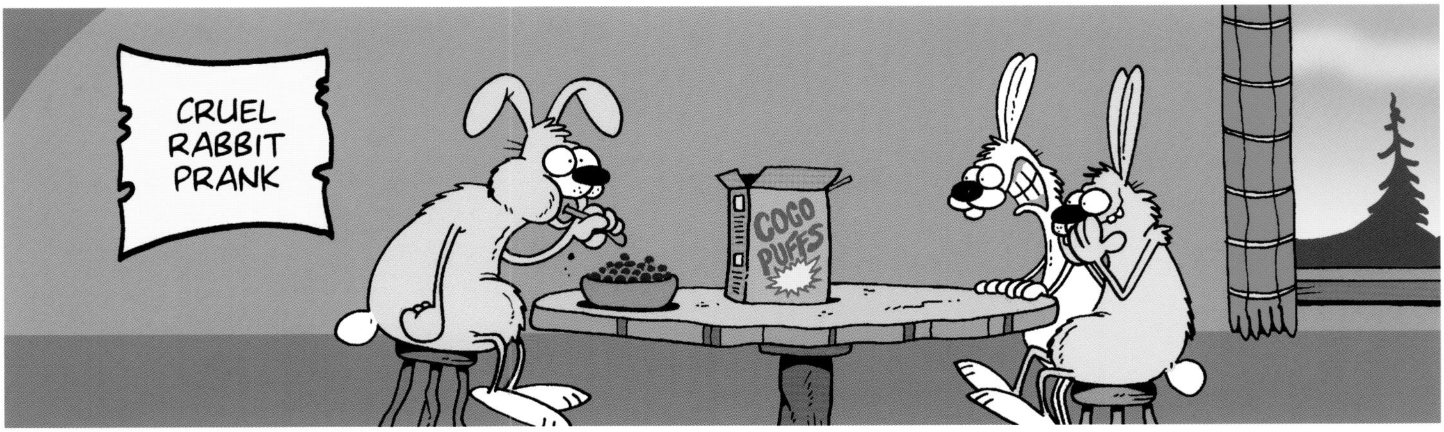
CRUEL RABBIT PRANK
COCO PUFFS

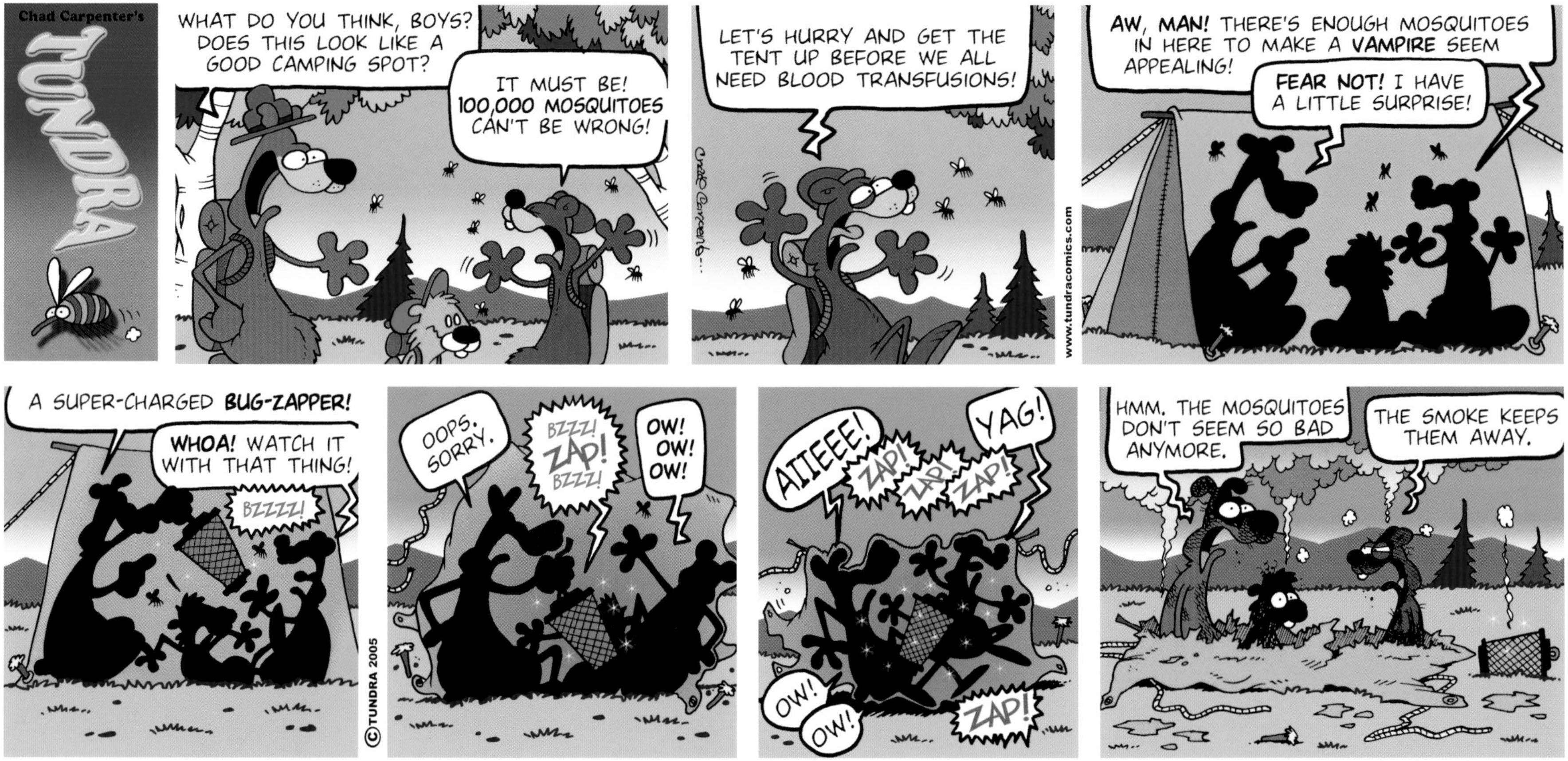
Chad Carpenter's
TUNDRA
WHAT DO YOU THINK, BOYS? DOES THIS LOOK LIKE A GOOD CAMPING SPOT?
IT MUST BE! 100,000 MOSQUITOES CAN'T BE WRONG!
LET'S HURRY AND GET THE TENT UP BEFORE WE ALL NEED BLOOD TRANSFUSIONS!
www.tundracomics.com
AW, MAN! THERE'S ENOUGH MOSQUITOES IN HERE TO MAKE A VAMPIRE SEEM APPEALING!
FEAR NOT! I HAVE A LITTLE SURPRISE!
A SUPER-CHARGED BUG-ZAPPER!
WHOA! WATCH IT WITH THAT THING!
BZZZZ!
©TUNDRA 2005
OOPS. SORRY.
BZZZ! ZAP! BZZZ!
OW! OW! OW!
AIIEEE!
ZAP! ZAP! ZAP!
YAG!
OW!
OW!
ZAP!
HMM. THE MOSQUITOES DON'T SEEM SO BAD ANYMORE.
THE SMOKE KEEPS THEM AWAY.

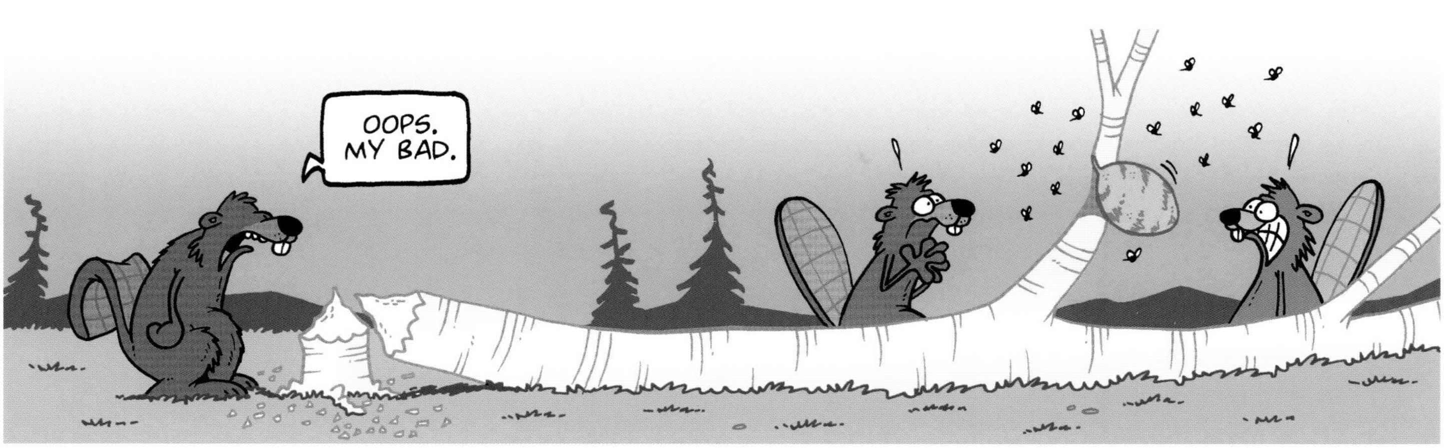
OOPS. MY BAD.

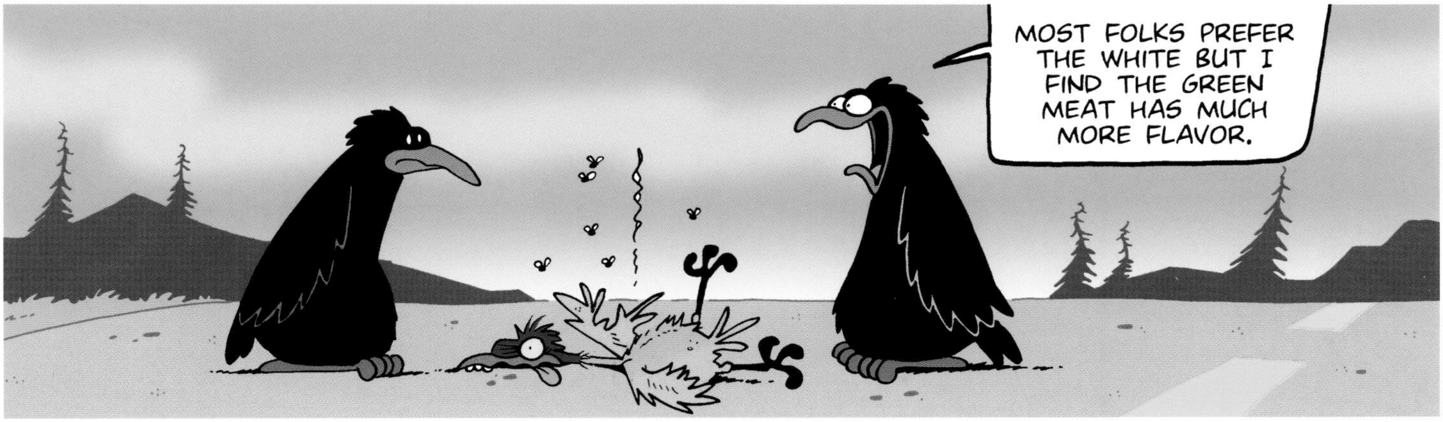
MOST FOLKS PREFER THE WHITE BUT I FIND THE GREEN MEAT HAS MUCH MORE FLAVOR.

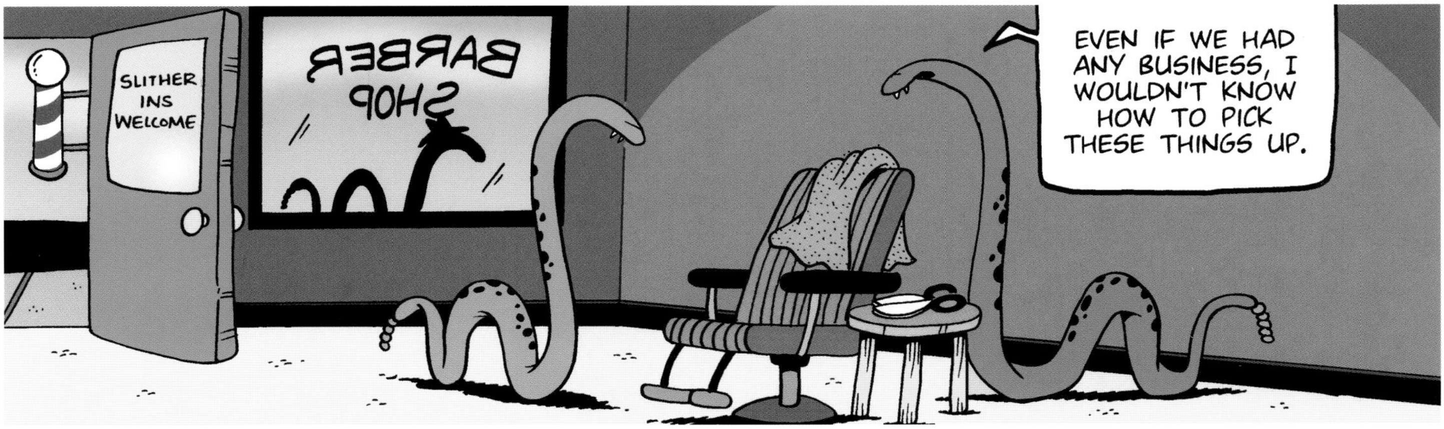
SLITHER INS WELCOME
BARBER SHOP
EVEN IF WE HAD ANY BUSINESS, I WOULDN'T KNOW HOW TO PICK THESE THINGS UP.

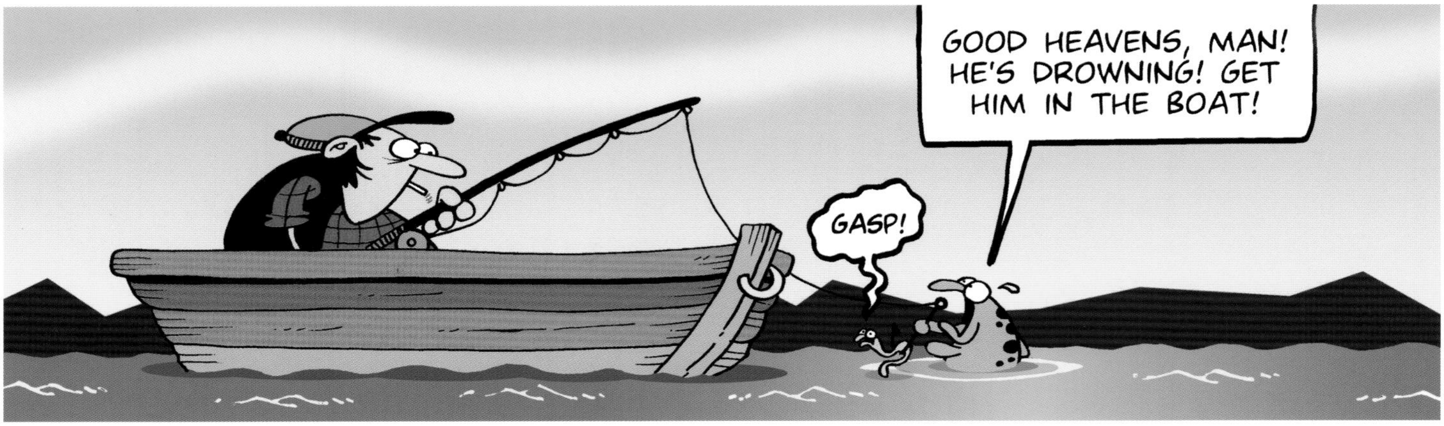
GOOD HEAVENS, MAN! HE'S DROWNING! GET HIM IN THE BOAT!
GASP!

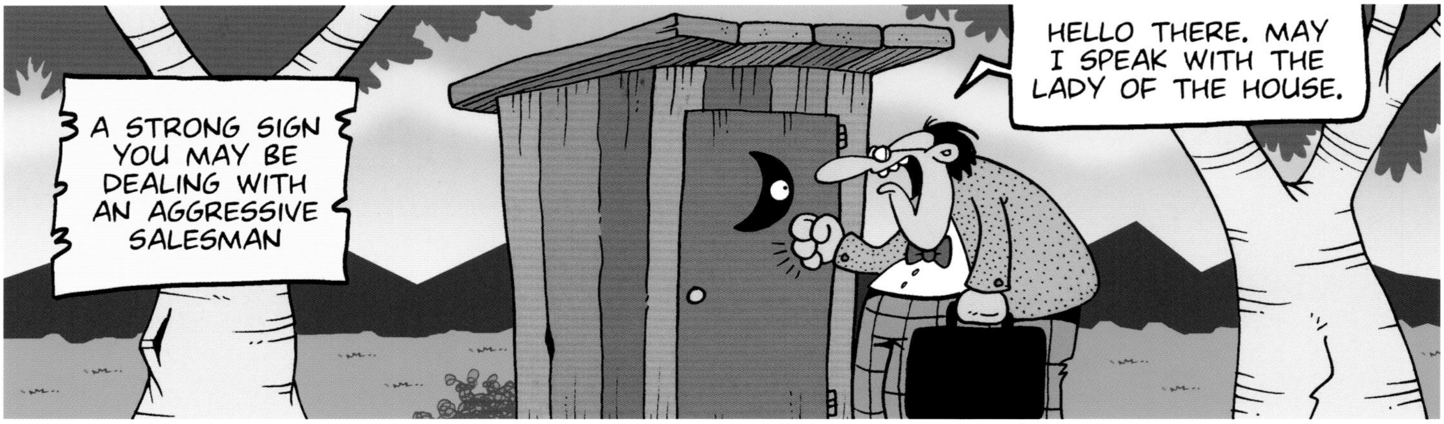
A STRONG SIGN YOU MAY BE DEALING WITH AN AGGRESSIVE SALESMAN
HELLO THERE. MAY I SPEAK WITH THE LADY OF THE HOUSE.

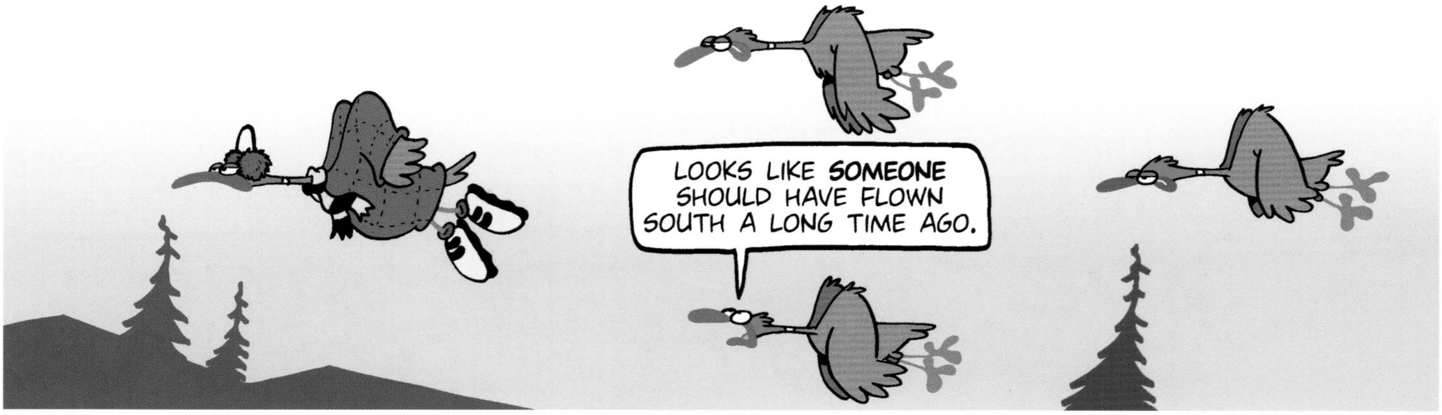
LOOKS LIKE SOMEONE SHOULD HAVE FLOWN SOUTH A LONG TIME AGO.

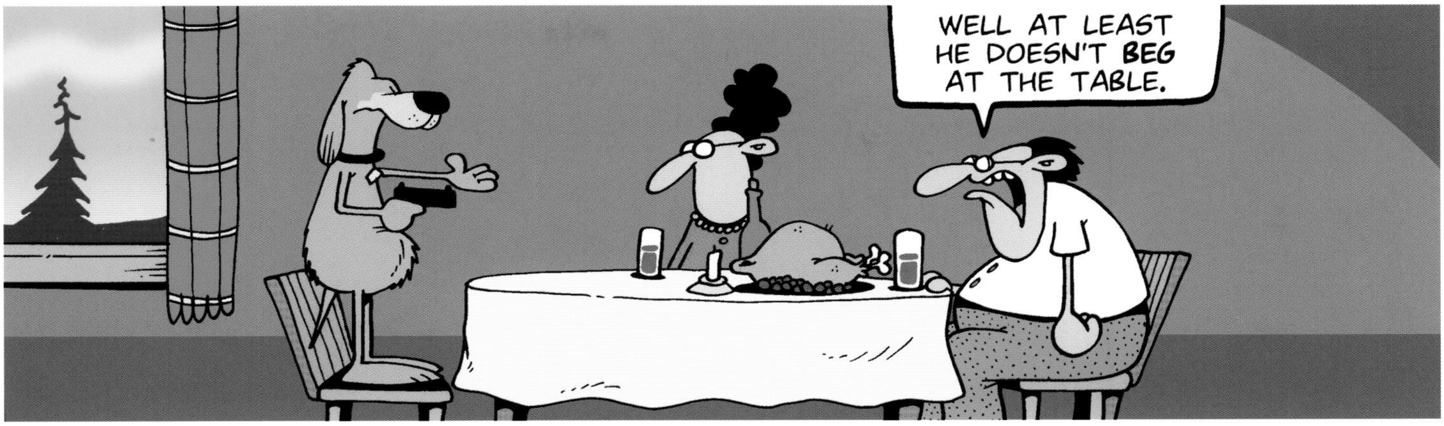
WELL AT LEAST HE DOESN'T **BEG** AT THE TABLE.

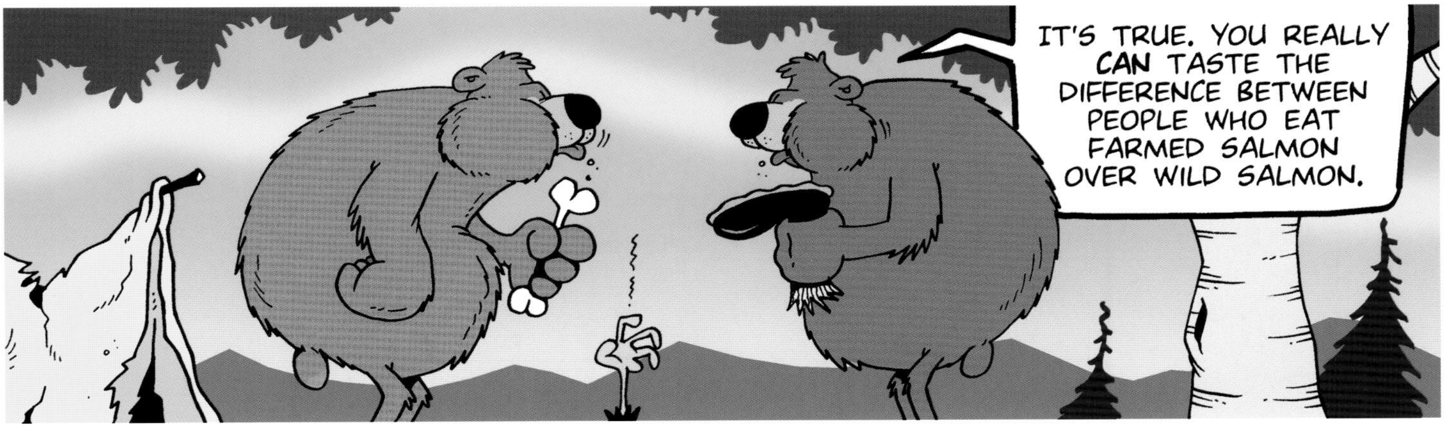
IT'S TRUE. YOU REALLY **CAN** TASTE THE DIFFERENCE BETWEEN PEOPLE WHO EAT FARMED SALMON OVER WILD SALMON.

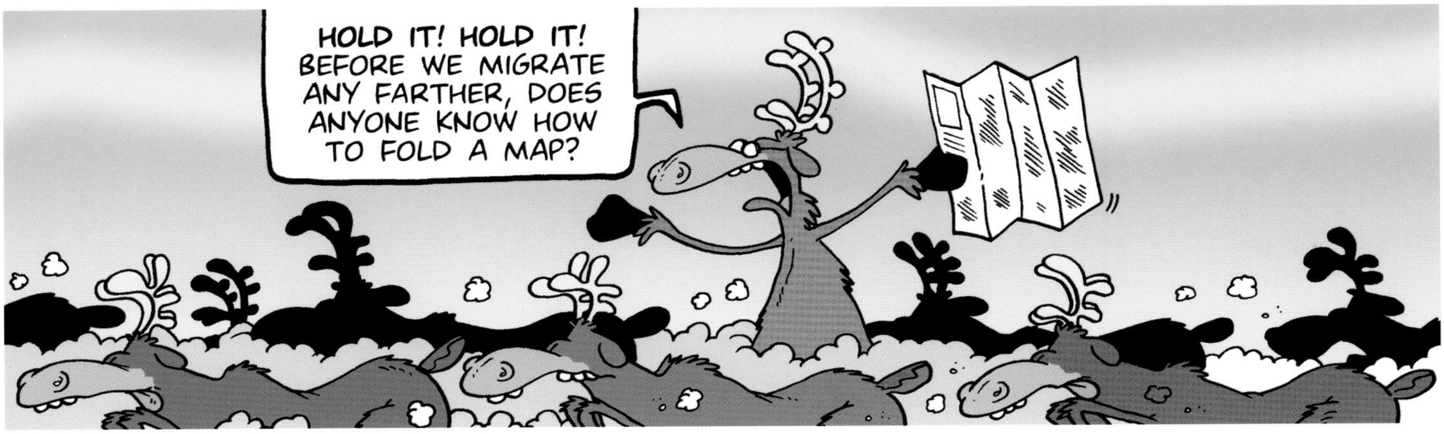
HOLD IT! HOLD IT! BEFORE WE MIGRATE ANY FARTHER, DOES ANYONE KNOW HOW TO FOLD A MAP?

Chad Carpenter's
TUNDRA
THIS STRIP IS BASED ON AN IDEA FROM:
TOM YOUNGBLOOD
ANCHORAGE, AK
AND
BILL ELLZEY
HOUMA, LA
WHAT THE...?! OH MAN! THIS IS ABSOLUTELY RIDICULOUS! I CAN'T FIGURE THIS THING OUT!
www.tundracomics.com
©TUNDRA 2005
PARDON ME, SIR. CAN I HELP YOU WITH THAT?
YAAAAG! A BEAR! AND SOME SORT OF SMALL RODENT!
YOU SEE, WHAT YOU NEED TO DO FIRST IS GRAB THE HANDLE LIKE THIS! THEN, SIMULTANIOUSLY PUSH THE LEVER HERE...!
STAY B-B-BACK!
...ALL THE WHILE WORKING THE LOWER PEDAL IN AN UP & DOWN MOTION AND THEN KICKING IT RIGHT HERE IN THE "SWEET-SPOT!"
D-D-DON'T EAT ME!
WHAP!
TA-DA!
POP!
IT'S NO WONDER HUMANS CAN'T OPERATE THOSE THINGS...
...YOU NEED FOUR PAWS TO GET THEM OPEN.
Bear Proof Trash Containers

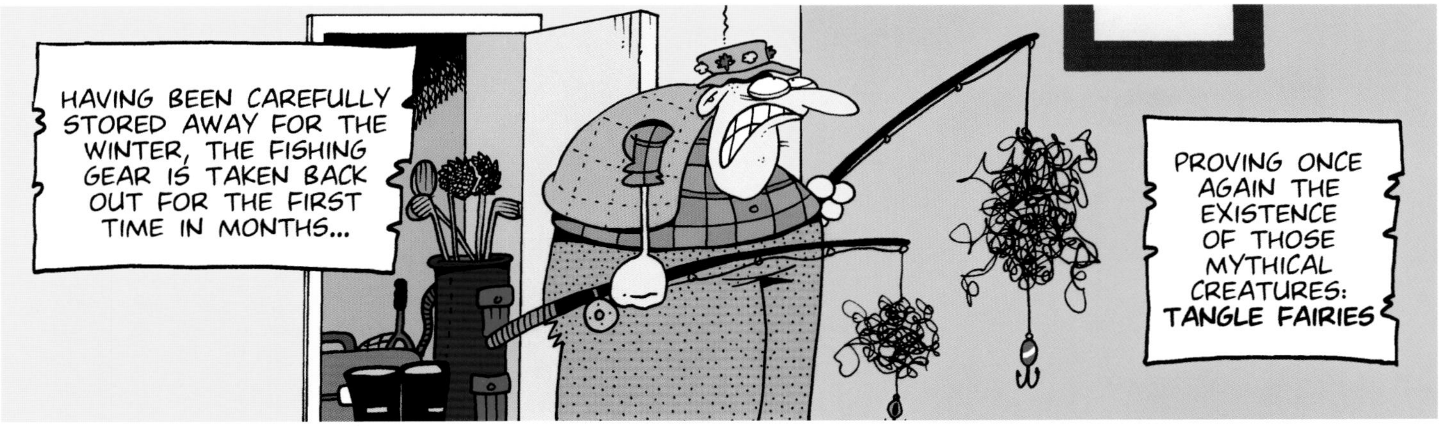
HAVING BEEN CAREFULLY STORED AWAY FOR THE WINTER, THE FISHING GEAR IS TAKEN BACK OUT FOR THE FIRST TIME IN MONTHS...
PROVING ONCE AGAIN THE EXISTENCE OF THOSE MYTHICAL CREATURES: TANGLE FAIRIES

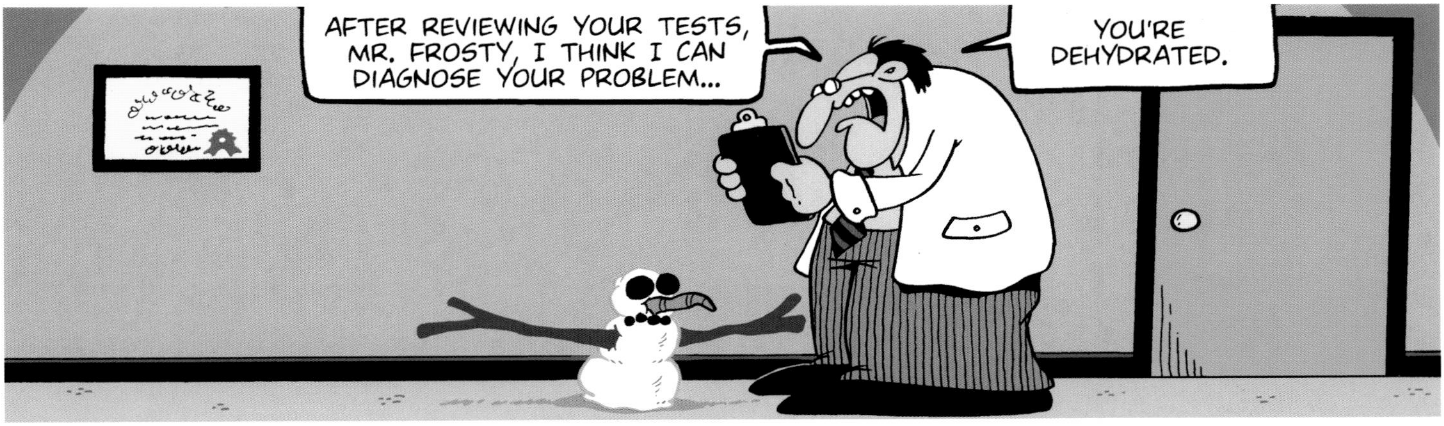
AFTER REVIEWING YOUR TESTS, MR. FROSTY, I THINK I CAN DIAGNOSE YOUR PROBLEM...
YOU'RE DEHYDRATED.

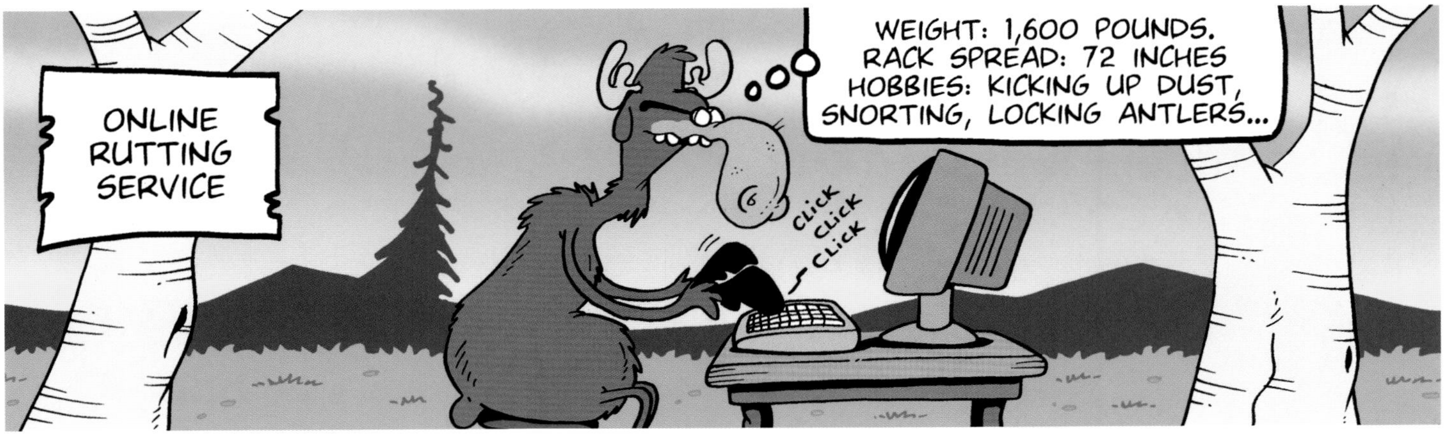
ONLINE RUTTING SERVICE
WEIGHT: 1,600 POUNDS. RACK SPREAD: 72 INCHES HOBBIES: KICKING UP DUST, SNORTING, LOCKING ANTLERS...
CLICK CLICK CLICK

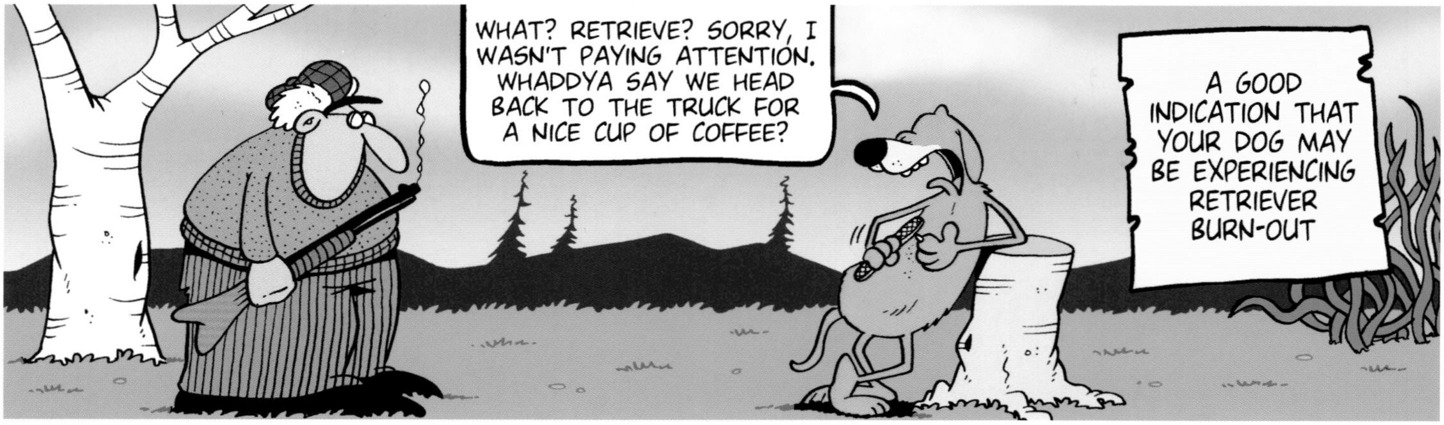
WHAT? RETRIEVE? SORRY, I WASN'T PAYING ATTENTION. WHADDYA SAY WE HEAD BACK TO THE TRUCK FOR A NICE CUP OF COFFEE?
A GOOD INDICATION THAT YOUR DOG MAY BE EXPERIENCING RETRIEVER BURN-OUT

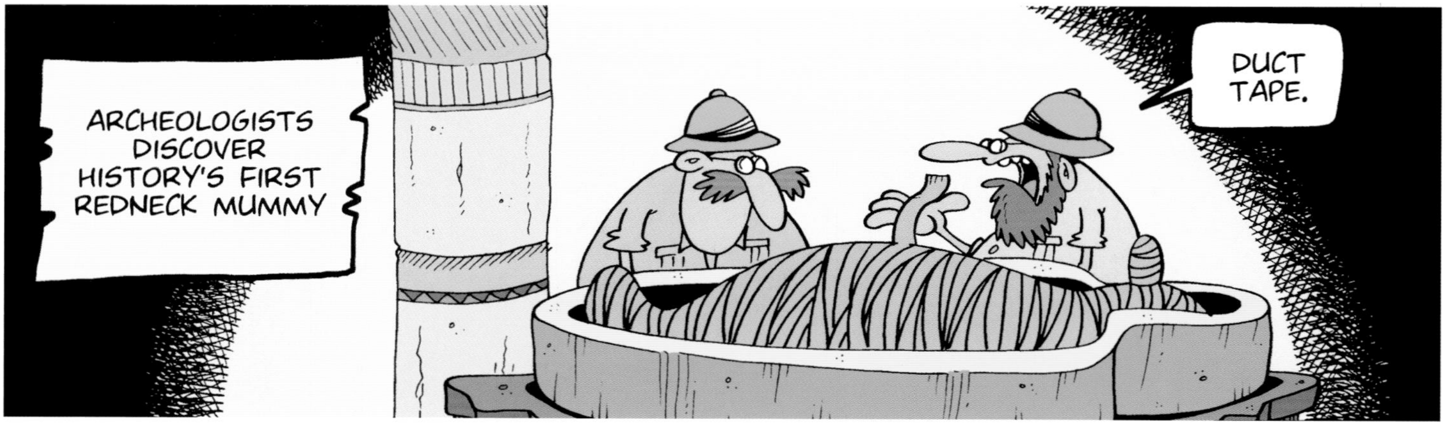
ARCHEOLOGISTS DISCOVER HISTORY'S FIRST REDNECK MUMMY
DUCT TAPE.

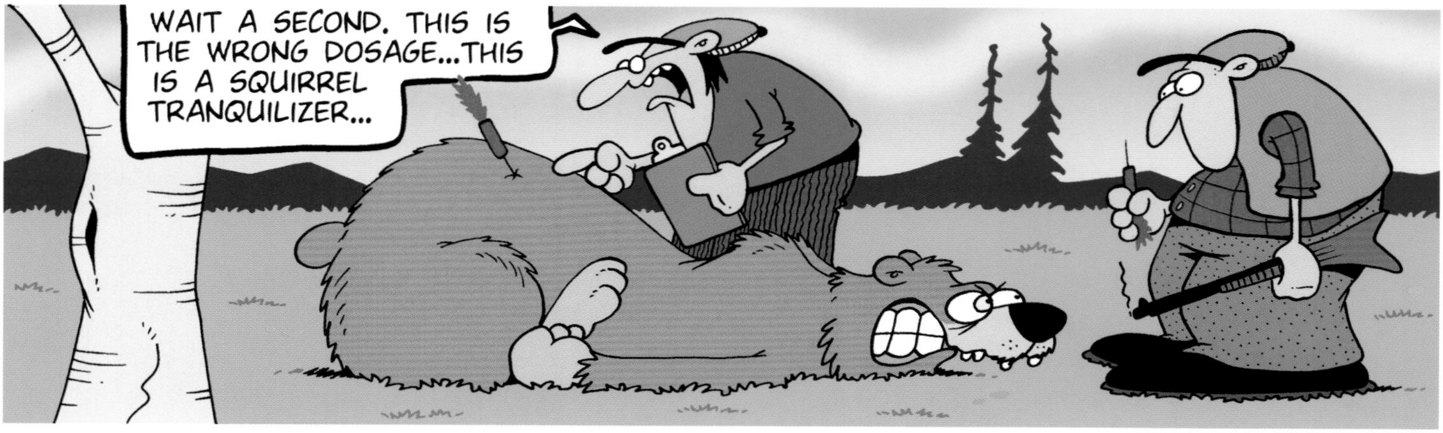
WAIT A SECOND. THIS IS THE WRONG DOSAGE...THIS IS A SQUIRREL TRANQUILIZER...

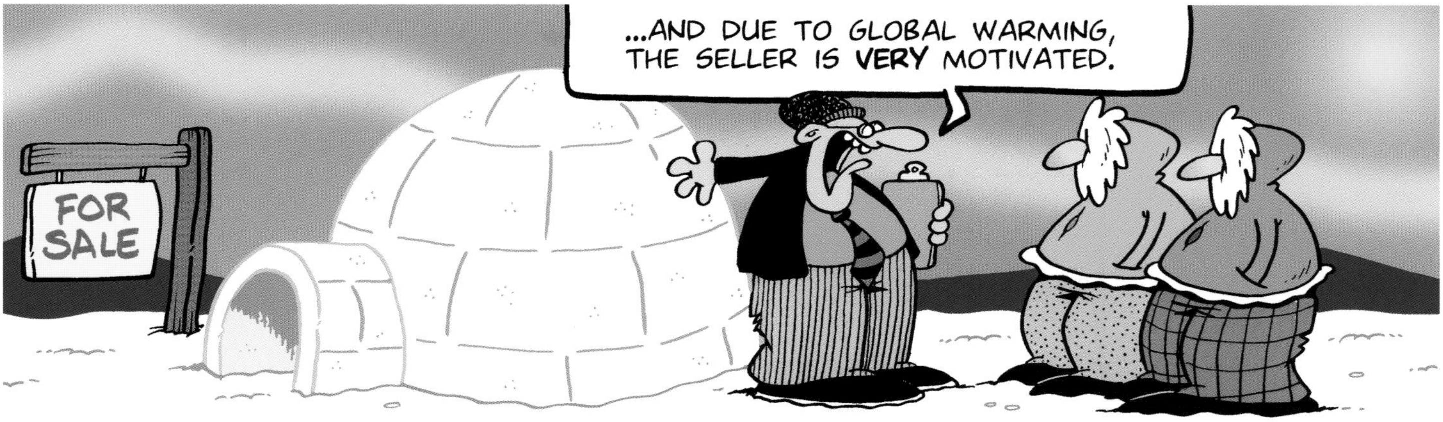
FOR SALE
...AND DUE TO GLOBAL WARMING, THE SELLER IS **VERY** MOTIVATED.

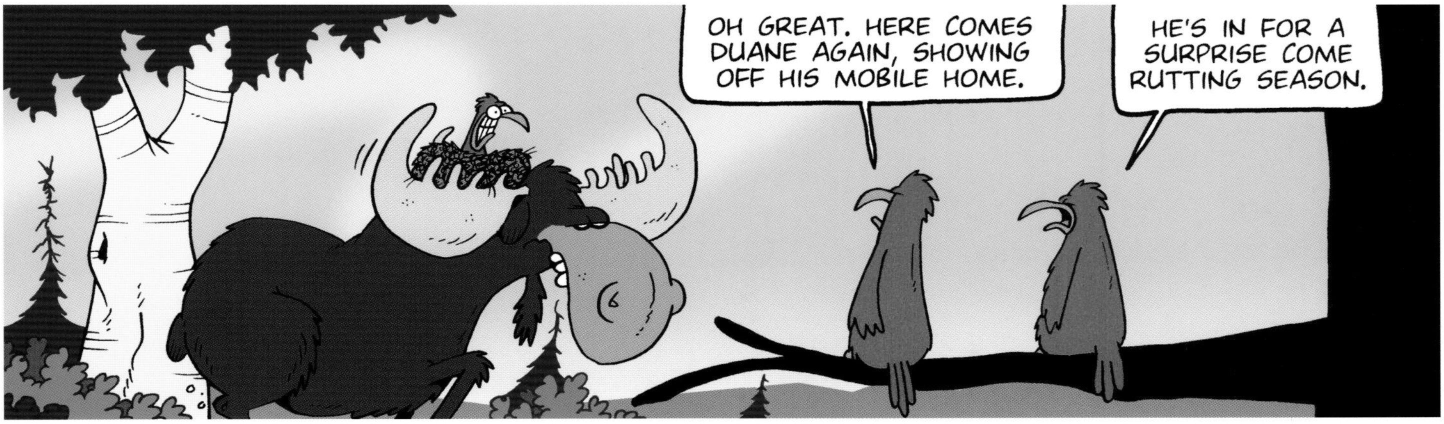
OH GREAT. HERE COMES DUANE AGAIN, SHOWING OFF HIS MOBILE HOME.
HE'S IN FOR A SURPRISE COME RUTTING SEASON.

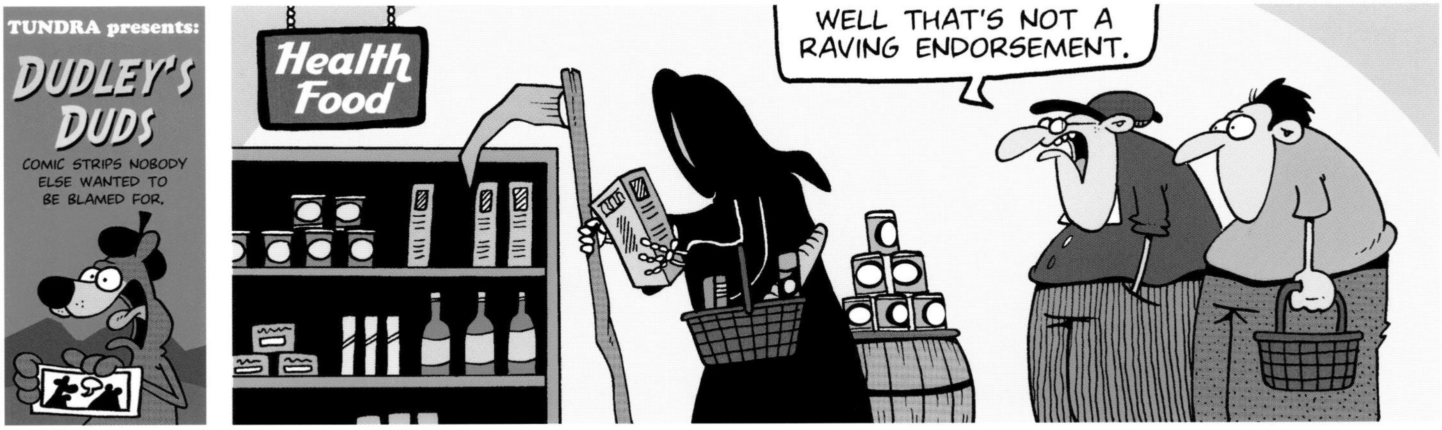
TUNDRA presents:
DUDLEY'S DUDS
COMIC STRIPS NOBODY ELSE WANTED TO BE BLAMED FOR.
Health Food
WELL THAT'S NOT A RAVING ENDORSEMENT.

Chad Carpenter's
TUNDRA
MAN O' MAN! THIS WEATHER IS HOTTER THAN **JALAPEÑO TOILET PAPER** AND **TWICE** AS UNCOMFORTABLE!
I THINK MY BRAIN IS MELTING.
www.tundracomics.com
IT JUST DOESN'T SEEM FAIR THAT WE FURRY WOODLAND FOLK SHOULD HAVE TO ENDURE THIS.
Chad Carpenter
THAT'S IT. I CAN'T TAKE THIS ANYMORE. **I'M** GOING TO DO SOMETHING ABOUT IT.
AHH. MUCH MORE REFRESHING.
YAAAG!
© TUNDRA 2005
AT LEAST I'M GLAD TO SEE YOU LEFT A FUR BATHING SUIT!
SPEAK FOR YOURSELF. **IT'S A THONG.**

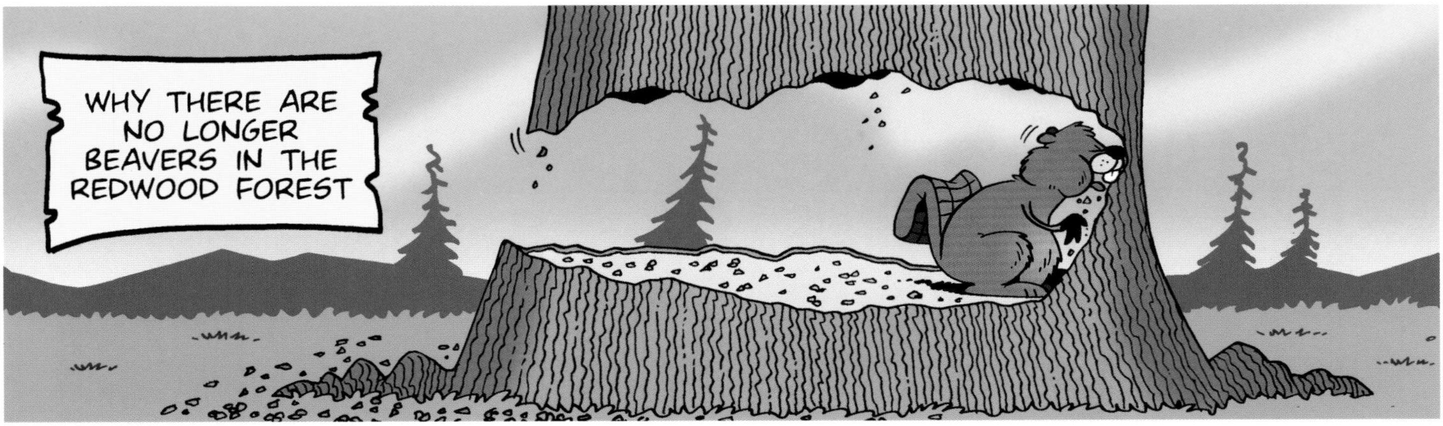
WHY THERE ARE NO LONGER BEAVERS IN THE REDWOOD FOREST

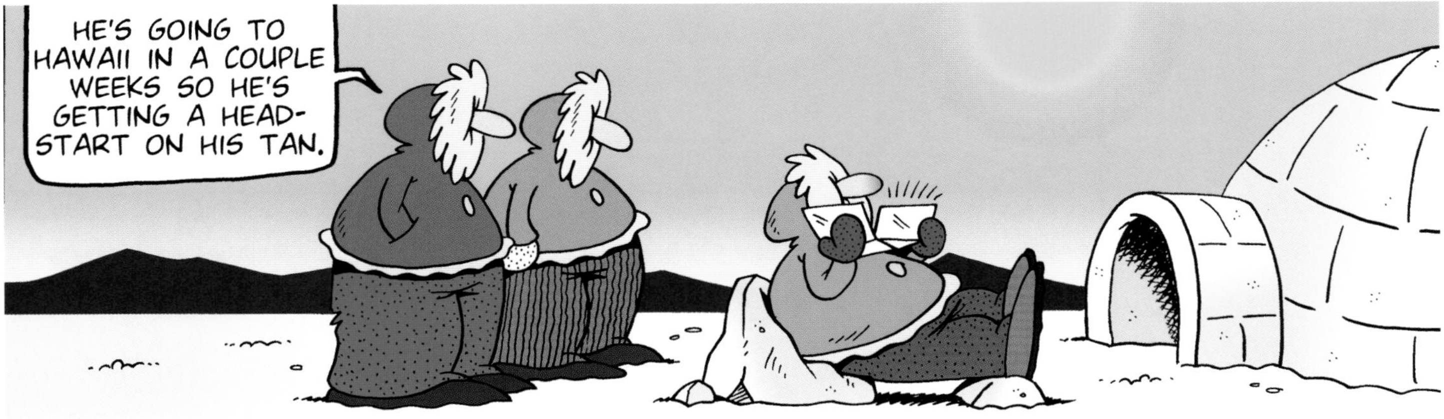
HE'S GOING TO HAWAII IN A COUPLE WEEKS SO HE'S GETTING A HEAD-START ON HIS TAN.

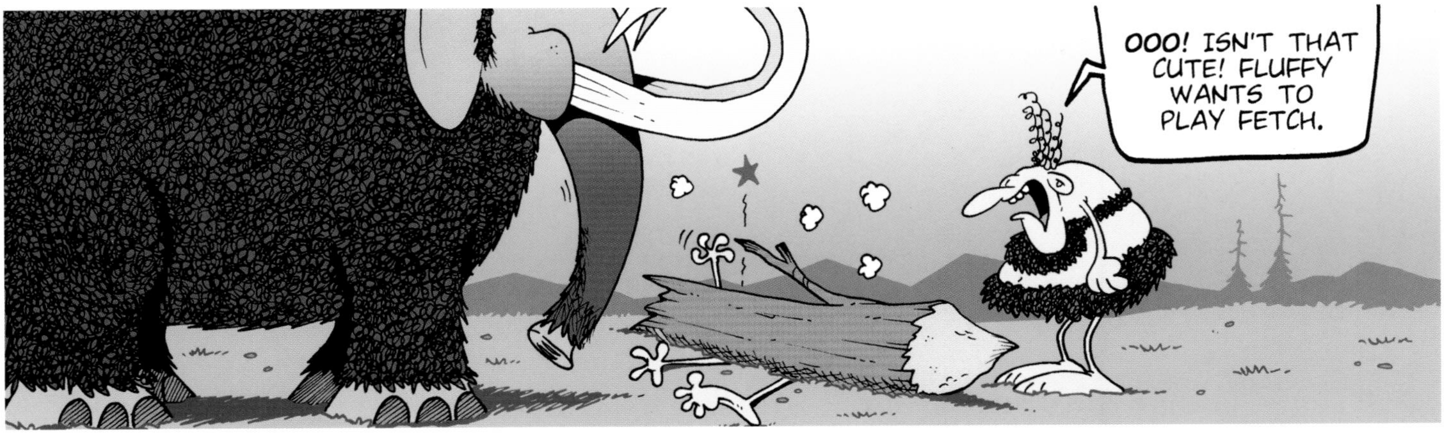
OOO! ISN'T THAT CUTE! FLUFFY WANTS TO PLAY FETCH.

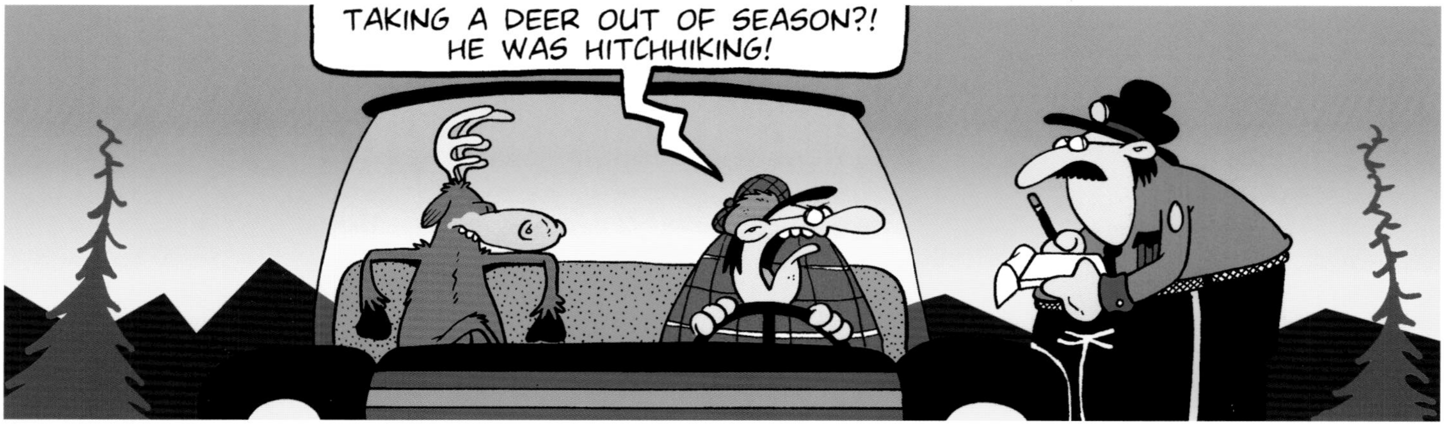
TAKING A DEER OUT OF SEASON?! HE WAS HITCHHIKING!

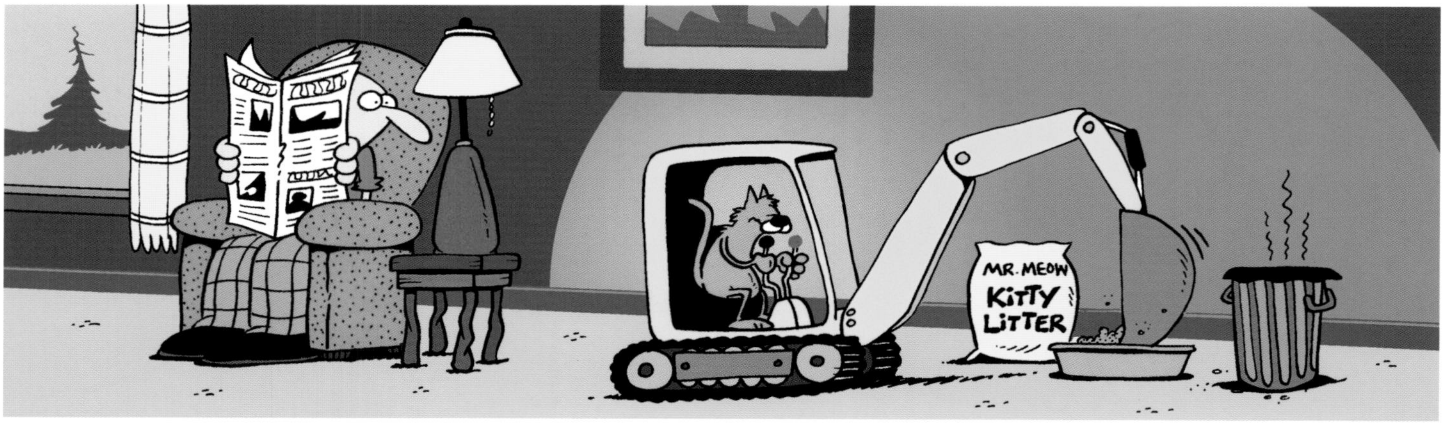
MR. MEOW
KITTY LITTER

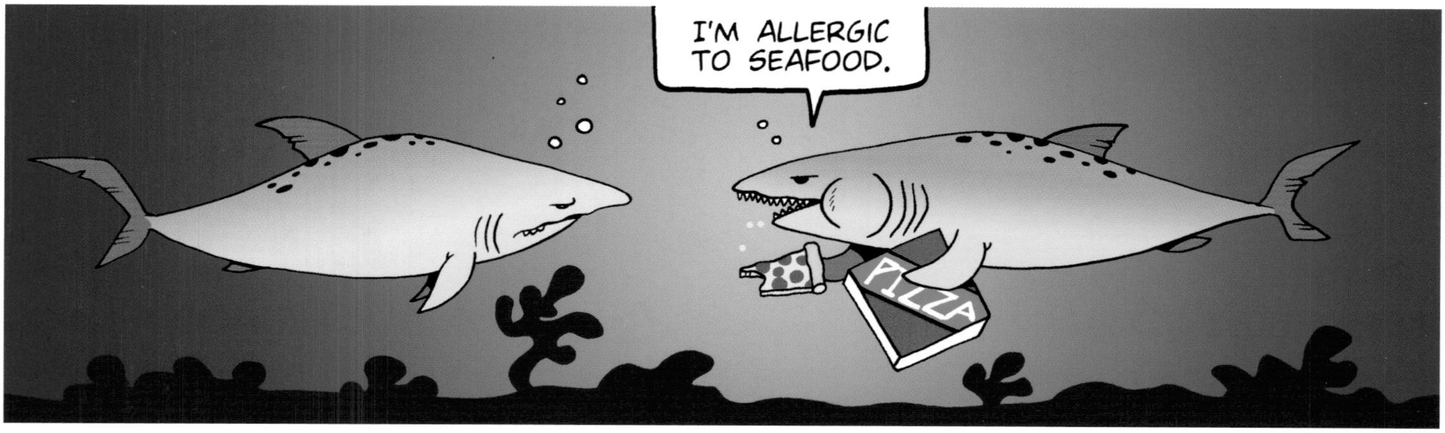
I'M ALLERGIC TO SEAFOOD.
PIZZA

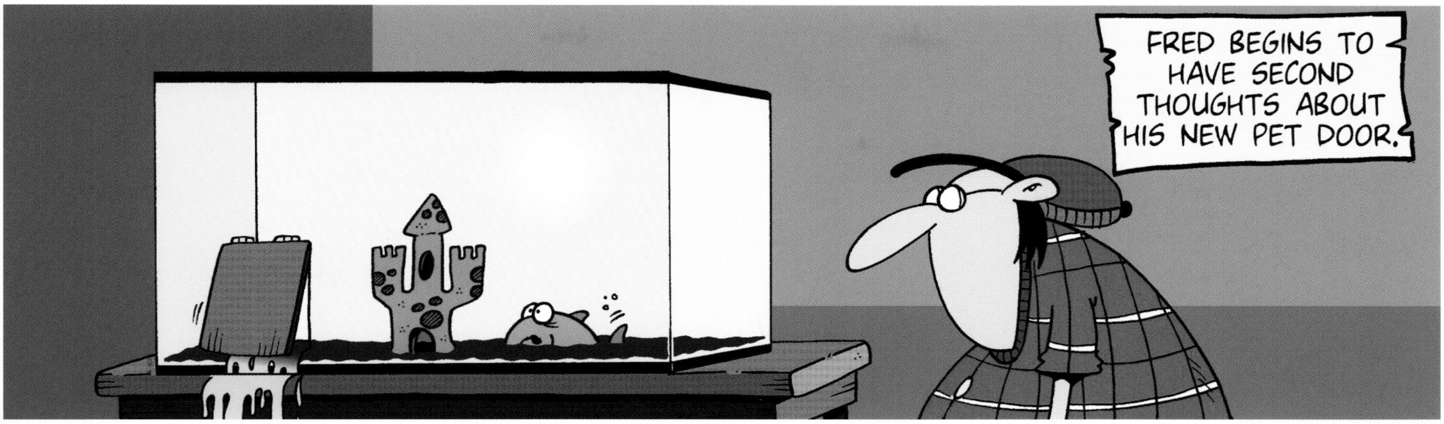
FRED BEGINS TO HAVE SECOND THOUGHTS ABOUT HIS NEW PET DOOR.

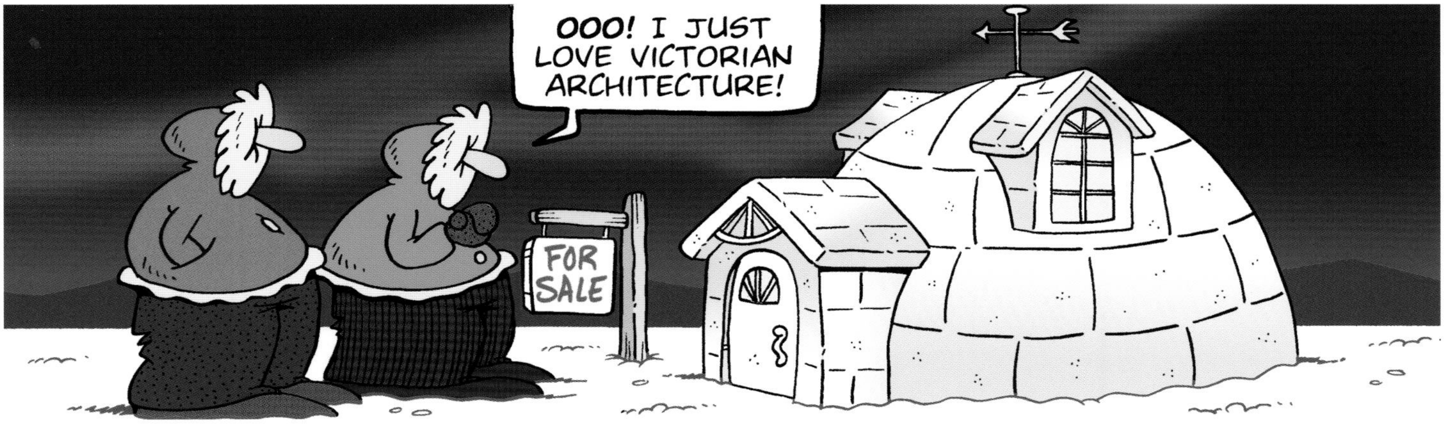
OOO! I JUST LOVE VICTORIAN ARCHITECTURE!
FOR SALE

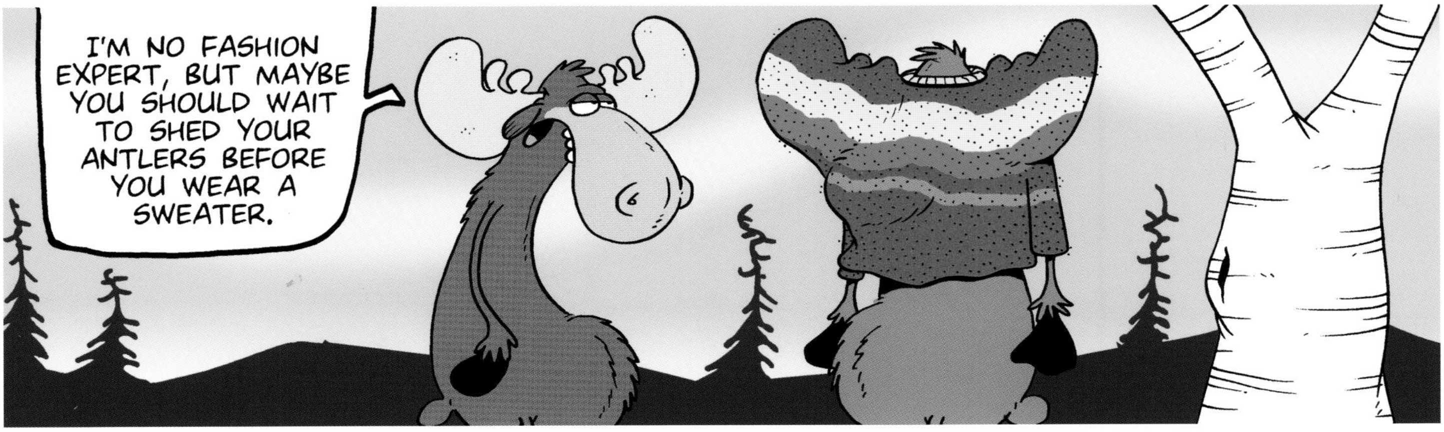
I'M NO FASHION EXPERT, BUT MAYBE YOU SHOULD WAIT TO SHED YOUR ANTLERS BEFORE YOU WEAR A SWEATER.

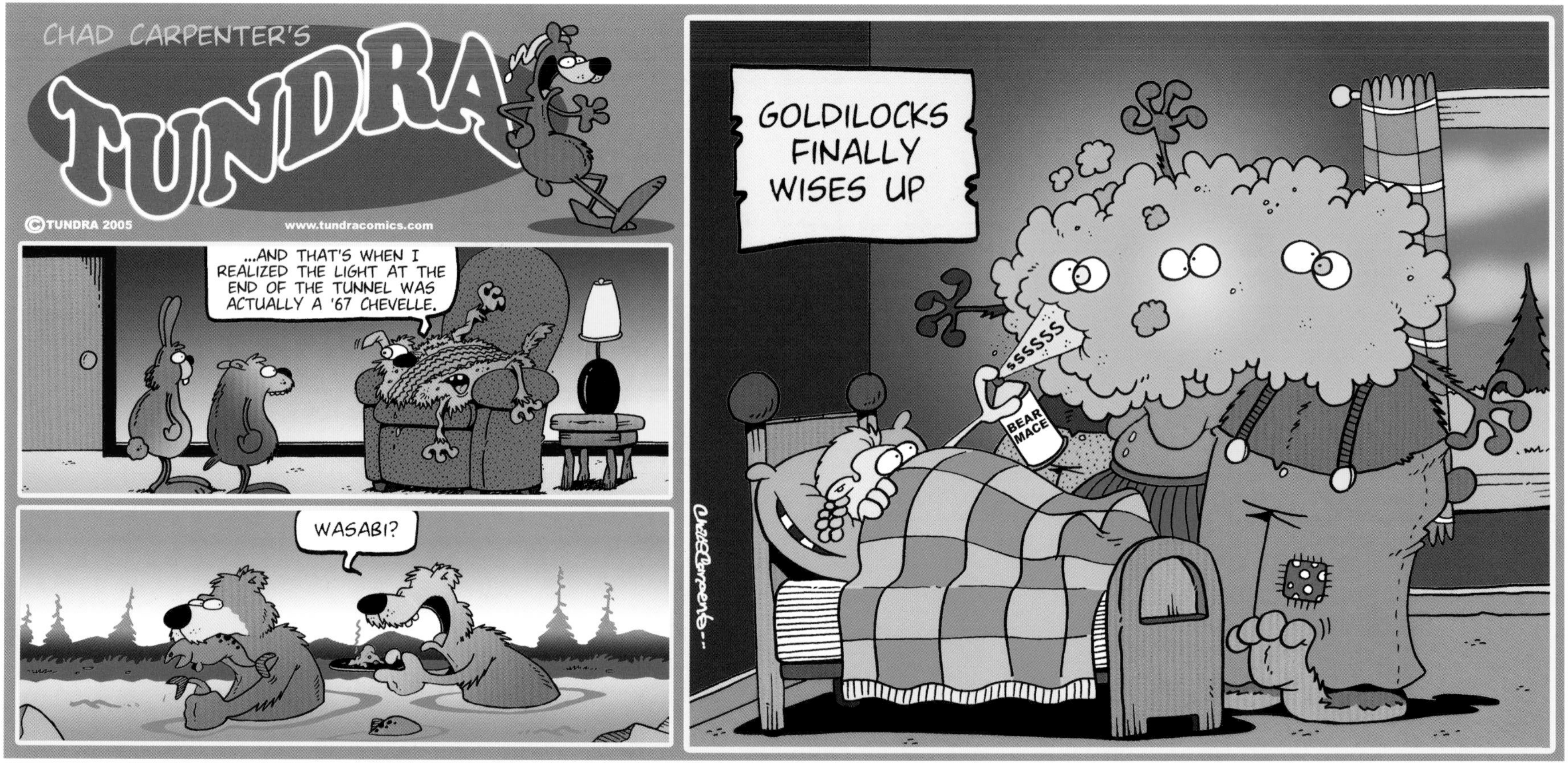
CHAD CARPENTER'S
TUNDRA
©TUNDRA 2005
www.tundracomics.com
...AND THAT'S WHEN I REALIZED THE LIGHT AT THE END OF THE TUNNEL WAS ACTUALLY A '67 CHEVELLE.
WASABI?
GOLDILOCKS FINALLY WISES UP
SSSSSS
BEAR MACE

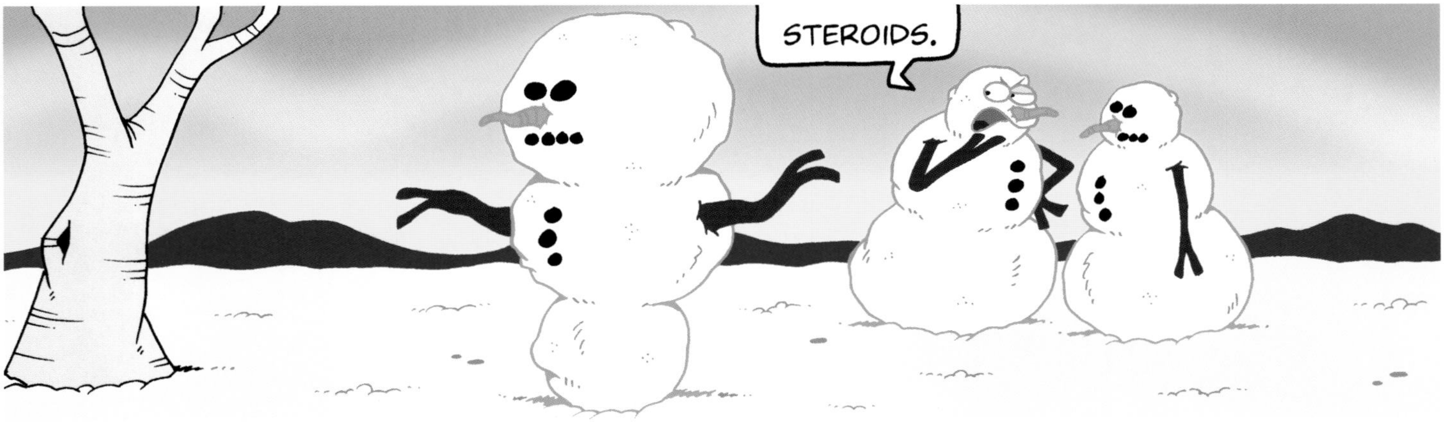
STEROIDS.

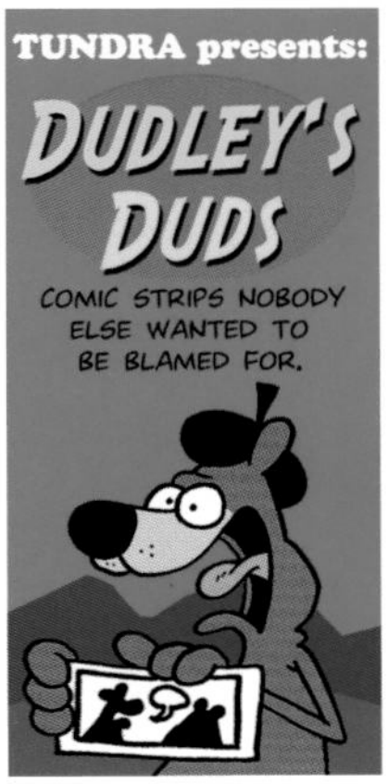
TUNDRA presents:
DUDLEY'S DUDS
COMIC STRIPS NOBODY ELSE WANTED TO BE BLAMED FOR.

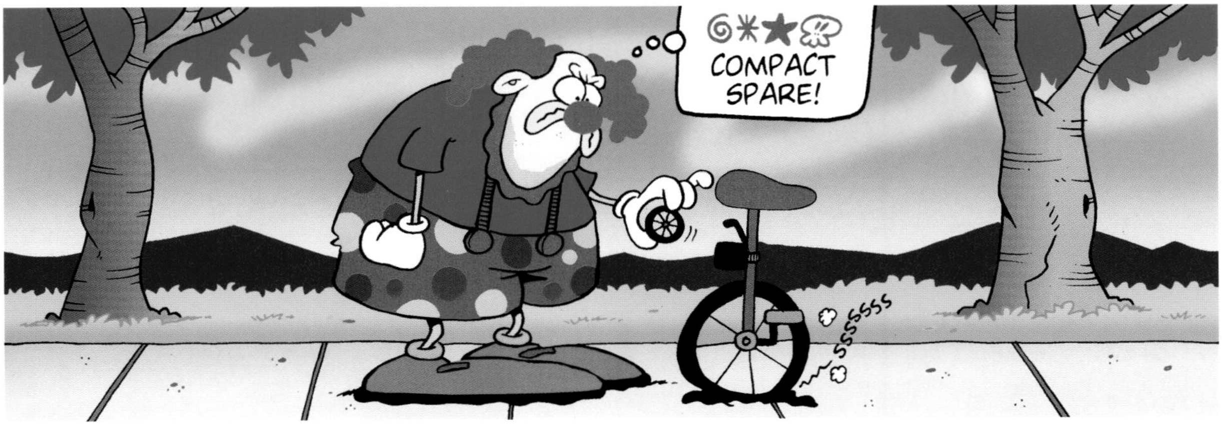
COMPACT SPARE!
SSSSSSS

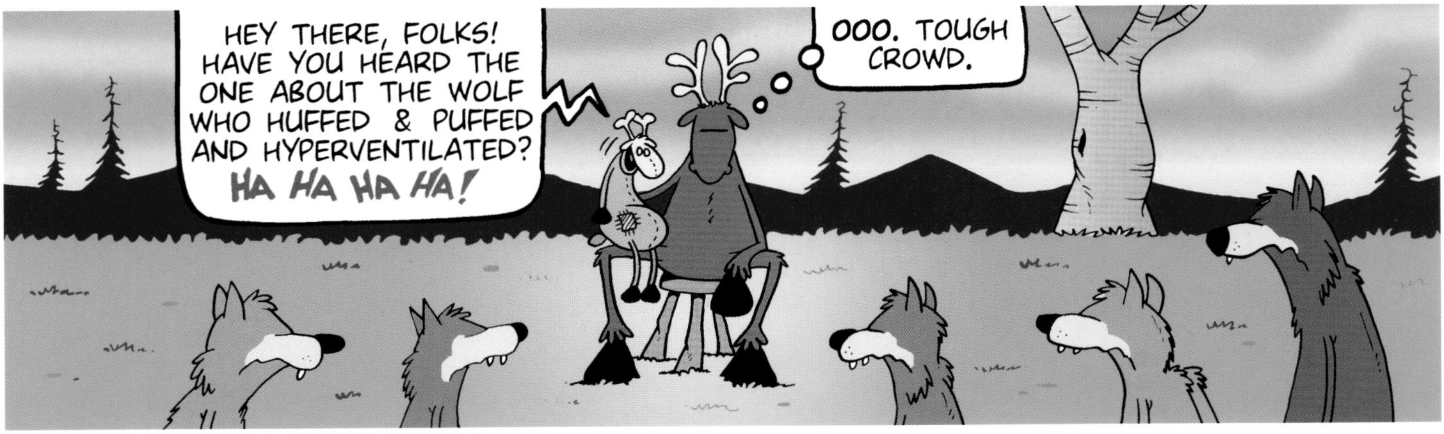
HEY THERE, FOLKS! HAVE YOU HEARD THE ONE ABOUT THE WOLF WHO HUFFED & PUFFED AND HYPERVENTILATED? HA HA HA HA!
OOO. TOUGH CROWD.

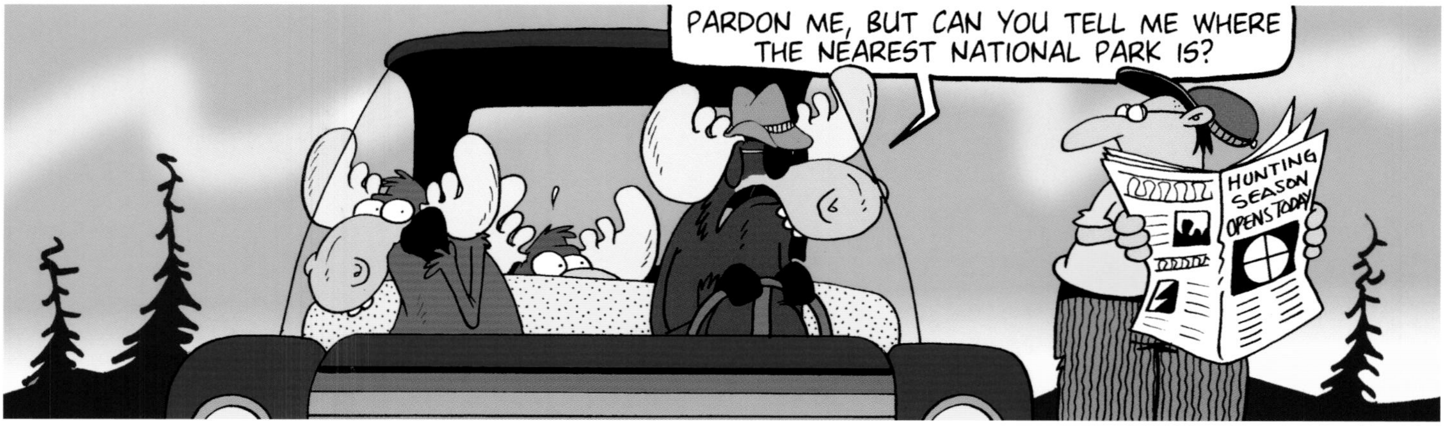
PARDON ME, BUT CAN YOU TELL ME WHERE THE NEAREST NATIONAL PARK IS?
HUNTING SEASON OPENS TODAY

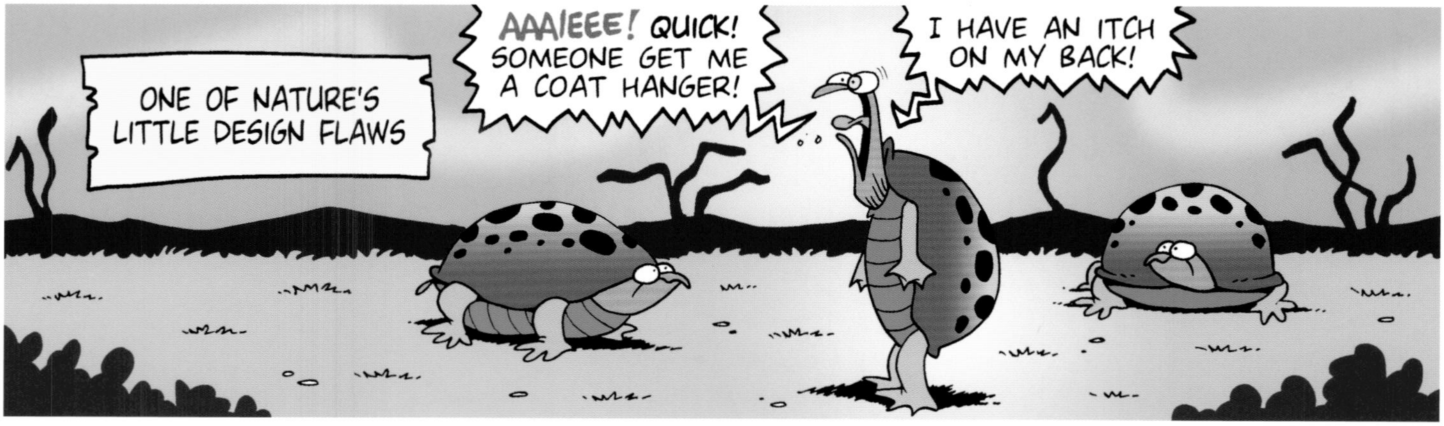
ONE OF NATURE'S LITTLE DESIGN FLAWS
AAAIEEE! QUICK! SOMEONE GET ME A COAT HANGER!
I HAVE AN ITCH ON MY BACK!

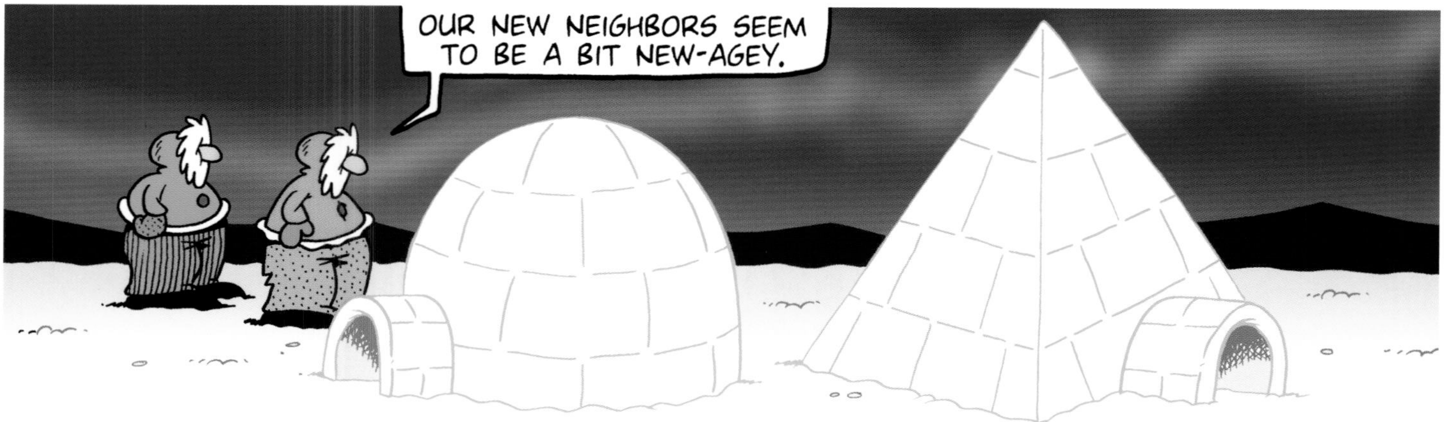
OUR NEW NEIGHBORS SEEM TO BE A BIT NEW-AGEY.

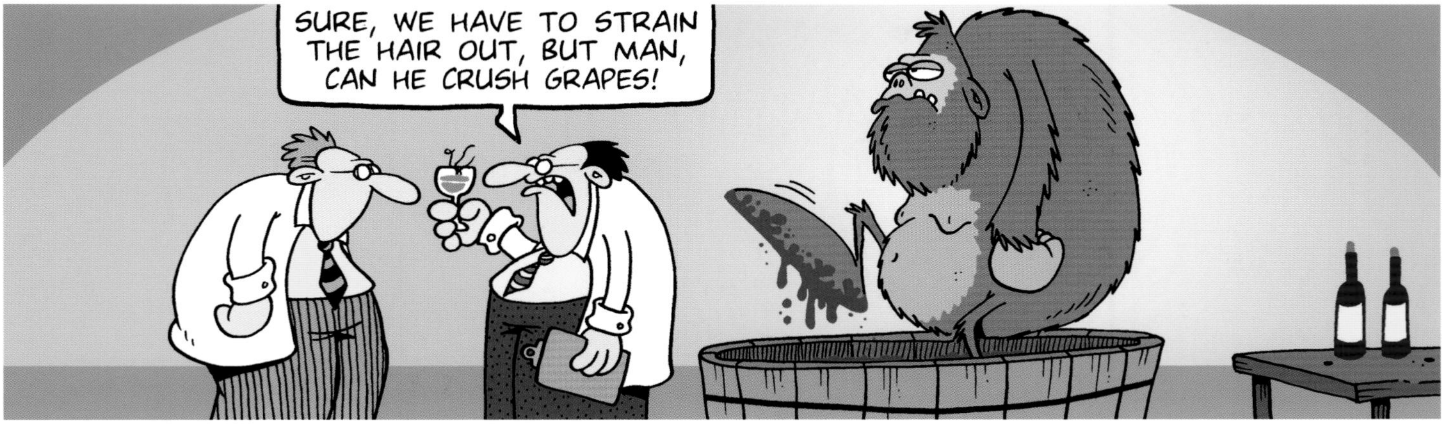
SURE, WE HAVE TO STRAIN THE HAIR OUT, BUT MAN, CAN HE CRUSH GRAPES!

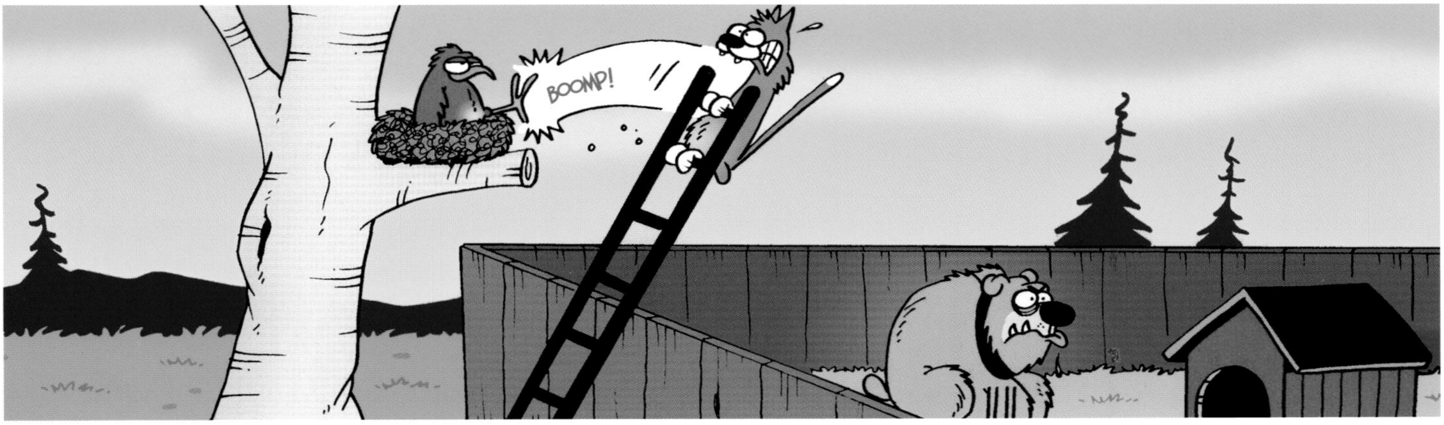
BOOMP!

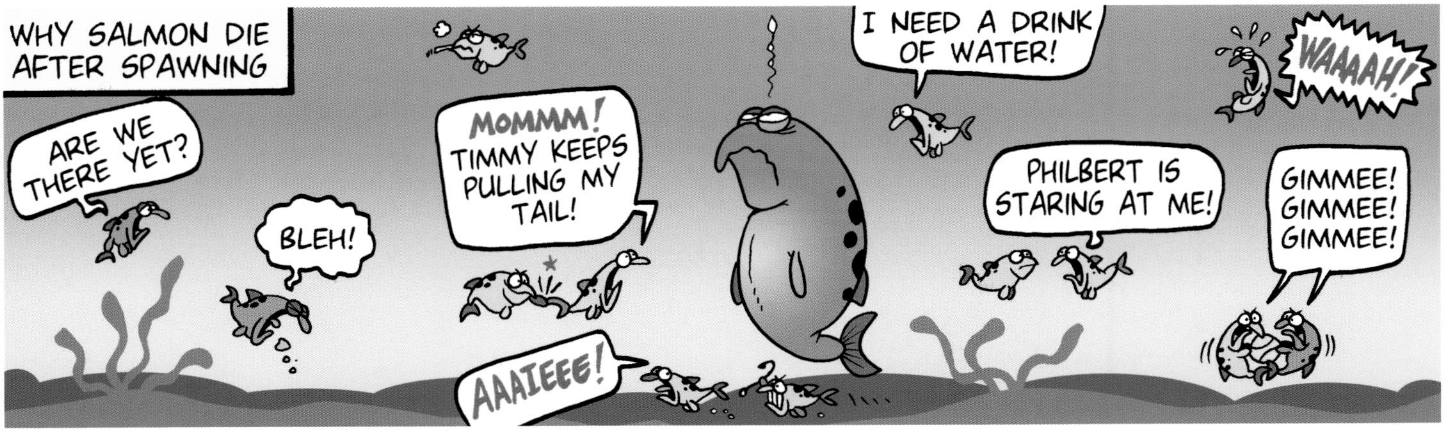
WHY SALMON DIE AFTER SPAWNING
ARE WE THERE YET?
BLEH!
MOMMM! TIMMY KEEPS PULLING MY TAIL!
AAAIEEE!
I NEED A DRINK OF WATER!
PHILBERT IS STARING AT ME!
WAAAAH!
GIMMEE! GIMMEE! GIMMEE!

Chad Carpenter's
TUNDRA
AW, MAN! YOU'RE NOT GOING TO ACTUALLY WATCH THIS REALITY-SHOW TRIPE ARE YOU?!
SHH. DONALD TRUMP'S HAIR IS LIKE WATCHING A TRAIN WRECK. YOU CAN'T HELP BUT STARE.
YOU'RE FIRED!
©TUNDRA 2005
THERE'S ABOUT AS MUCH REALITY INVOLVED WITH THIS GARBAGE AS THERE IS IN PAMELA ANDERSON'S PHYSIQUE.
OKAY, OKAY! I'LL CHANGE THE LOUSY CHANNEL!
Click!
LOOK OUT SHERIFF!
HOW'D YOU DO THAT? WHERE'S THE REMOTE?
HE'S SITTING ON IT.
SITTING ON IT?!
YUP. SITTING ON IT. LEAVES MY HANDS FREE FOR MORE IMPORTANT THINGS, SUCH AS SNACKING!
YOU SEE, WHEN YOU HAVE A POSTERIOR AS LARGE AS MINE, YOU LEARN TO USE IT TO YOUR ADVANTAGE.
JUST LIKE KIRSTIE ALLEY.
www.tundracomics.com
I THINK I'M GOING TO BE SICK!
MIND IF I TURN UP THE VOLUME?
YOU SHOULD SEE HIM PLAY VIDEO GAMES!

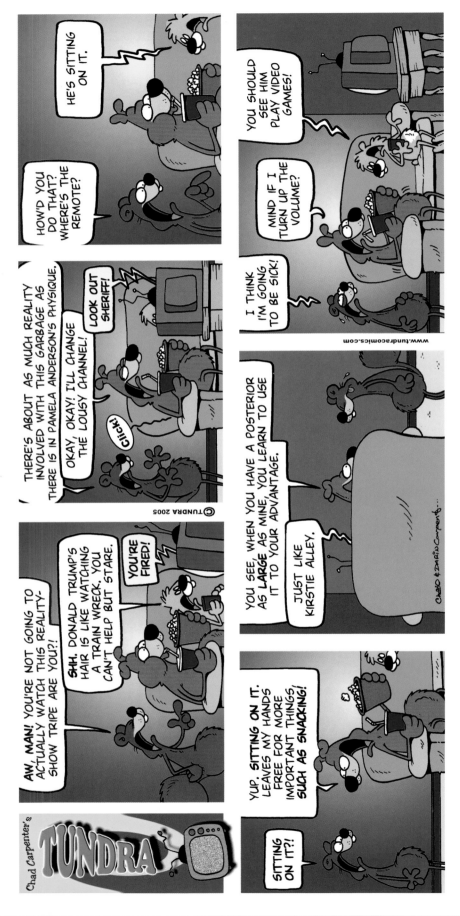

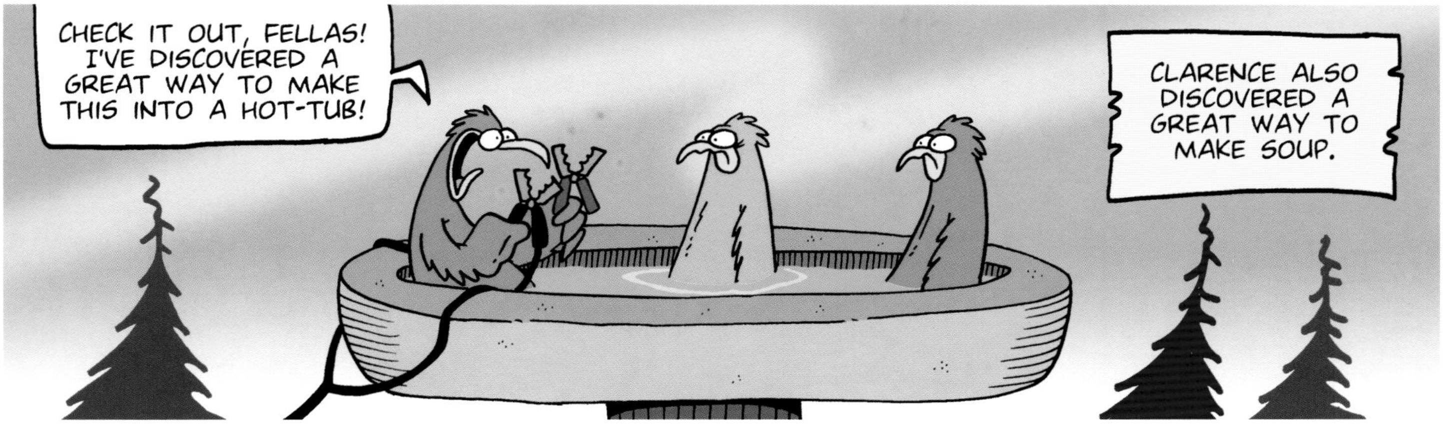
CHECK IT OUT, FELLAS! I'VE DISCOVERED A GREAT WAY TO MAKE THIS INTO A HOT-TUB!
CLARENCE ALSO DISCOVERED A GREAT WAY TO MAKE SOUP.

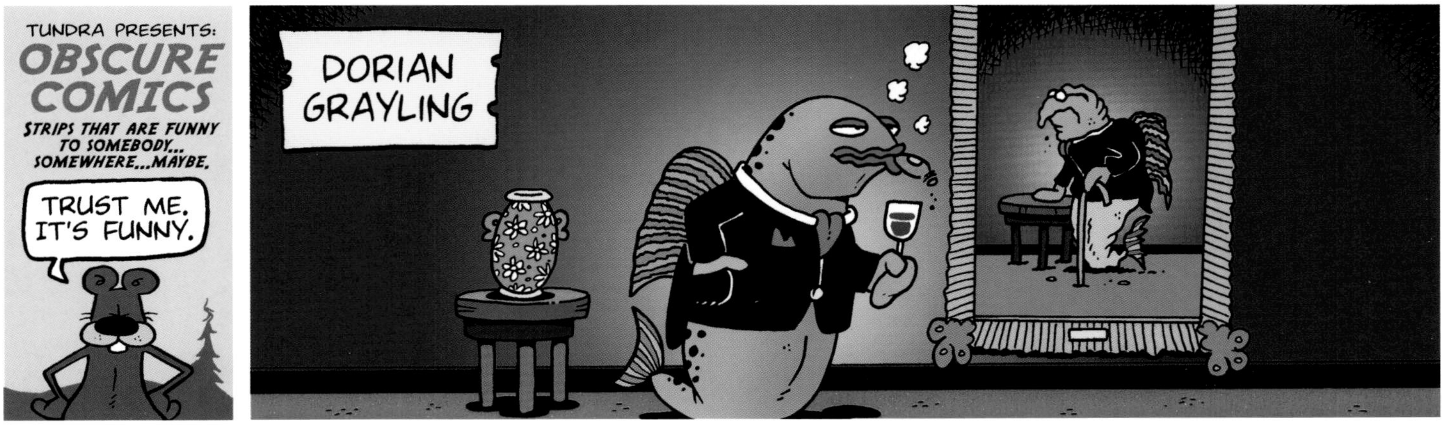
TUNDRA PRESENTS:
OBSCURE COMICS
STRIPS THAT ARE FUNNY TO SOMEBODY... SOMEWHERE...MAYBE.
TRUST ME. IT'S FUNNY.
DORIAN GRAYLING

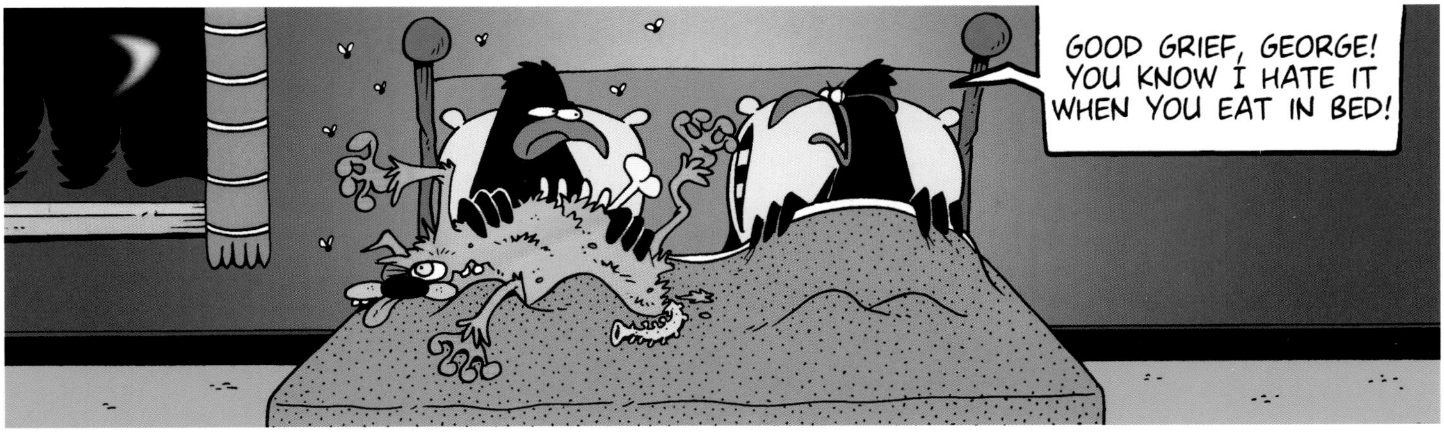
GOOD GRIEF, GEORGE! YOU KNOW I HATE IT WHEN YOU EAT IN BED!

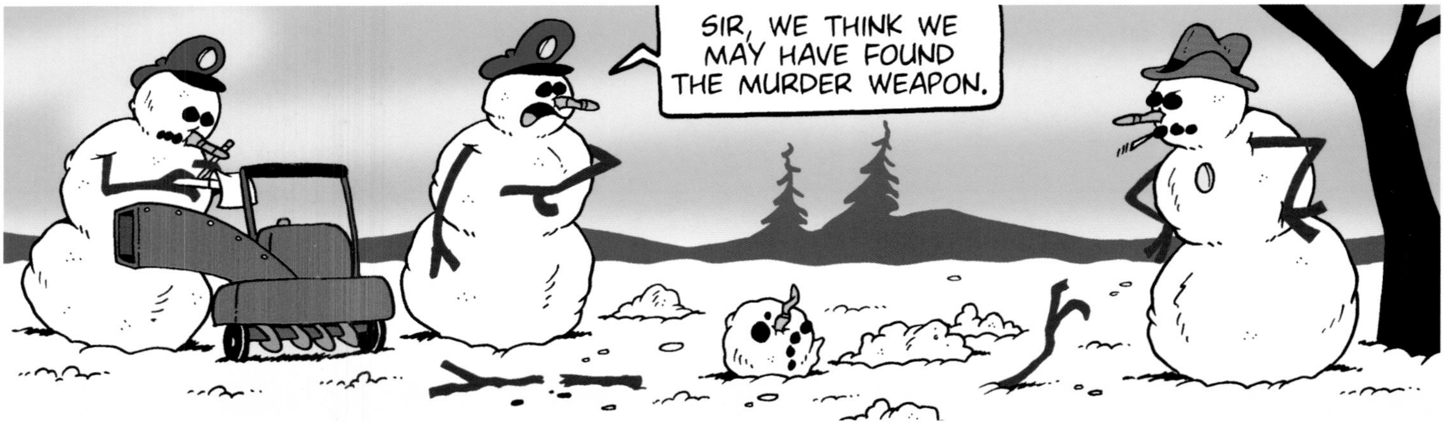
SIR, WE THINK WE MAY HAVE FOUND THE MURDER WEAPON.

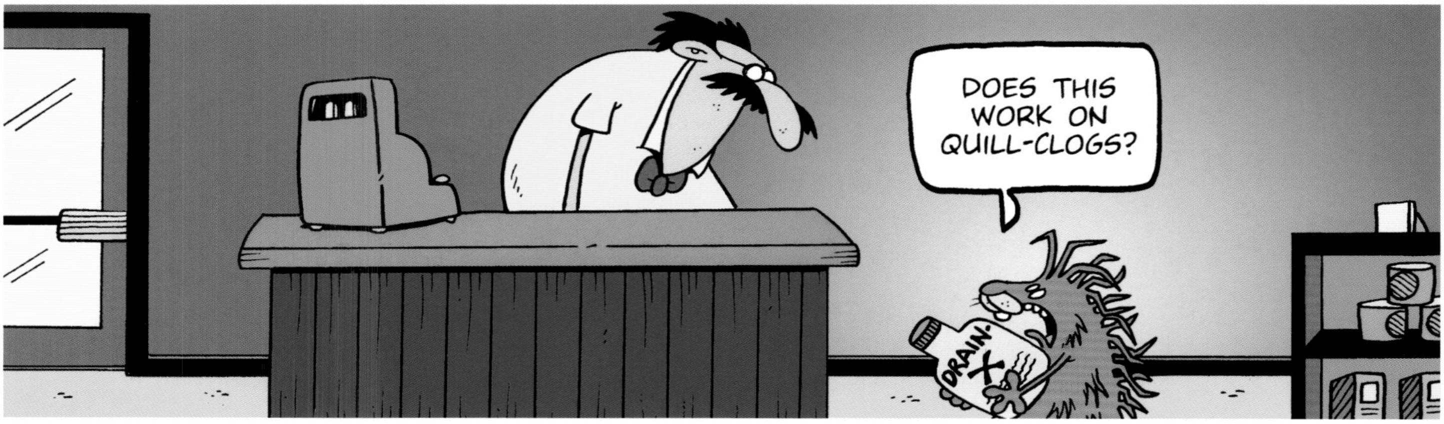
DOES THIS WORK ON QUILL-CLOGS?
DRAIN-X

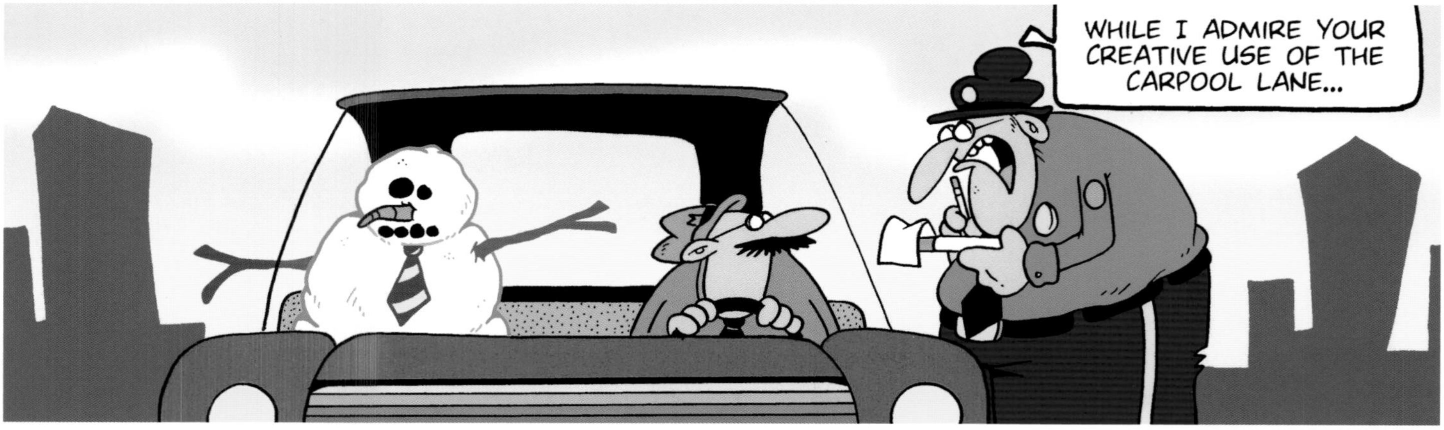
WHILE I ADMIRE YOUR CREATIVE USE OF THE CARPOOL LANE...

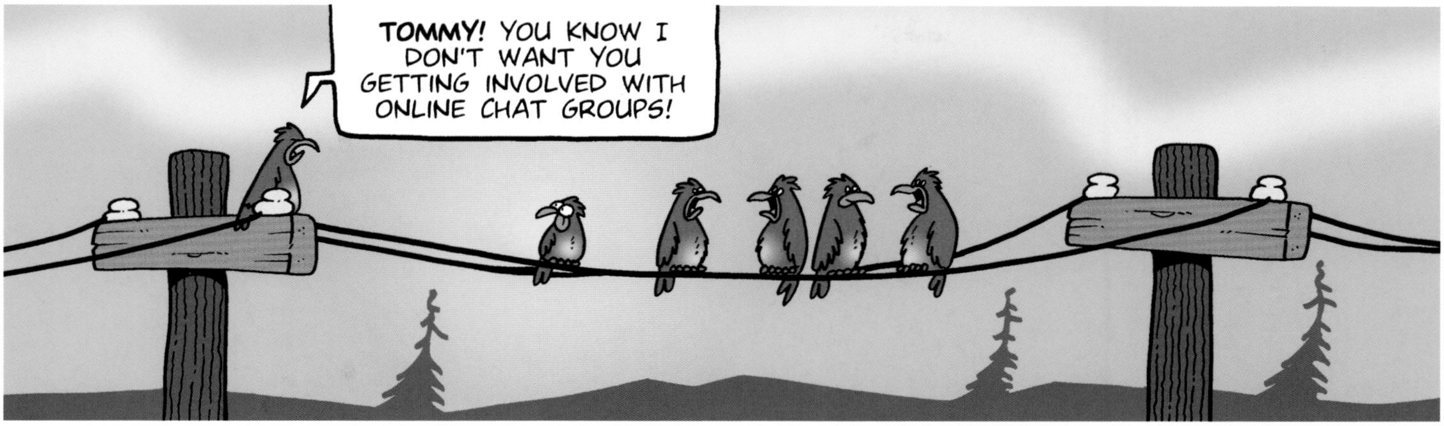
TOMMY! YOU KNOW I DON'T WANT YOU GETTING INVOLVED WITH ONLINE CHAT GROUPS!

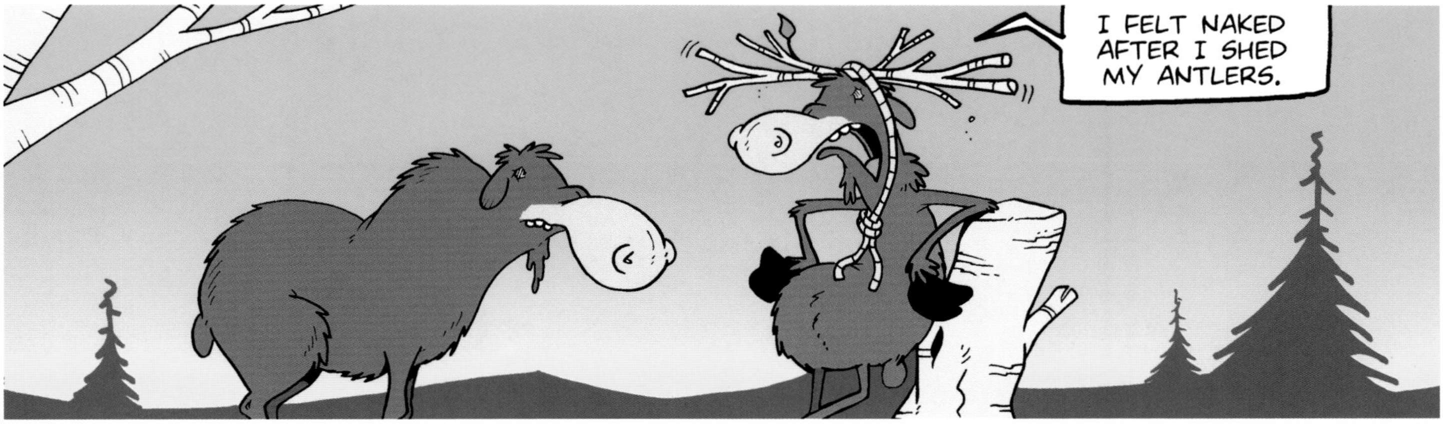
I FELT NAKED AFTER I SHED MY ANTLERS.

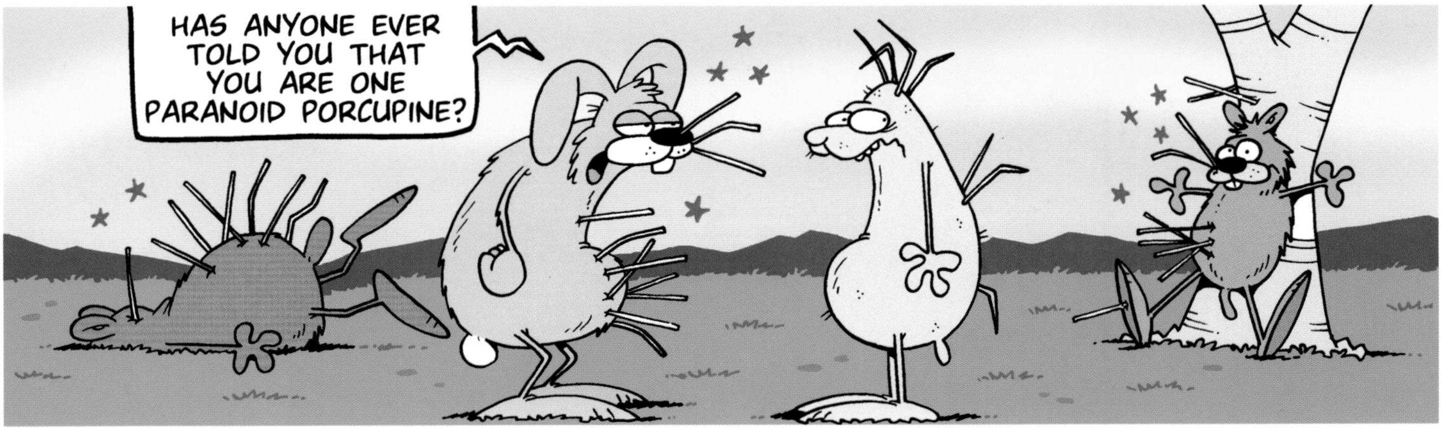
HAS ANYONE EVER TOLD YOU THAT YOU ARE ONE PARANOID PORCUPINE?

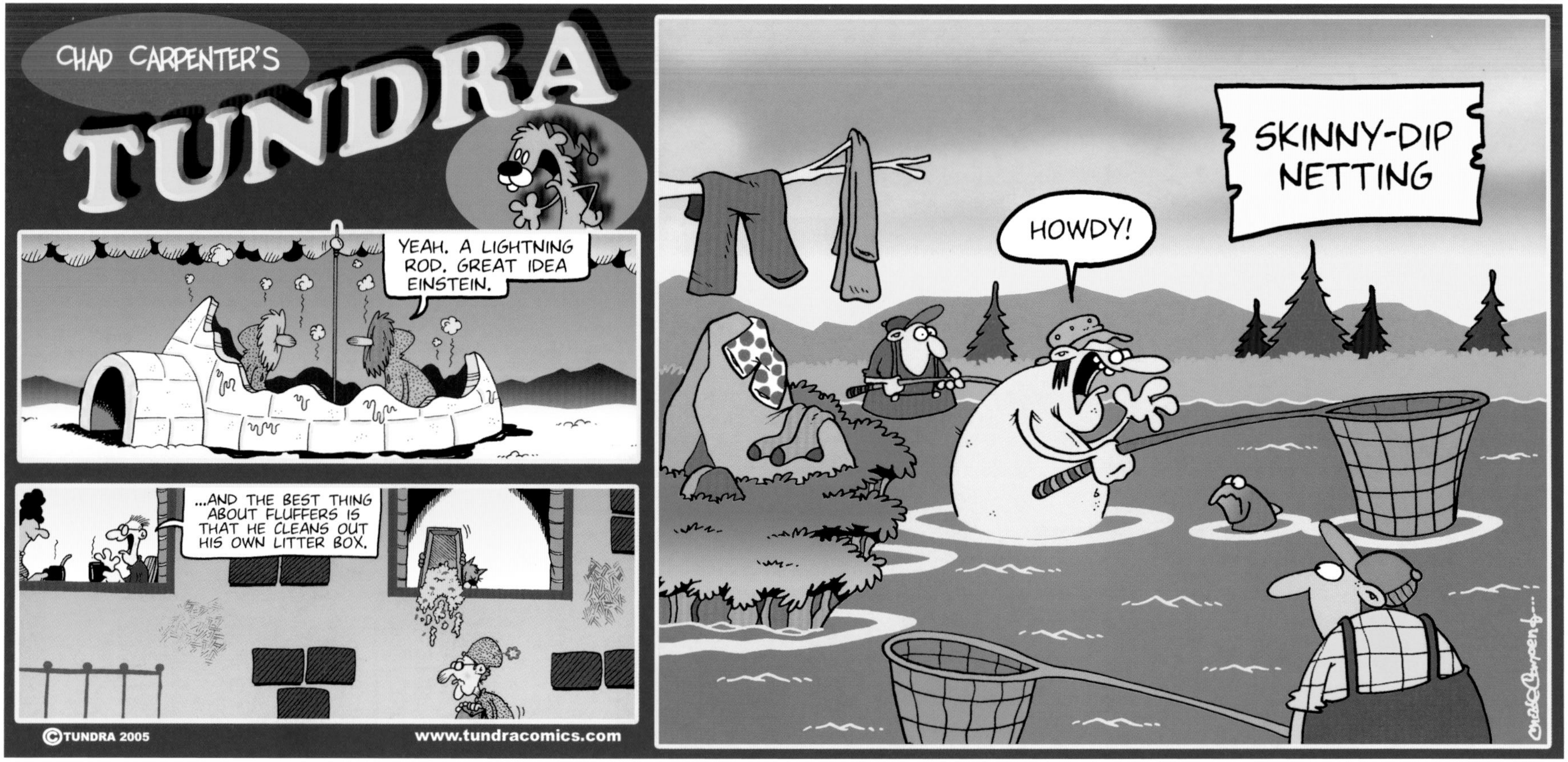
CHAD CARPENTER'S
TUNDRA
YEAH. A LIGHTNING ROD. GREAT IDEA EINSTEIN.
...AND THE BEST THING ABOUT FLUFFERS IS THAT HE CLEANS OUT HIS OWN LITTER BOX.
©TUNDRA 2005
www.tundracomics.com
SKINNY-DIP NETTING
HOWDY!

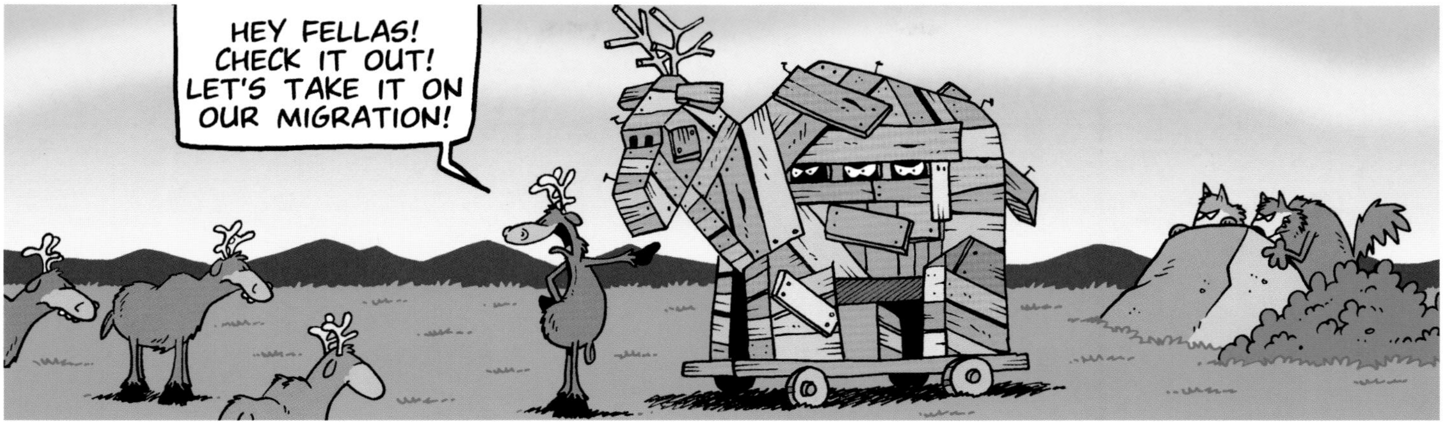
HEY FELLAS! CHECK IT OUT! LET'S TAKE IT ON OUR MIGRATION!

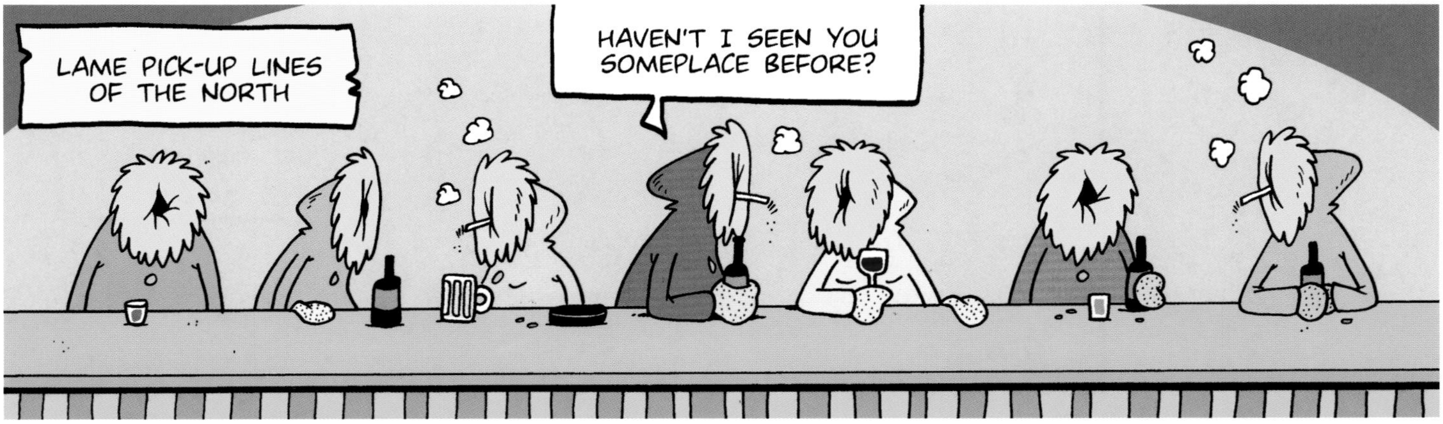
LAME PICK-UP LINES OF THE NORTH
HAVEN'T I SEEN YOU SOMEPLACE BEFORE?

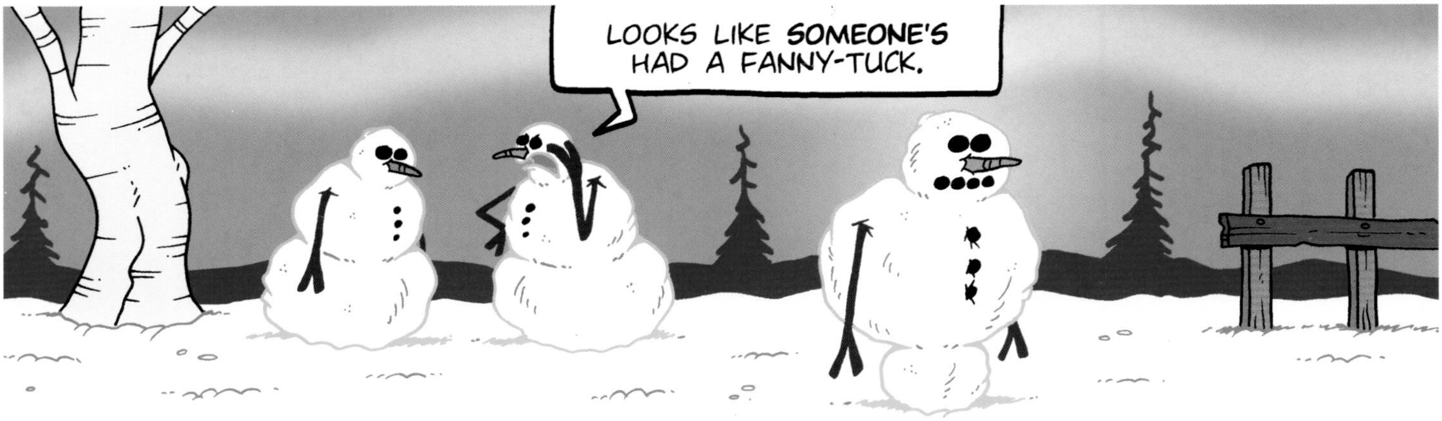
LOOKS LIKE SOMEONE'S HAD A FANNY-TUCK.

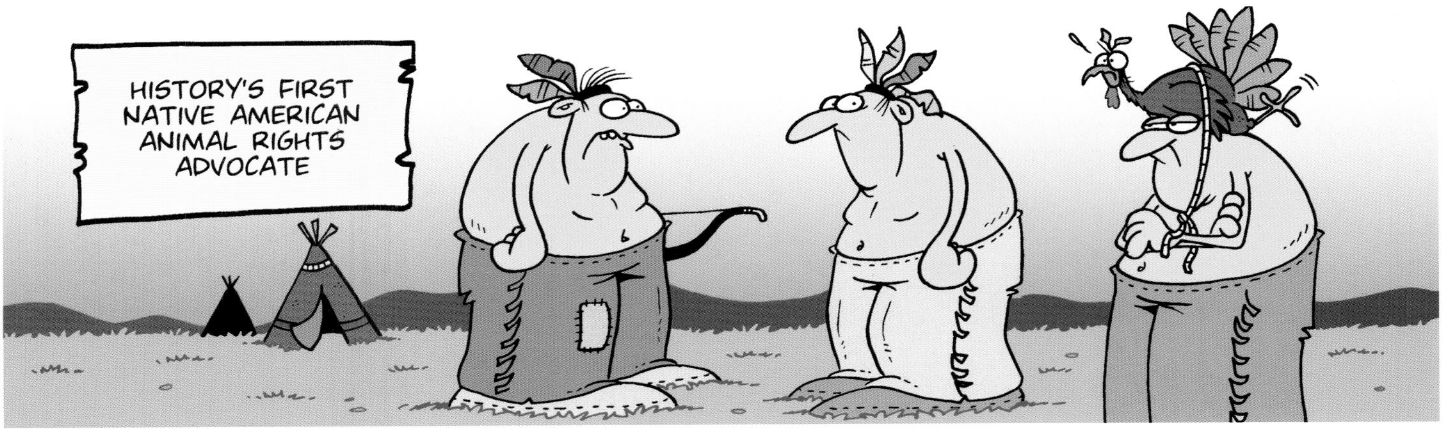
HISTORY'S FIRST NATIVE AMERICAN ANIMAL RIGHTS ADVOCATE

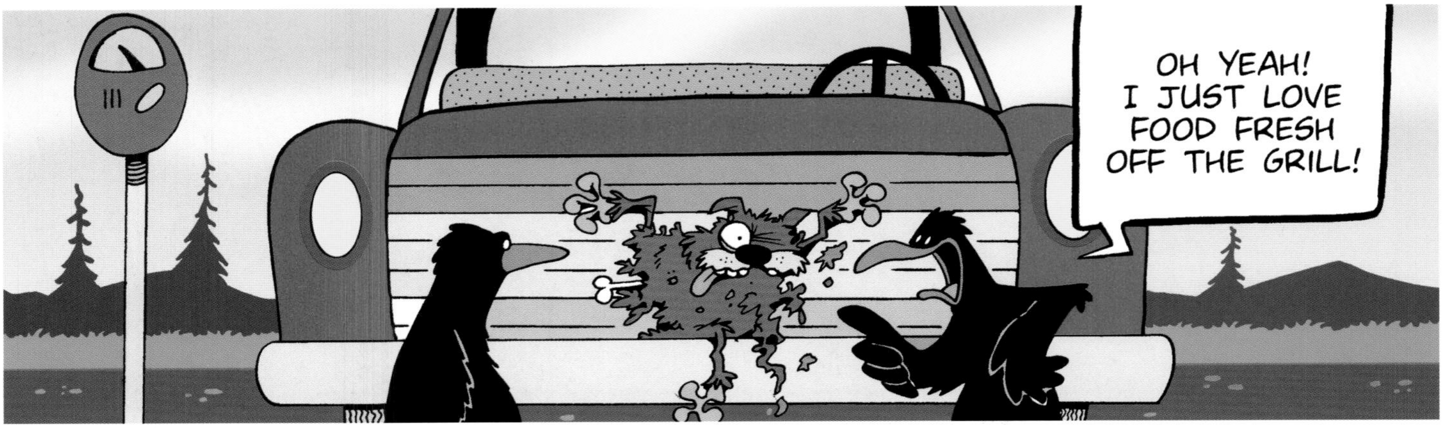
OH YEAH! I JUST LOVE FOOD FRESH OFF THE GRILL!

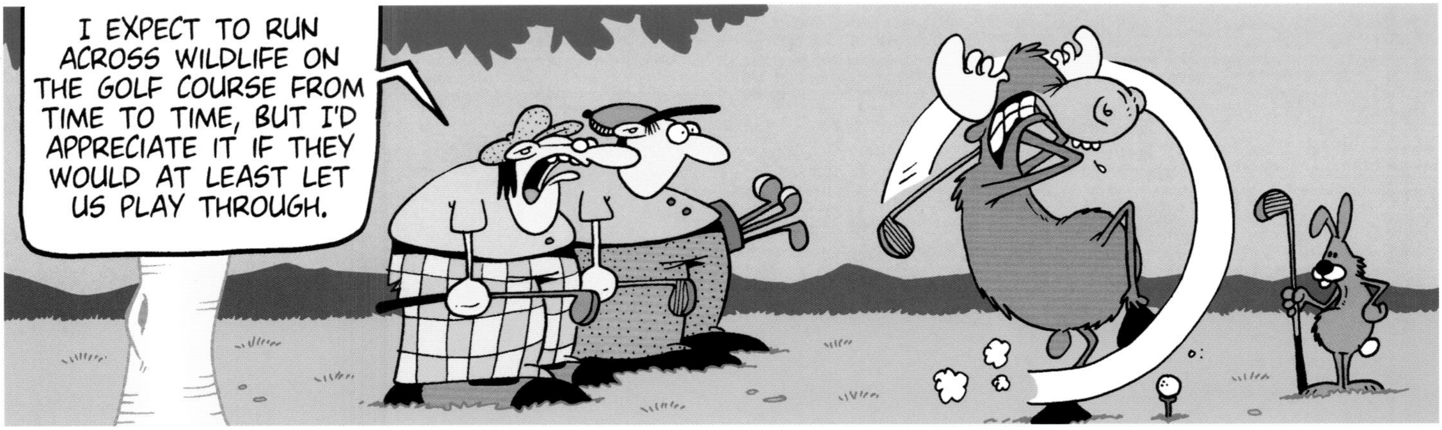
I EXPECT TO RUN ACROSS WILDLIFE ON THE GOLF COURSE FROM TIME TO TIME, BUT I'D APPRECIATE IT IF THEY WOULD AT LEAST LET US PLAY THROUGH.

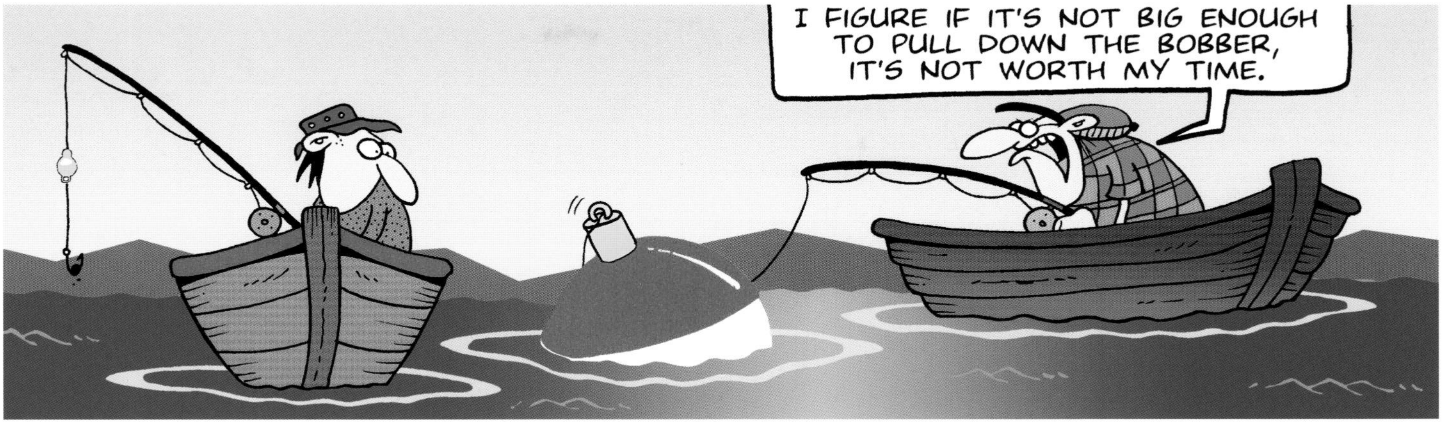
I FIGURE IF IT'S NOT BIG ENOUGH TO PULL DOWN THE BOBBER, IT'S NOT WORTH MY TIME.

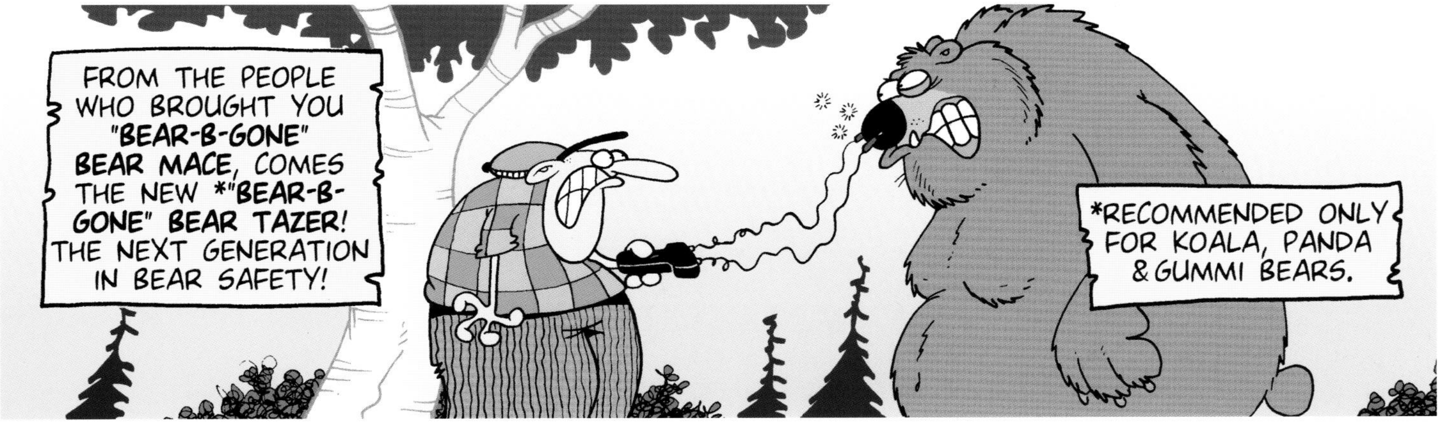
FROM THE PEOPLE WHO BROUGHT YOU "BEAR-B-GONE" BEAR MACE, COMES THE NEW *"BEAR-B-GONE" BEAR TAZER! THE NEXT GENERATION IN BEAR SAFETY!
*RECOMMENDED ONLY FOR KOALA, PANDA & GUMMI BEARS.

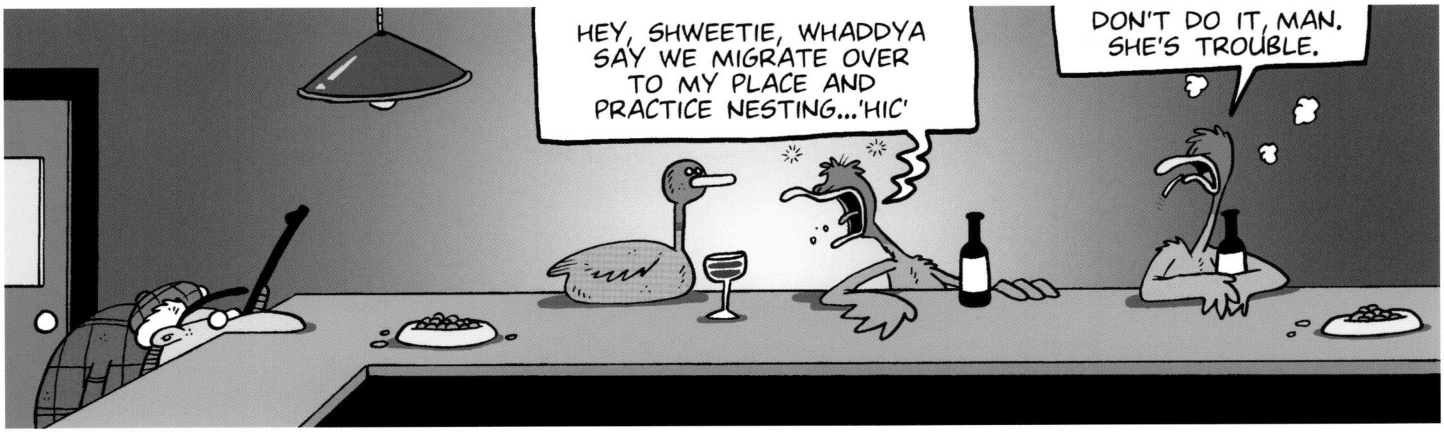
HEY, SHWEETIE, WHADDYA SAY WE MIGRATE OVER TO MY PLACE AND PRACTICE NESTING...'HIC'
DON'T DO IT, MAN. SHE'S TROUBLE.

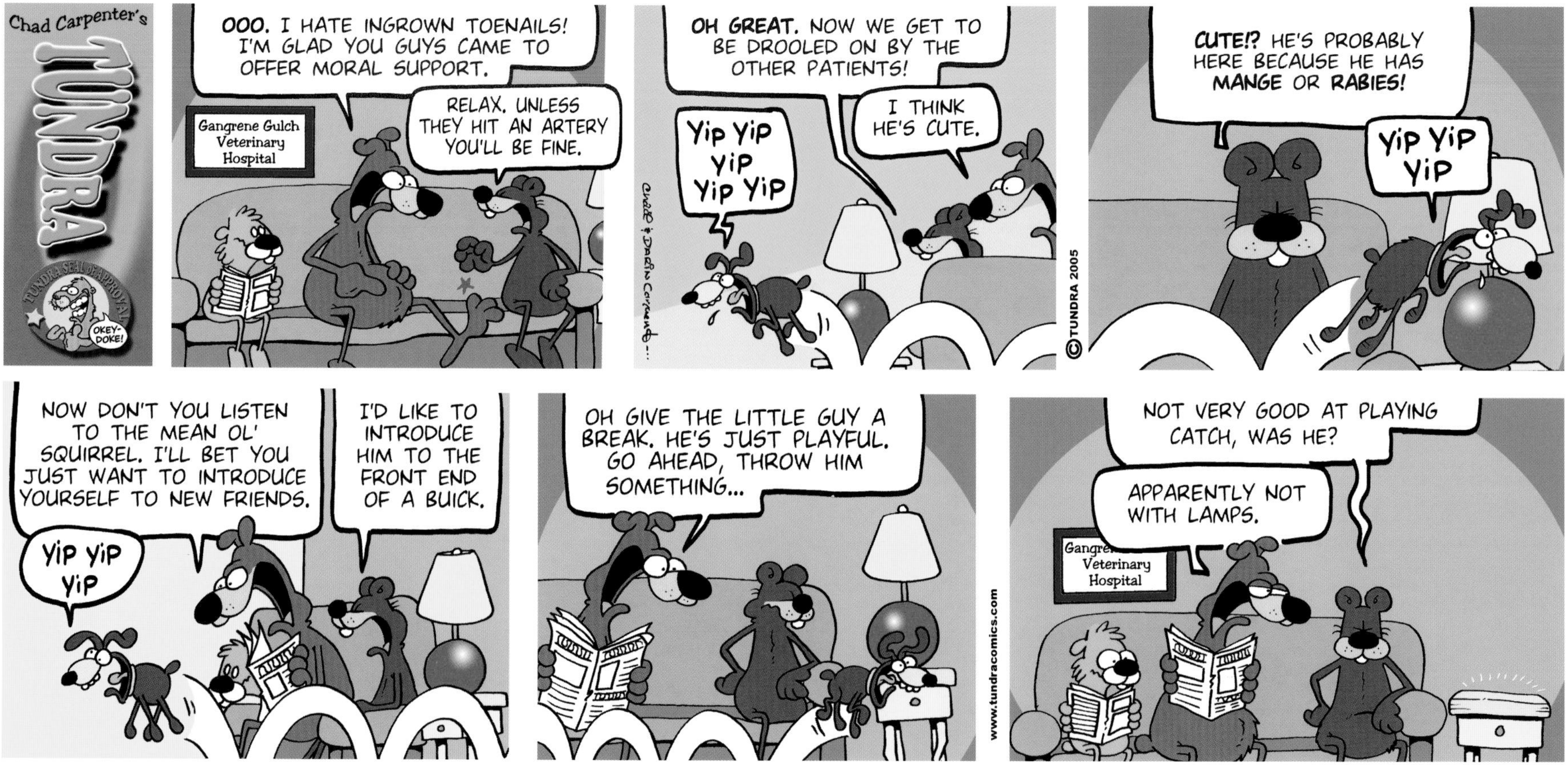
Chad Carpenter's
TUNDRA
TUNDRA SEAL OF APPROVAL
OKEY-DOKE!
OOO. I HATE INGROWN TOENAILS! I'M GLAD YOU GUYS CAME TO OFFER MORAL SUPPORT.
RELAX. UNLESS THEY HIT AN ARTERY YOU'LL BE FINE.
Gangrene Gulch Veterinary Hospital
OH GREAT. NOW WE GET TO BE DROOLED ON BY THE OTHER PATIENTS!
Yip Yip Yip Yip Yip
I THINK HE'S CUTE.
CUTE!? HE'S PROBABLY HERE BECAUSE HE HAS MANGE OR RABIES!
Yip Yip Yip
© TUNDRA 2005
NOW DON'T YOU LISTEN TO THE MEAN OL' SQUIRREL. I'LL BET YOU JUST WANT TO INTRODUCE YOURSELF TO NEW FRIENDS.
Yip Yip Yip
I'D LIKE TO INTRODUCE HIM TO THE FRONT END OF A BUICK.
OH GIVE THE LITTLE GUY A BREAK. HE'S JUST PLAYFUL. GO AHEAD, THROW HIM SOMETHING...
www.tundracomics.com
NOT VERY GOOD AT PLAYING CATCH, WAS HE?
APPARENTLY NOT WITH LAMPS.
Veterinary Hospital

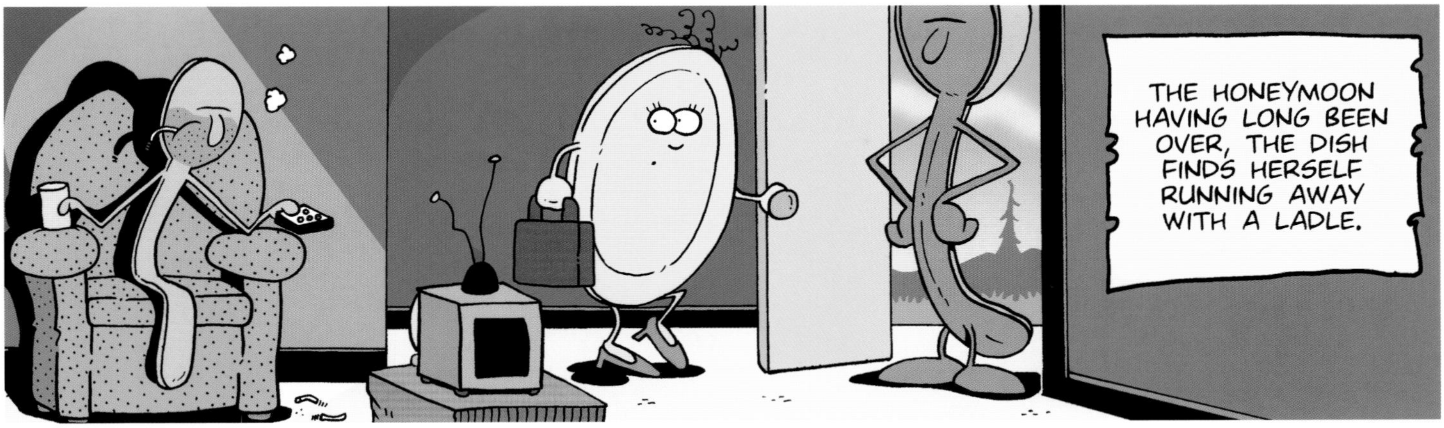
THE HONEYMOON HAVING LONG BEEN OVER, THE DISH FINDS HERSELF RUNNING AWAY WITH A LADLE.

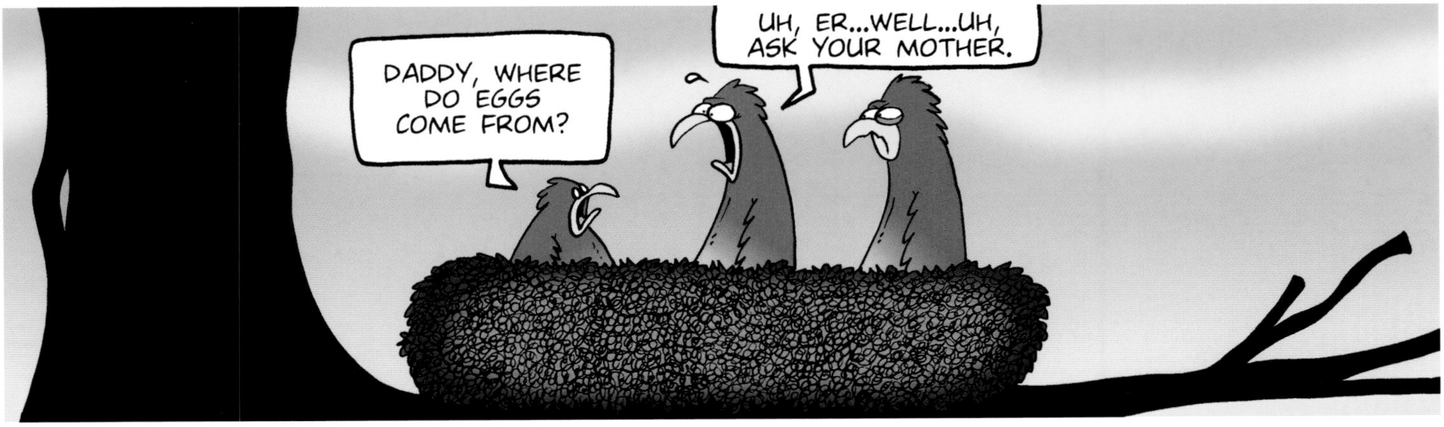
DADDY, WHERE DO EGGS COME FROM?
UH, ER...WELL...UH, ASK YOUR MOTHER.

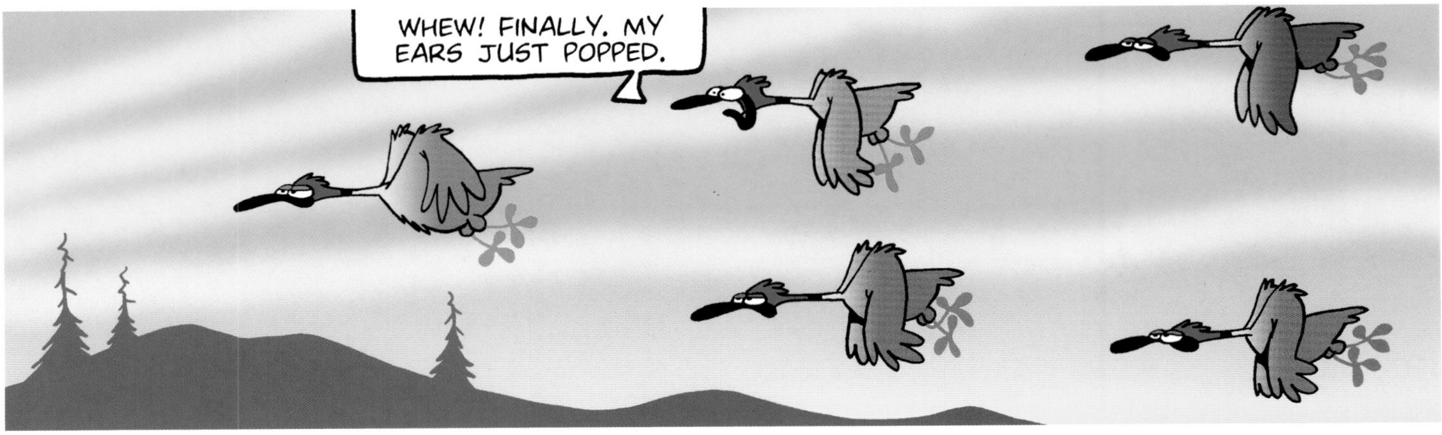
WHEW! FINALLY. MY EARS JUST POPPED.

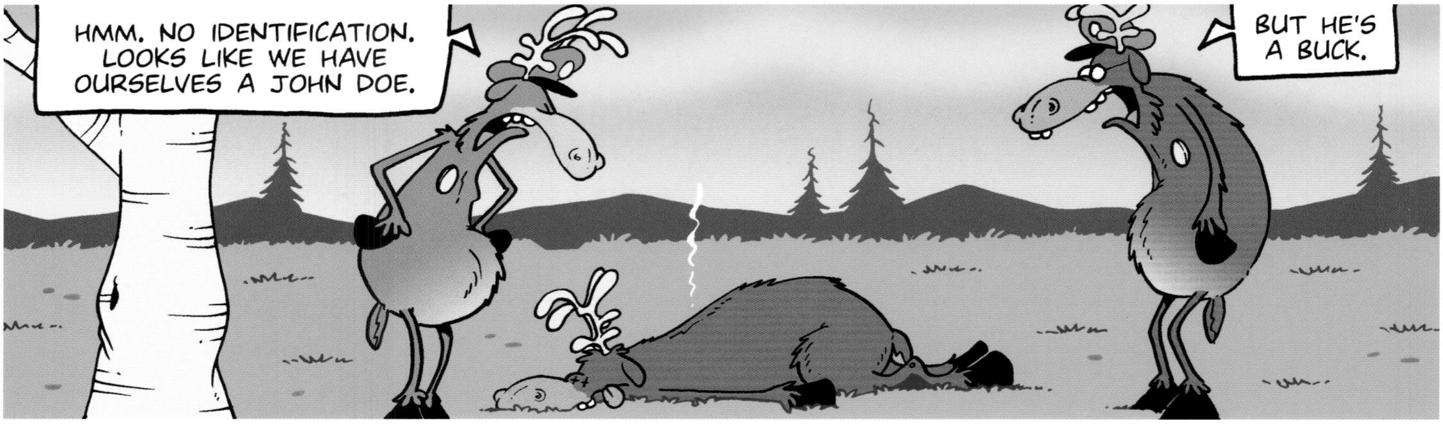
HMM. NO IDENTIFICATION. LOOKS LIKE WE HAVE OURSELVES A JOHN DOE.
BUT HE'S A BUCK.

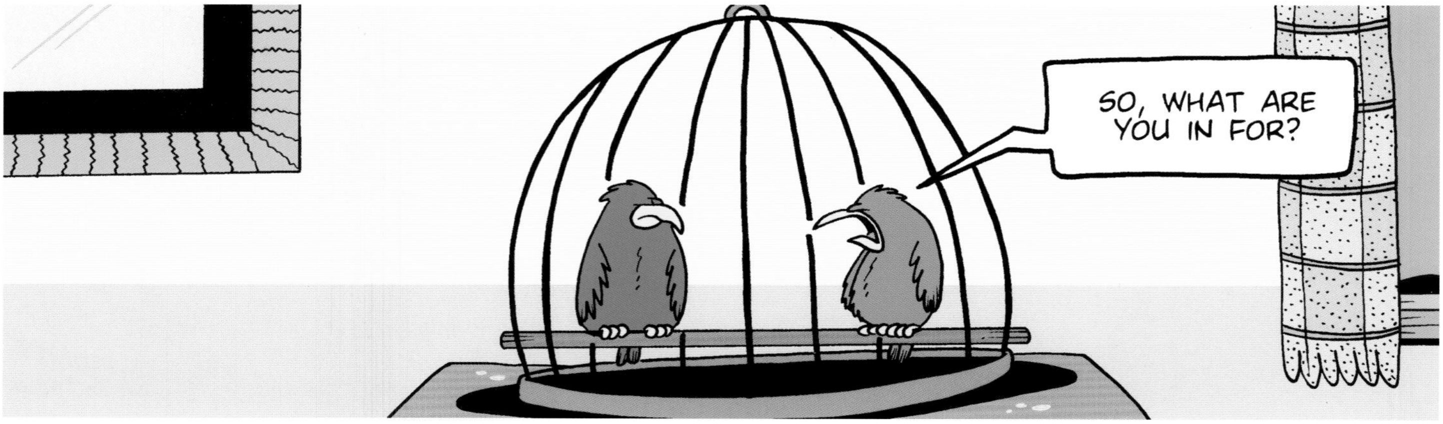
SO, WHAT ARE YOU IN FOR?

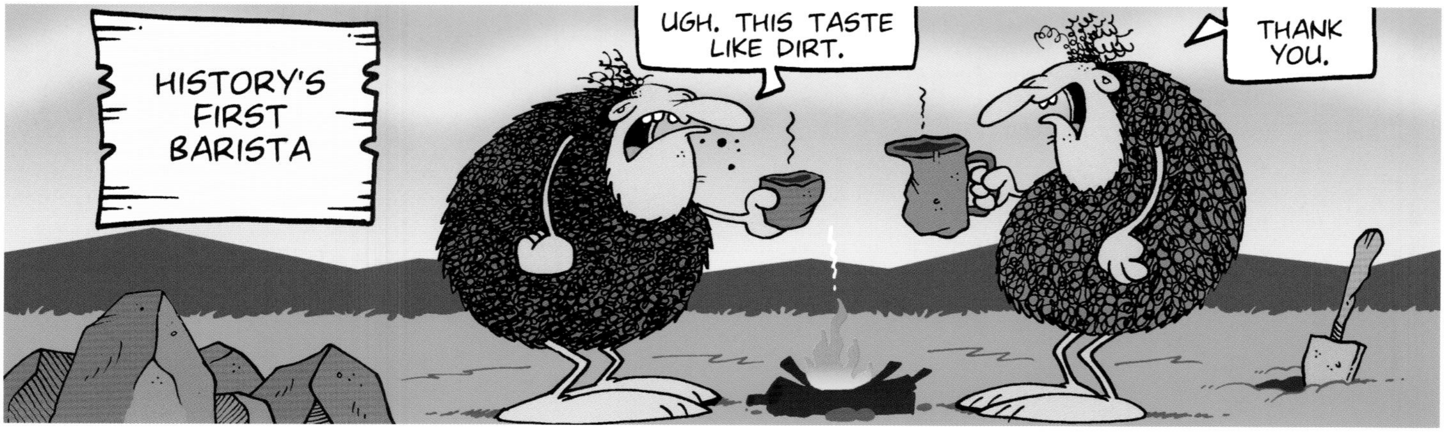
HISTORY'S FIRST BARISTA
UGH. THIS TASTE LIKE DIRT.
THANK YOU.

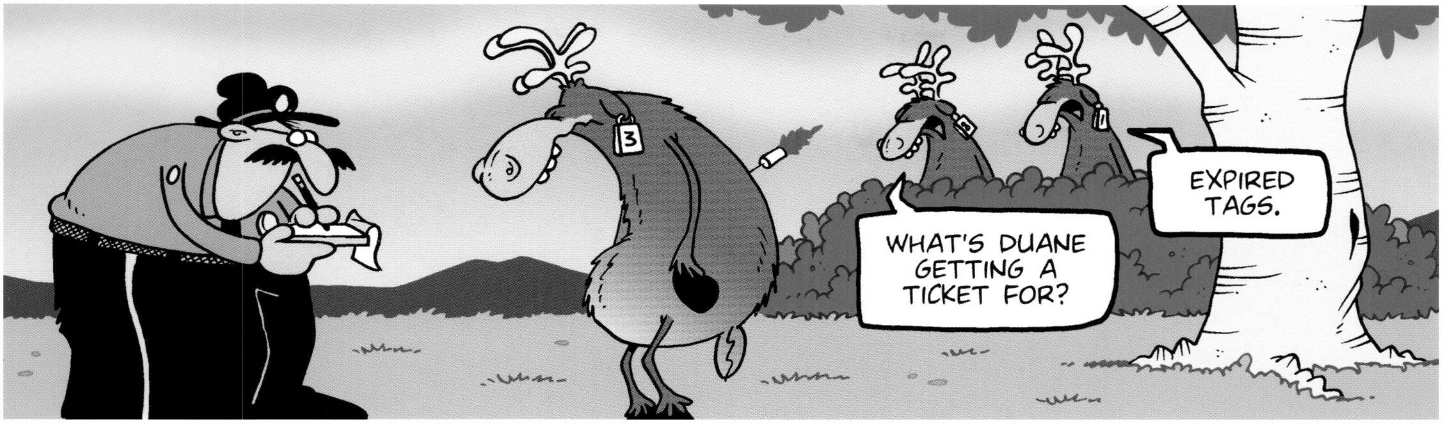
WHAT'S DUANE GETTING A TICKET FOR?
EXPIRED TAGS.

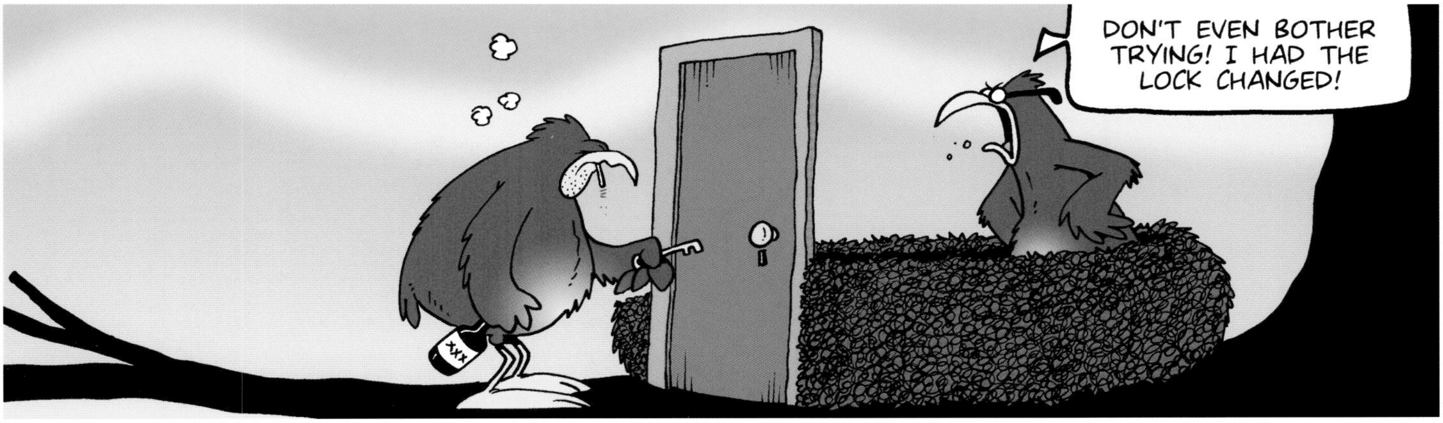
XXX
DON'T EVEN BOTHER TRYING! I HAD THE LOCK CHANGED!

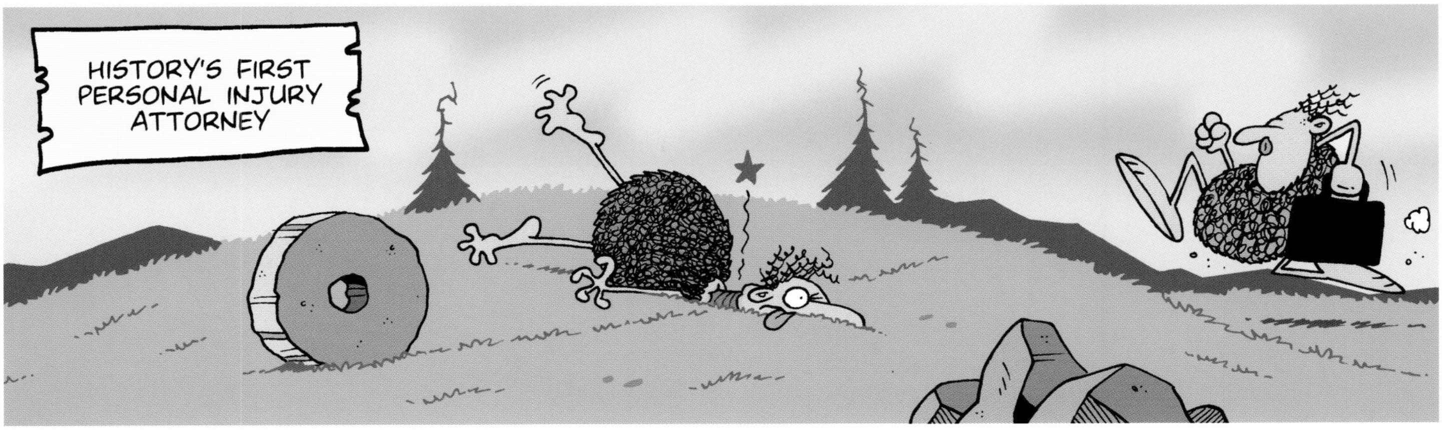
HISTORY'S FIRST PERSONAL INJURY ATTORNEY

Chad Carpenter's
TUNDRA
WHERE YOU OFF TO, SHERM?
ANDY AND I GOT PICKED FOR JURY DUTY.
©TUNDRA 2005
WE'RE OFF TO DO OUR PART IN ASSURING SOME POOR SAP GETS A FAIR, UNBIASED TRIAL BY HIS PEERS.
UNBIASED, HUH? SO WHAT'S THE ROPE FOR?
WHAT? OH...THIS THING? UH...I WAS JUST PRACTICING SOME BOY SCOUT KNOTS.
YOU DO REALIZE WE DON'T HAVE THE DEATH PENALTY IN THIS STATE.
OH.
ANDY! NIX THE RIFLE AND BLINDFOLD. WE'RE GOING TO HAVE TO SETTLE WITH A GOOD OLD-FASHIONED CANING!
WOW. CAN YOU BELIEVE IT? I MADE IT TO THE JURY!
APPARENTLY YOU FOUND THE WEAK LINK IN THEIR BACKGROUND CHECKS.
WATCH AND LEARN, ANDY. TO FIND THE TRUTH, YOU SOMETIMES HAVE TO THINK LIKE A CRIMINAL.
OH. DO YOU THINK OTHER WAYS TOO?
MY CLIENT IS INNOCENT OF THIS HEINOUS CRIME! DNA TESTS ON THE TRUE PERPETRATOR'S HAIR SAMPLE SHOW THAT IT BELONGS TO A LARGE BROWN SQUIRREL WITH LOW MORAL STANDARDS!
EXHIBIT A
www.tundracomics.com
HMM. I THOUGHT THE VICTIM LOOKED FAMILIAR.

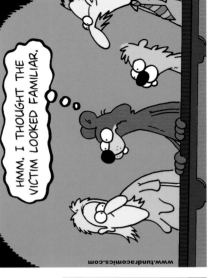

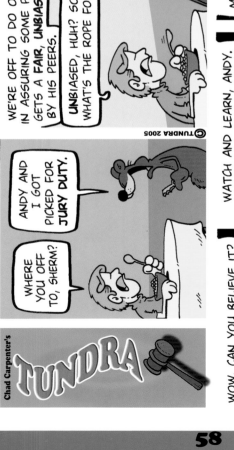

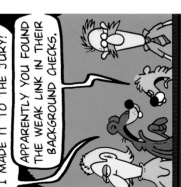

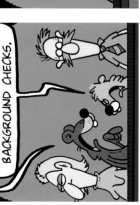

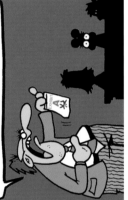

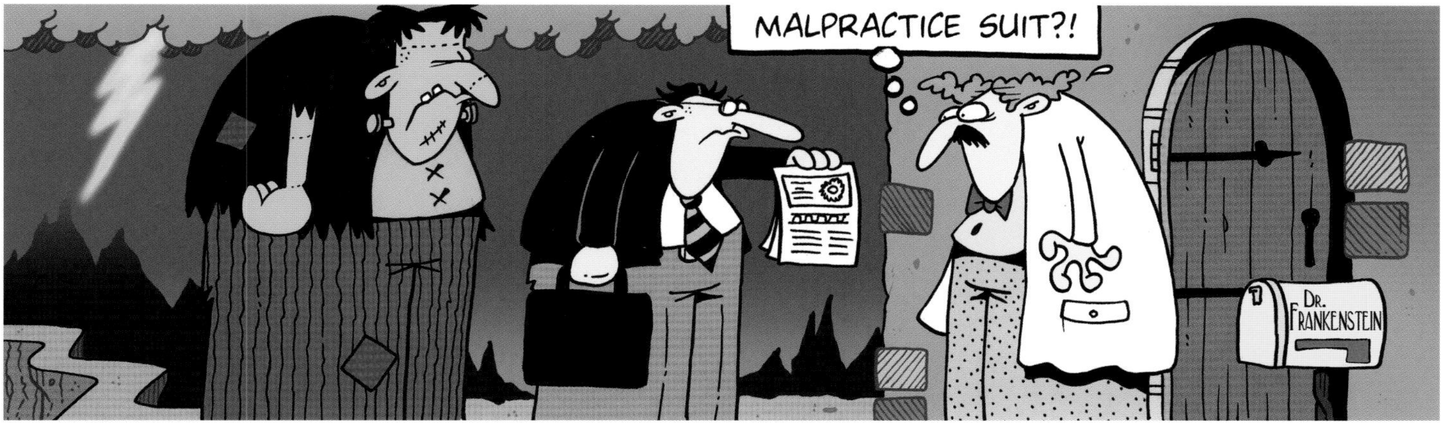
MALPRACTICE SUIT?!
DR. FRANKENSTEIN

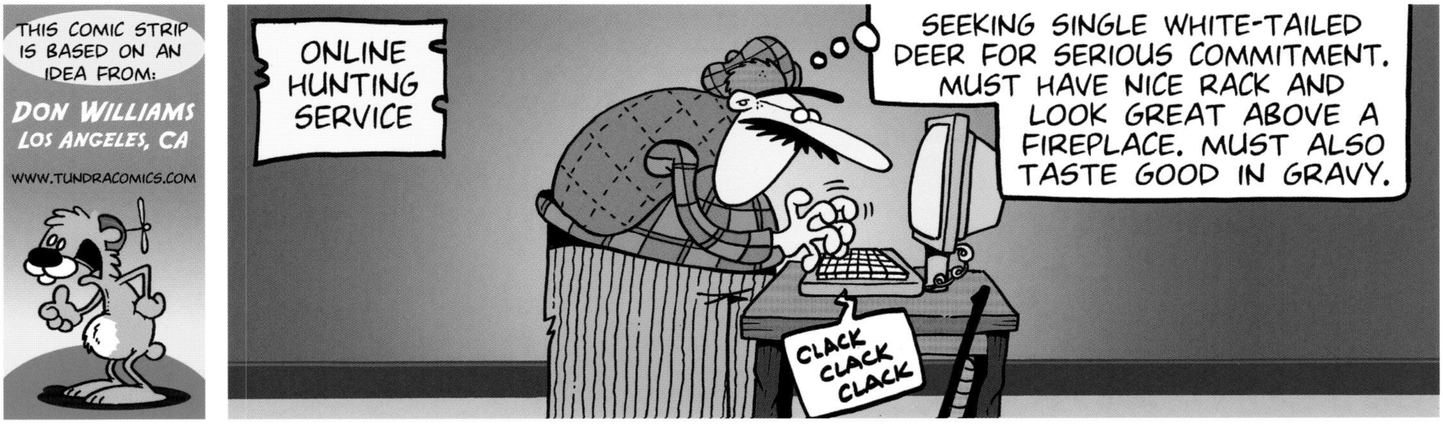
THIS COMIC STRIP IS BASED ON AN IDEA FROM:
DON WILLIAMS
LOS ANGELES, CA
WWW.TUNDRACOMICS.COM
ONLINE HUNTING SERVICE
SEEKING SINGLE WHITE-TAILED DEER FOR SERIOUS COMMITMENT. MUST HAVE NICE RACK AND LOOK GREAT ABOVE A FIREPLACE. MUST ALSO TASTE GOOD IN GRAVY.
CLACK CLACK CLACK

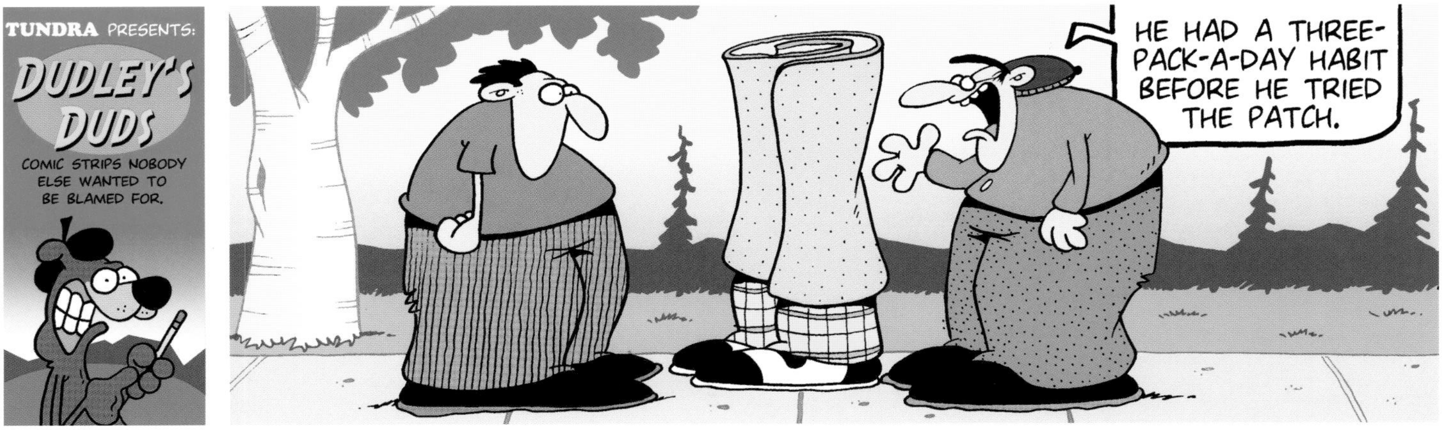
TUNDRA PRESENTS:
DUDLEY'S DUDS
COMIC STRIPS NOBODY ELSE WANTED TO BE BLAMED FOR.
HE HAD A THREE-PACK-A-DAY HABIT BEFORE HE TRIED THE PATCH.

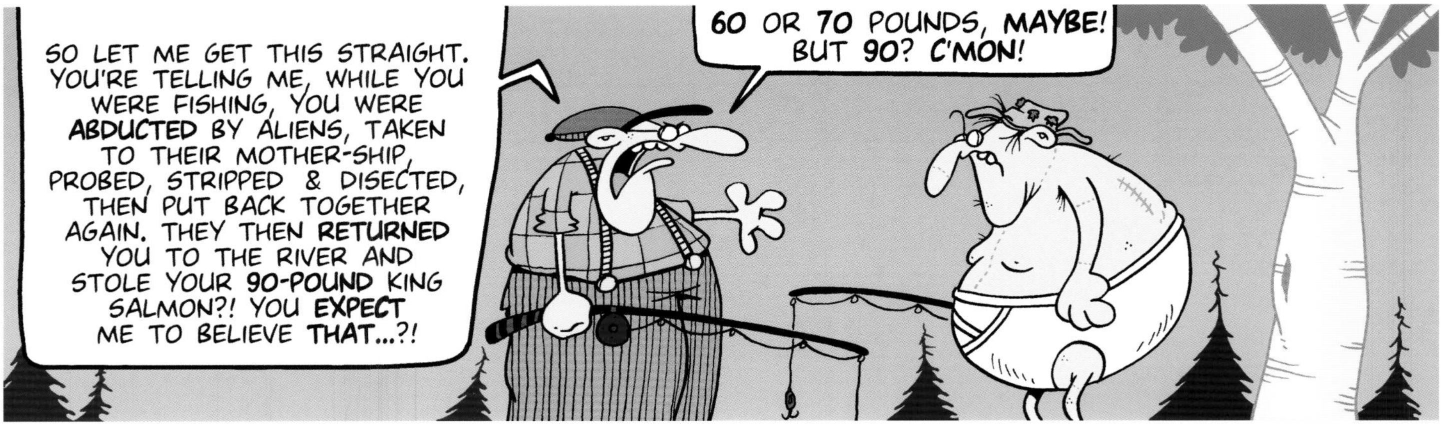
SO LET ME GET THIS STRAIGHT. YOU'RE TELLING ME, WHILE YOU WERE FISHING, YOU WERE ABDUCTED BY ALIENS, TAKEN TO THEIR MOTHER-SHIP, PROBED, STRIPPED & DISECTED, THEN PUT BACK TOGETHER AGAIN. THEY THEN RETURNED YOU TO THE RIVER AND STOLE YOUR 90-POUND KING SALMON?! YOU EXPECT ME TO BELIEVE THAT...?!
60 OR 70 POUNDS, MAYBE! BUT 90? C'MON!

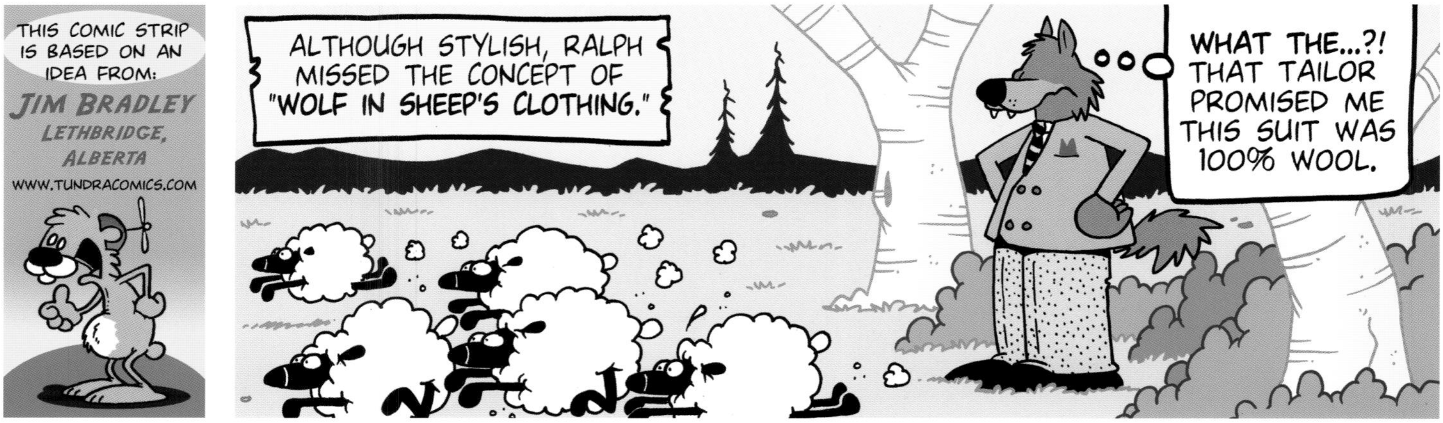
THIS COMIC STRIP IS BASED ON AN IDEA FROM:
JIM BRADLEY
LETHBRIDGE, ALBERTA
WWW.TUNDRACOMICS.COM
ALTHOUGH STYLISH, RALPH MISSED THE CONCEPT OF "WOLF IN SHEEP'S CLOTHING."
WHAT THE...?! THAT TAILOR PROMISED ME THIS SUIT WAS 100% WOOL.

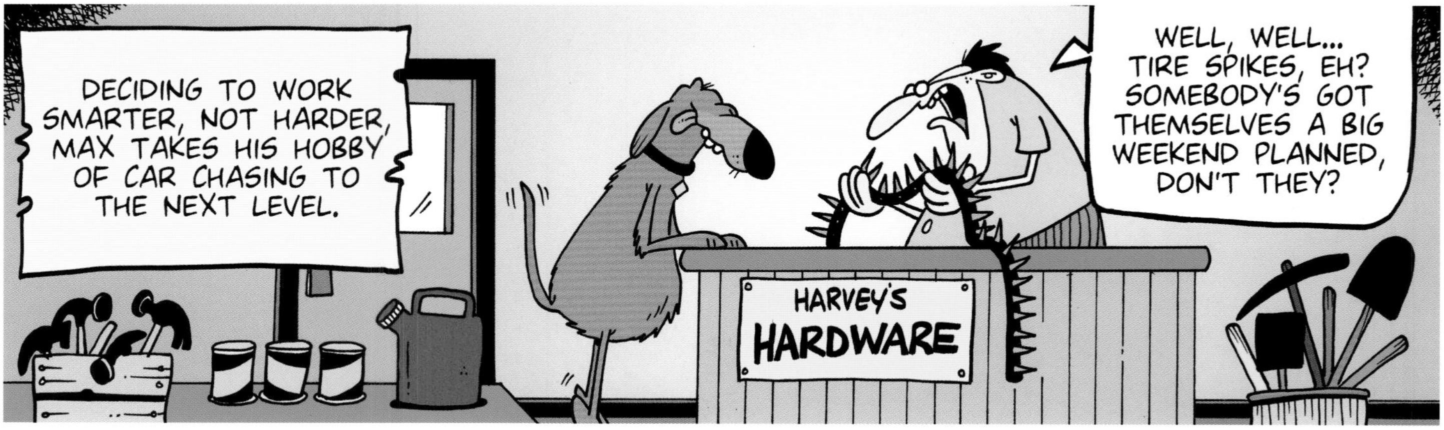
DECIDING TO WORK SMARTER, NOT HARDER, MAX TAKES HIS HOBBY OF CAR CHASING TO THE NEXT LEVEL.
WELL, WELL... TIRE SPIKES, EH? SOMEBODY'S GOT THEMSELVES A BIG WEEKEND PLANNED, DON'T THEY?
HARVEY'S HARDWARE

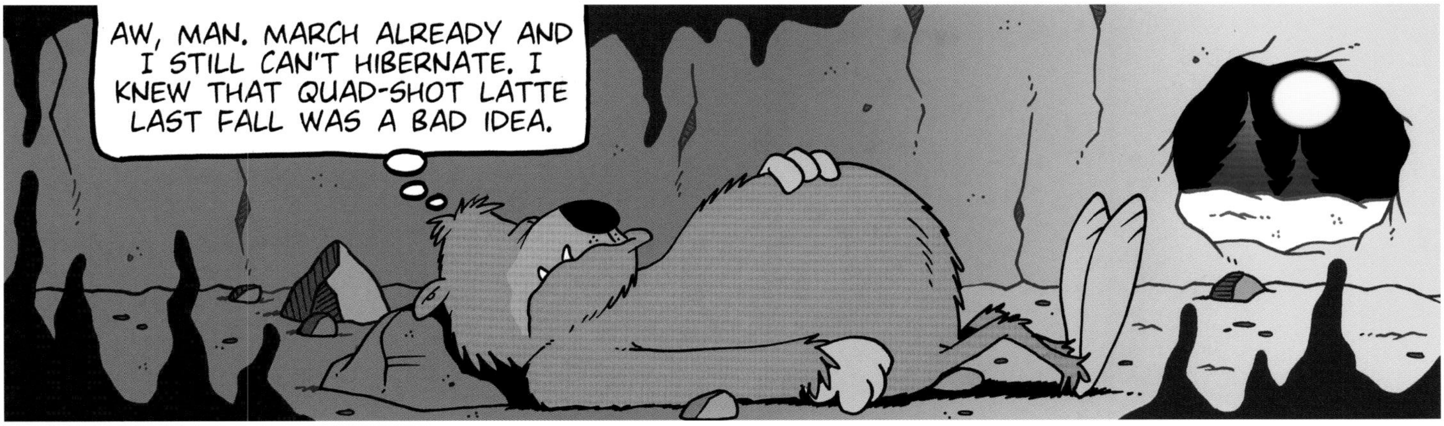
AW, MAN. MARCH ALREADY AND I STILL CAN'T HIBERNATE. I KNEW THAT QUAD-SHOT LATTE LAST FALL WAS A BAD IDEA.

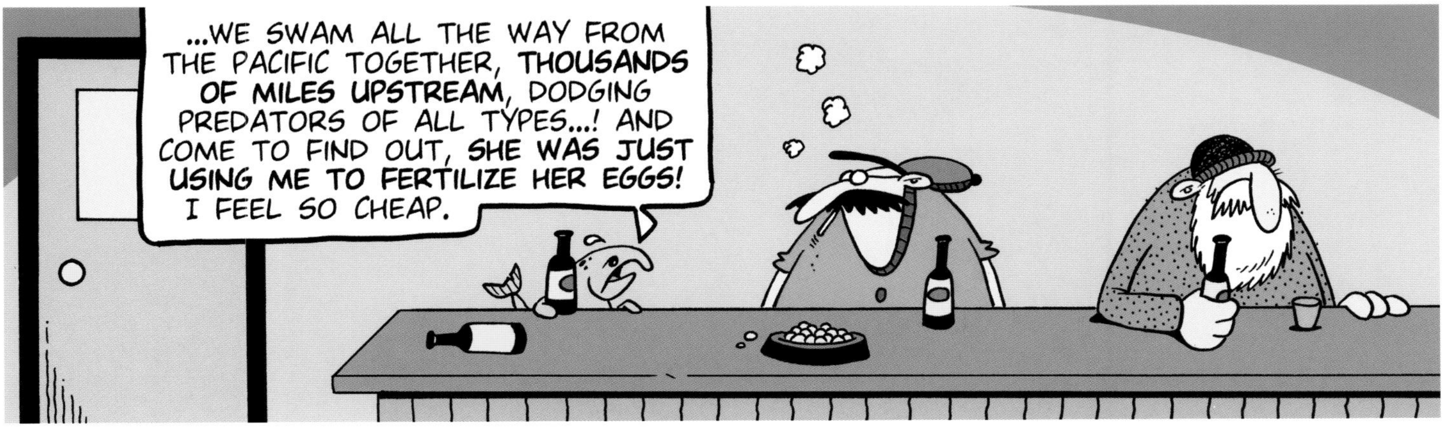
...WE SWAM ALL THE WAY FROM THE PACIFIC TOGETHER, THOUSANDS OF MILES UPSTREAM, DODGING PREDATORS OF ALL TYPES...! AND COME TO FIND OUT, SHE WAS JUST USING ME TO FERTILIZE HER EGGS! I FEEL SO CHEAP.

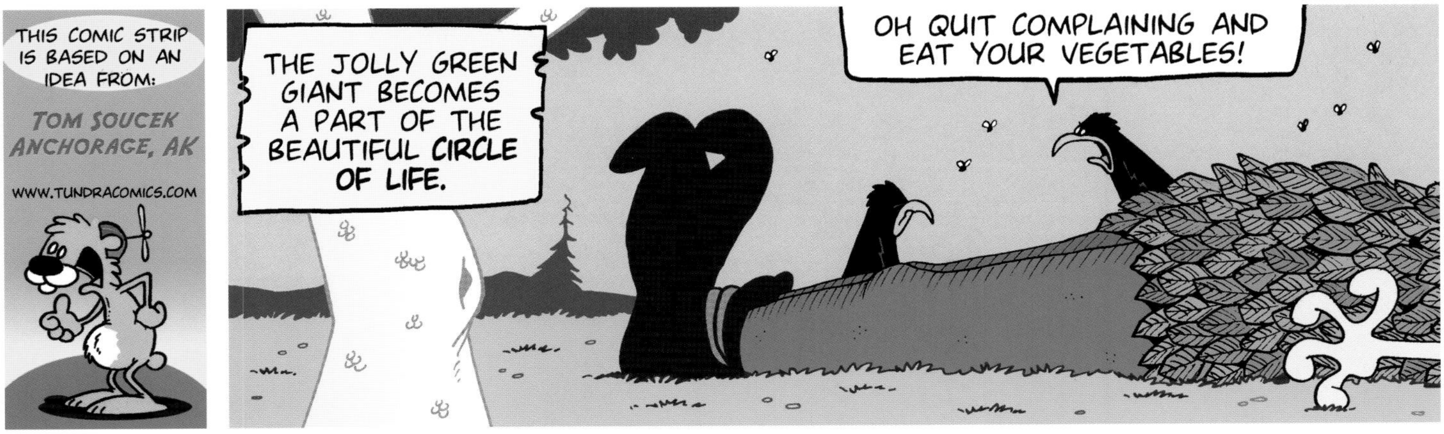
THIS COMIC STRIP IS BASED ON AN IDEA FROM:
TOM SOUCEK
ANCHORAGE, AK
WWW.TUNDRACOMICS.COM
THE JOLLY GREEN GIANT BECOMES A PART OF THE BEAUTIFUL CIRCLE OF LIFE.
OH QUIT COMPLAINING AND EAT YOUR VEGETABLES!

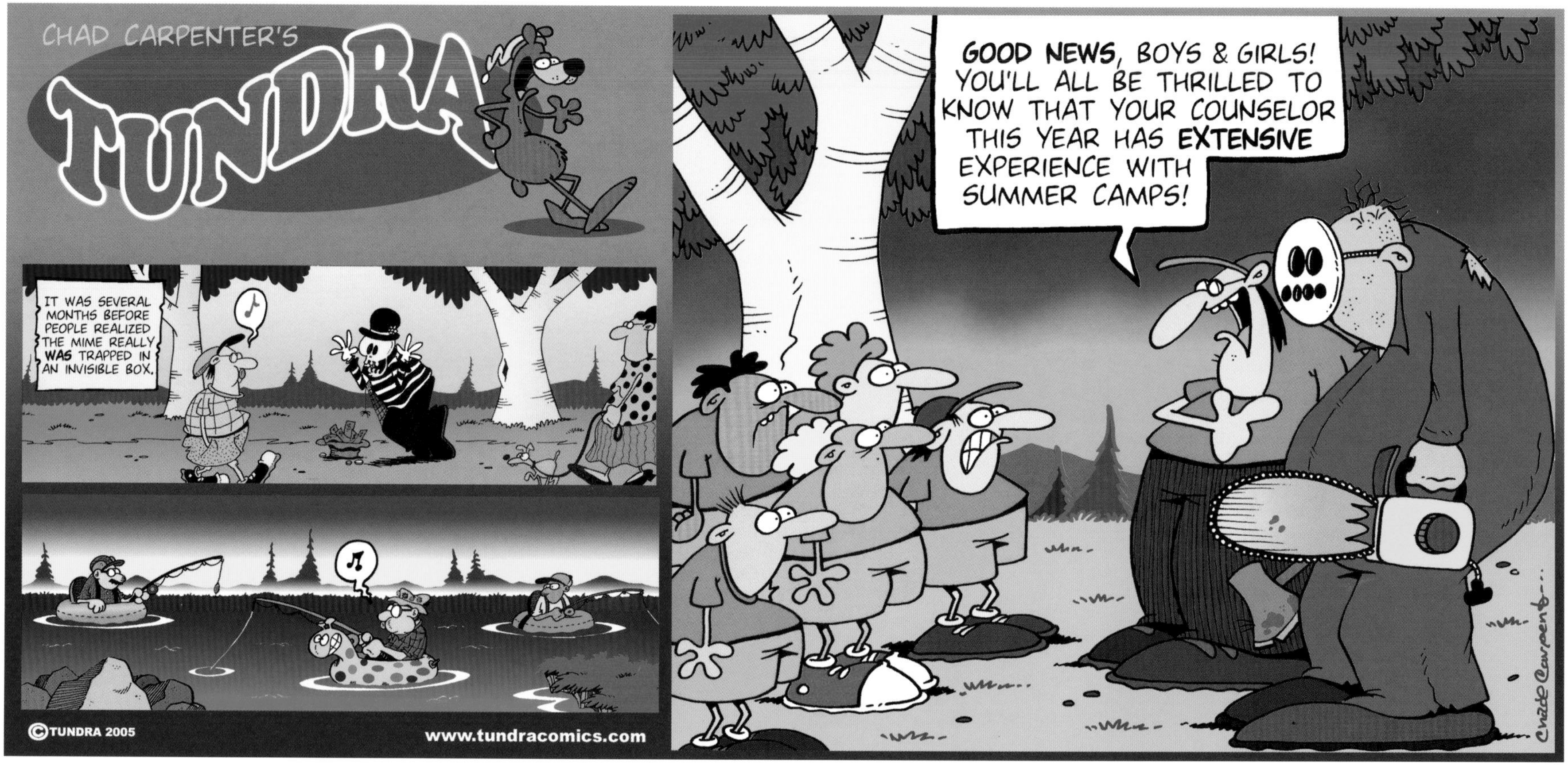
CHAD CARPENTER'S
TUNDRA
IT WAS SEVERAL MONTHS BEFORE PEOPLE REALIZED THE MIME REALLY WAS TRAPPED IN AN INVISIBLE BOX.
©TUNDRA 2005
www.tundracomics.com
GOOD NEWS, BOYS & GIRLS! YOU'LL ALL BE THRILLED TO KNOW THAT YOUR COUNSELOR THIS YEAR HAS EXTENSIVE EXPERIENCE WITH SUMMER CAMPS!

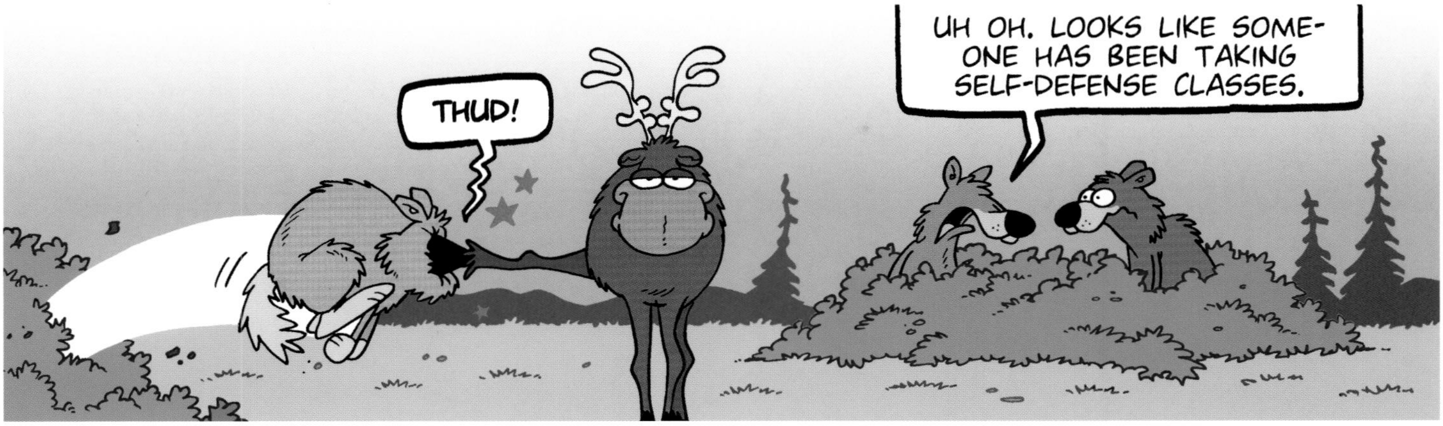
THUD!
UH OH. LOOKS LIKE SOME-ONE HAS BEEN TAKING SELF-DEFENSE CLASSES.

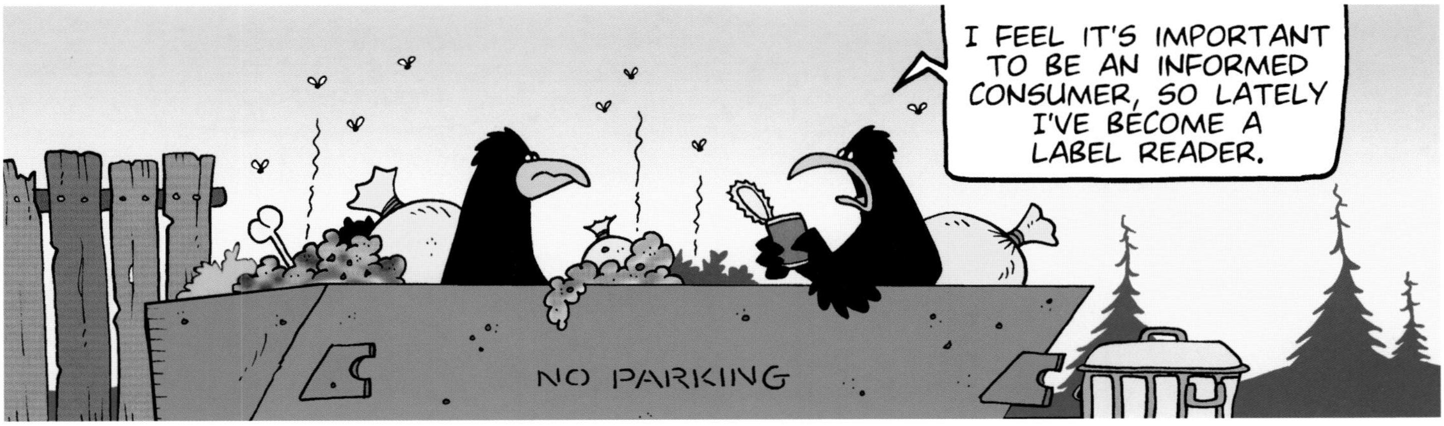
I FEEL IT'S IMPORTANT TO BE AN INFORMED CONSUMER, SO LATELY I'VE BECOME A LABEL READER.
NO PARKING

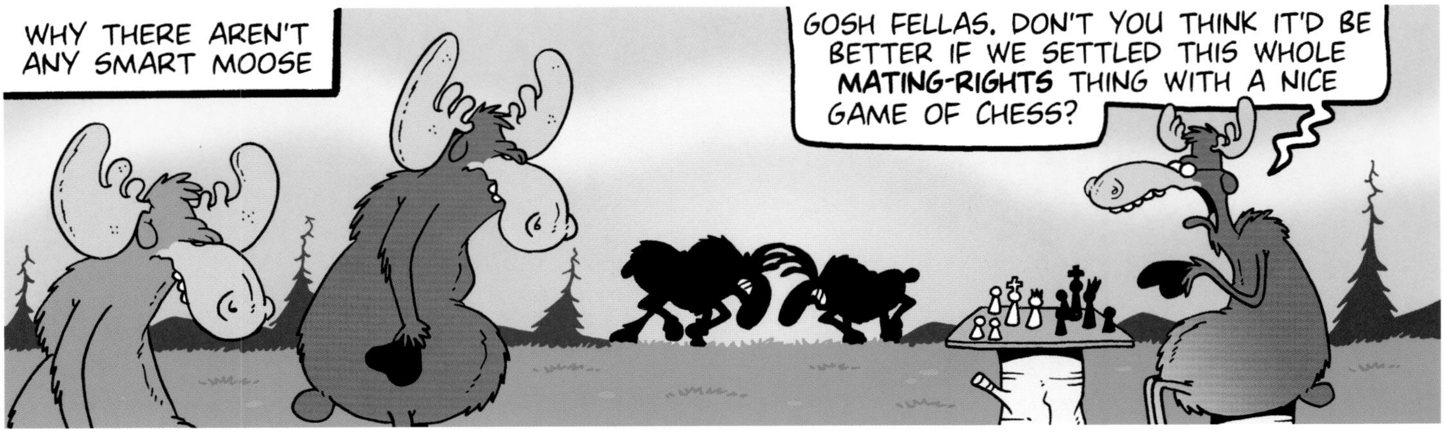
WHY THERE AREN'T ANY SMART MOOSE
GOSH FELLAS. DON'T YOU THINK IT'D BE BETTER IF WE SETTLED THIS WHOLE **MATING-RIGHTS** THING WITH A NICE GAME OF CHESS?

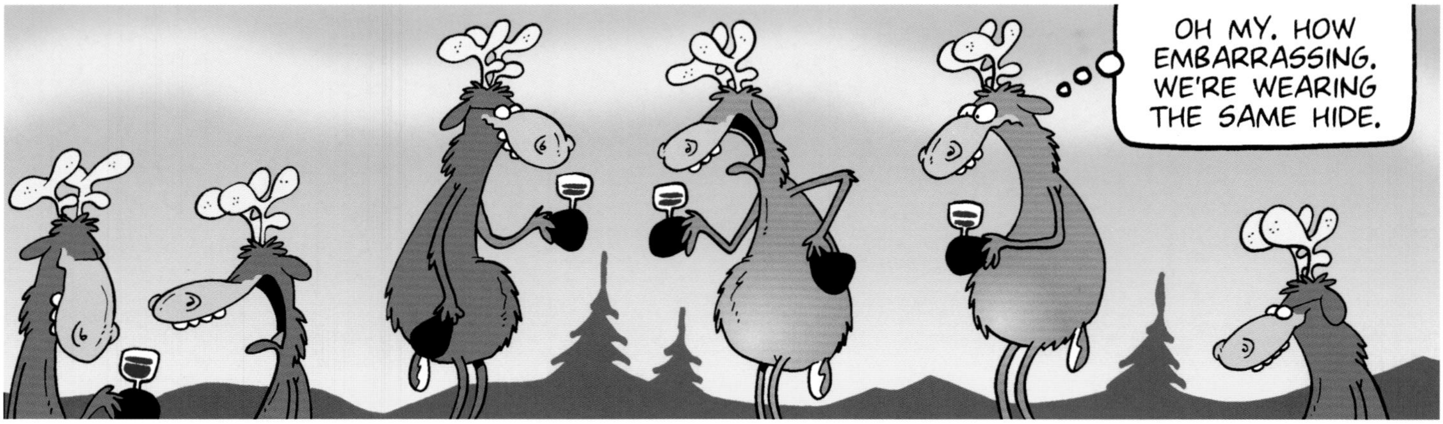
OH MY. HOW EMBARRASSING. WE'RE WEARING THE SAME HIDE.

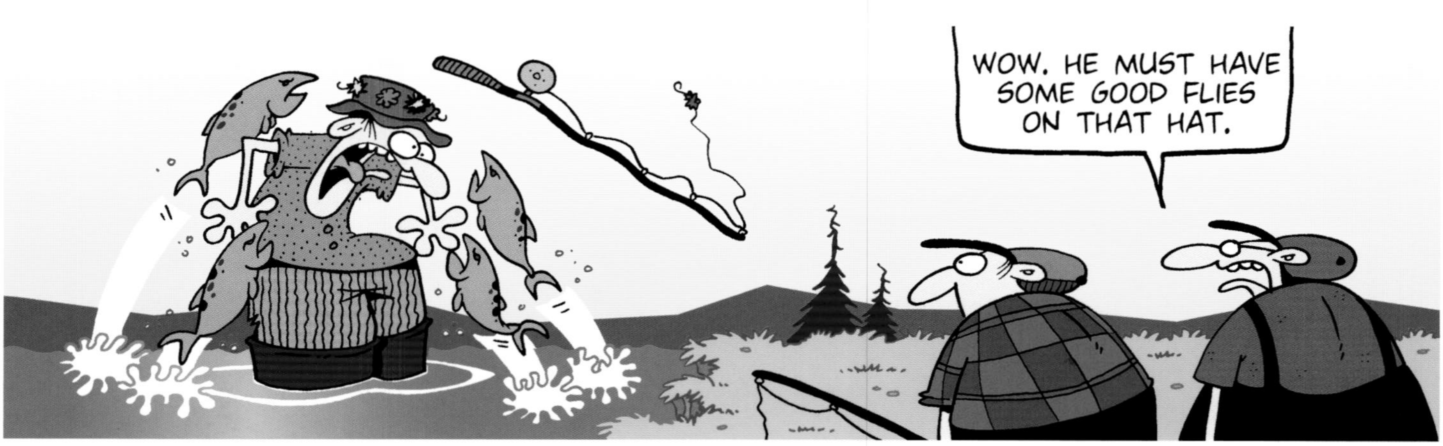
WOW. HE MUST HAVE SOME GOOD FLIES ON THAT HAT.

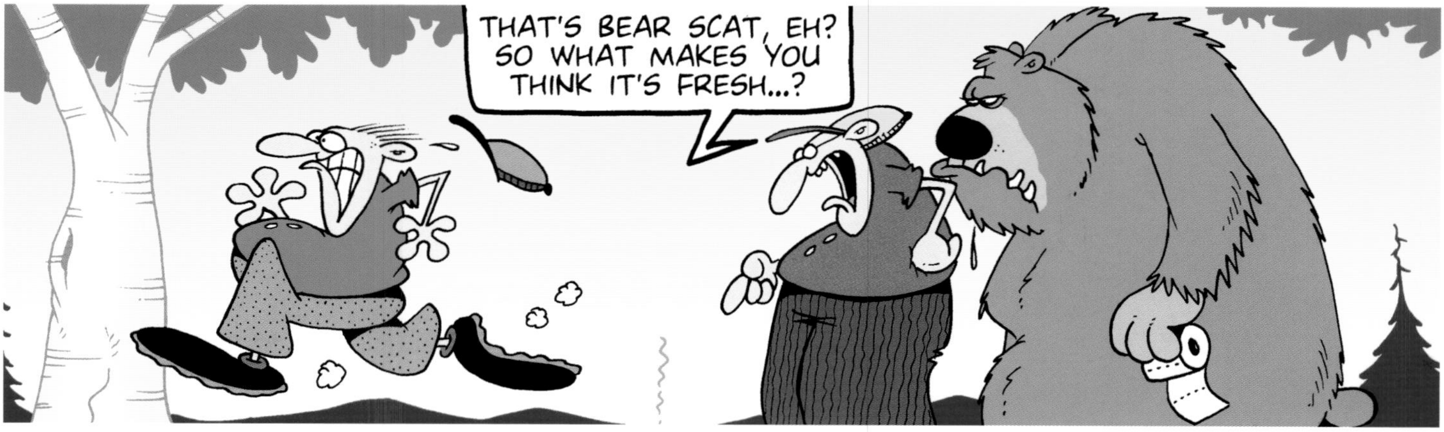
THAT'S BEAR SCAT, EH? SO WHAT MAKES YOU THINK IT'S FRESH...?

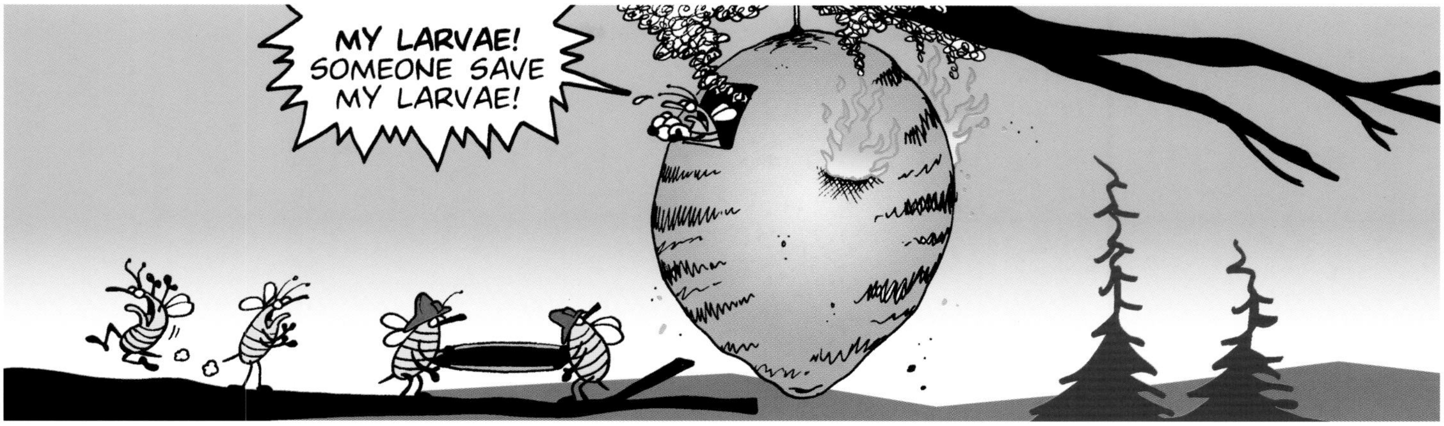
MY LARVAE! SOMEONE SAVE MY LARVAE!

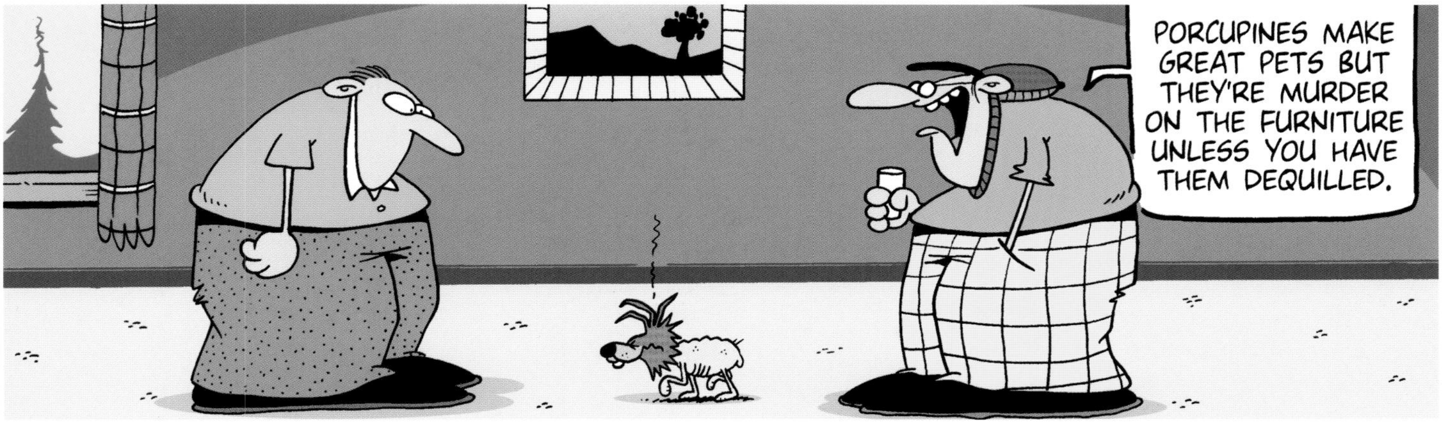
PORCUPINES MAKE GREAT PETS BUT THEY'RE MURDER ON THE FURNITURE UNLESS YOU HAVE THEM DEQUILLED.

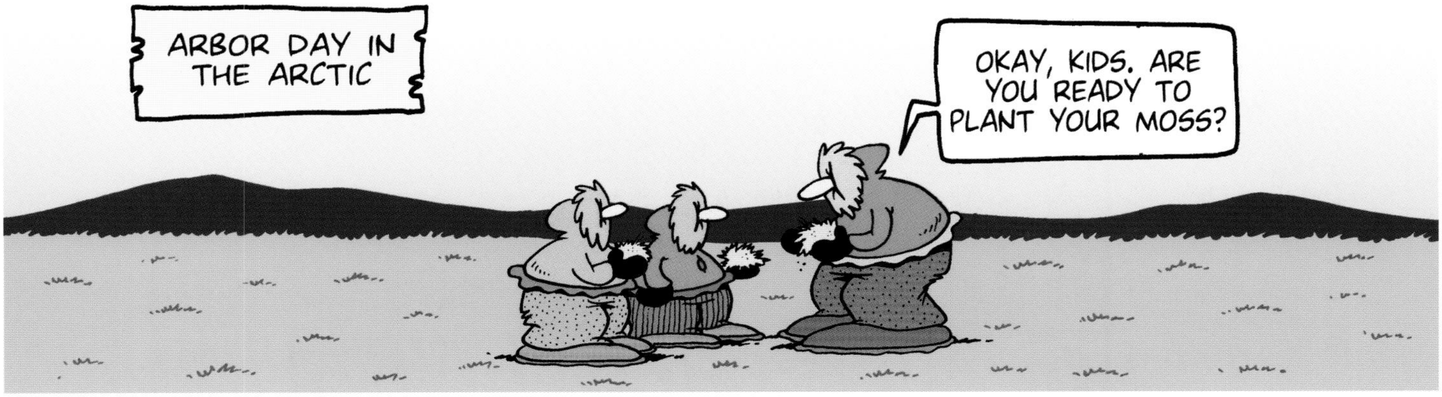
ARBOR DAY IN THE ARCTIC
OKAY, KIDS. ARE YOU READY TO PLANT YOUR MOSS?

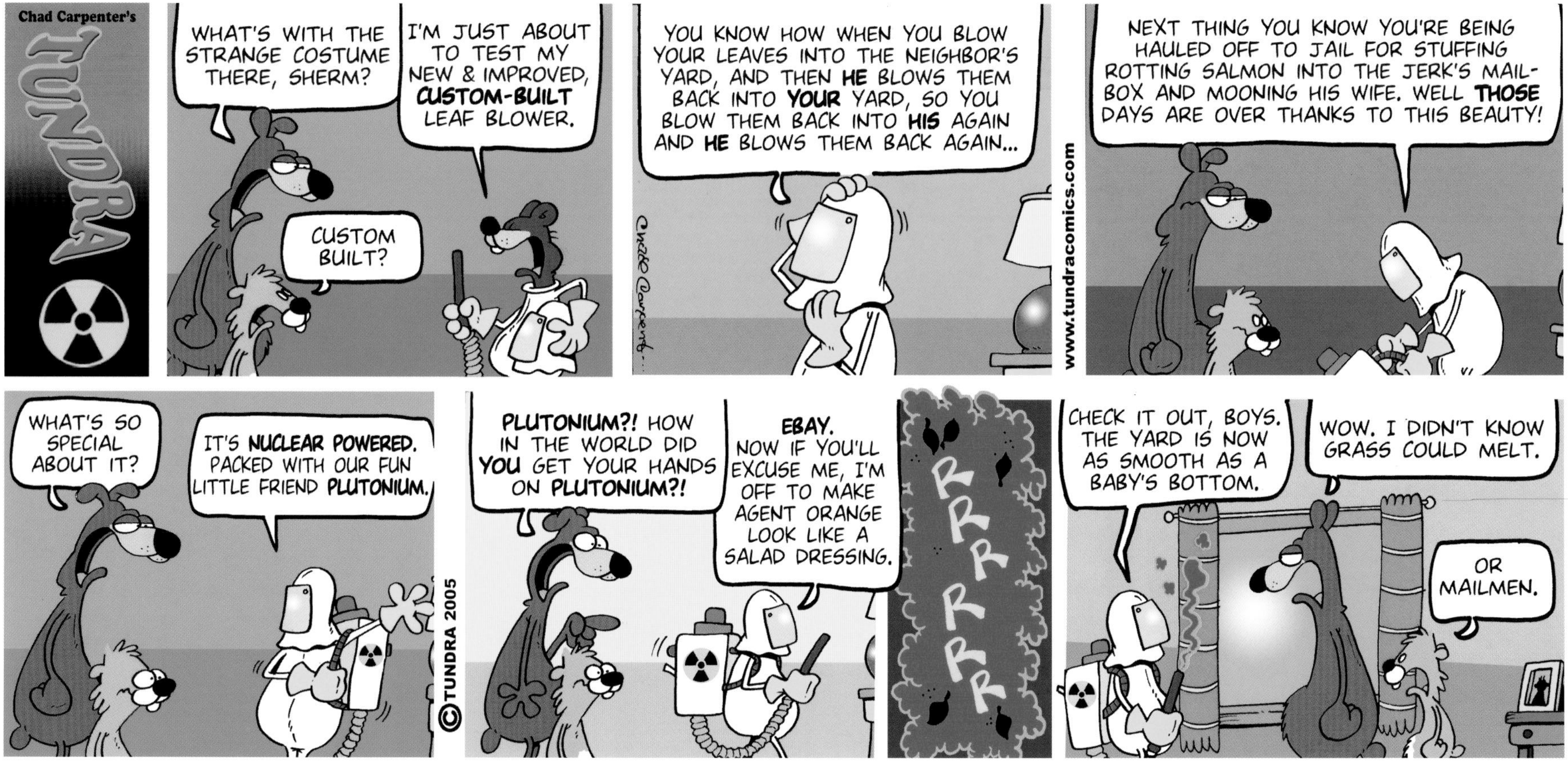
Chad Carpenter's
TUNDRA
WHAT'S WITH THE STRANGE COSTUME THERE, SHERM?
I'M JUST ABOUT TO TEST MY NEW & IMPROVED, **CUSTOM-BUILT** LEAF BLOWER.
CUSTOM BUILT?
YOU KNOW HOW WHEN YOU BLOW YOUR LEAVES INTO THE NEIGHBOR'S YARD, AND THEN **HE** BLOWS THEM BACK INTO **YOUR** YARD, SO YOU BLOW THEM BACK INTO **HIS** AGAIN AND **HE** BLOWS THEM BACK AGAIN...
www.tundracomics.com
NEXT THING YOU KNOW YOU'RE BEING HAULED OFF TO JAIL FOR STUFFING ROTTING SALMON INTO THE JERK'S MAIL-BOX AND MOONING HIS WIFE. WELL **THOSE** DAYS ARE OVER THANKS TO THIS BEAUTY!
WHAT'S SO SPECIAL ABOUT IT?
IT'S **NUCLEAR POWERED.** PACKED WITH OUR FUN LITTLE FRIEND **PLUTONIUM.**
©TUNDRA 2005
PLUTONIUM?! HOW IN THE WORLD DID **YOU** GET YOUR HANDS ON **PLUTONIUM?!**
EBAY. NOW IF YOU'LL EXCUSE ME, I'M OFF TO MAKE AGENT ORANGE LOOK LIKE A SALAD DRESSING.
RRRRRR
CHECK IT OUT, BOYS. THE YARD IS NOW AS SMOOTH AS A BABY'S BOTTOM.
WOW. I DIDN'T KNOW GRASS COULD MELT.
OR MAILMEN.

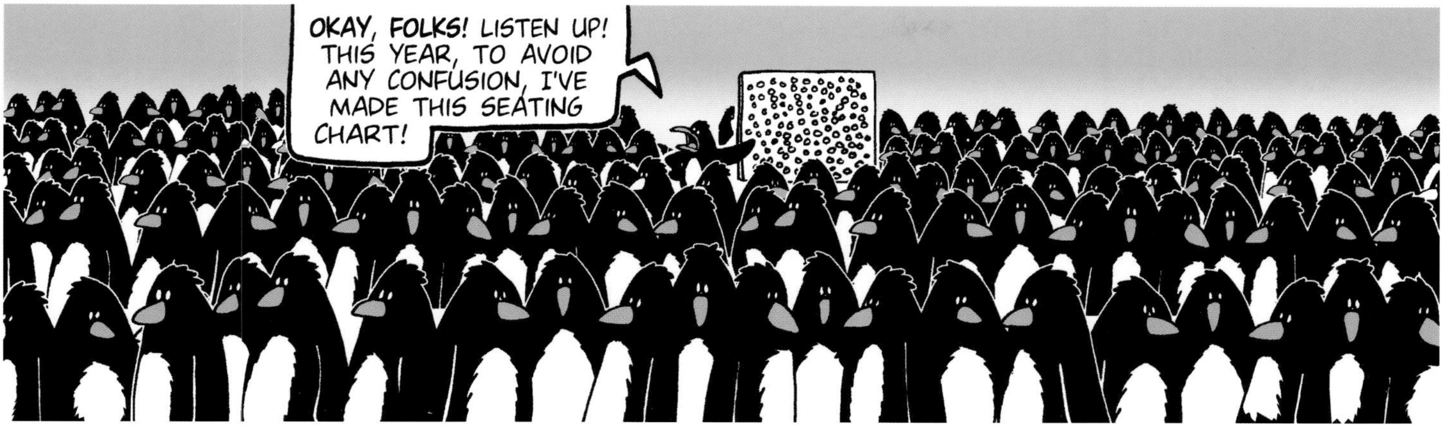
OKAY, FOLKS! LISTEN UP! THIS YEAR, TO AVOID ANY CONFUSION, I'VE MADE THIS SEATING CHART!

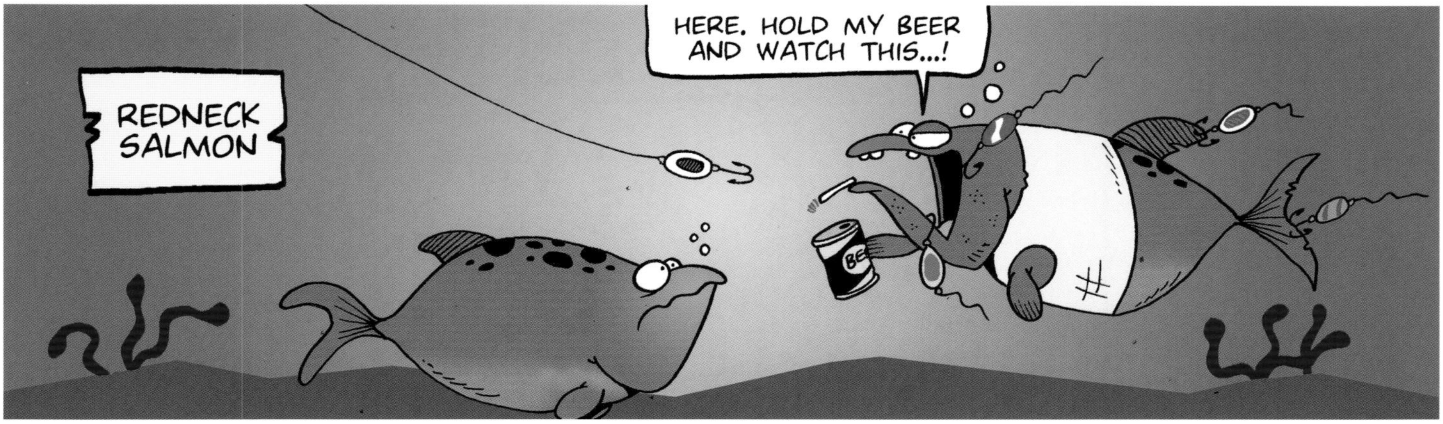
REDNECK SALMON
HERE. HOLD MY BEER AND WATCH THIS...!

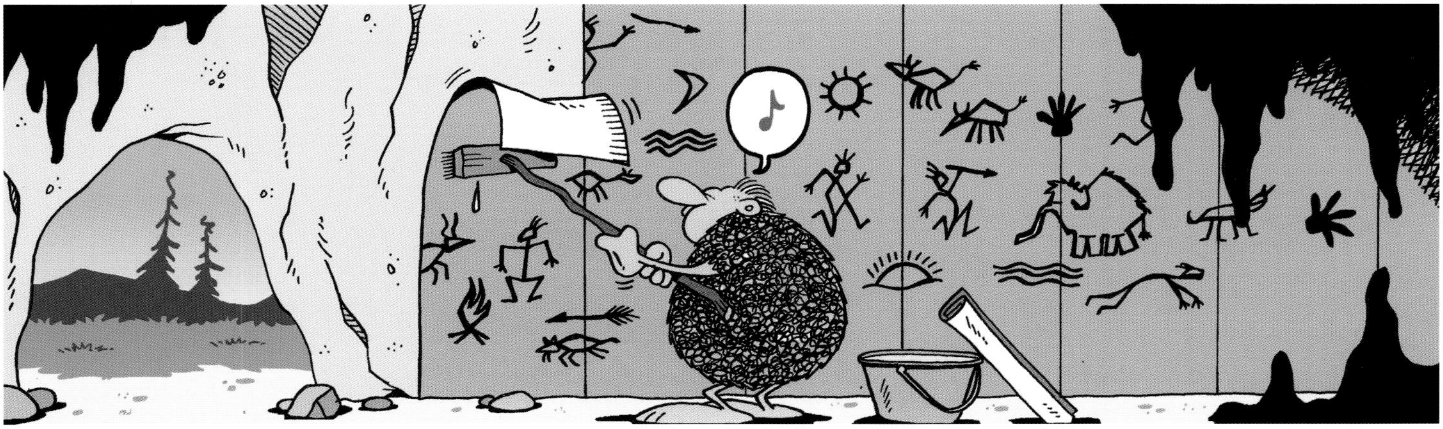

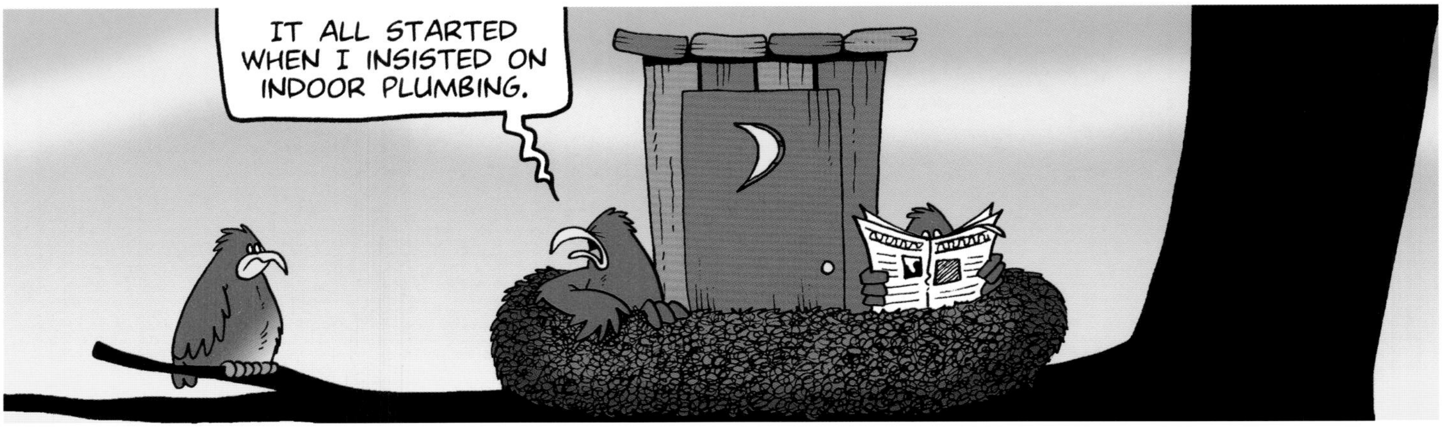
IT ALL STARTED WHEN I INSISTED ON INDOOR PLUMBING.

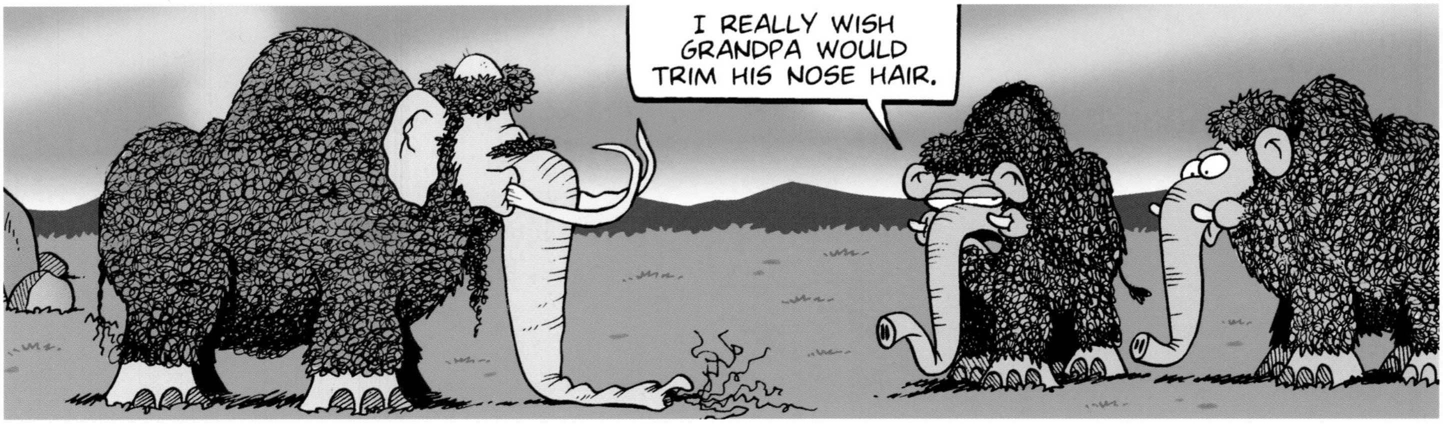
I REALLY WISH GRANDPA WOULD TRIM HIS NOSE HAIR.

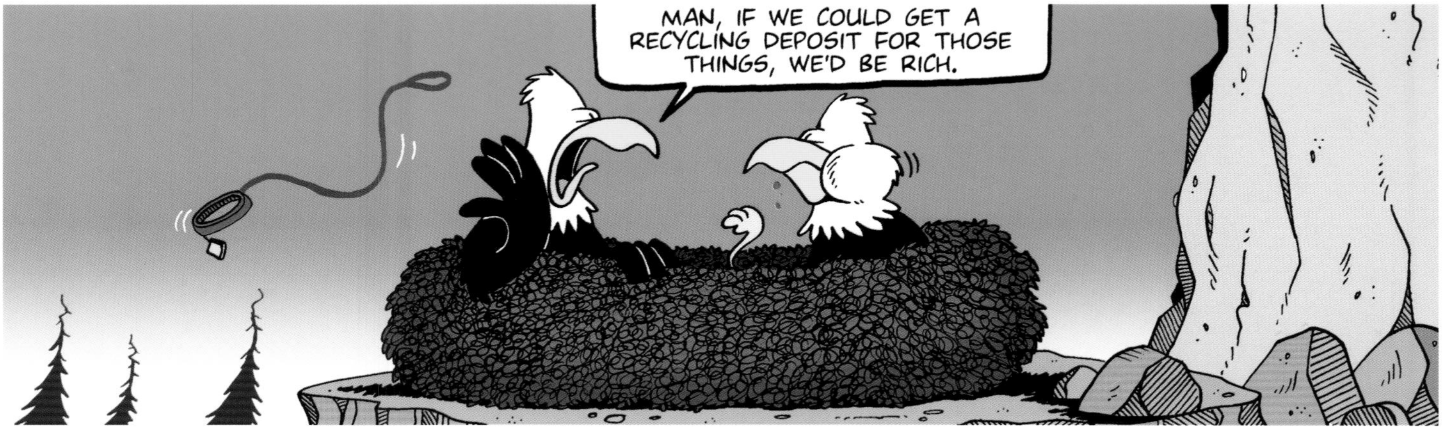
MAN, IF WE COULD GET A RECYCLING DEPOSIT FOR THOSE THINGS, WE'D BE RICH.

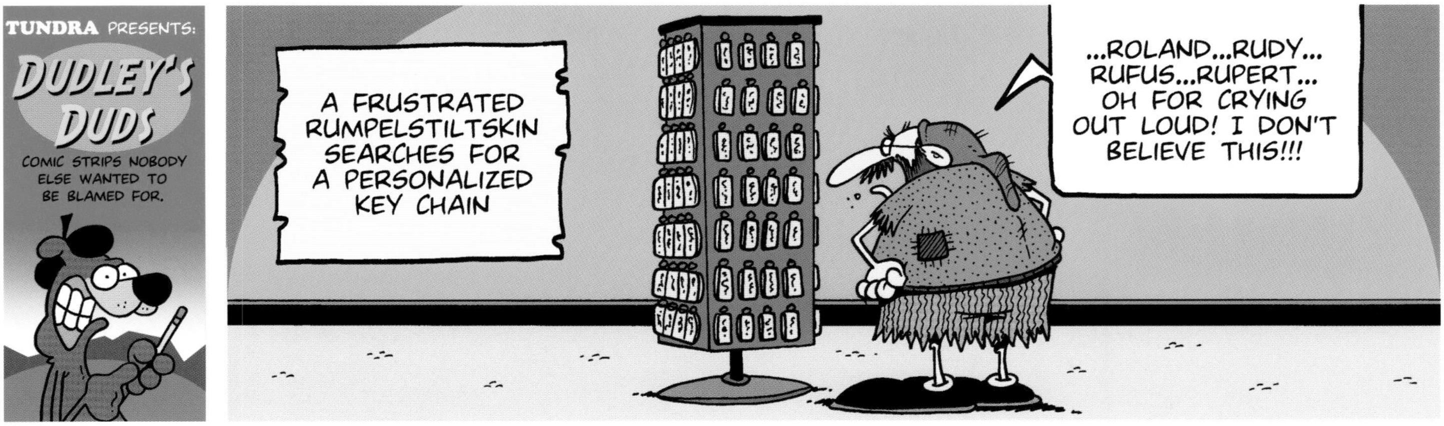
TUNDRA PRESENTS:
DUDLEY'S DUDS
COMIC STRIPS NOBODY ELSE WANTED TO BE BLAMED FOR.
A FRUSTRATED RUMPELSTILTSKIN SEARCHES FOR A PERSONALIZED KEY CHAIN
...ROLAND...RUDY... RUFUS...RUPERT... OH FOR CRYING OUT LOUD! I DON'T BELIEVE THIS!!!

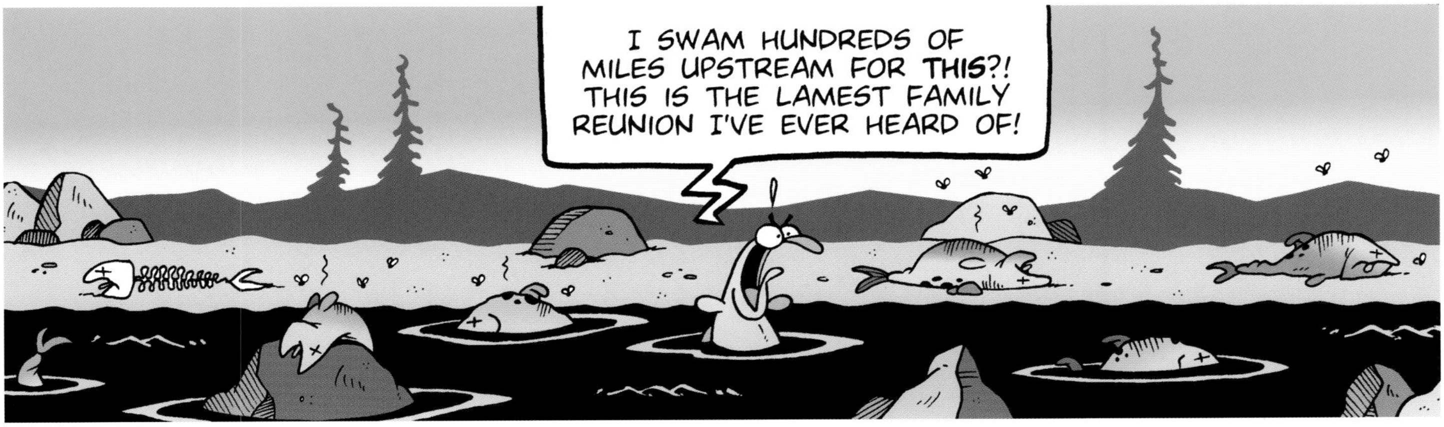
I SWAM HUNDREDS OF MILES UPSTREAM FOR THIS?! THIS IS THE LAMEST FAMILY REUNION I'VE EVER HEARD OF!

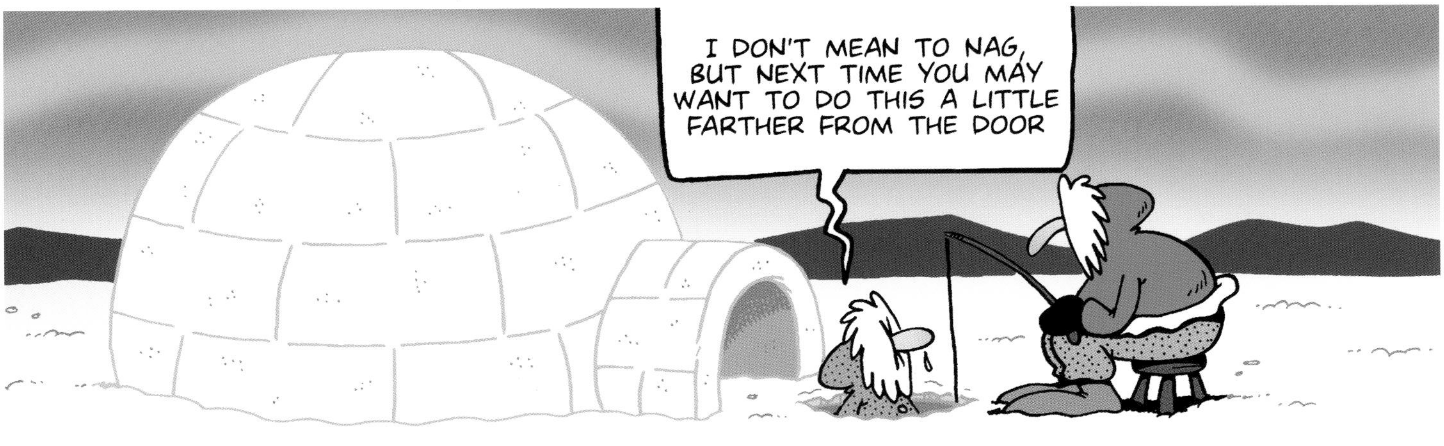
I DON'T MEAN TO NAG, BUT NEXT TIME YOU MAY WANT TO DO THIS A LITTLE FARTHER FROM THE DOOR

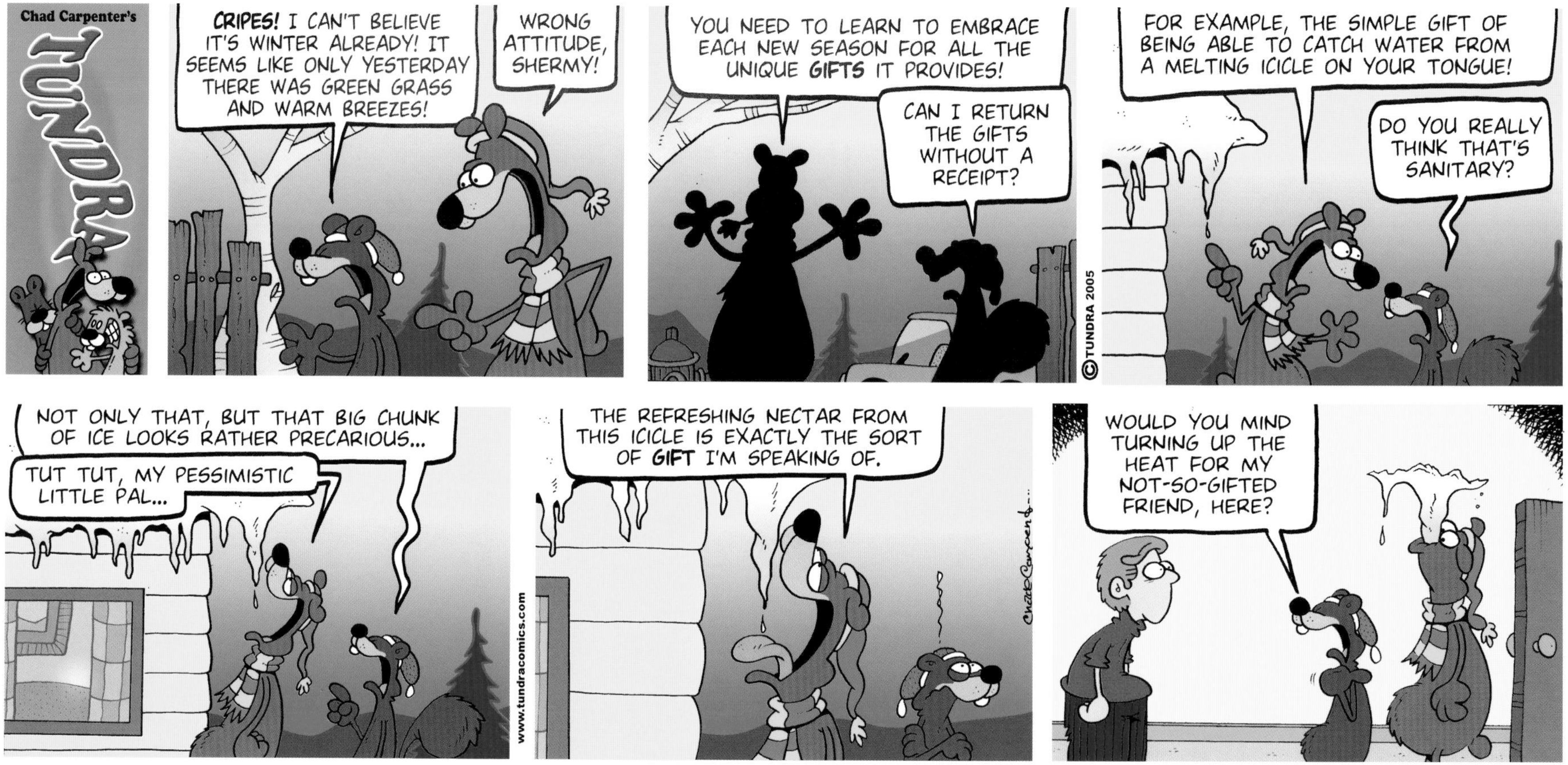
Chad Carpenter's
TUNDRA
CRIPES! I CAN'T BELIEVE IT'S WINTER ALREADY! IT SEEMS LIKE ONLY YESTERDAY THERE WAS GREEN GRASS AND WARM BREEZES!
WRONG ATTITUDE, SHERMY!
YOU NEED TO LEARN TO EMBRACE EACH NEW SEASON FOR ALL THE UNIQUE GIFTS IT PROVIDES!
CAN I RETURN THE GIFTS WITHOUT A RECEIPT?
©TUNDRA 2005
FOR EXAMPLE, THE SIMPLE GIFT OF BEING ABLE TO CATCH WATER FROM A MELTING ICICLE ON YOUR TONGUE!
DO YOU REALLY THINK THAT'S SANITARY?
NOT ONLY THAT, BUT THAT BIG CHUNK OF ICE LOOKS RATHER PRECARIOUS...
TUT TUT, MY PESSIMISTIC LITTLE PAL...
www.tundracomics.com
THE REFRESHING NECTAR FROM THIS ICICLE IS EXACTLY THE SORT OF GIFT I'M SPEAKING OF.
WOULD YOU MIND TURNING UP THE HEAT FOR MY NOT-SO-GIFTED FRIEND, HERE?

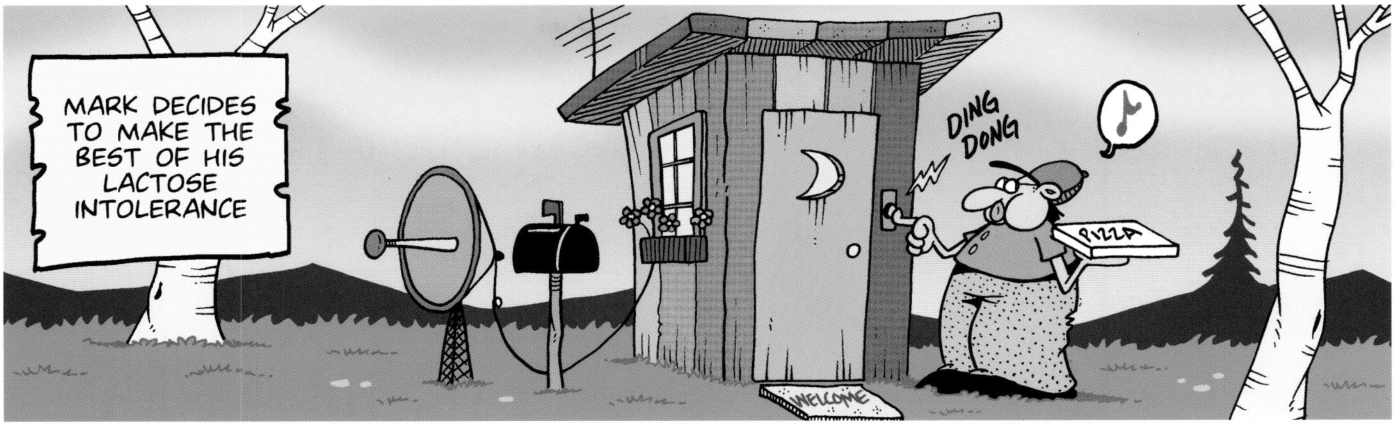
MARK DECIDES TO MAKE THE BEST OF HIS LACTOSE INTOLERANCE
DING DONG
PIZZA
WELCOME

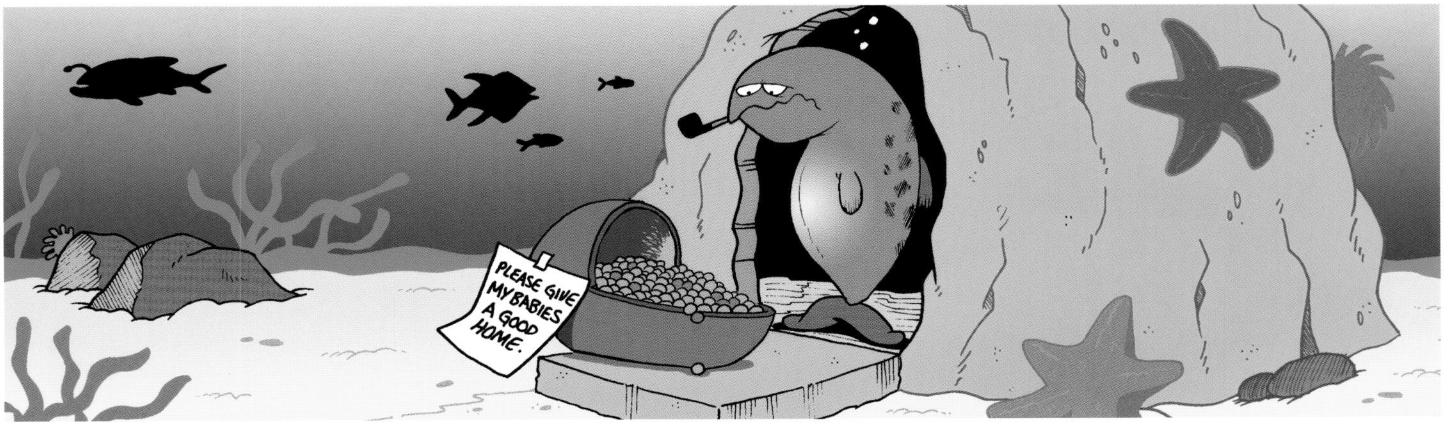
PLEASE GIVE MY BABIES A GOOD HOME.

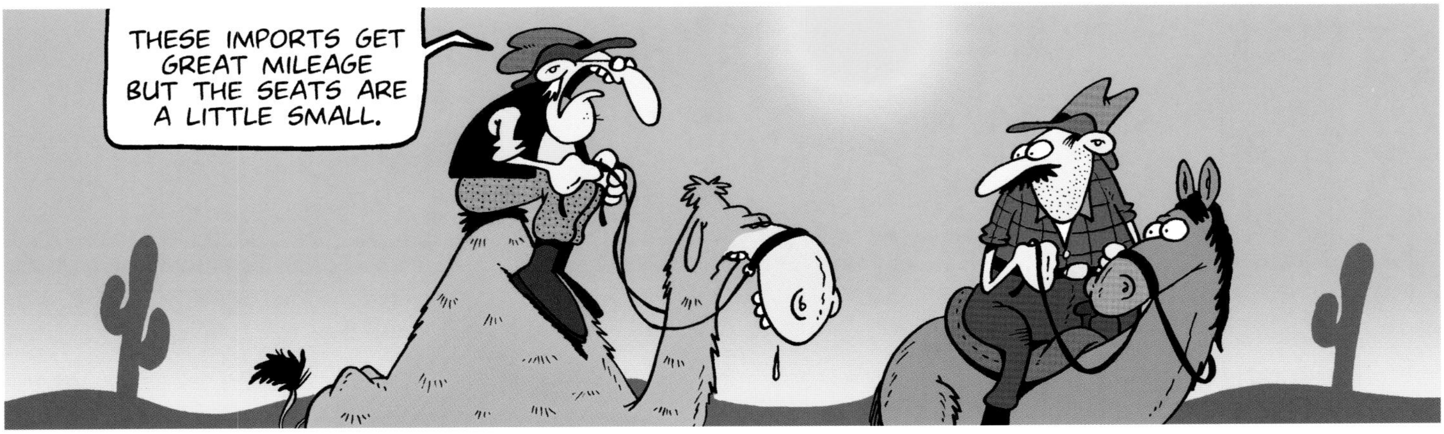
THESE IMPORTS GET GREAT MILEAGE BUT THE SEATS ARE A LITTLE SMALL.

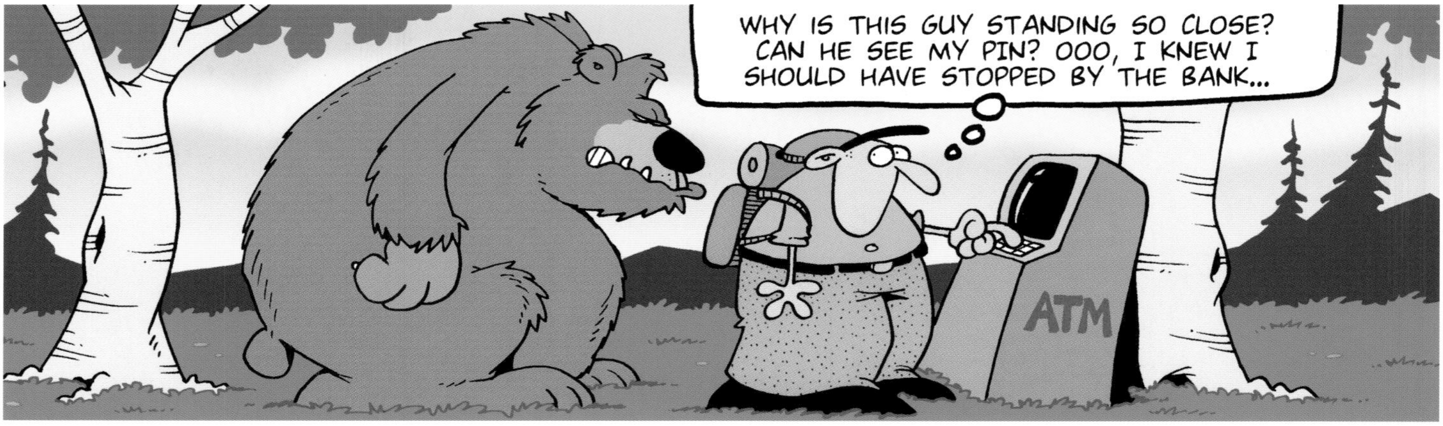
WHY IS THIS GUY STANDING SO CLOSE? CAN HE SEE MY PIN? OOO, I KNEW I SHOULD HAVE STOPPED BY THE BANK...
ATM

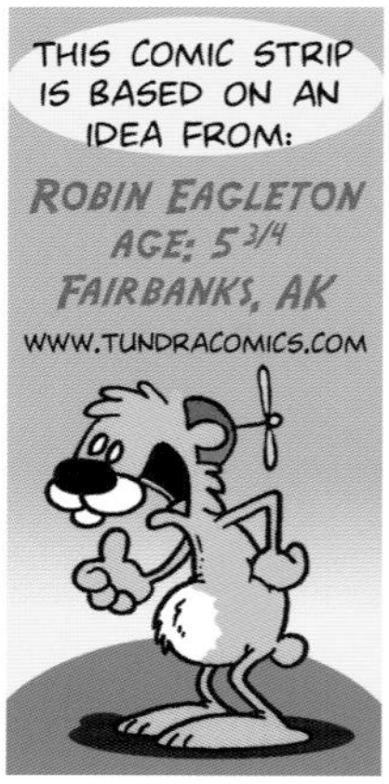
THIS COMIC STRIP IS BASED ON AN IDEA FROM:
ROBIN EAGLETON
AGE: 5 3/4
FAIRBANKS, AK
WWW.TUNDRACOMICS.COM

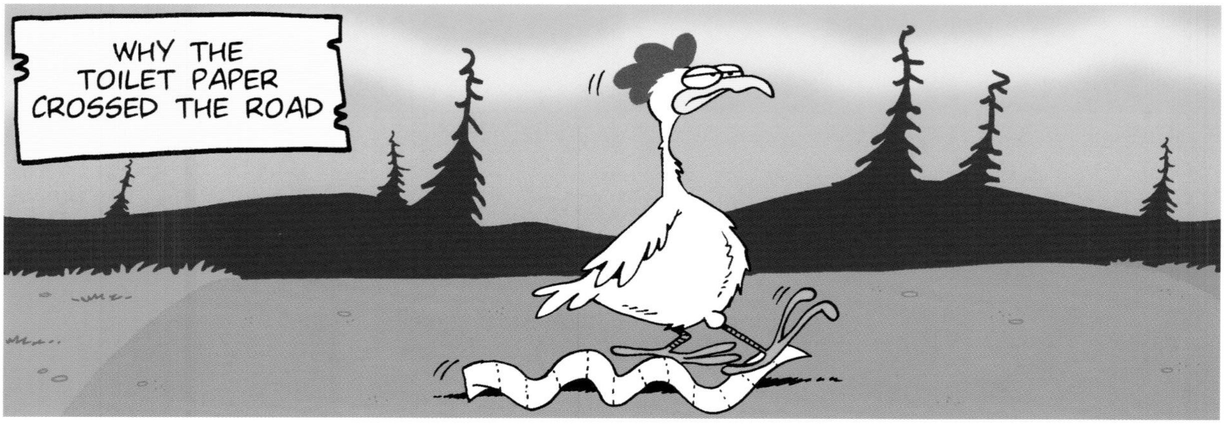
WHY THE TOILET PAPER CROSSED THE ROAD

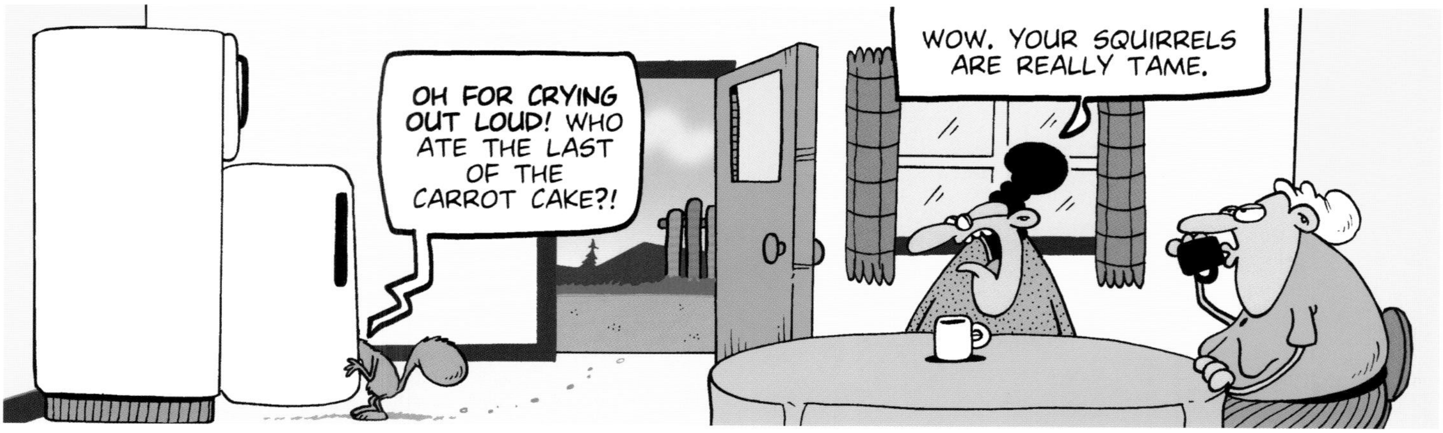
OH FOR CRYING OUT LOUD! WHO ATE THE LAST OF THE CARROT CAKE?!
WOW. YOUR SQUIRRELS ARE REALLY TAME.

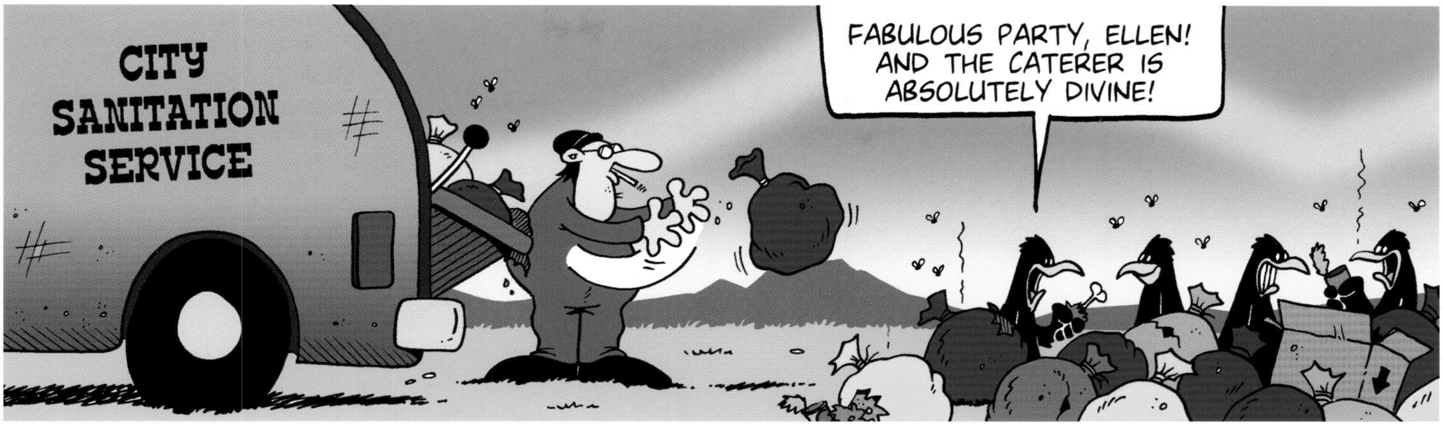
CITY SANITATION SERVICE
FABULOUS PARTY, ELLEN! AND THE CATERER IS ABSOLUTELY DIVINE!

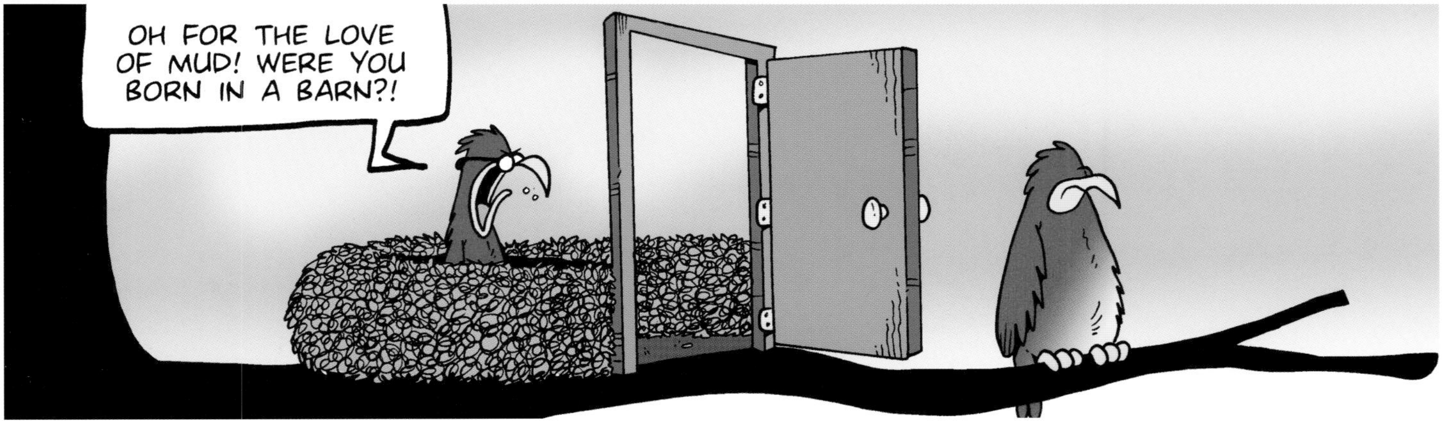
OH FOR THE LOVE OF MUD! WERE YOU BORN IN A BARN?!

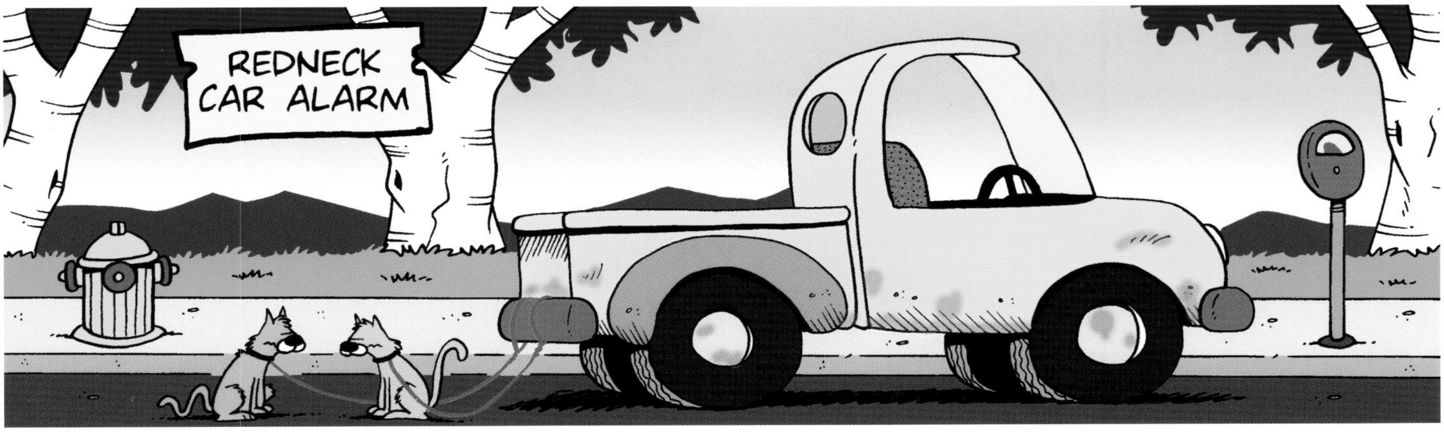
REDNECK CAR ALARM

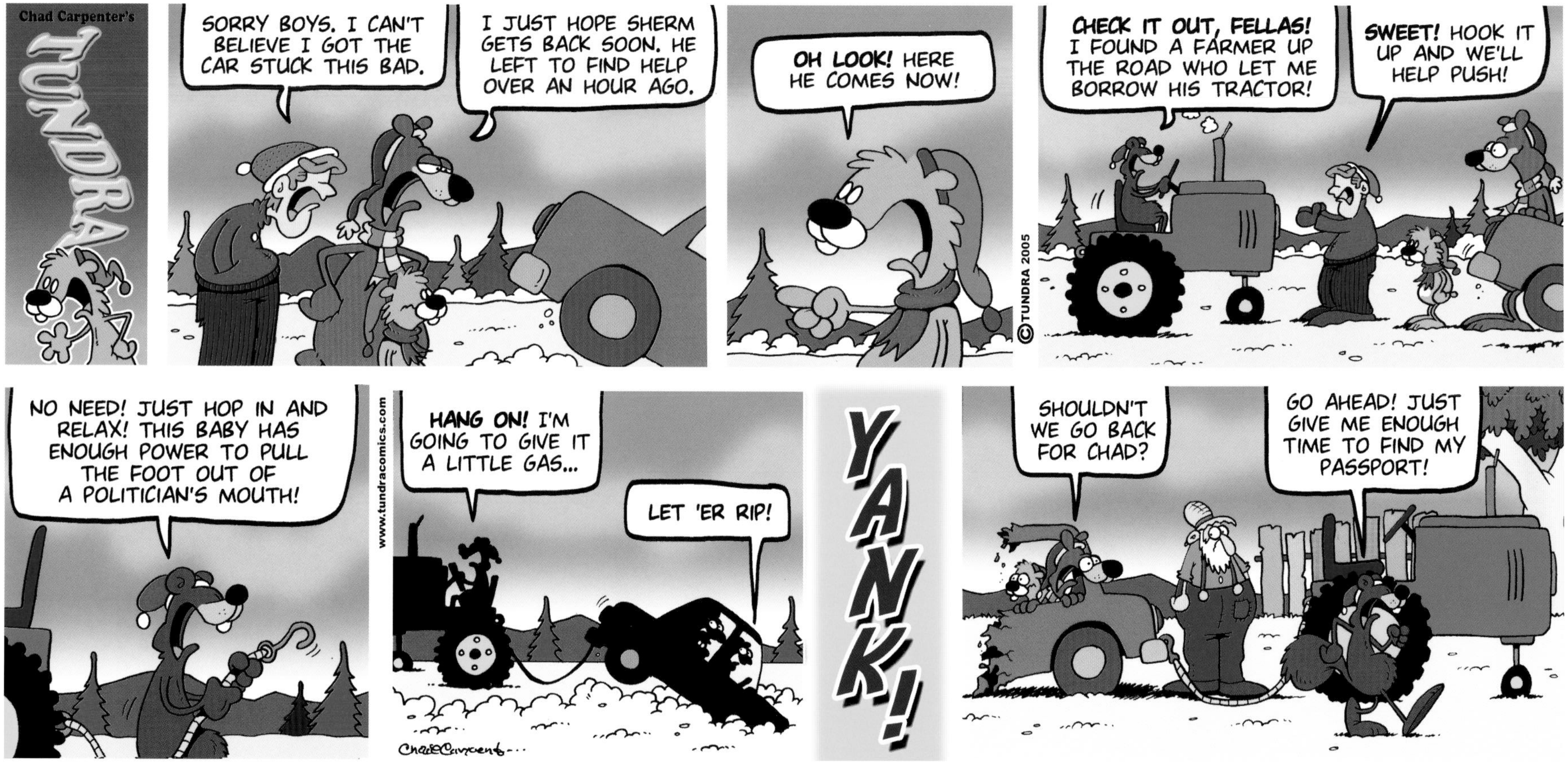
Chad Carpenter's
TUNDRA
SORRY BOYS. I CAN'T BELIEVE I GOT THE CAR STUCK THIS BAD.
I JUST HOPE SHERM GETS BACK SOON. HE LEFT TO FIND HELP OVER AN HOUR AGO.
OH LOOK! HERE HE COMES NOW!
©TUNDRA 2005
CHECK IT OUT, FELLAS! I FOUND A FARMER UP THE ROAD WHO LET ME BORROW HIS TRACTOR!
SWEET! HOOK IT UP AND WE'LL HELP PUSH!
NO NEED! JUST HOP IN AND RELAX! THIS BABY HAS ENOUGH POWER TO PULL THE FOOT OUT OF A POLITICIAN'S MOUTH!
www.tundracomics.com
HANG ON! I'M GOING TO GIVE IT A LITTLE GAS...
LET 'ER RIP!
YANK!
SHOULDN'T WE GO BACK FOR CHAD?
GO AHEAD! JUST GIVE ME ENOUGH TIME TO FIND MY PASSPORT!

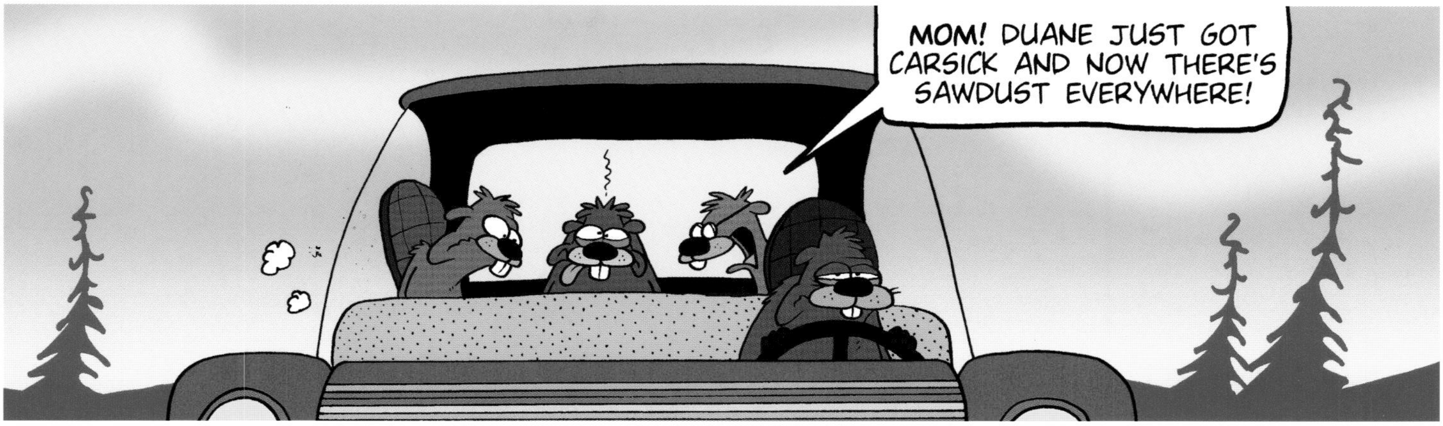
MOM! DUANE JUST GOT CARSICK AND NOW THERE'S SAWDUST EVERYWHERE!

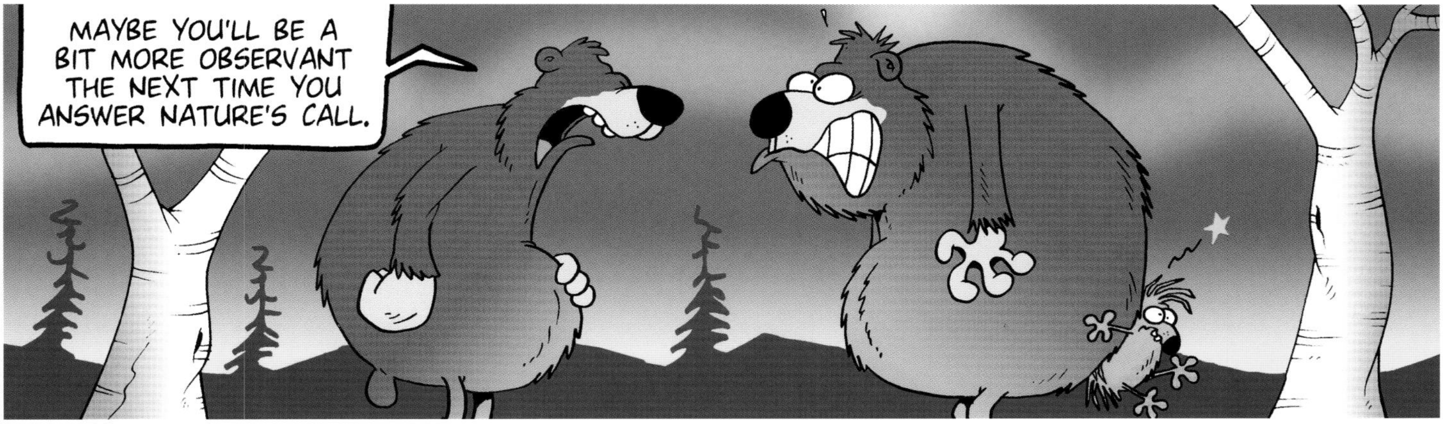
MAYBE YOU'LL BE A BIT MORE OBSERVANT THE NEXT TIME YOU ANSWER NATURE'S CALL.

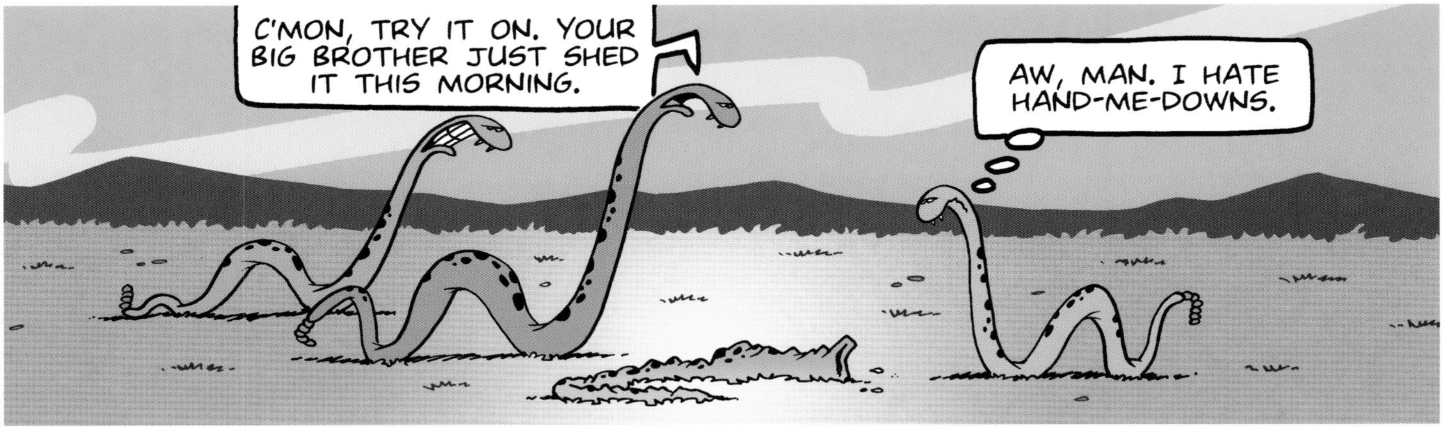
C'MON, TRY IT ON. YOUR BIG BROTHER JUST SHED IT THIS MORNING.
AW, MAN. I HATE HAND-ME-DOWNS.

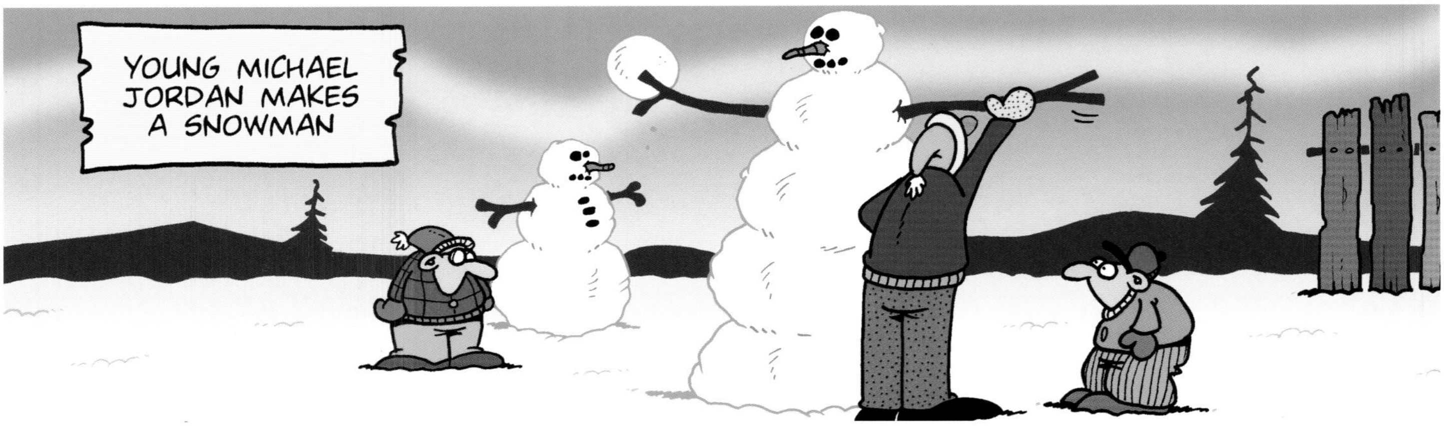
YOUNG MICHAEL JORDAN MAKES A SNOWMAN

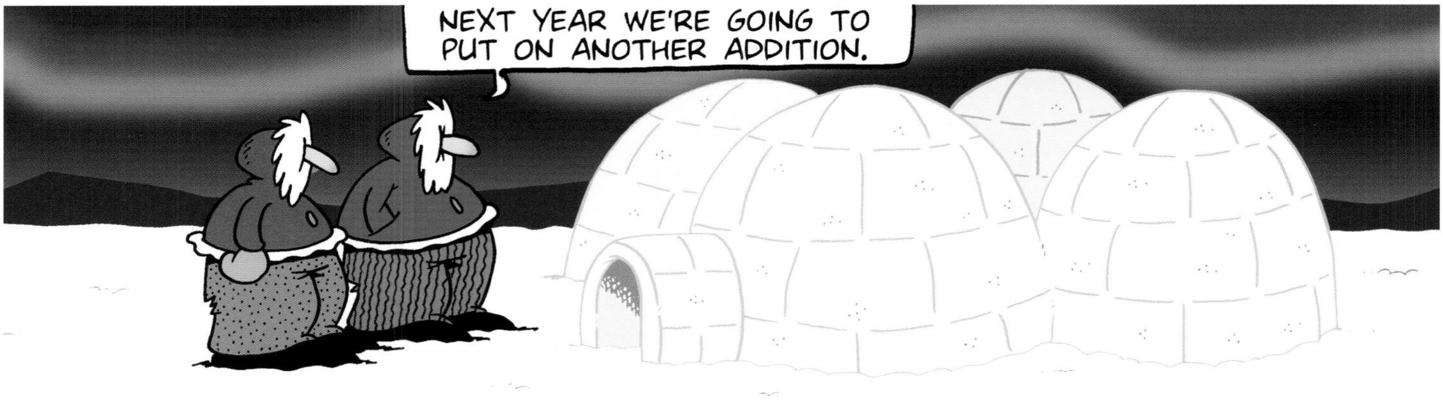
NEXT YEAR WE'RE GOING TO PUT ON ANOTHER ADDITION.

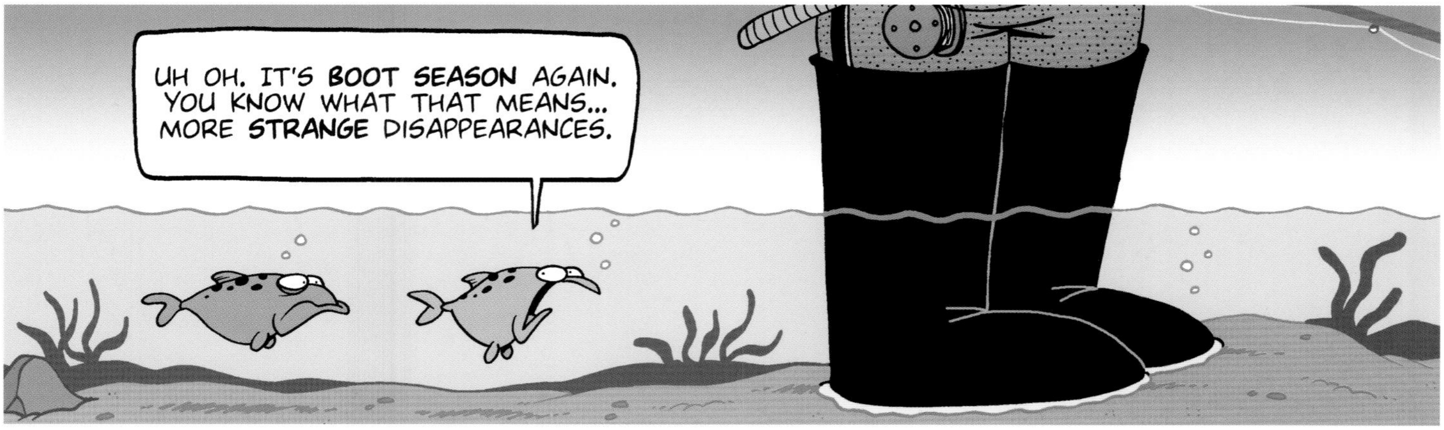
UH OH. IT'S **BOOT SEASON** AGAIN. YOU KNOW WHAT THAT MEANS... MORE **STRANGE** DISAPPEARANCES.

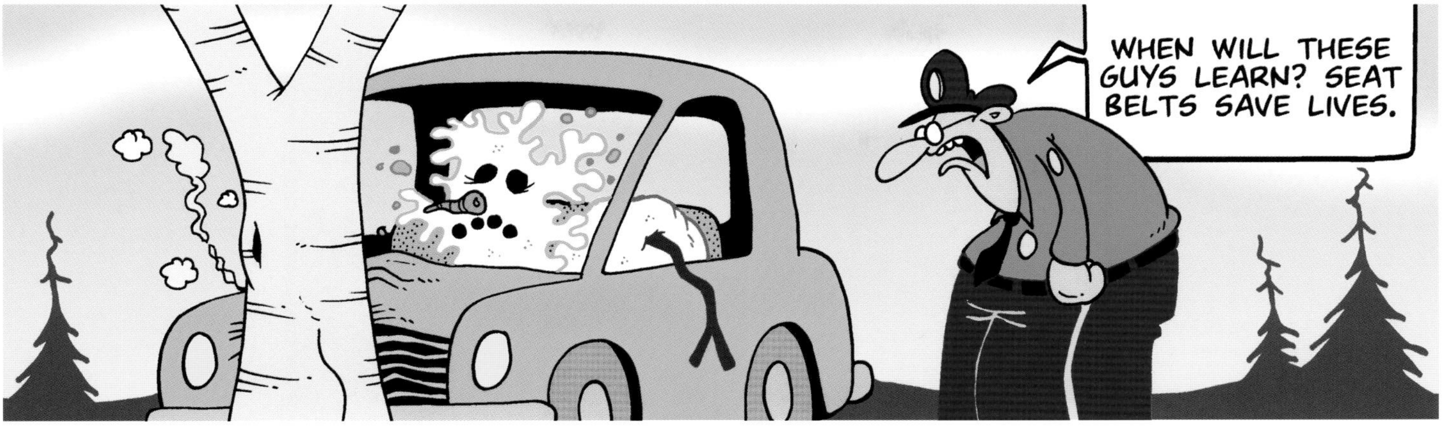
WHEN WILL THESE GUYS LEARN? SEAT BELTS SAVE LIVES.

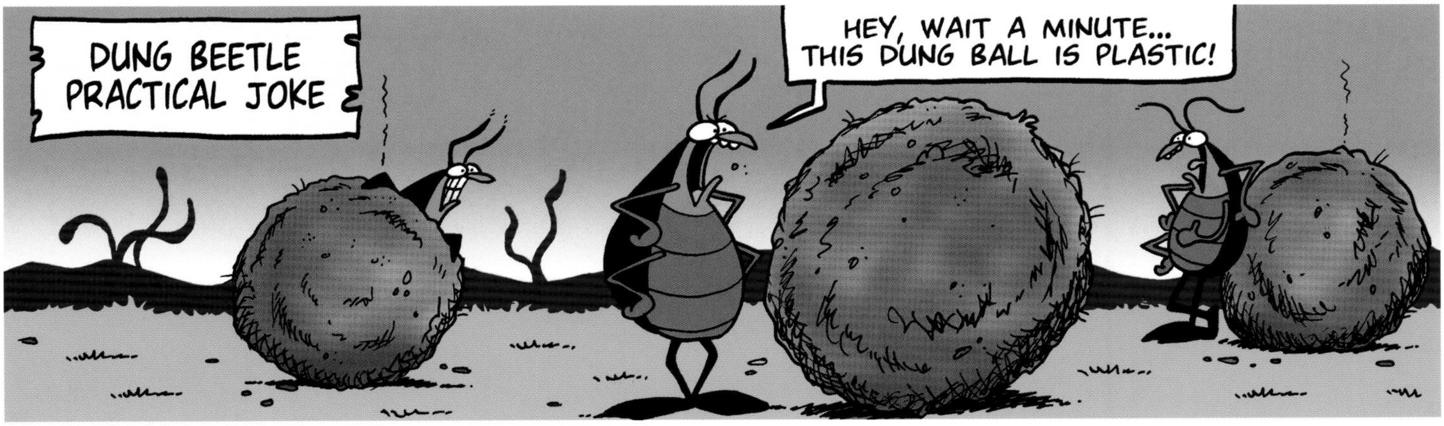
DUNG BEETLE PRACTICAL JOKE
HEY, WAIT A MINUTE... THIS DUNG BALL IS PLASTIC!

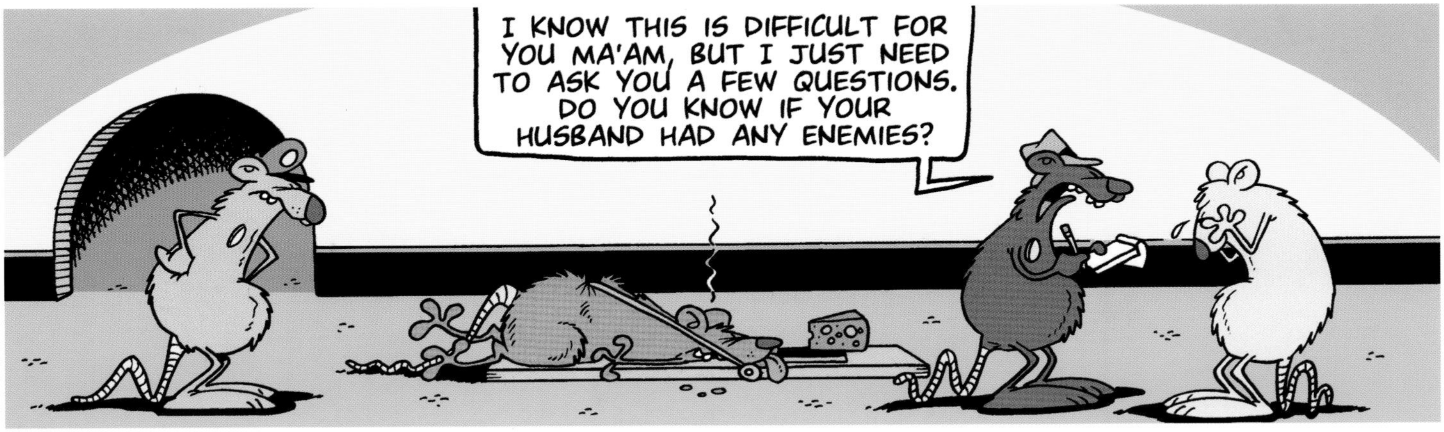
I KNOW THIS IS DIFFICULT FOR YOU MA'AM, BUT I JUST NEED TO ASK YOU A FEW QUESTIONS. DO YOU KNOW IF YOUR HUSBAND HAD ANY ENEMIES?

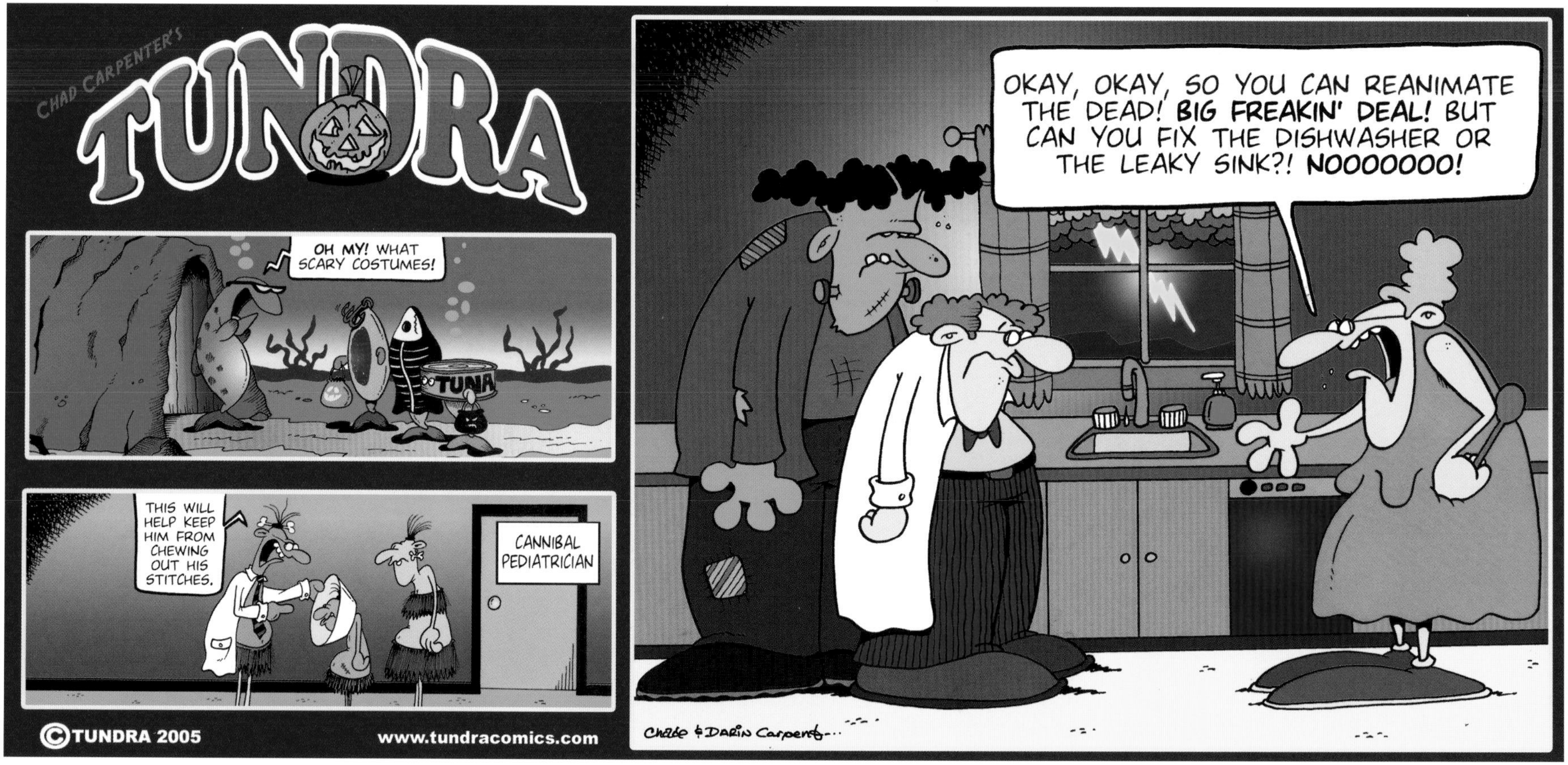
CHAD CARPENTER'S
TUNDRA
OH MY! WHAT SCARY COSTUMES!
TUNA
THIS WILL HELP KEEP HIM FROM CHEWING OUT HIS STITCHES.
CANNIBAL PEDIATRICIAN
©TUNDRA 2005
www.tundracomics.com
OKAY, OKAY, SO YOU CAN REANIMATE THE DEAD! BIG FREAKIN' DEAL! BUT CAN YOU FIX THE DISHWASHER OR THE LEAKY SINK?! NOOOOOOO!
Chad & Darin Carpenter...

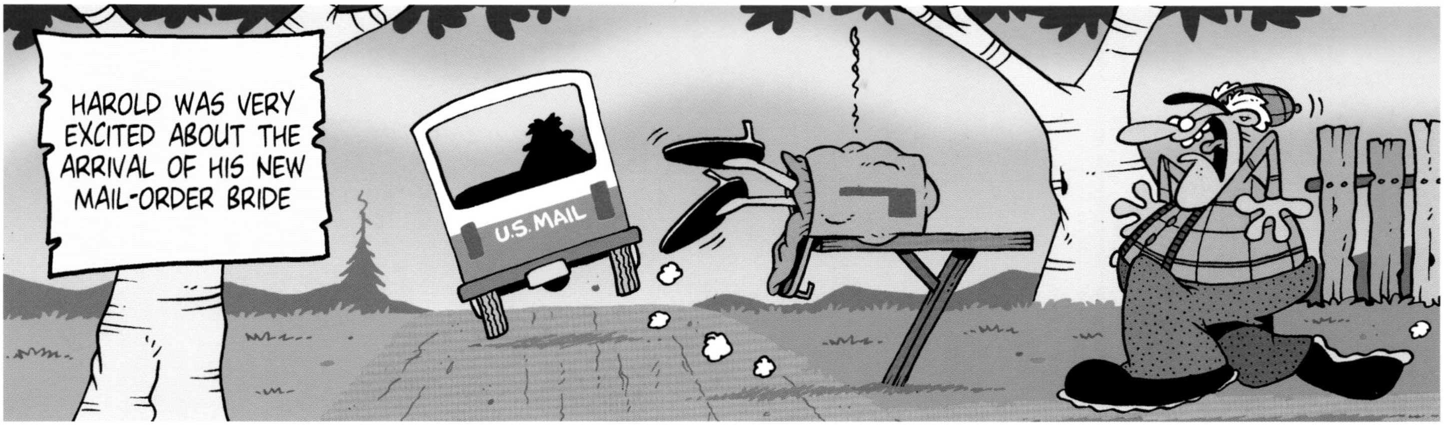
HAROLD WAS VERY EXCITED ABOUT THE ARRIVAL OF HIS NEW MAIL-ORDER BRIDE
U.S. MAIL

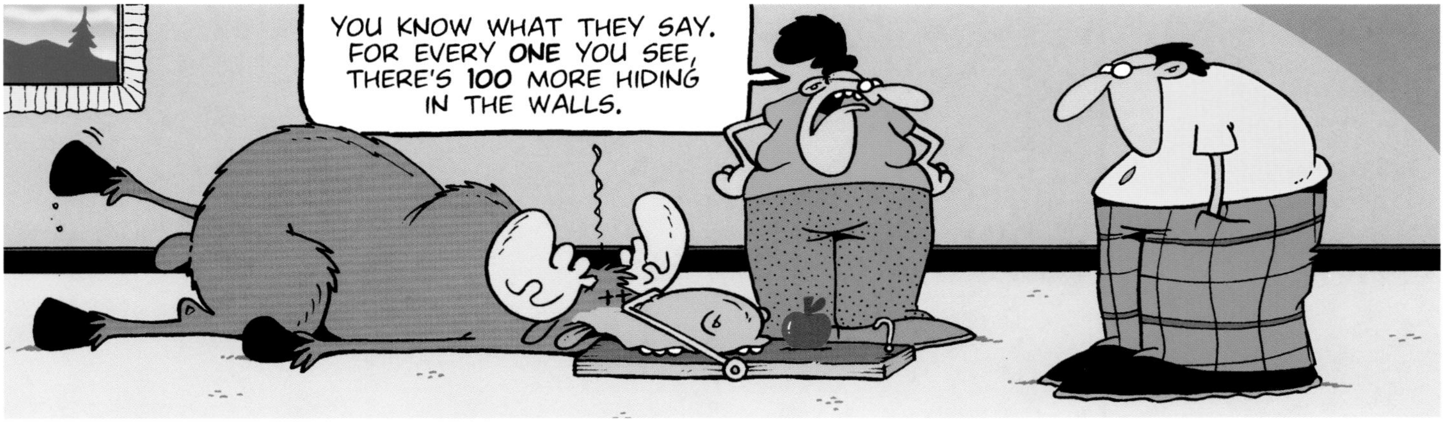
YOU KNOW WHAT THEY SAY. FOR EVERY ONE YOU SEE, THERE'S 100 MORE HIDING IN THE WALLS.

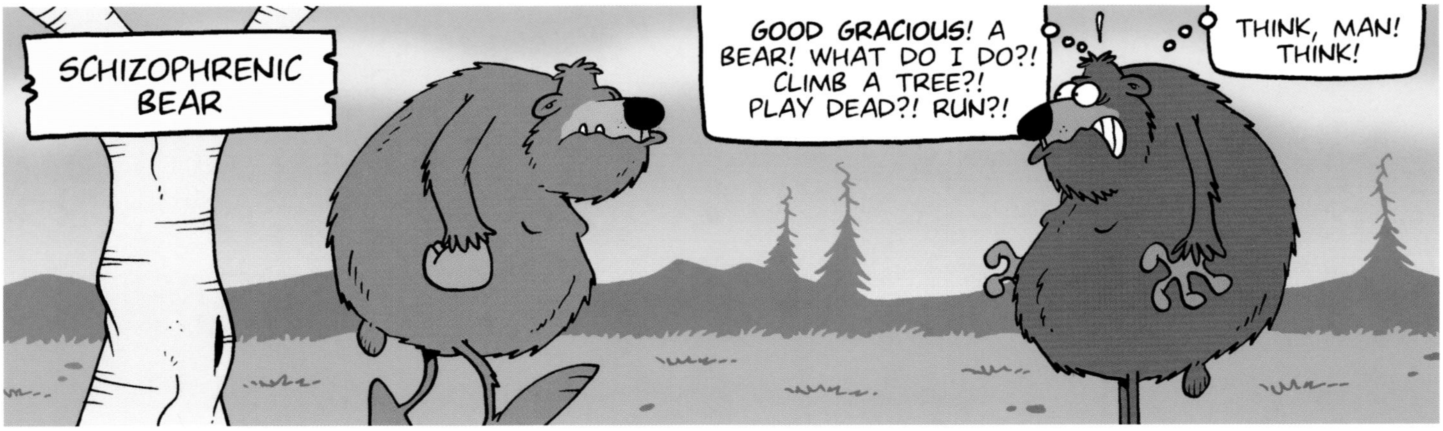
SCHIZOPHRENIC BEAR
GOOD GRACIOUS! A BEAR! WHAT DO I DO?! CLIMB A TREE?! PLAY DEAD?! RUN?!
THINK, MAN! THINK!

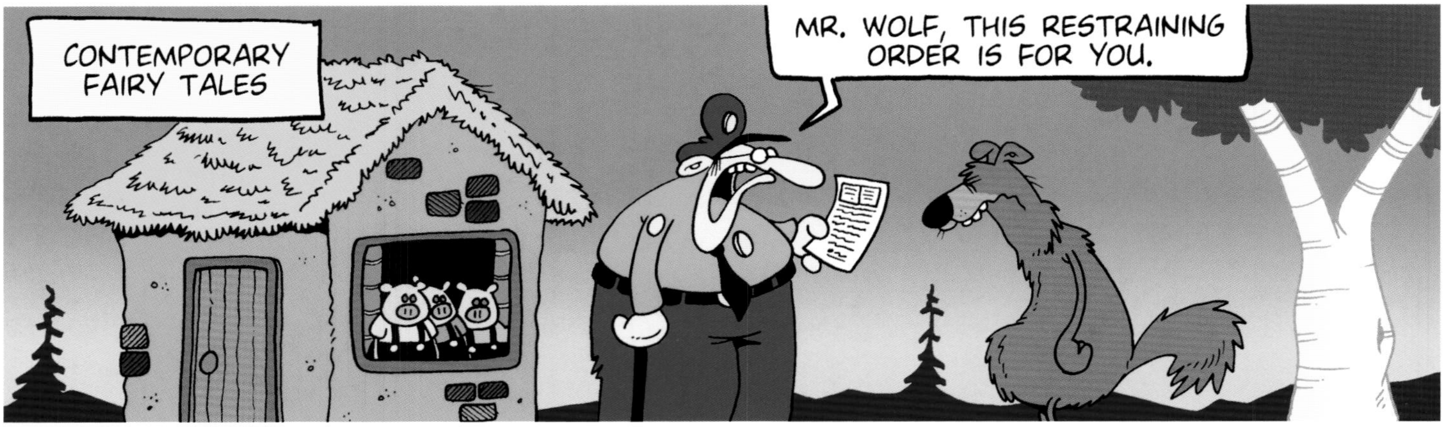
CONTEMPORARY FAIRY TALES
MR. WOLF, THIS RESTRAINING ORDER IS FOR YOU.

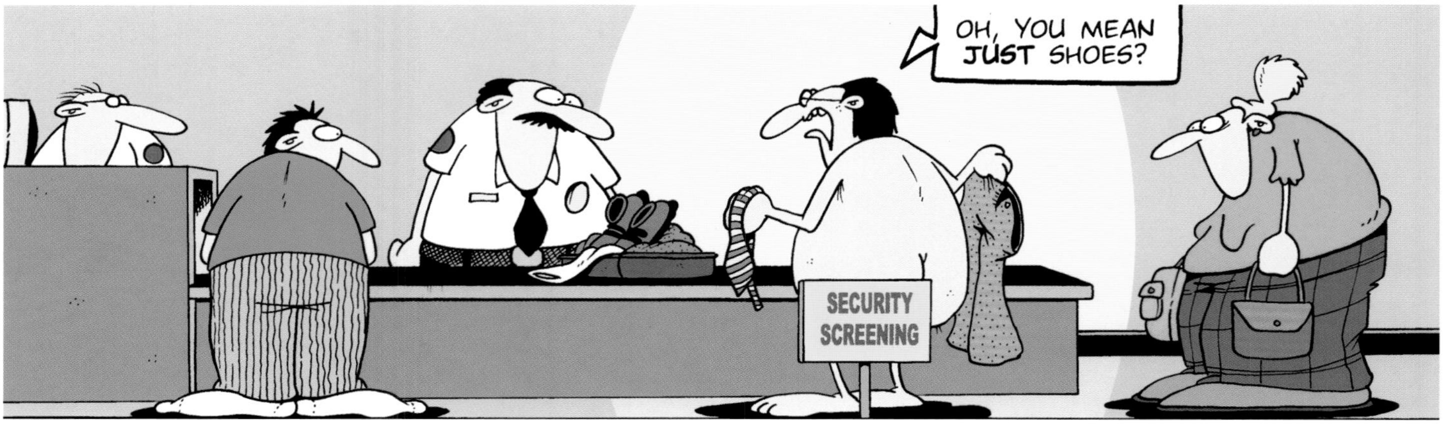
SECURITY SCREENING
OH, YOU MEAN **JUST** SHOES?

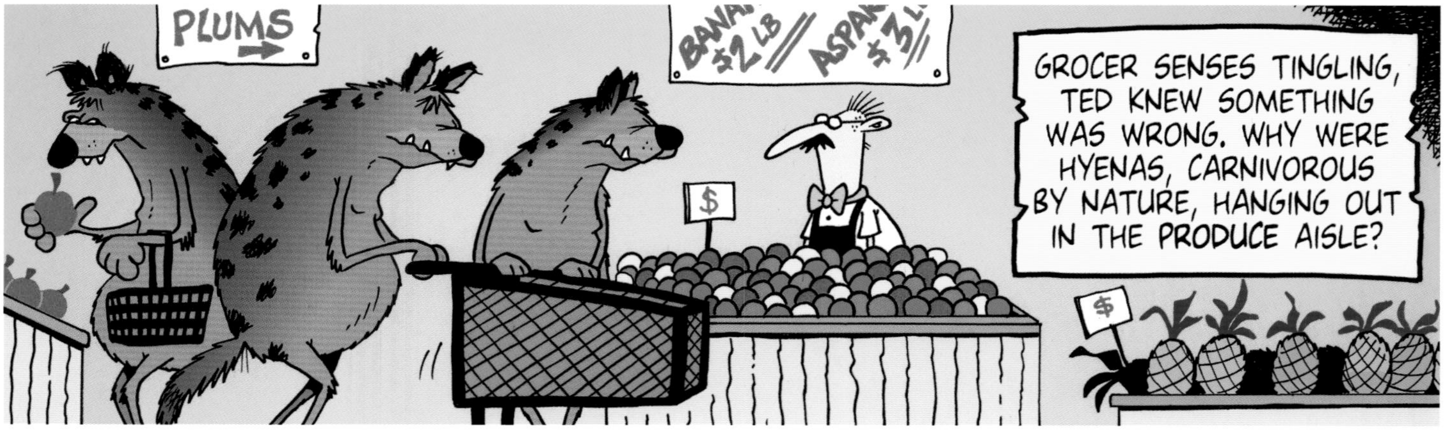
PLUMS
GROCER SENSES TINGLING, TED KNEW SOMETHING WAS WRONG. WHY WERE HYENAS, CARNIVOROUS BY NATURE, HANGING OUT IN THE PRODUCE AISLE?

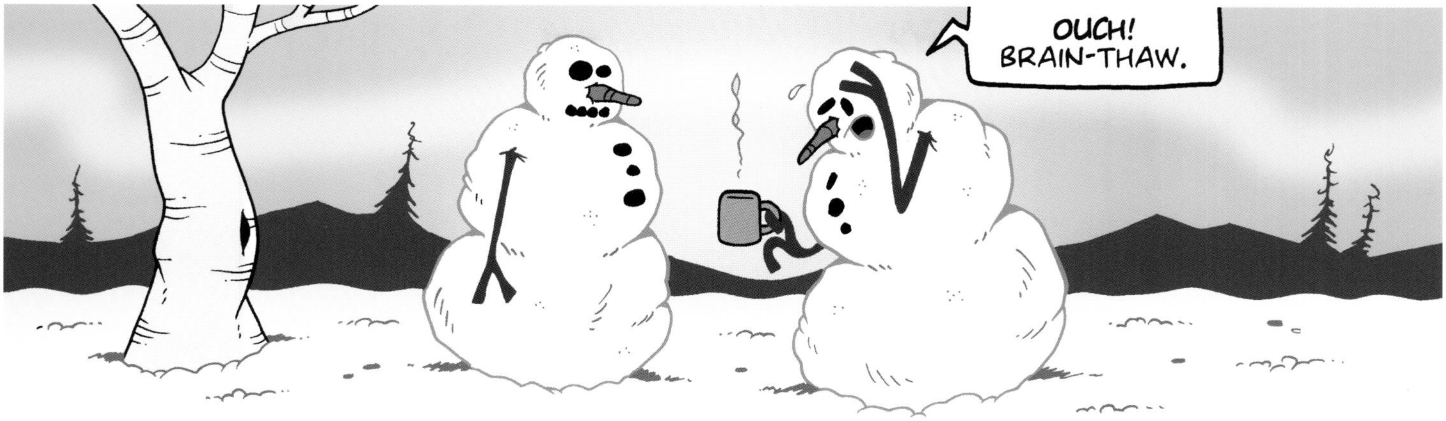
OUCH! BRAIN-THAW.

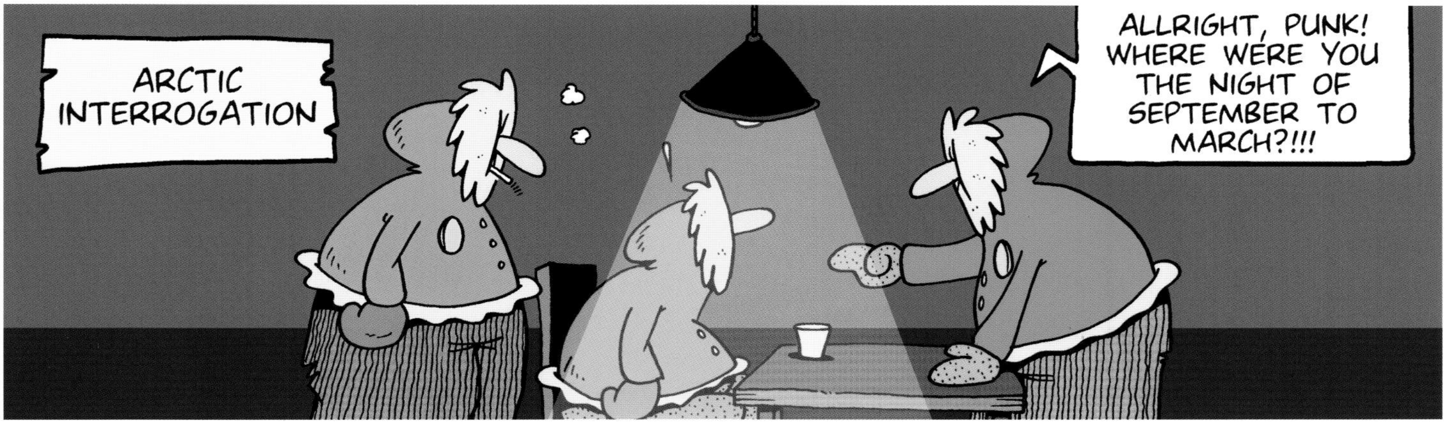
ARCTIC INTERROGATION
ALLRIGHT, PUNK! WHERE WERE YOU THE NIGHT OF SEPTEMBER TO MARCH?!!!

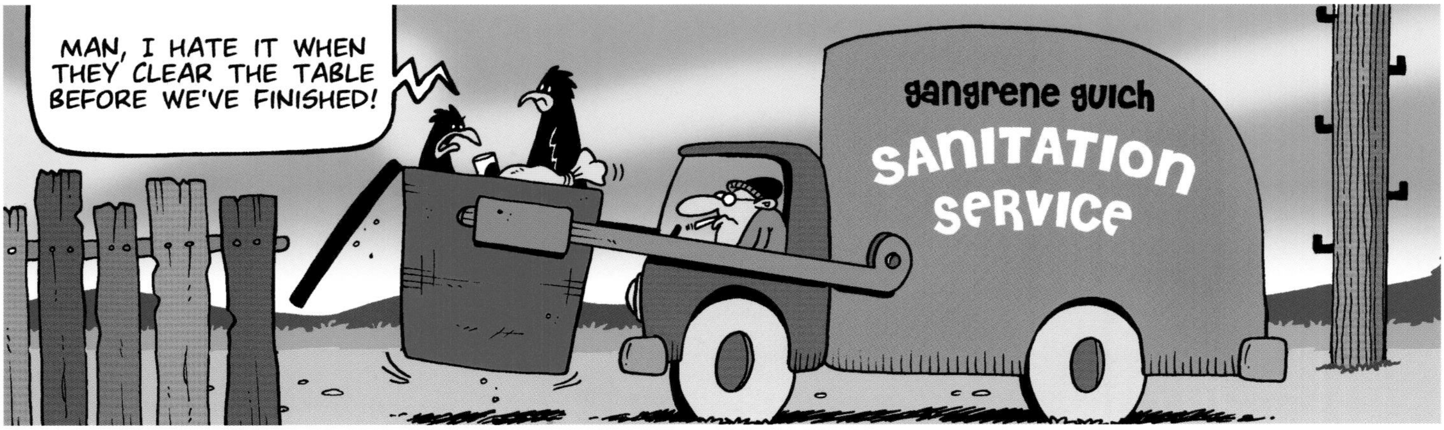
MAN, I HATE IT WHEN THEY CLEAR THE TABLE BEFORE WE'VE FINISHED!
gangrene gulch
SANITATION
SERVICE

WHAT ARE YOU DOING CREEPING AROUND MALLS ALREADY?! DID YOUR OLD LADY FINALLY GET SICK OF LOOKING AT YOUR HAIRY MUG AND TOSS YOU OUT?!

WOW, FOR BEING A JOLLY OLD ELF, HE SURE PACKS A PUNCH.

DO YOU THINK THIS WOULD BE A BAD TIME TO GO BACK IN AND ASK FOR A PONY?

HEY TUBS! THESE KIDS ARE STILL NAUSEOUS FROM ALL THEIR **TRICK-OR-TREAT LOOT** AND YOU'RE ALREADY TRYING TO STUFF YOUR CANDY-CANES IN THEIR GREEDY FACES!

Chad Carpend....

HOW DO YOU SLEEP AT NIGHT KNOWING SOMEWHERE OUT THERE, SOME POOR YAK IS FREEZING BECAUSE YOU HAVE HIS **KEISTER HAIR** STRAPPED TO YOUR FACE?!

OH FOR THE LOVE OF MUD! WOULD YOU LOOK AT THIS! JUST BARELY PAST **HALLOWEEN** AND ALREADY WE HAVE TO PUT UP WITH A **MALL SANTA!**

SANTA

SPEAKING OF HAIR, I'VE SEEN BETTER LOOKING BEARDS ON EAST GERMAN BALLERINAS!

Chad Carpenter's

TUNDRA

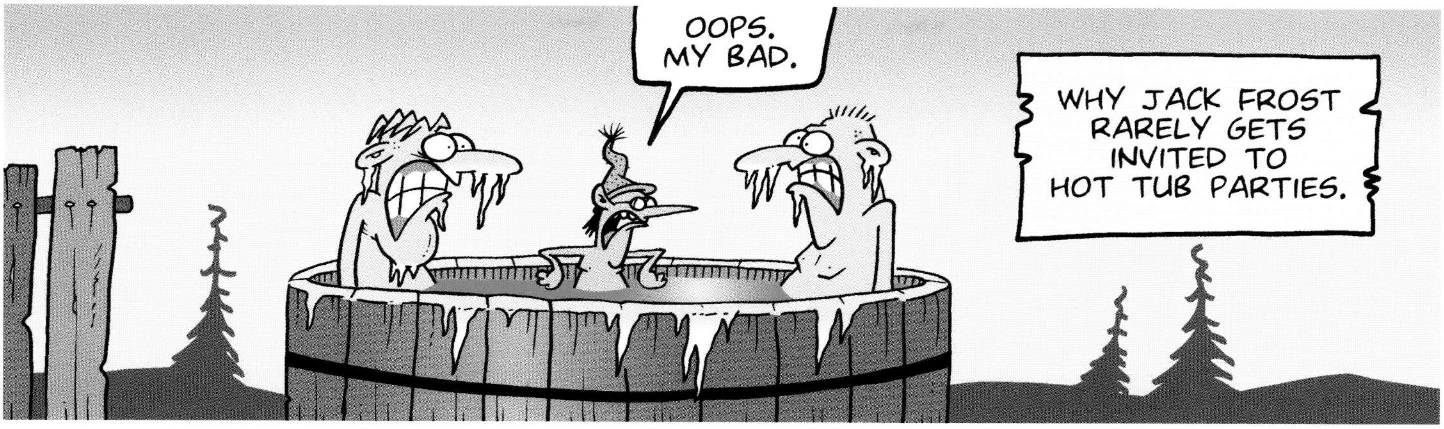
OOPS. MY BAD.
WHY JACK FROST RARELY GETS INVITED TO HOT TUB PARTIES.

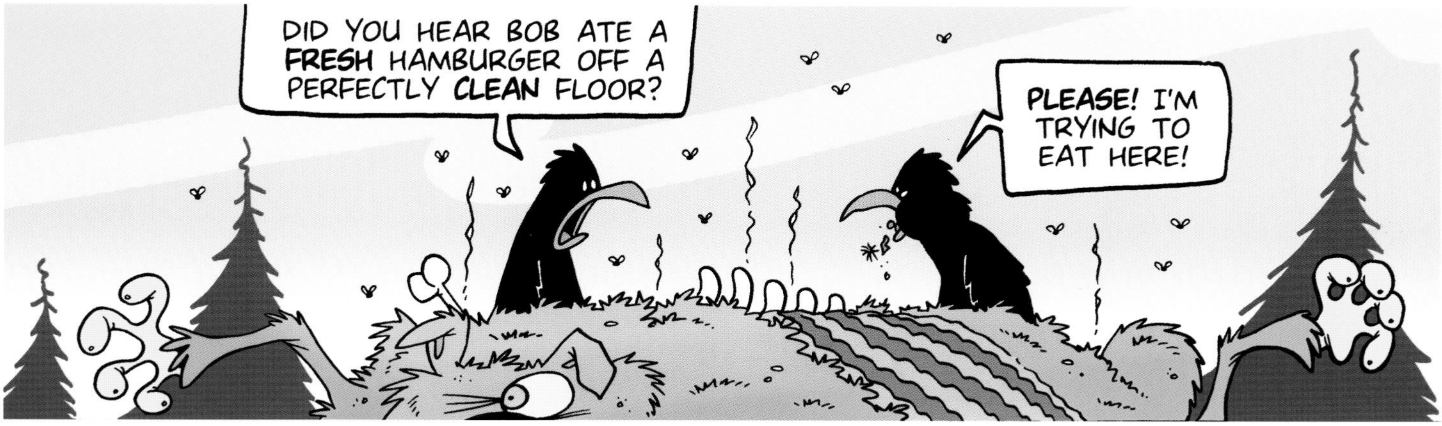
DID YOU HEAR BOB ATE A **FRESH** HAMBURGER OFF A PERFECTLY **CLEAN** FLOOR?
PLEASE! I'M TRYING TO EAT HERE!

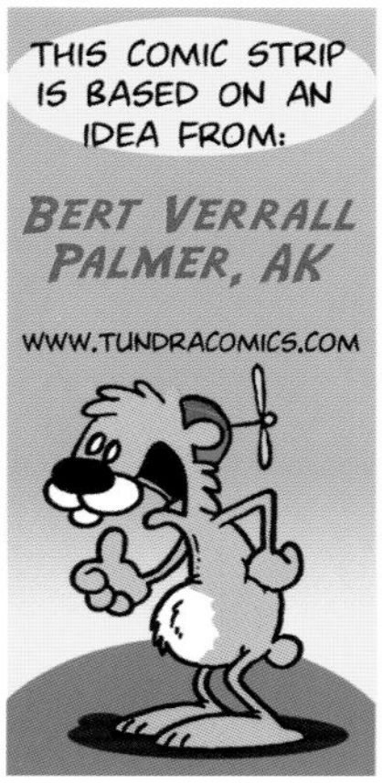
THIS COMIC STRIP IS BASED ON AN IDEA FROM:
BERT VERRALL
PALMER, AK
WWW.TUNDRACOMICS.COM

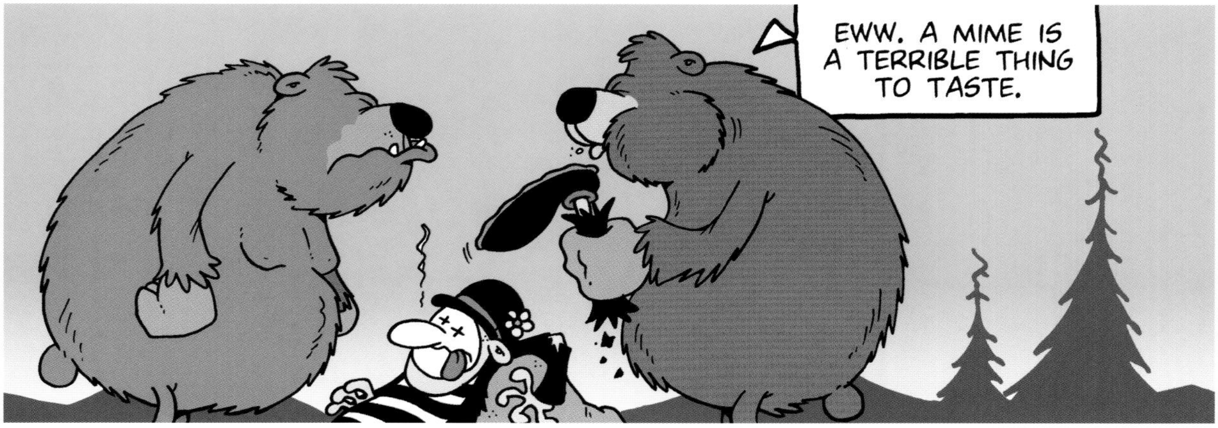
EWW. A MIME IS A TERRIBLE THING TO TASTE.

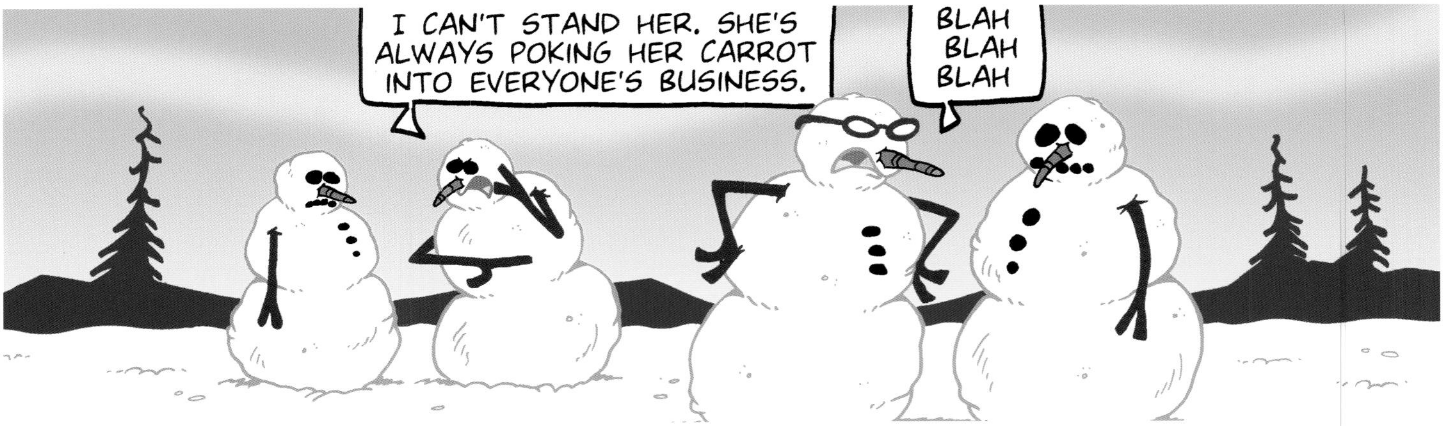
I CAN'T STAND HER. SHE'S ALWAYS POKING HER CARROT INTO EVERYONE'S BUSINESS.
BLAH BLAH BLAH

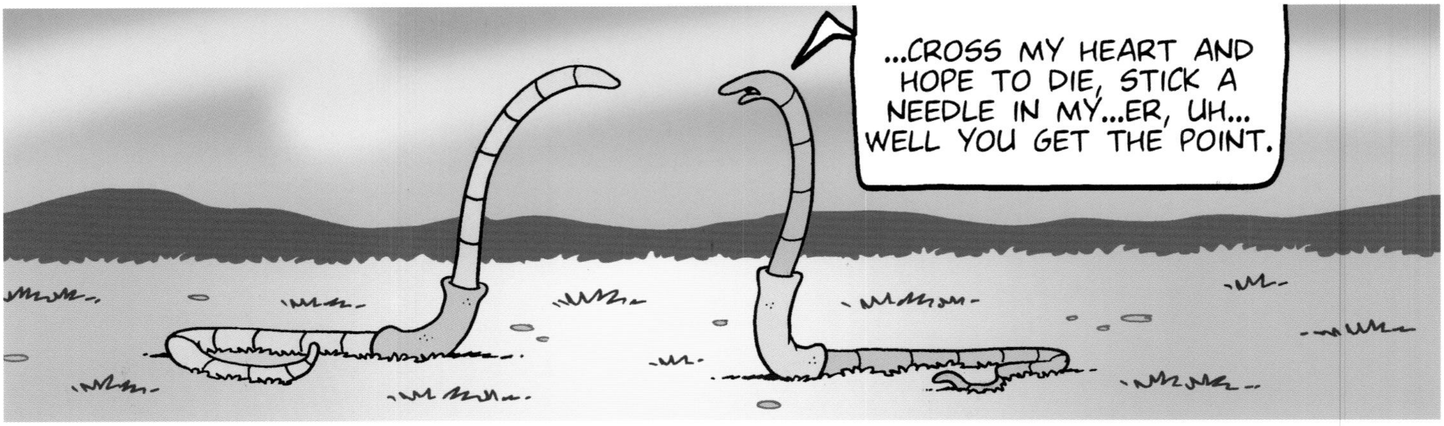
...CROSS MY HEART AND HOPE TO DIE, STICK A NEEDLE IN MY...ER, UH... WELL YOU GET THE POINT.

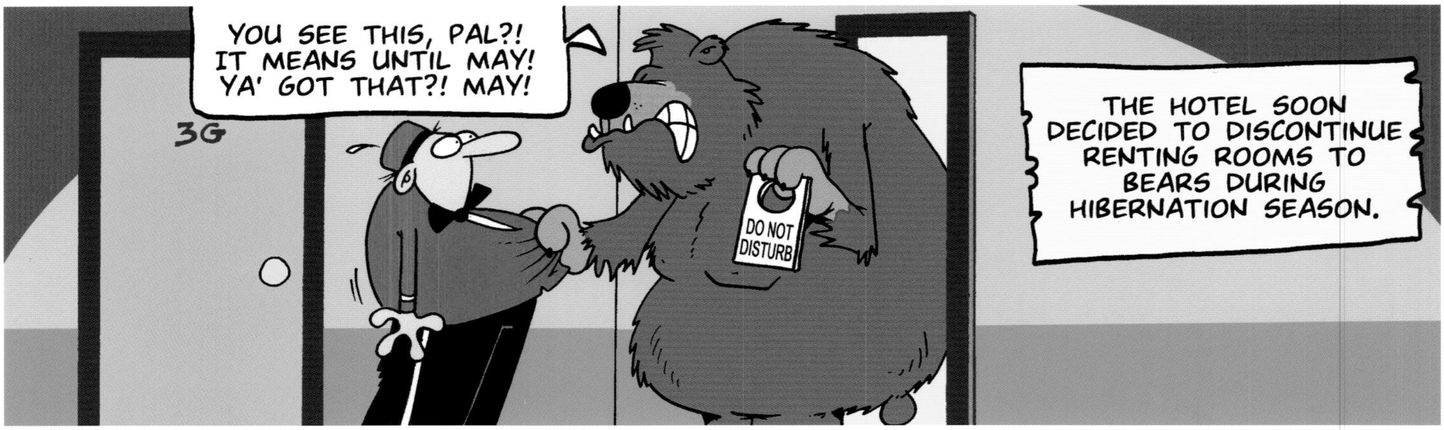
YOU SEE THIS, PAL?! IT MEANS UNTIL MAY! YA' GOT THAT?! MAY!
3G
DO NOT DISTURB
THE HOTEL SOON DECIDED TO DISCONTINUE RENTING ROOMS TO BEARS DURING HIBERNATION SEASON.

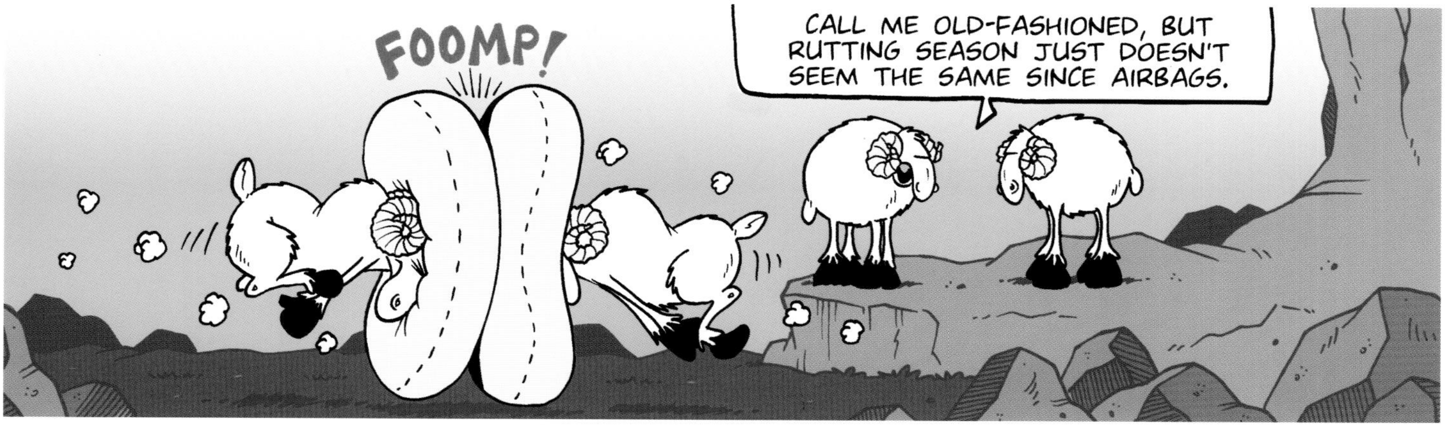
FOOMP!
CALL ME OLD-FASHIONED, BUT RUTTING SEASON JUST DOESN'T SEEM THE SAME SINCE AIRBAGS.

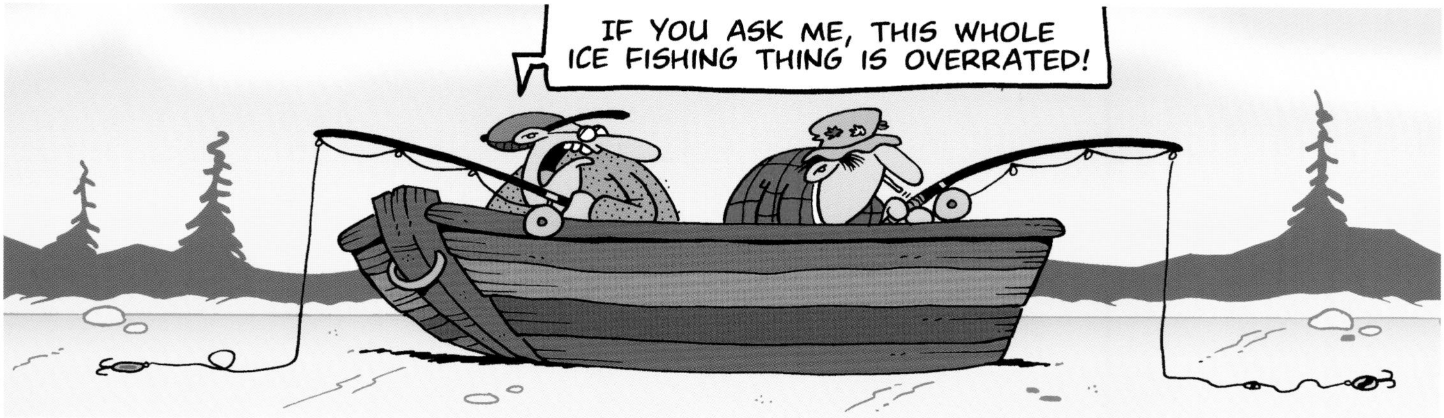
IF YOU ASK ME, THIS WHOLE ICE FISHING THING IS OVERRATED!

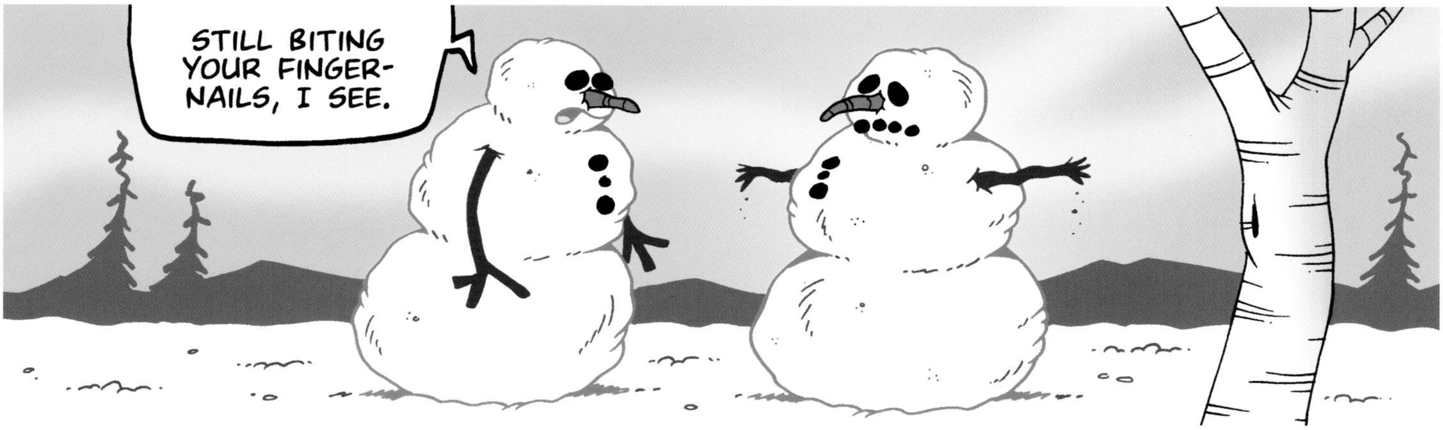
STILL BITING YOUR FINGER-NAILS, I SEE.

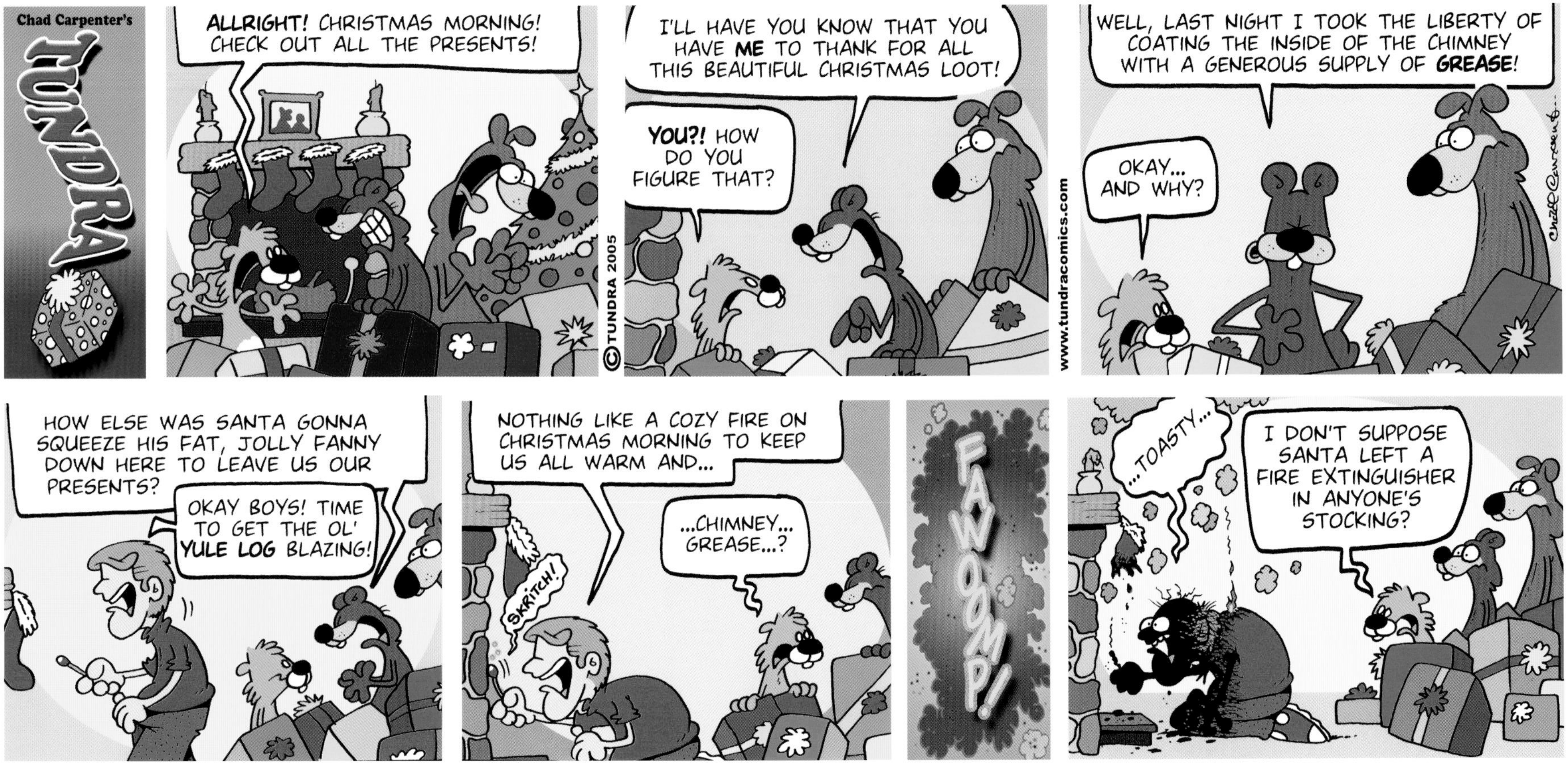
Chad Carpenter's
TUNDRA
ALLRIGHT! CHRISTMAS MORNING! CHECK OUT ALL THE PRESENTS!
©TUNDRA 2005
I'LL HAVE YOU KNOW THAT YOU HAVE ME TO THANK FOR ALL THIS BEAUTIFUL CHRISTMAS LOOT!
YOU?! HOW DO YOU FIGURE THAT?
www.tundracomics.com
WELL, LAST NIGHT I TOOK THE LIBERTY OF COATING THE INSIDE OF THE CHIMNEY WITH A GENEROUS SUPPLY OF GREASE!
OKAY... AND WHY?
HOW ELSE WAS SANTA GONNA SQUEEZE HIS FAT, JOLLY FANNY DOWN HERE TO LEAVE US OUR PRESENTS?
OKAY BOYS! TIME TO GET THE OL' YULE LOG BLAZING!
NOTHING LIKE A COZY FIRE ON CHRISTMAS MORNING TO KEEP US ALL WARM AND...
SKRITCH!
...CHIMNEY... GREASE...?
FAWOOMP!
...TOASTY...
I DON'T SUPPOSE SANTA LEFT A FIRE EXTINGUISHER IN ANYONE'S STOCKING?

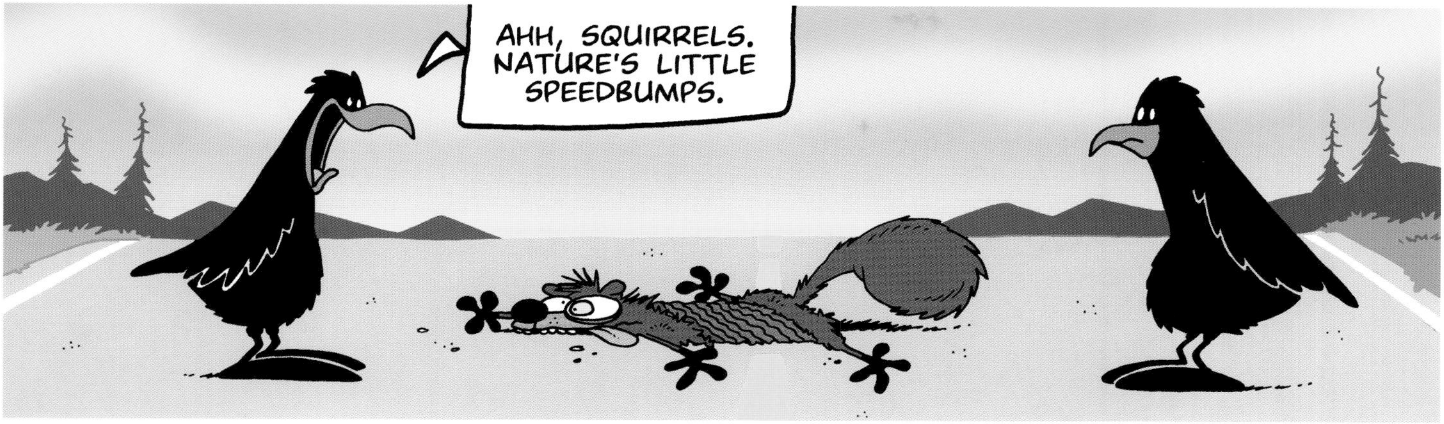
AHH, SQUIRRELS. NATURE'S LITTLE SPEEDBUMPS.

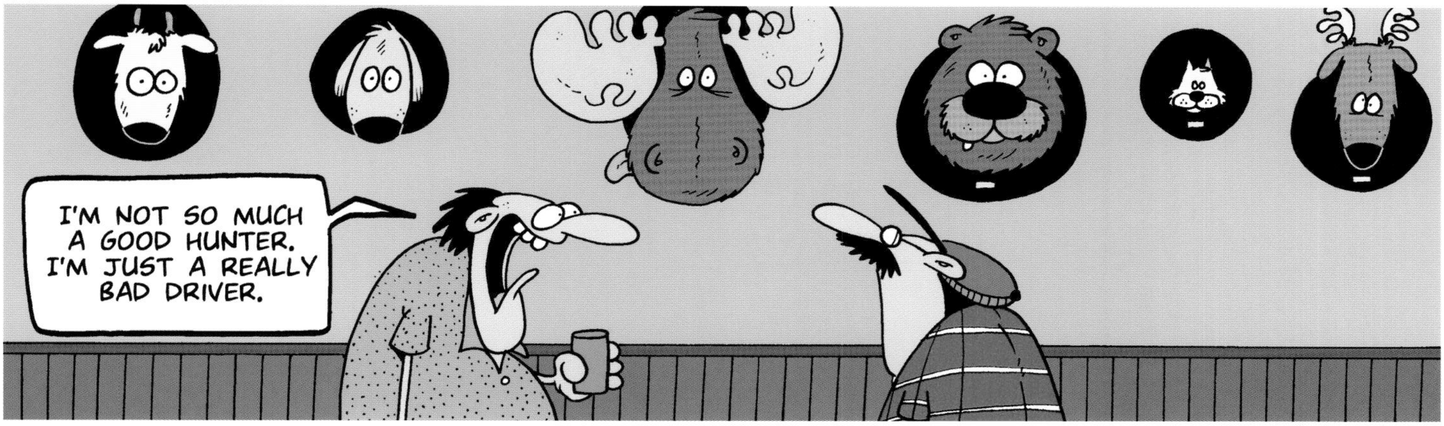
I'M NOT SO MUCH A GOOD HUNTER. I'M JUST A REALLY BAD DRIVER.

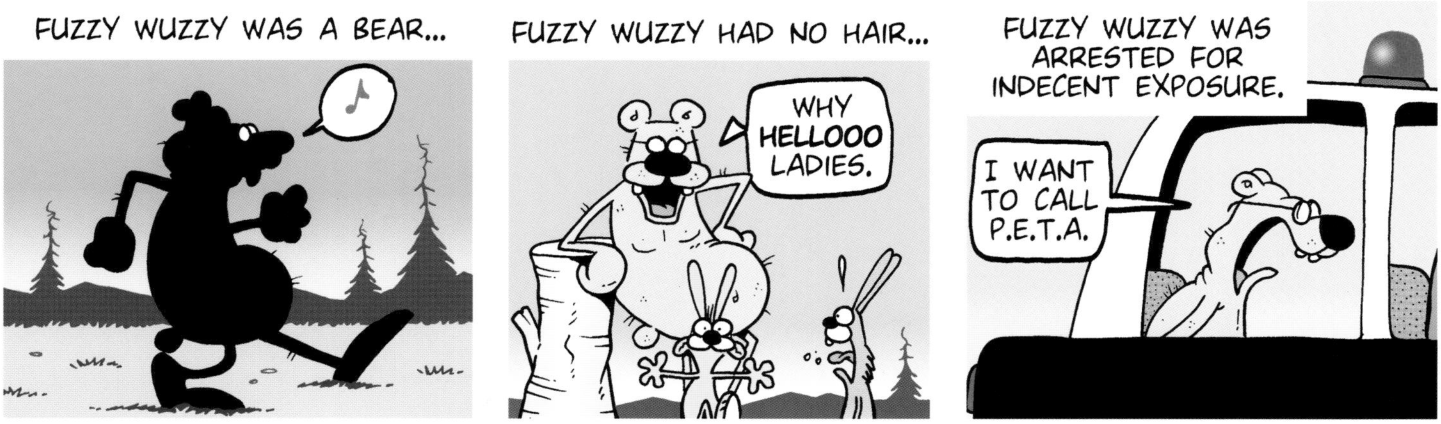
FUZZY WUZZY WAS A BEAR...
FUZZY WUZZY HAD NO HAIR...
WHY **HELLOOO** LADIES.
FUZZY WUZZY WAS ARRESTED FOR INDECENT EXPOSURE.
I WANT TO CALL P.E.T.A.

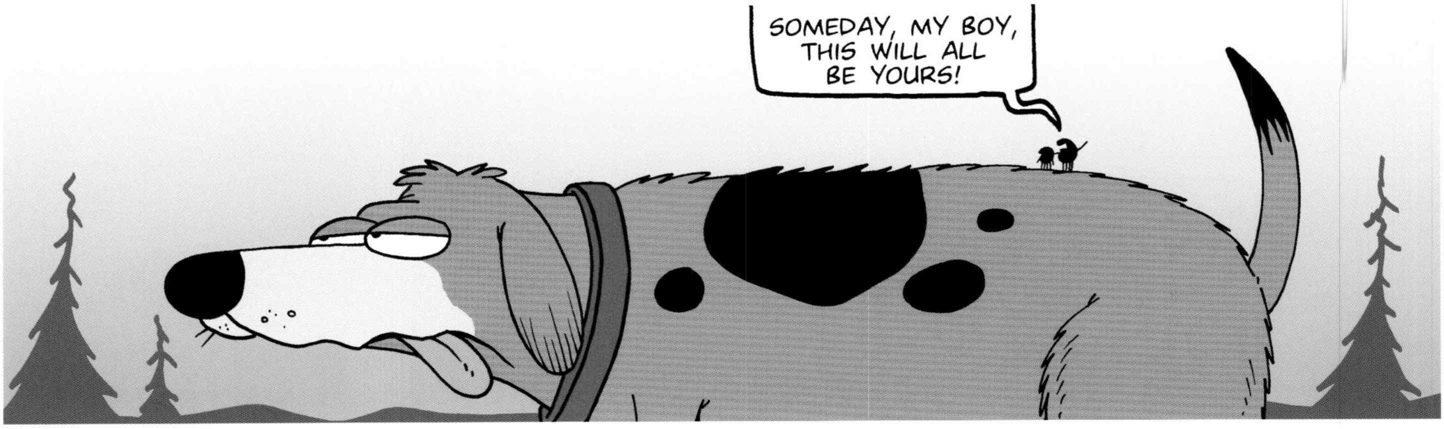
SOMEDAY, MY BOY, THIS WILL ALL BE YOURS!

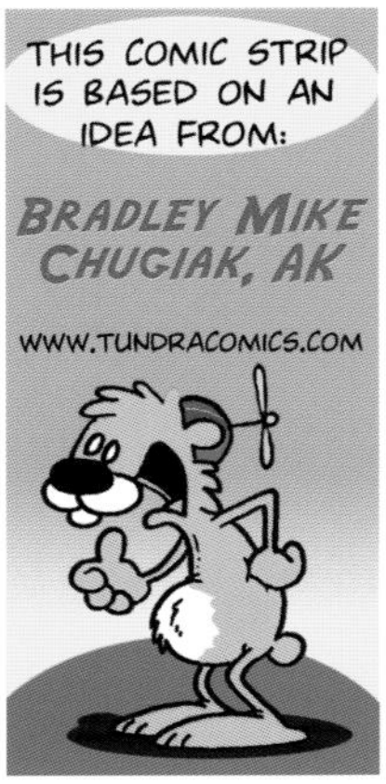
THIS COMIC STRIP IS BASED ON AN IDEA FROM:
BRADLEY MIKE
CHUGIAK, AK
WWW.TUNDRACOMICS.COM

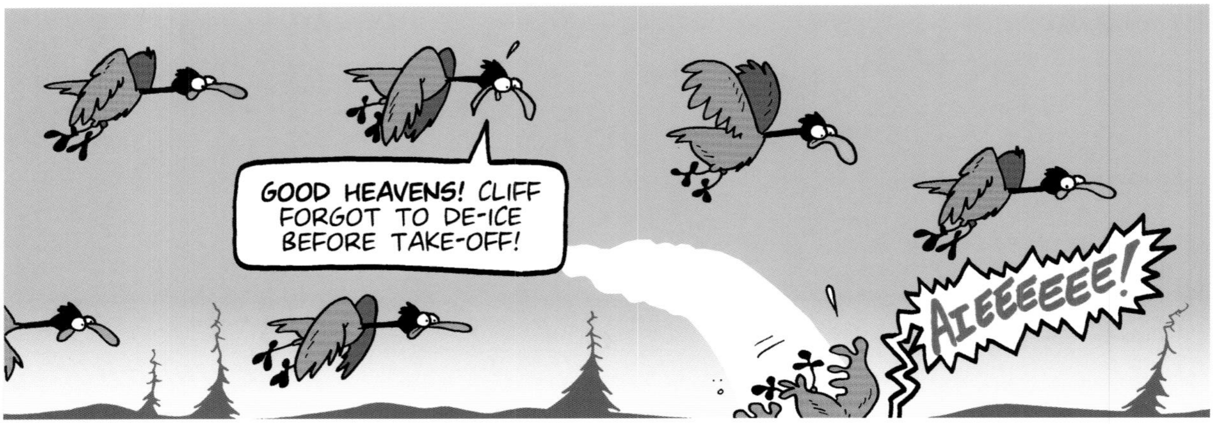
GOOD HEAVENS! CLIFF FORGOT TO DE-ICE BEFORE TAKE-OFF!
AIEEEEEE!

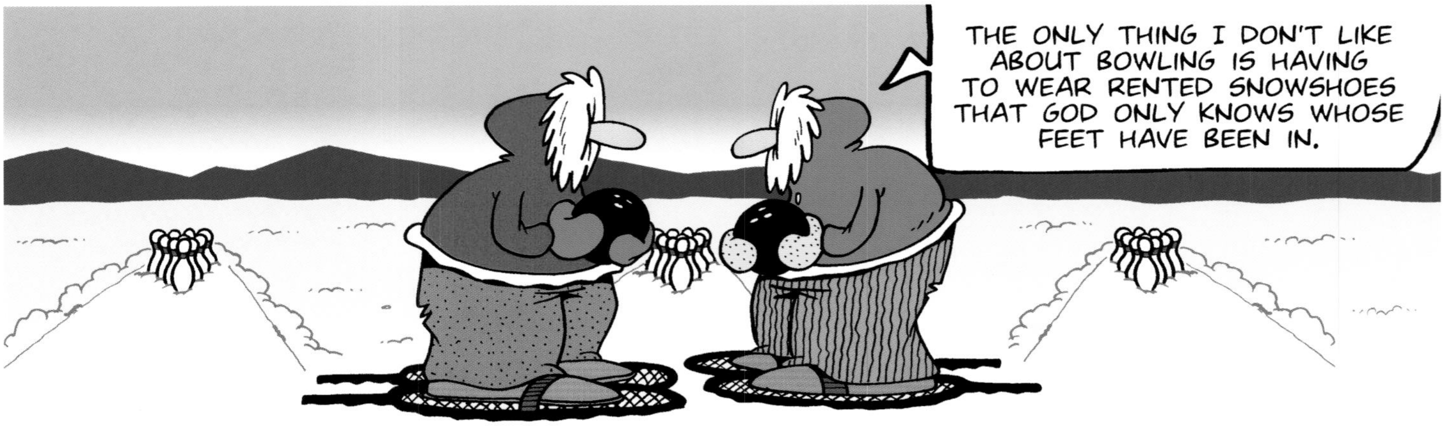
THE ONLY THING I DON'T LIKE ABOUT BOWLING IS HAVING TO WEAR RENTED SNOWSHOES THAT GOD ONLY KNOWS WHOSE FEET HAVE BEEN IN.

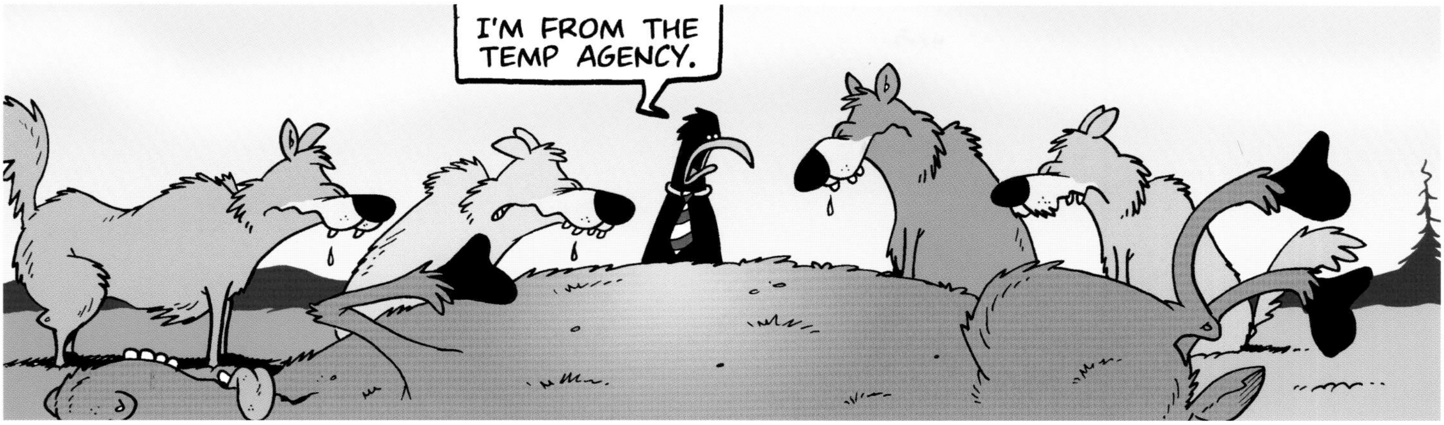
I'M FROM THE TEMP AGENCY.

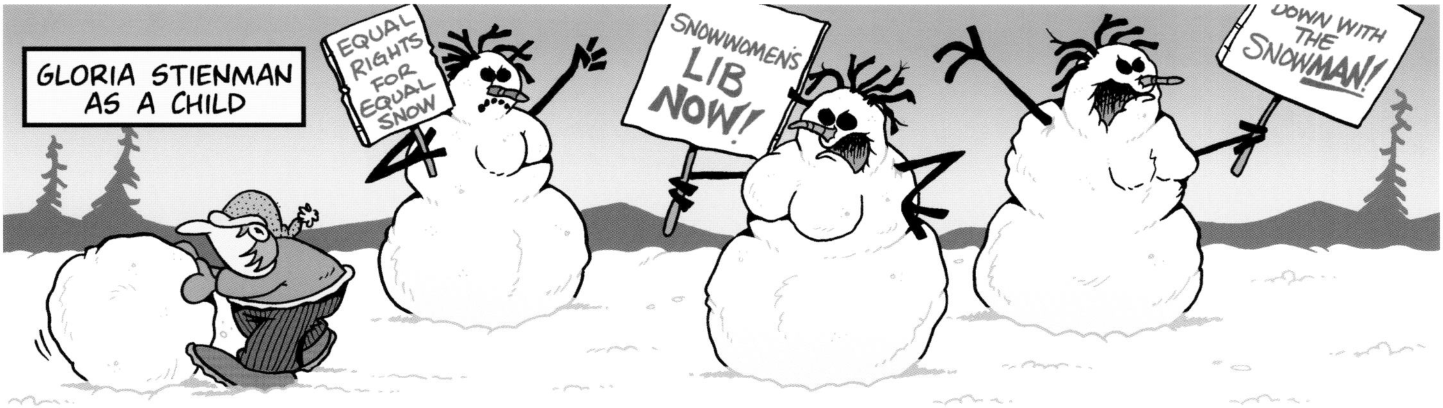
GLORIA STIENMAN AS A CHILD
EQUAL RIGHTS FOR EQUAL SNOW
SNOWWOMEN'S LIB NOW!
DOWN WITH THE SNOWMAN!

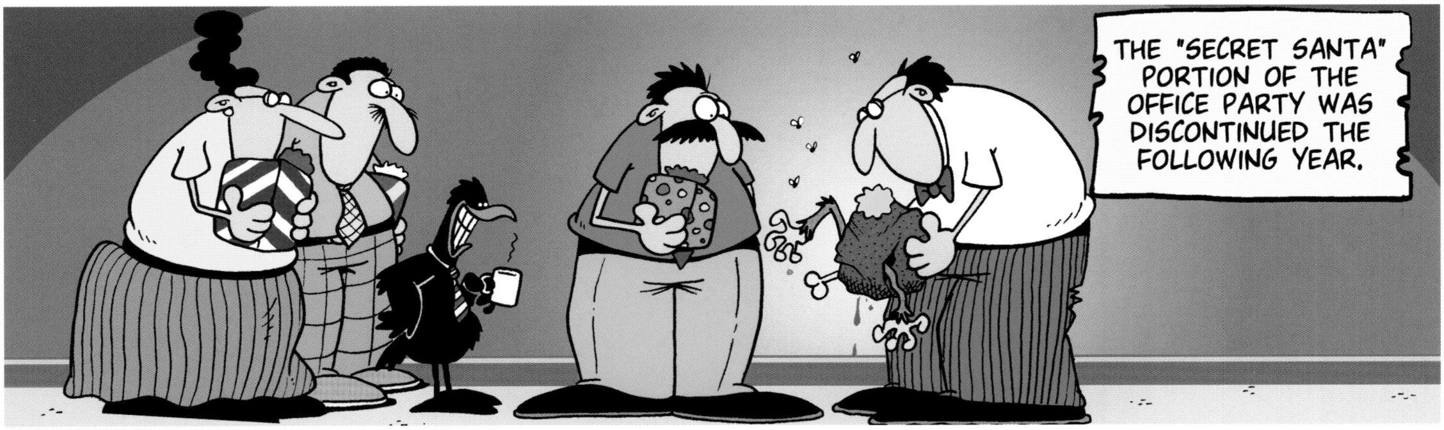
THE "SECRET SANTA" PORTION OF THE OFFICE PARTY WAS DISCONTINUED THE FOLLOWING YEAR.

CHAD CARPENTER'S
TUNDRA
NEW YEAR
WOW. THAT'S QUITE A NOVEL YOU'RE WRITING THERE, SHERMY OL' PAL!
IT'S A LIST OF NEW YEAR RESOLUTIONS. CARE TO HEAR THEM?
YOU BET!
AS OF THIS DAY, I VOW TO START BEING KINDER TO OTHERS, BEING MORE GENEROUS WITH MY MONEY AND OFFERING TO GIVE OUT **FREE** FOOT MASSAGES. I ALSO VOW TO IMPROVE MY AIM IN THE BATHROOM.
YES. VERY BOLD.
©TUNDRA 2006
I WILL ALSO IMPROVE MY PERSONAL HYGIENE, STOP CHEWING WITH MY MOUTH OPEN AND REFRAIN FROM GIGGLING AT MY OWN RUDE BODY NOISES.
GOOD POINT.
THAT'S JUST THE BASICS OF COURSE. I'VE STILL GOT A **LOT** OF WRITING TO DO.
I AM TRULY IMPRESSED!
www.tundracomics.com
YESSIREE! MAKING A LIST LIKE THAT IS A SIGN OF PERSONAL GROWTH AND MATURITY! I'M PROUD OF YOU, SHERM! I HOPE YOU'RE ABLE TO STICK TO IT!
ME? I'M MAKING THIS LIST FOR **YOU.**

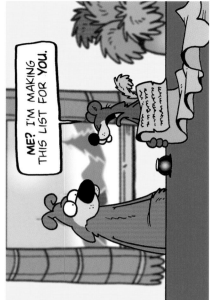

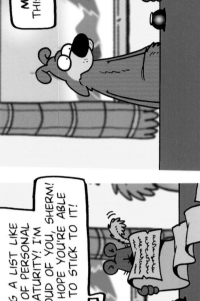

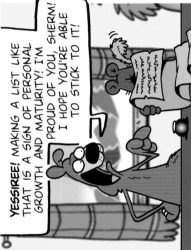

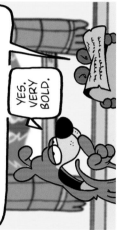

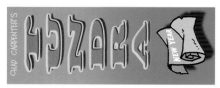

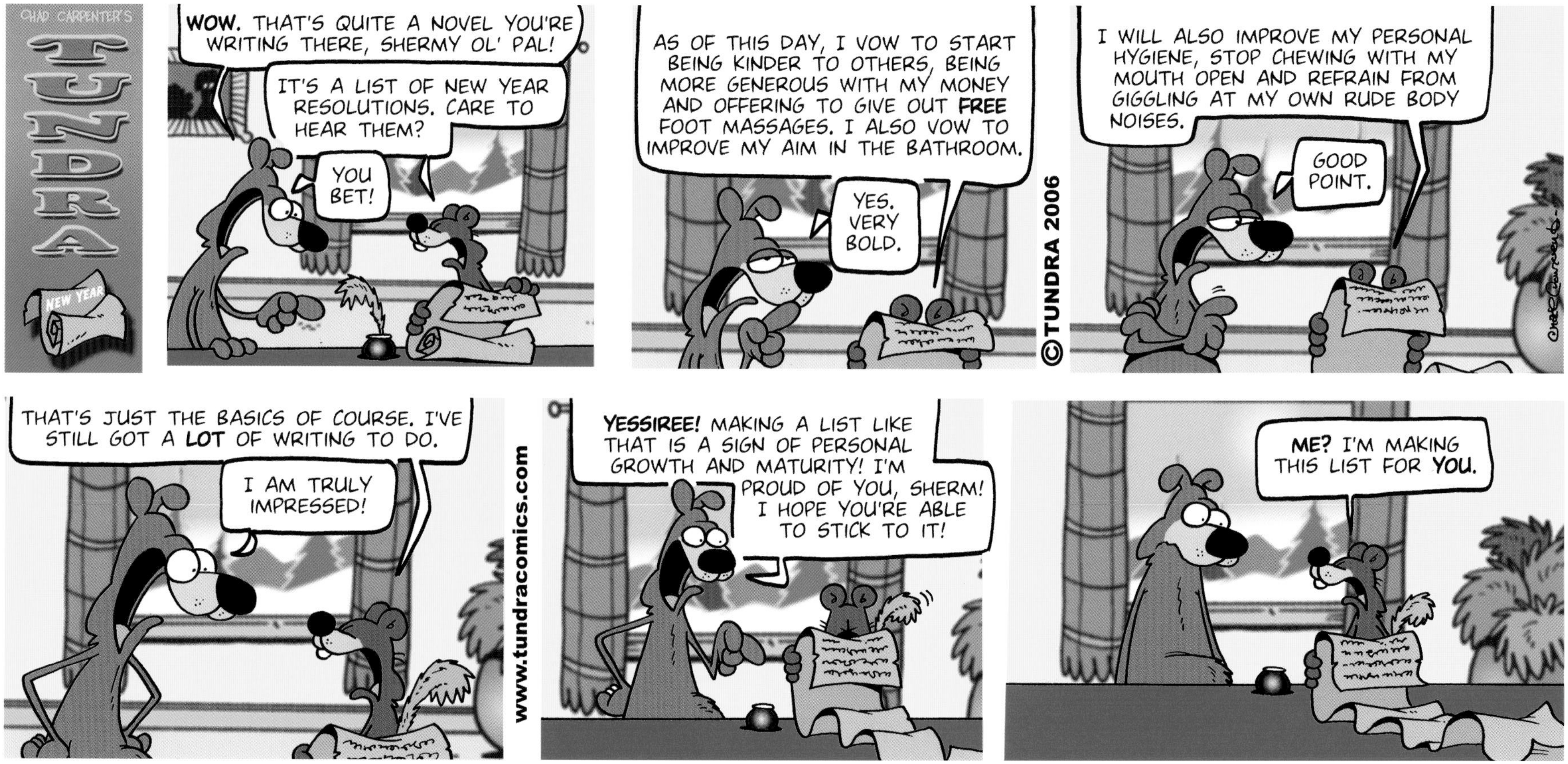

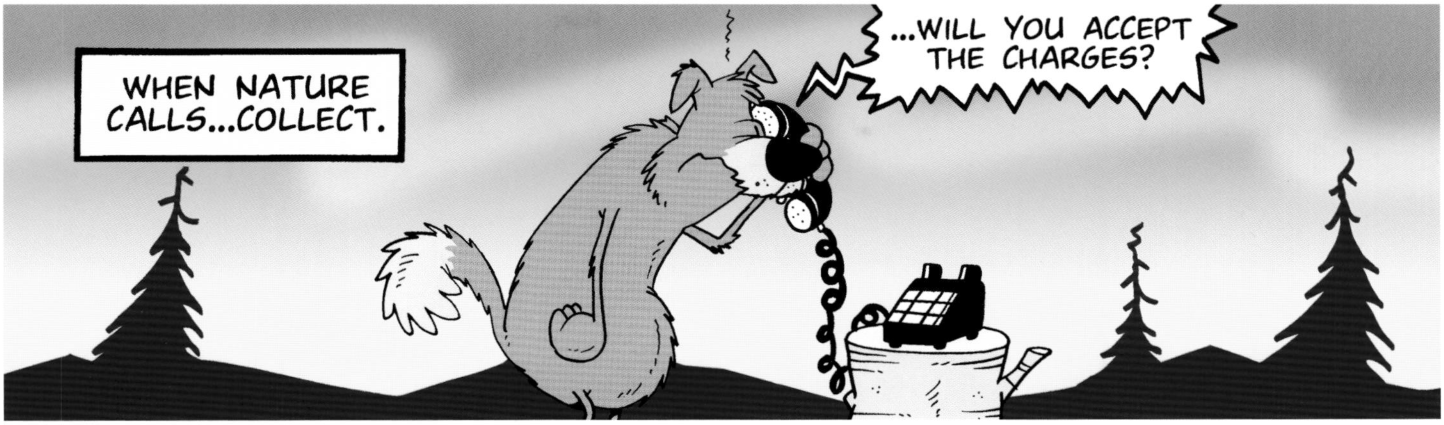
WHEN NATURE CALLS...COLLECT.
...WILL YOU ACCEPT THE CHARGES?

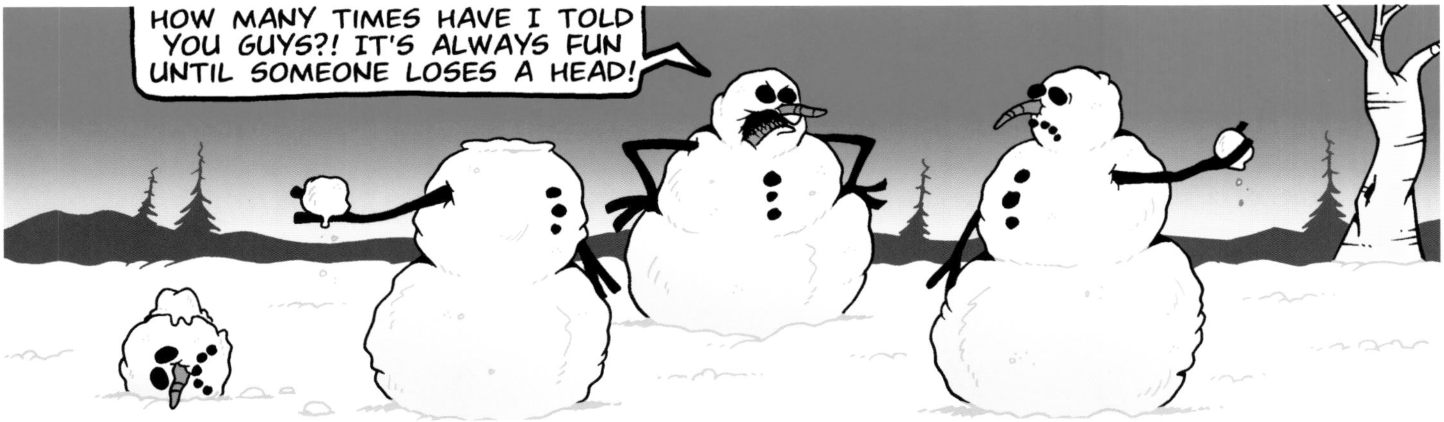
HOW MANY TIMES HAVE I TOLD YOU GUYS?! IT'S ALWAYS FUN UNTIL SOMEONE LOSES A HEAD!

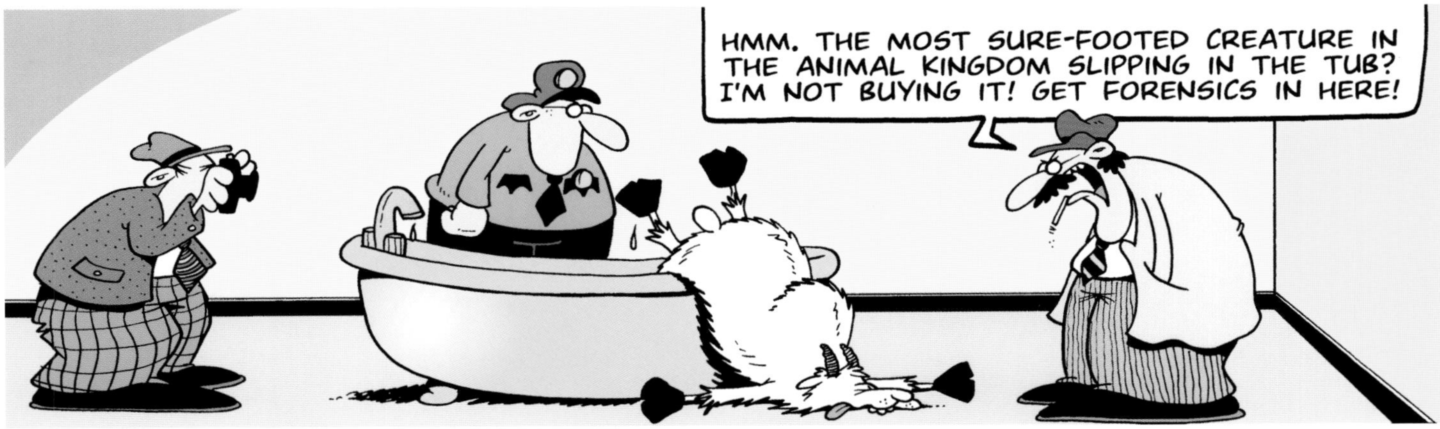
HMM. THE MOST SURE-FOOTED CREATURE IN THE ANIMAL KINGDOM SLIPPING IN THE TUB? I'M NOT BUYING IT! GET FORENSICS IN HERE!

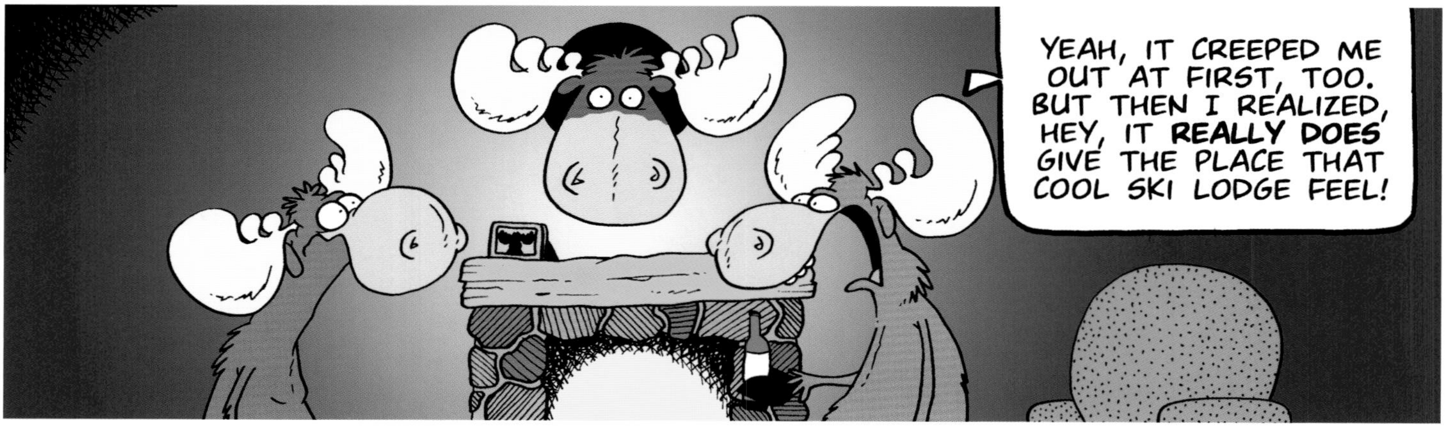
YEAH, IT CREEPED ME OUT AT FIRST, TOO. BUT THEN I REALIZED, HEY, IT **REALLY DOES** GIVE THE PLACE THAT COOL SKI LODGE FEEL!

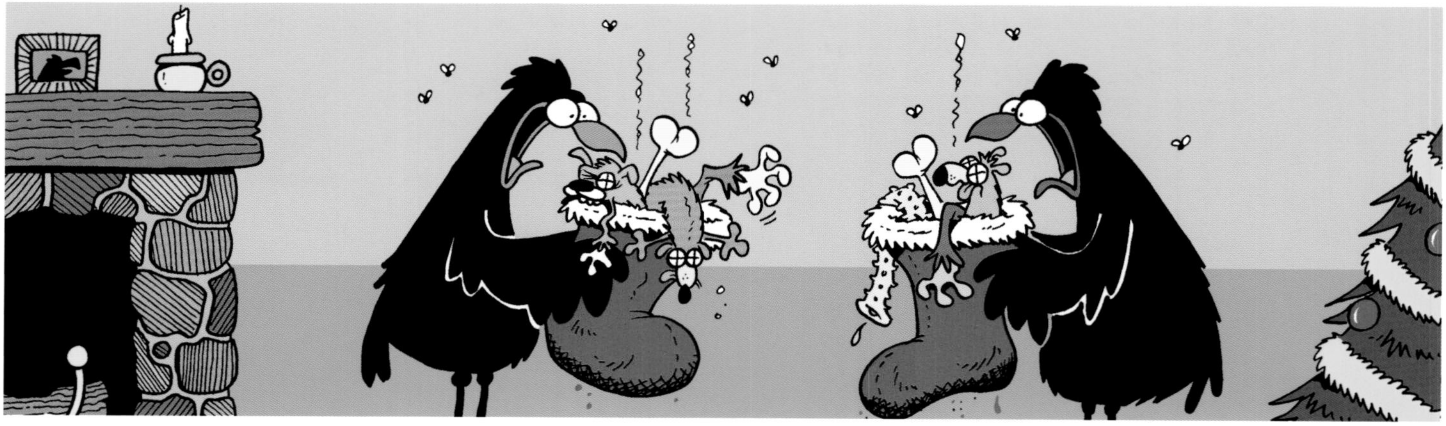

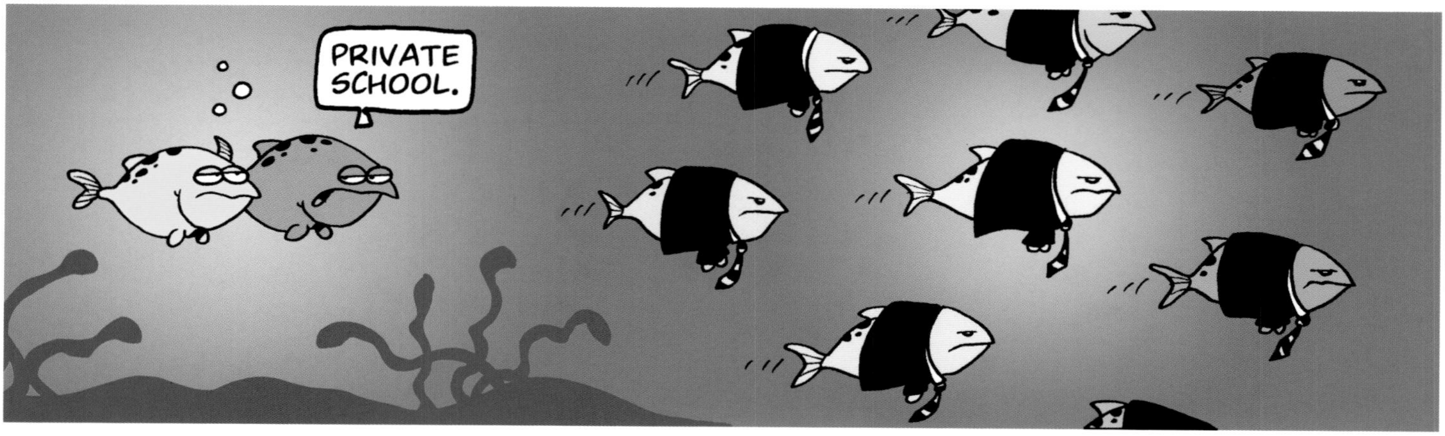
PRIVATE SCHOOL.

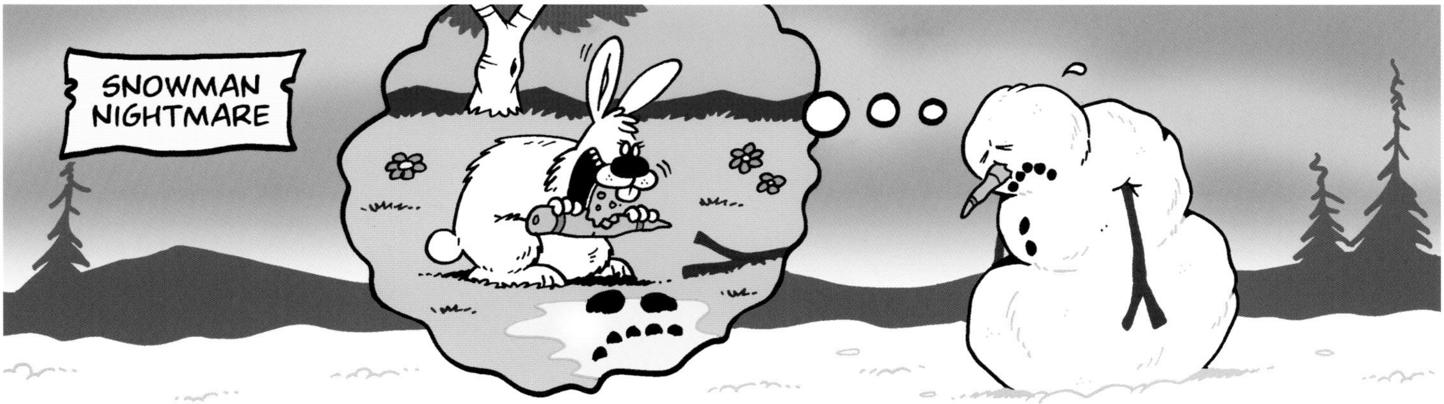
SNOWMAN NIGHTMARE

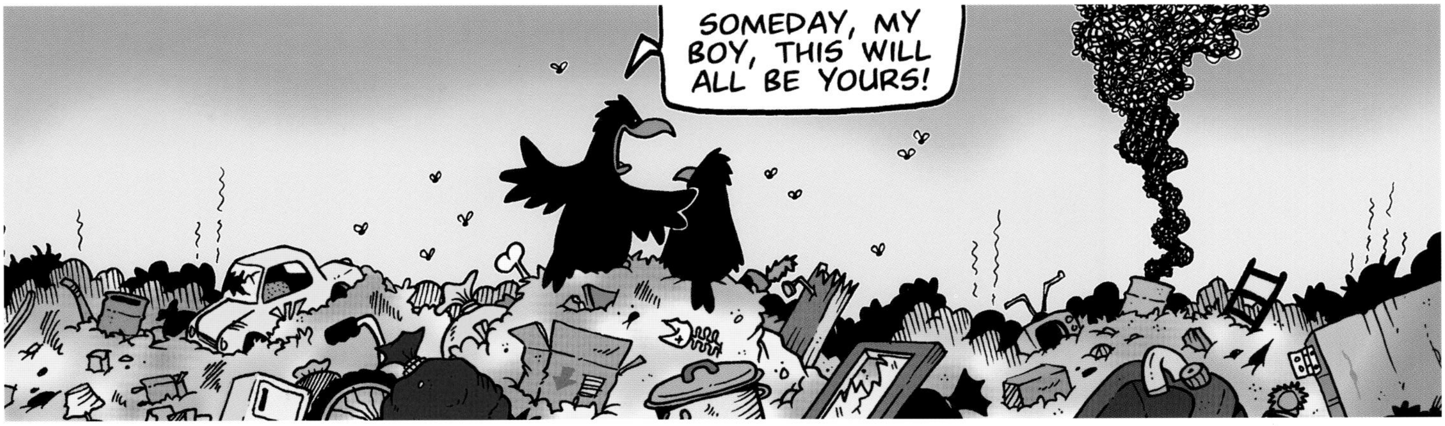
SOMEDAY, MY BOY, THIS WILL ALL BE YOURS!

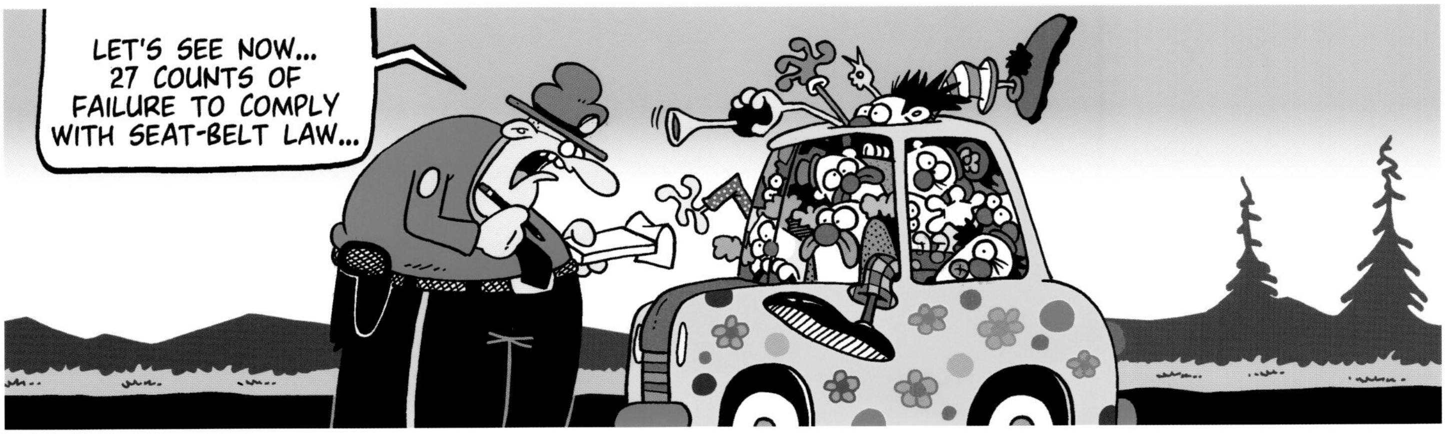
LET'S SEE NOW... 27 COUNTS OF FAILURE TO COMPLY WITH SEAT-BELT LAW...

CHAD CARPENTER'S
TUNDRA
www.tundracomics.com
SNIFF
SNIFF
SNIFF
SNIFF
© TUNDRA 2006

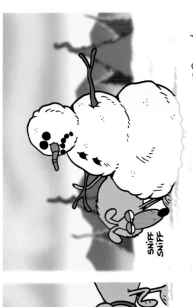

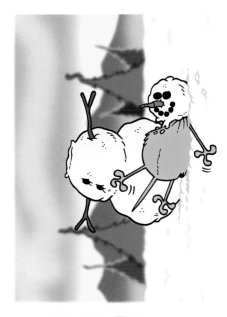

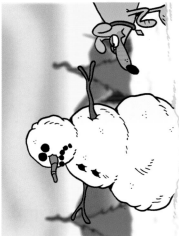

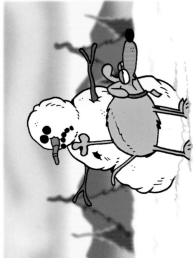

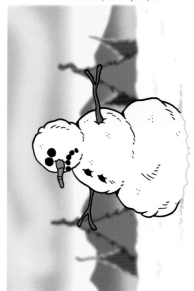

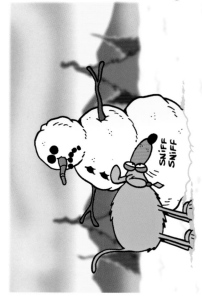

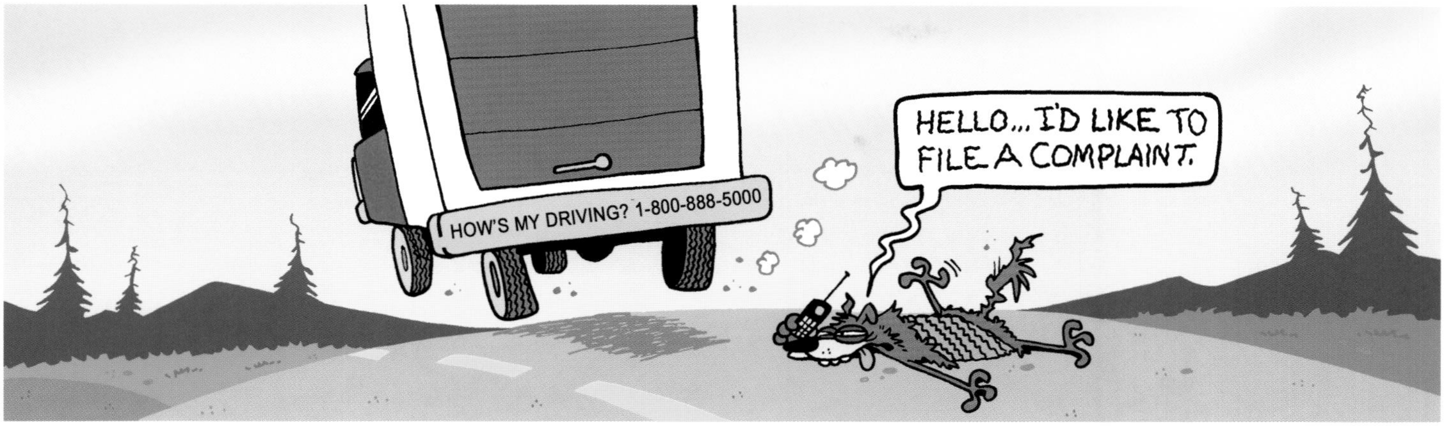
HOW'S MY DRIVING? 1-800-888-5000
HELLO... I'D LIKE TO FILE A COMPLAINT.

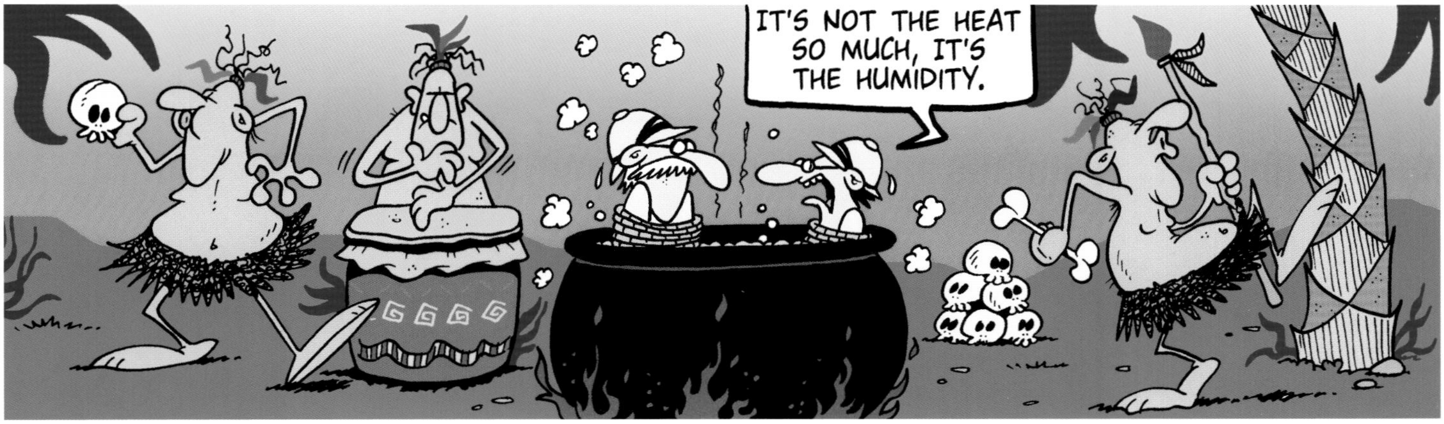
IT'S NOT THE HEAT SO MUCH, IT'S THE HUMIDITY.

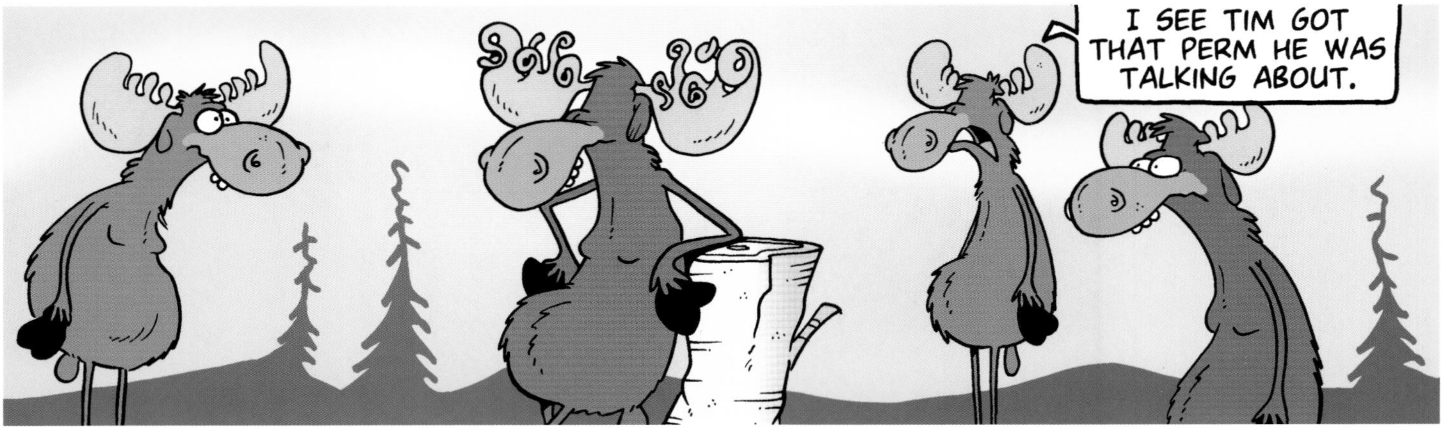
I SEE TIM GOT THAT PERM HE WAS TALKING ABOUT.

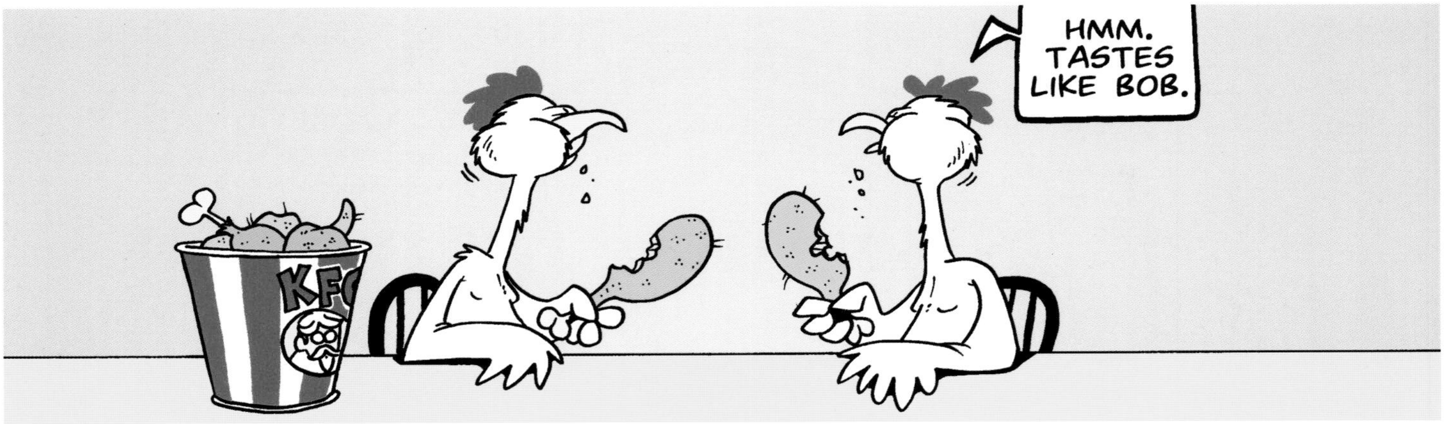
HMM. TASTES LIKE BOB.
KFC

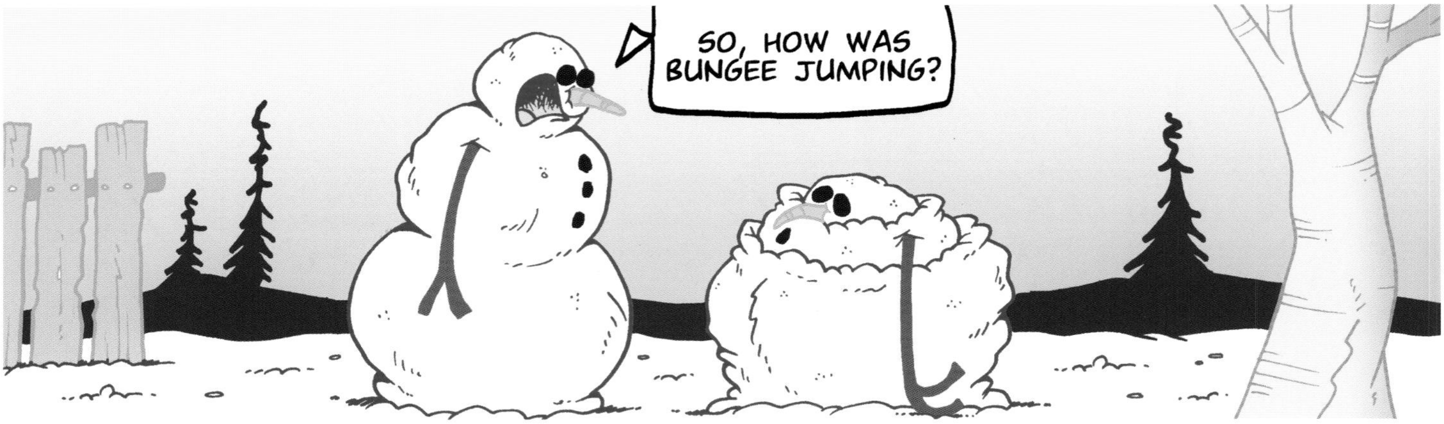
SO, HOW WAS BUNGEE JUMPING?

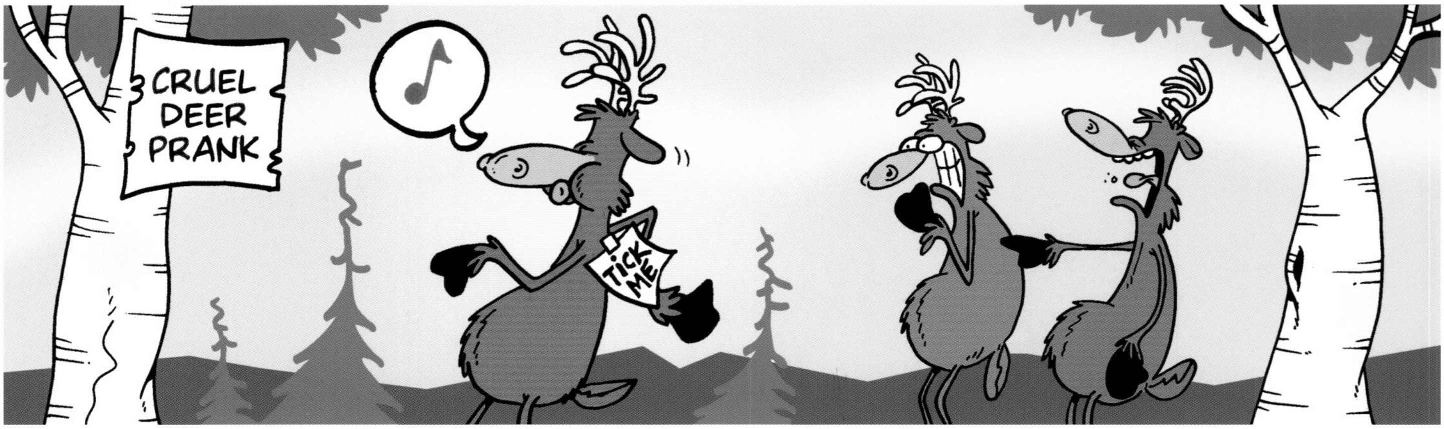
CRUEL DEER PRANK
TICK ME

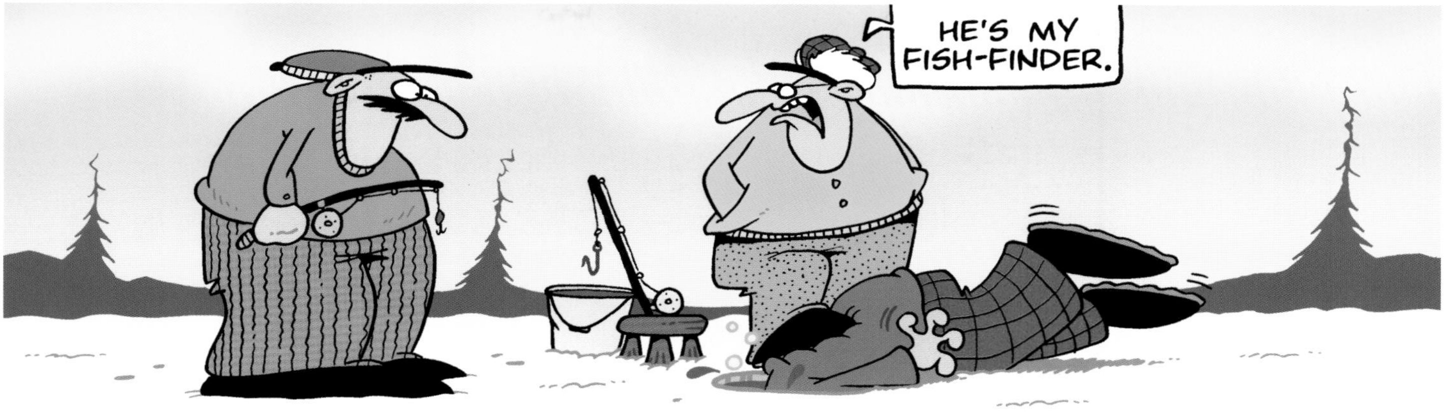
HE'S MY FISH-FINDER.

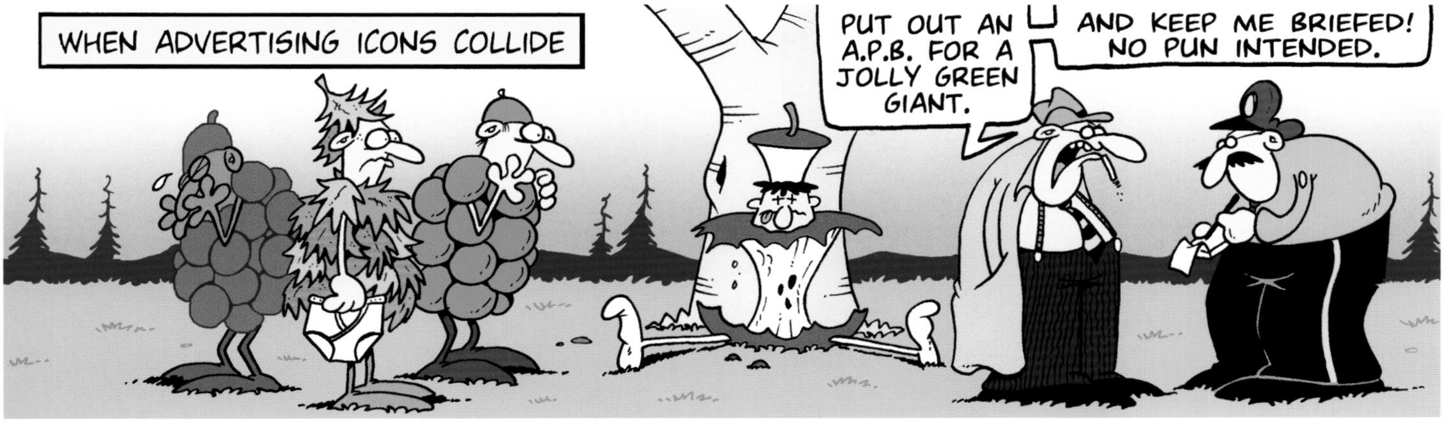
WHEN ADVERTISING ICONS COLLIDE
PUT OUT AN A.P.B. FOR A JOLLY GREEN GIANT.
AND KEEP ME BRIEFED! NO PUN INTENDED.

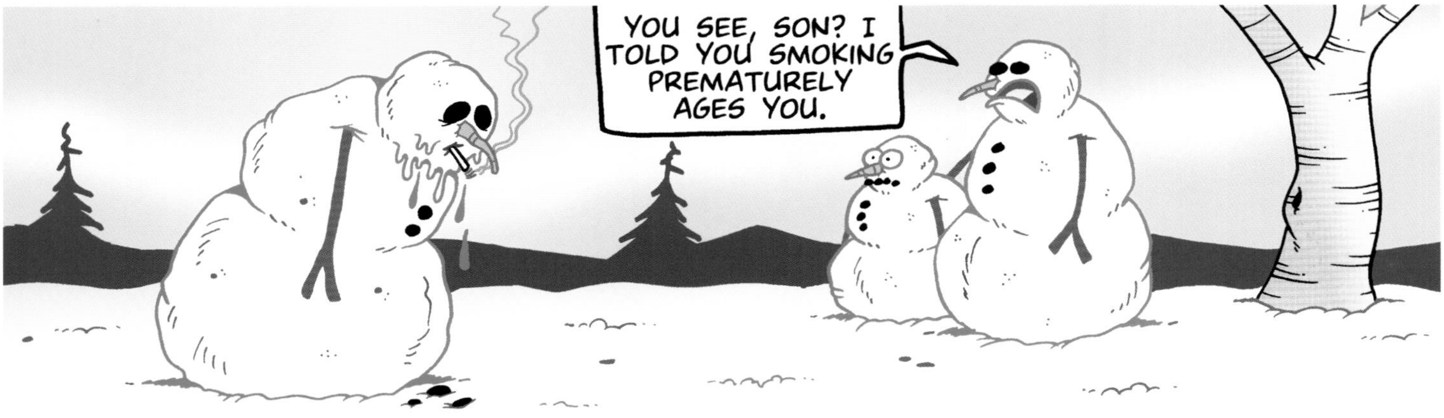
YOU SEE, SON? I TOLD YOU SMOKING PREMATURELY AGES YOU.

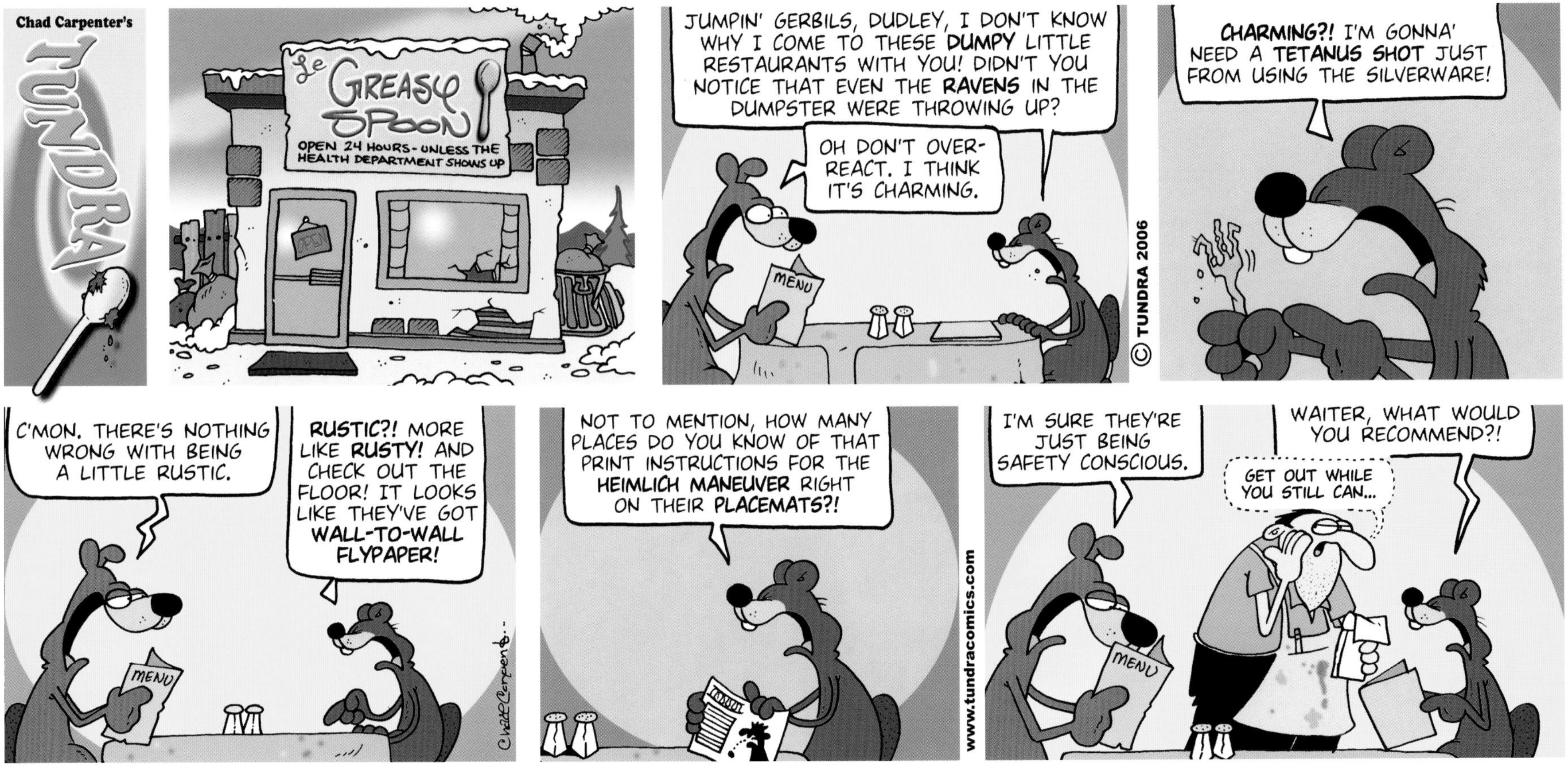
Chad Carpenter's
TUNDRA
Le GREASY SPOON
OPEN 24 HOURS - UNLESS THE HEALTH DEPARTMENT SHOWS UP
OPEN
JUMPIN' GERBILS, DUDLEY, I DON'T KNOW WHY I COME TO THESE **DUMPY** LITTLE RESTAURANTS WITH YOU! DIDN'T YOU NOTICE THAT EVEN THE **RAVENS** IN THE DUMPSTER WERE THROWING UP?
OH DON'T OVER-REACT. I THINK IT'S CHARMING.
MENU
© TUNDRA 2006
CHARMING?! I'M GONNA' NEED A **TETANUS SHOT** JUST FROM USING THE SILVERWARE!
C'MON. THERE'S NOTHING WRONG WITH BEING A LITTLE RUSTIC.
RUSTIC?! MORE LIKE **RUSTY!** AND CHECK OUT THE FLOOR! IT LOOKS LIKE THEY'VE GOT **WALL-TO-WALL FLYPAPER!**
MENU
NOT TO MENTION, HOW MANY PLACES DO YOU KNOW OF THAT PRINT INSTRUCTIONS FOR THE **HEIMLICH MANEUVER** RIGHT ON THEIR **PLACEMATS?!**
www.tundracomics.com
I'M SURE THEY'RE JUST BEING SAFETY CONSCIOUS.
WAITER, WHAT WOULD YOU RECOMMEND?!
GET OUT WHILE YOU STILL CAN...
MENU

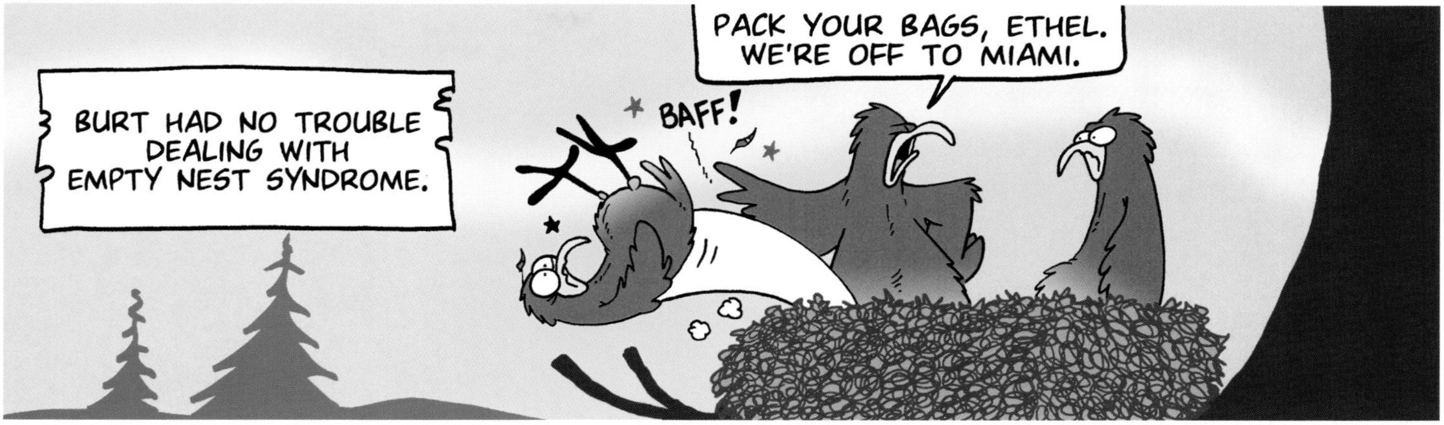
BURT HAD NO TROUBLE DEALING WITH EMPTY NEST SYNDROME.
PACK YOUR BAGS, ETHEL. WE'RE OFF TO MIAMI.
BAFF!

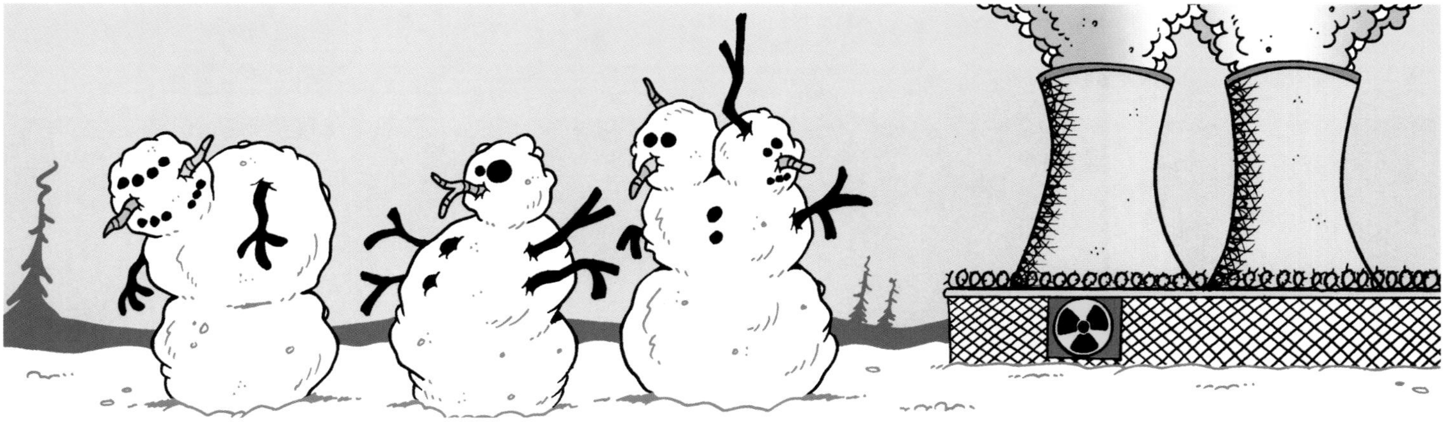

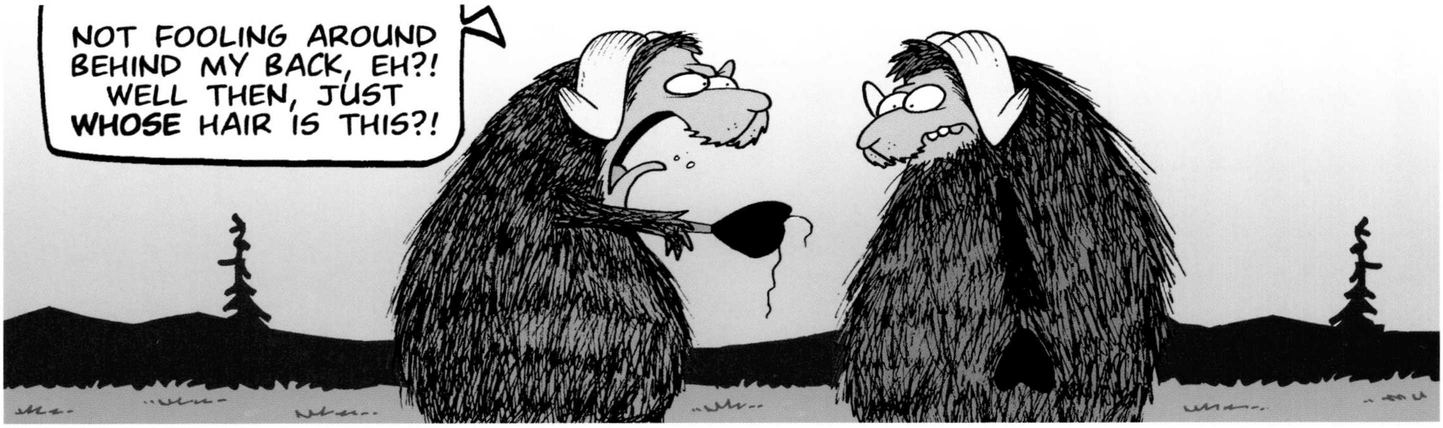
NOT FOOLING AROUND BEHIND MY BACK, EH?! WELL THEN, JUST **WHOSE** HAIR IS THIS?!

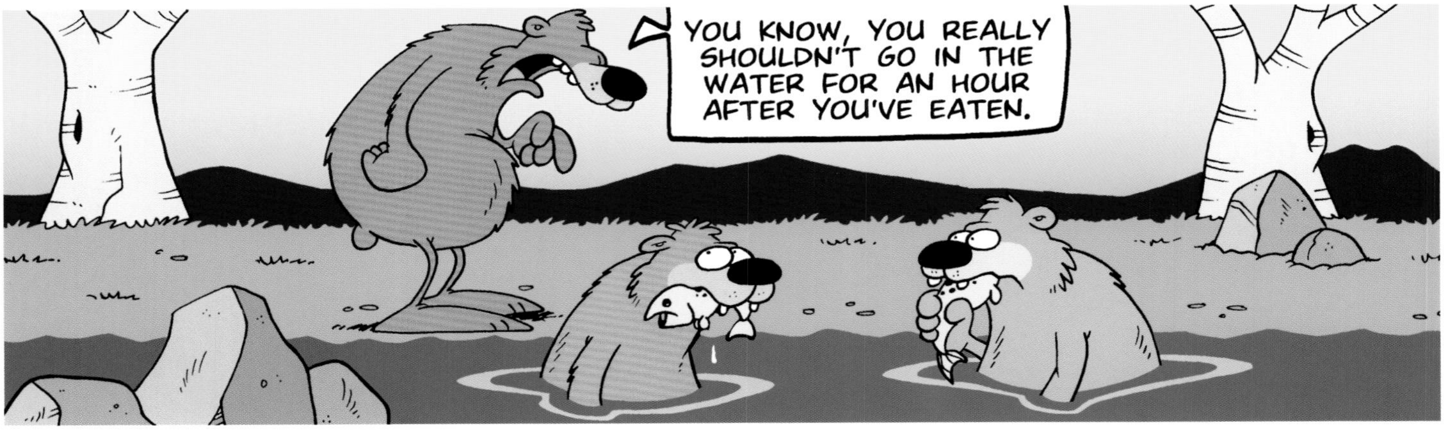
YOU KNOW, YOU REALLY SHOULDN'T GO IN THE WATER FOR AN HOUR AFTER YOU'VE EATEN.

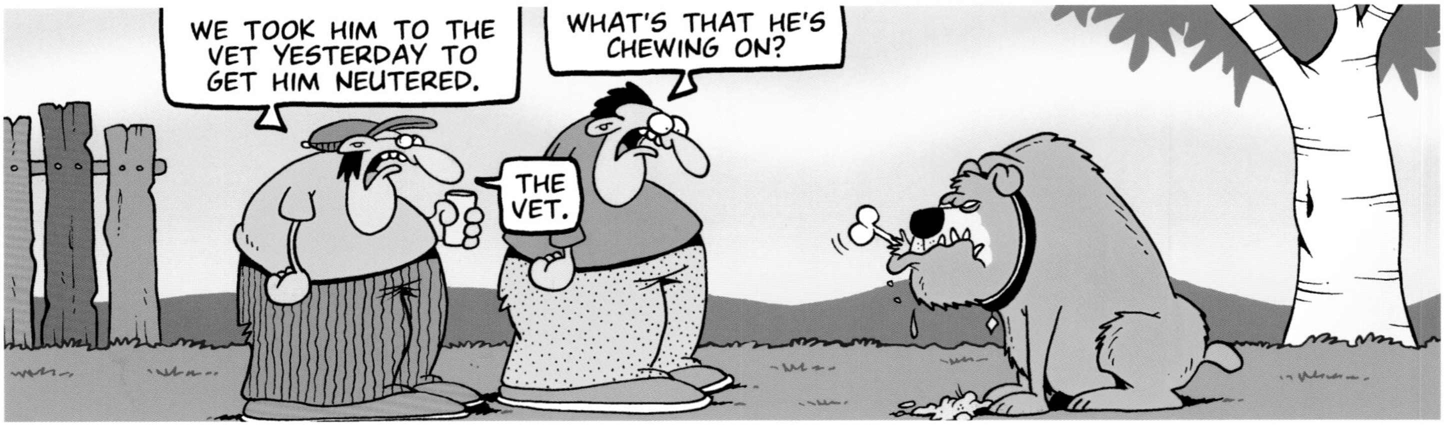
WE TOOK HIM TO THE VET YESTERDAY TO GET HIM NEUTERED.
WHAT'S THAT HE'S CHEWING ON?
THE VET.

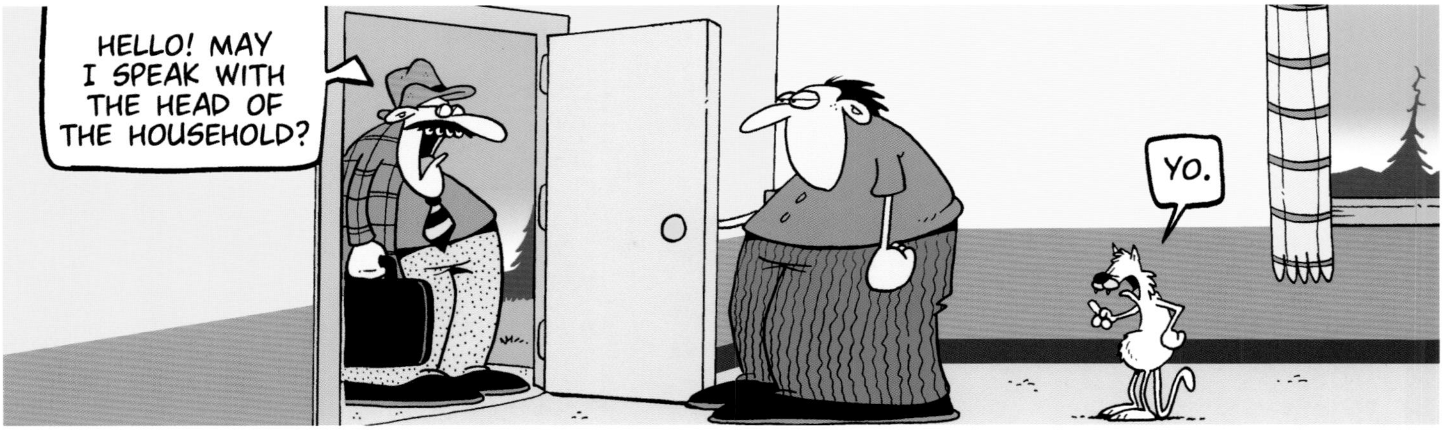
HELLO! MAY I SPEAK WITH THE HEAD OF THE HOUSEHOLD?
YO.

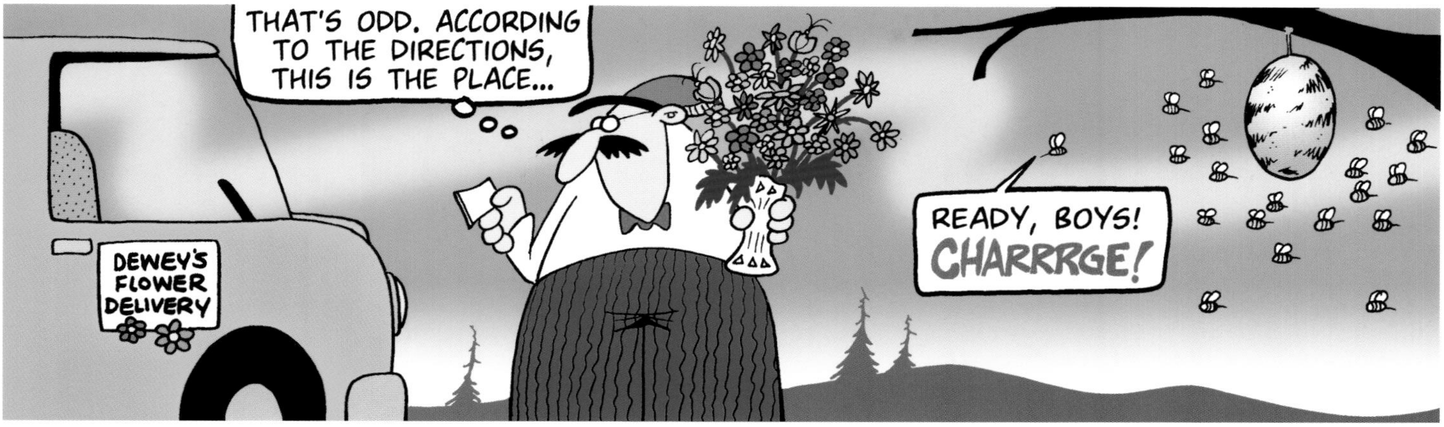
THAT'S ODD. ACCORDING TO THE DIRECTIONS, THIS IS THE PLACE...
DEWEY'S FLOWER DELIVERY
READY, BOYS! CHARRRGE!

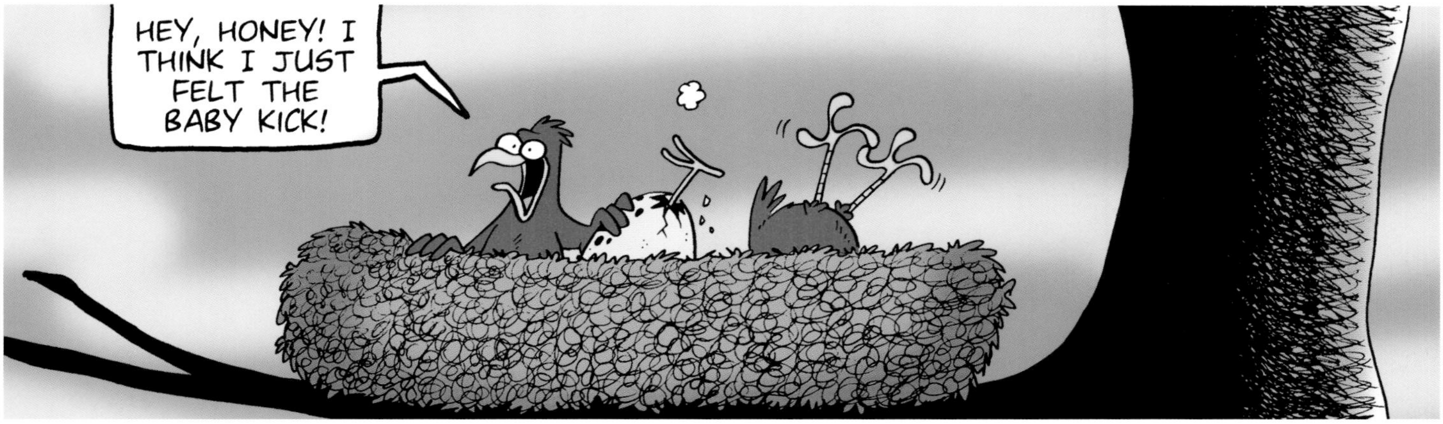
HEY, HONEY! I THINK I JUST FELT THE BABY KICK!

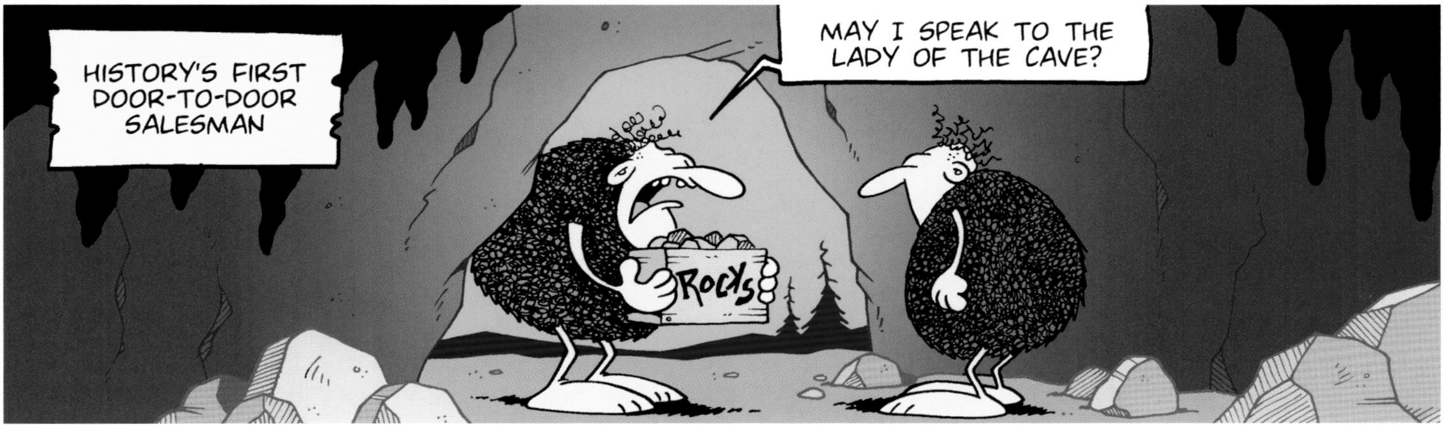
HISTORY'S FIRST DOOR-TO-DOOR SALESMAN
MAY I SPEAK TO THE LADY OF THE CAVE?
ROCKS

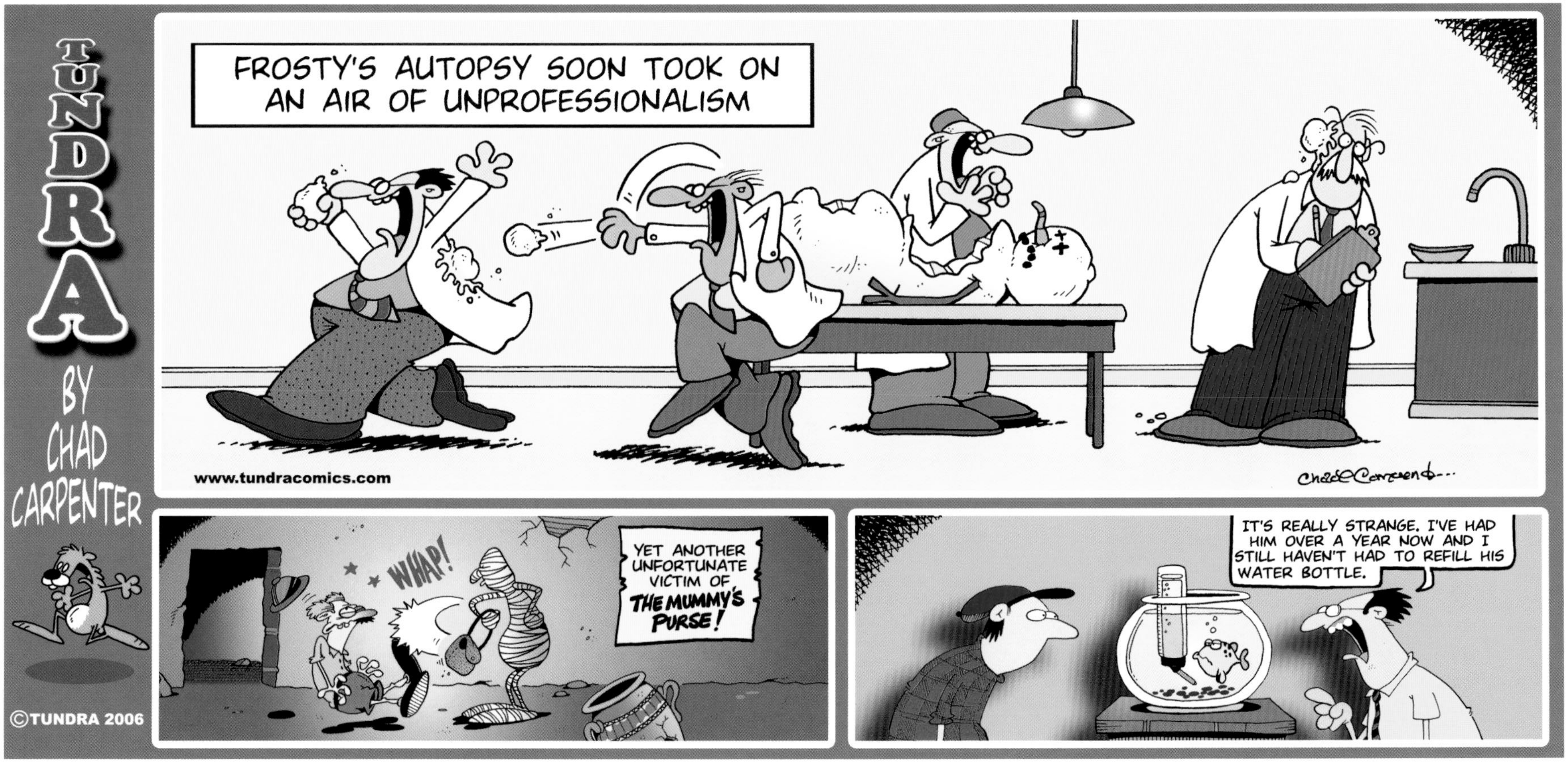
TUNDRA
BY CHAD CARPENTER
©TUNDRA 2006
FROSTY'S AUTOPSY SOON TOOK ON AN AIR OF UNPROFESSIONALISM
www.tundracomics.com
YET ANOTHER UNFORTUNATE VICTIM OF THE MUMMY'S PURSE!
WHAP!
IT'S REALLY STRANGE. I'VE HAD HIM OVER A YEAR NOW AND I STILL HAVEN'T HAD TO REFILL HIS WATER BOTTLE.

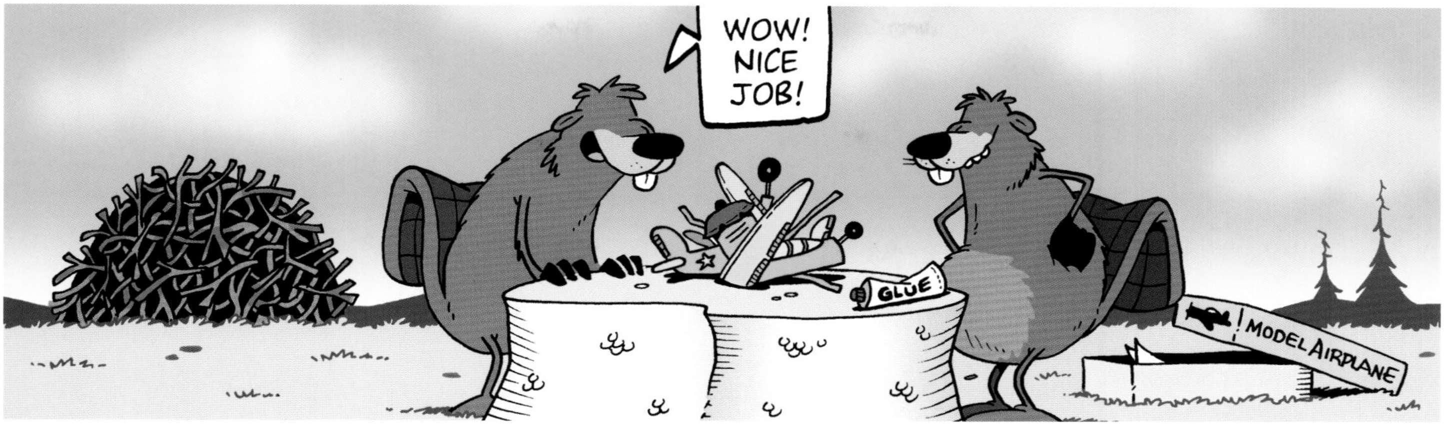
WOW! NICE JOB!
GLUE
MODEL AIRPLANE

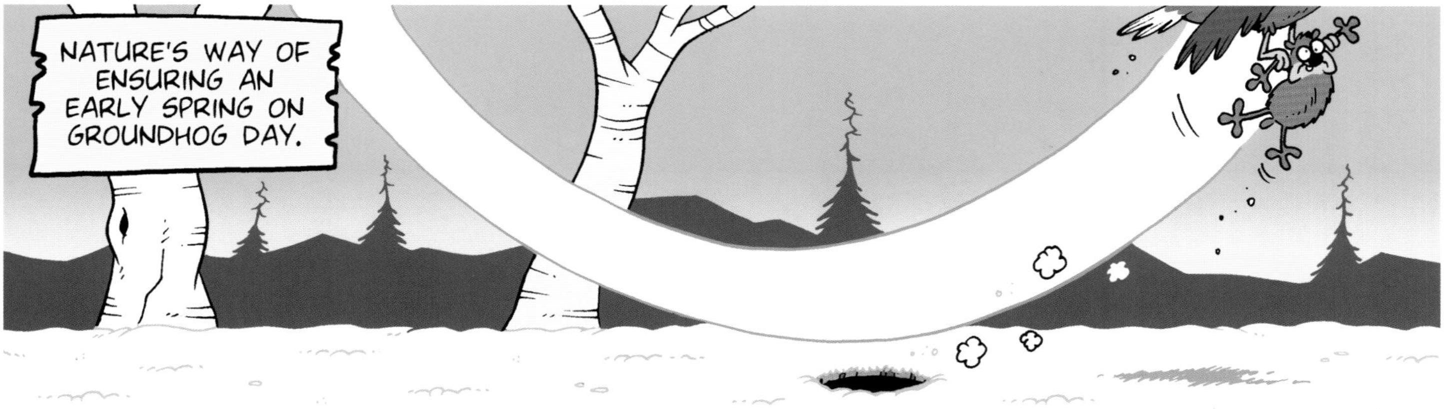
NATURE'S WAY OF ENSURING AN EARLY SPRING ON GROUNDHOG DAY.

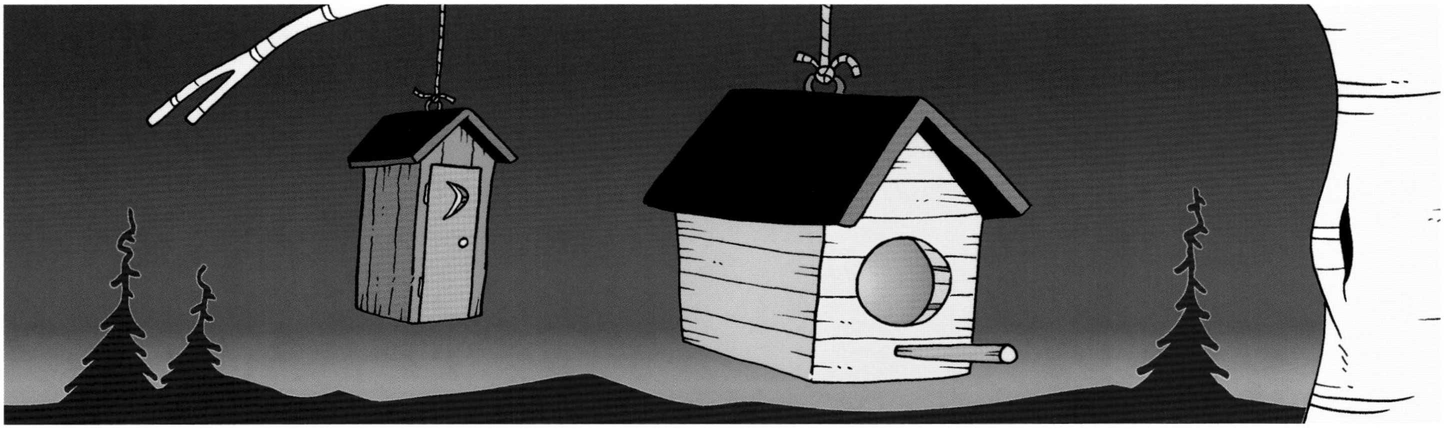

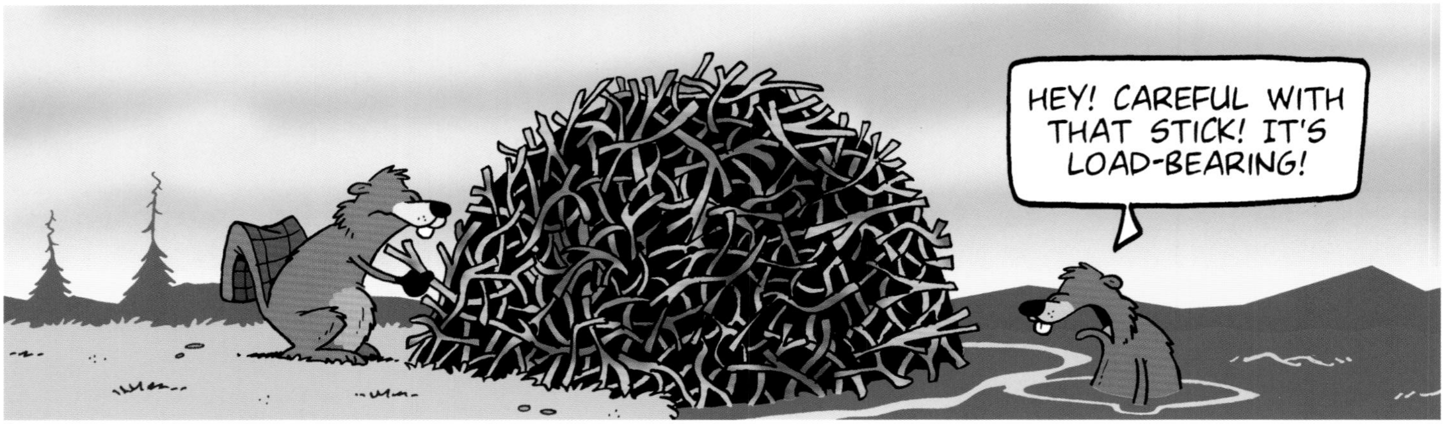
HEY! CAREFUL WITH THAT STICK! IT'S LOAD-BEARING!

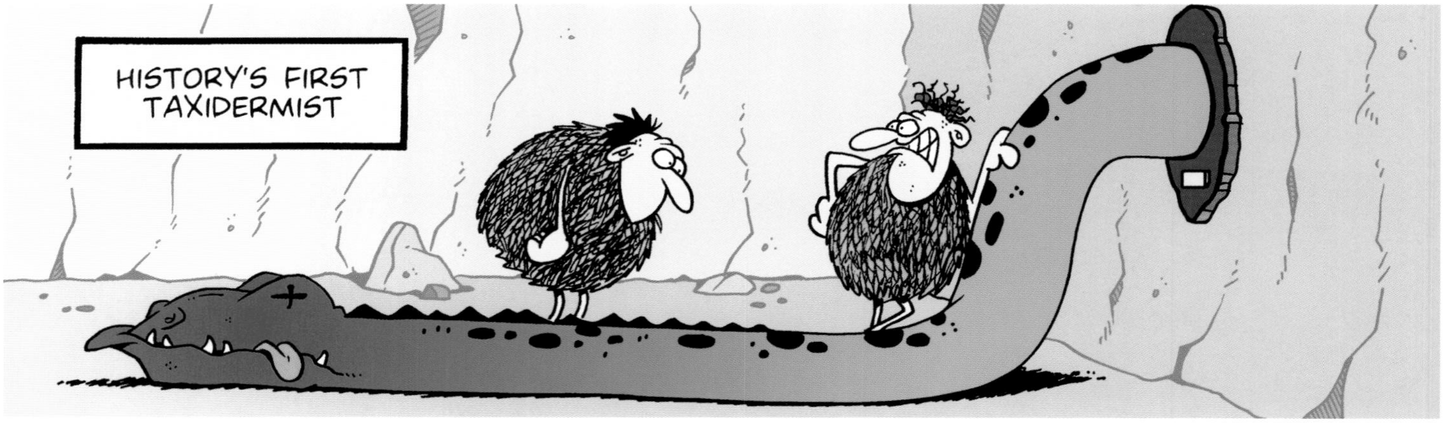
HISTORY'S FIRST TAXIDERMIST

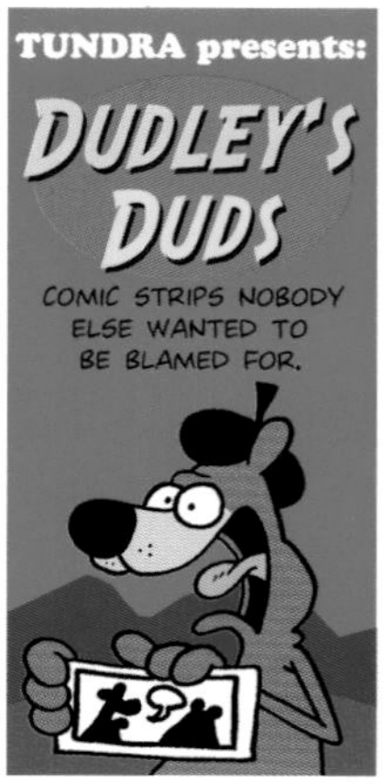
TUNDRA presents:
DUDLEY'S DUDS
COMIC STRIPS NOBODY ELSE WANTED TO BE BLAMED FOR.

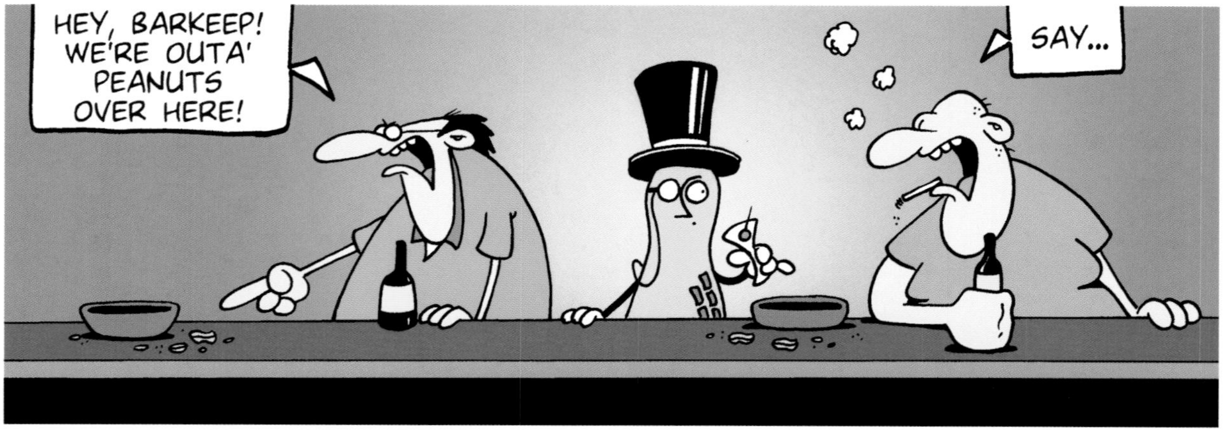
HEY, BARKEEP! WE'RE OUTA' PEANUTS OVER HERE!
SAY...

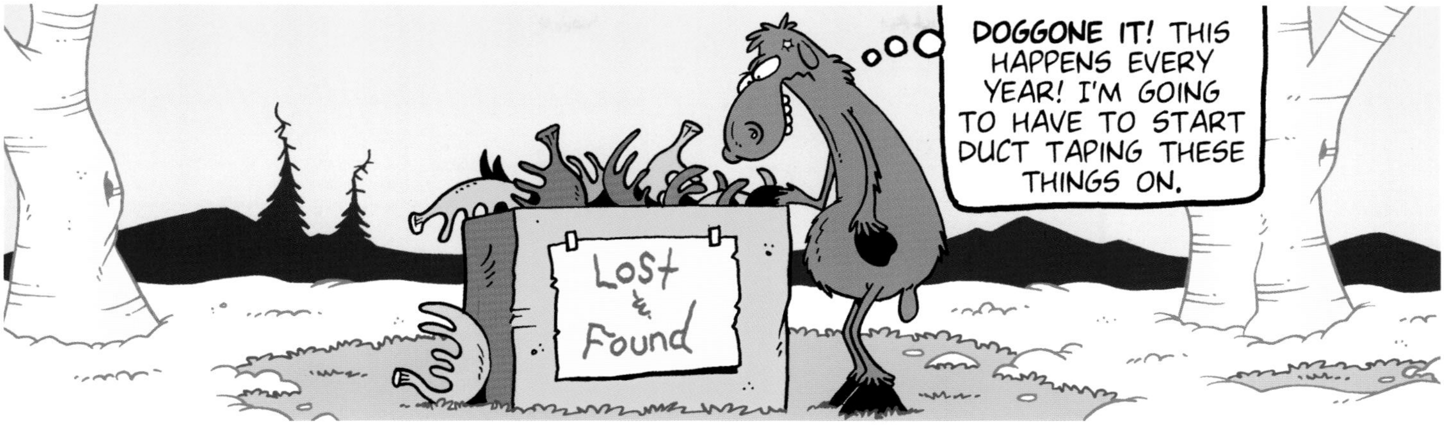
DOGGONE IT! THIS HAPPENS EVERY YEAR! I'M GOING TO HAVE TO START DUCT TAPING THESE THINGS ON.
Lost & Found

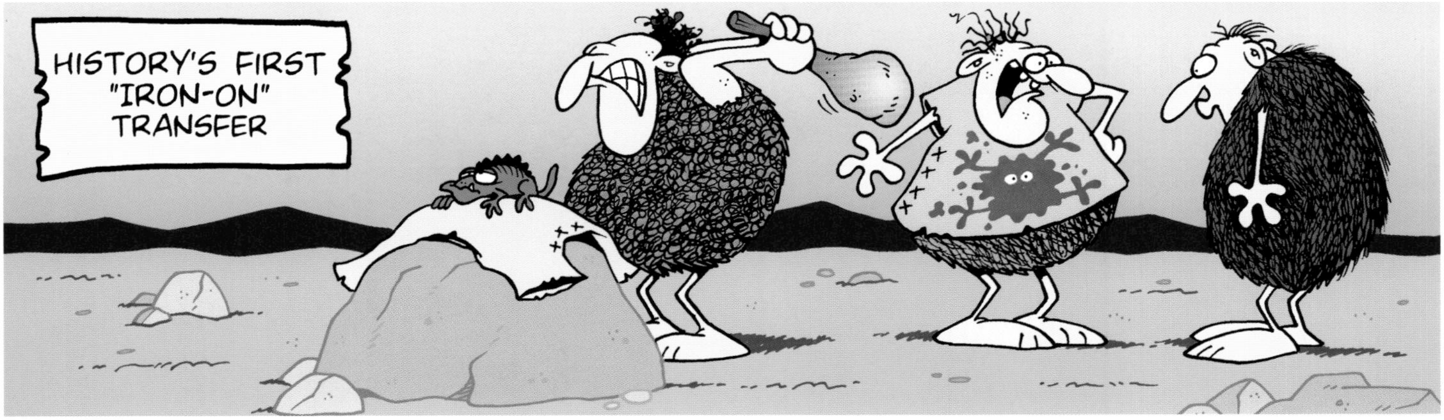
HISTORY'S FIRST "IRON-ON" TRANSFER

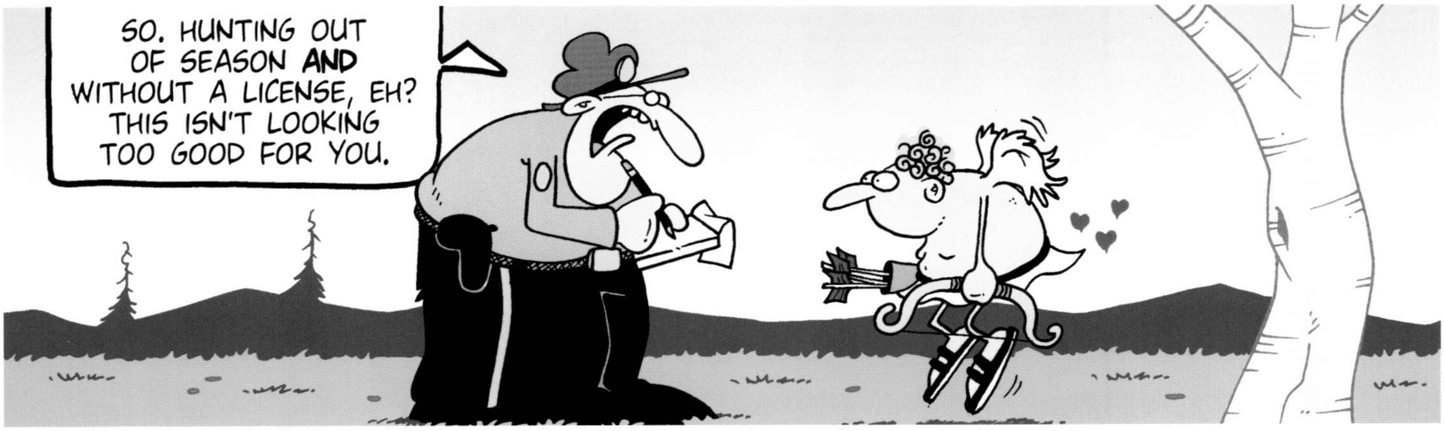
SO. HUNTING OUT OF SEASON AND WITHOUT A LICENSE, EH? THIS ISN'T LOOKING TOO GOOD FOR YOU.

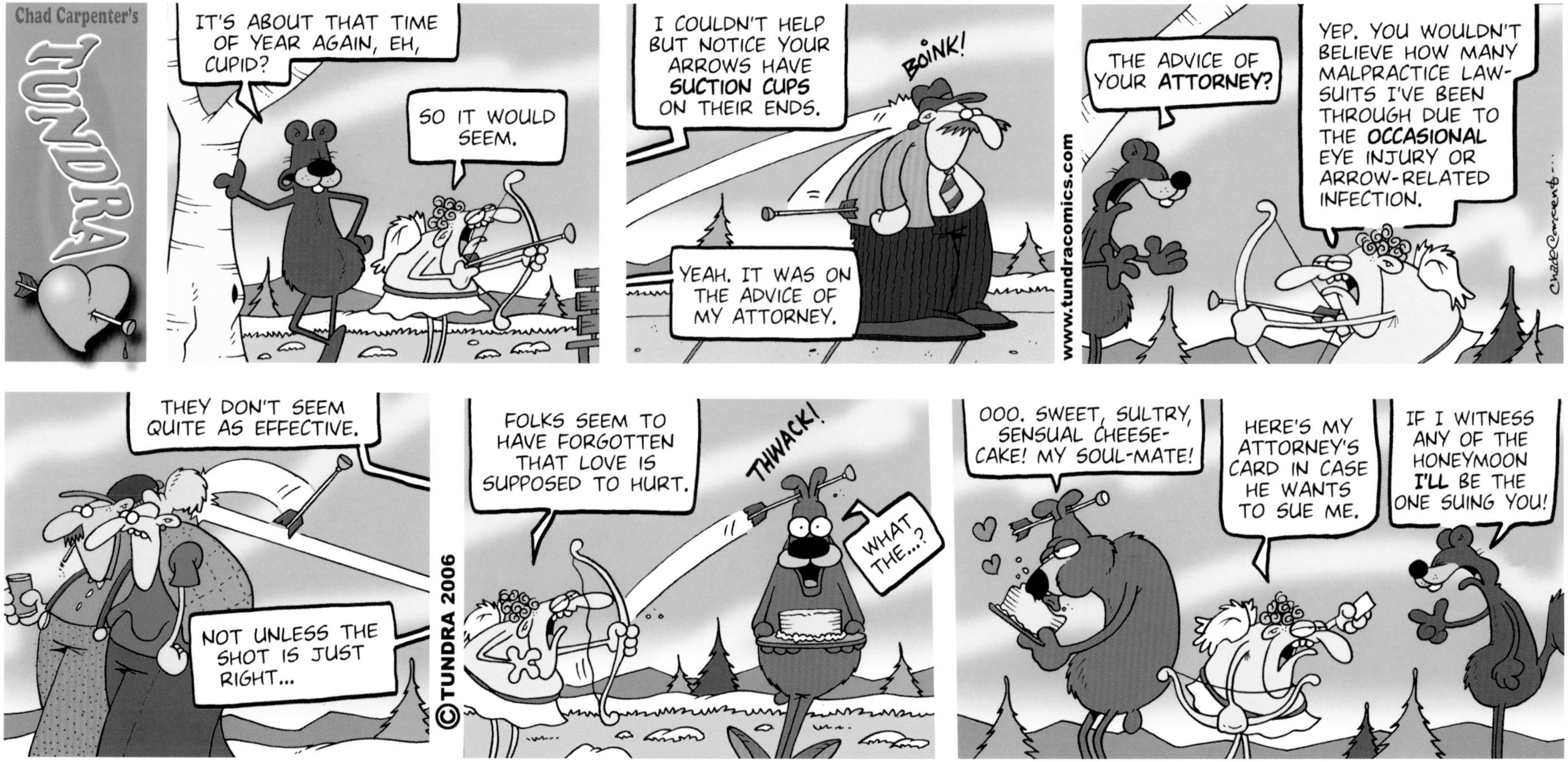
Chad Carpenter's
TUNDRA
IT'S ABOUT THAT TIME OF YEAR AGAIN, EH, CUPID?
SO IT WOULD SEEM.
I COULDN'T HELP BUT NOTICE YOUR ARROWS HAVE **SUCTION CUPS** ON THEIR ENDS.
BOINK!
YEAH. IT WAS ON THE ADVICE OF MY ATTORNEY.
www.tundracomics.com
THE ADVICE OF YOUR **ATTORNEY?**
YEP. YOU WOULDN'T BELIEVE HOW MANY MALPRACTICE LAW-SUITS I'VE BEEN THROUGH DUE TO THE **OCCASIONAL** EYE INJURY OR ARROW-RELATED INFECTION.
THEY DON'T SEEM QUITE AS EFFECTIVE.
NOT UNLESS THE SHOT IS JUST RIGHT...
©TUNDRA 2006
FOLKS SEEM TO HAVE FORGOTTEN THAT LOVE IS SUPPOSED TO HURT.
THWACK!
WHAT THE...?
OOO. SWEET, SULTRY, SENSUAL CHEESE-CAKE! MY SOUL-MATE!
HERE'S MY ATTORNEY'S CARD IN CASE HE WANTS TO SUE ME.
IF I WITNESS ANY OF THE HONEYMOON **I'LL** BE THE ONE SUING YOU!

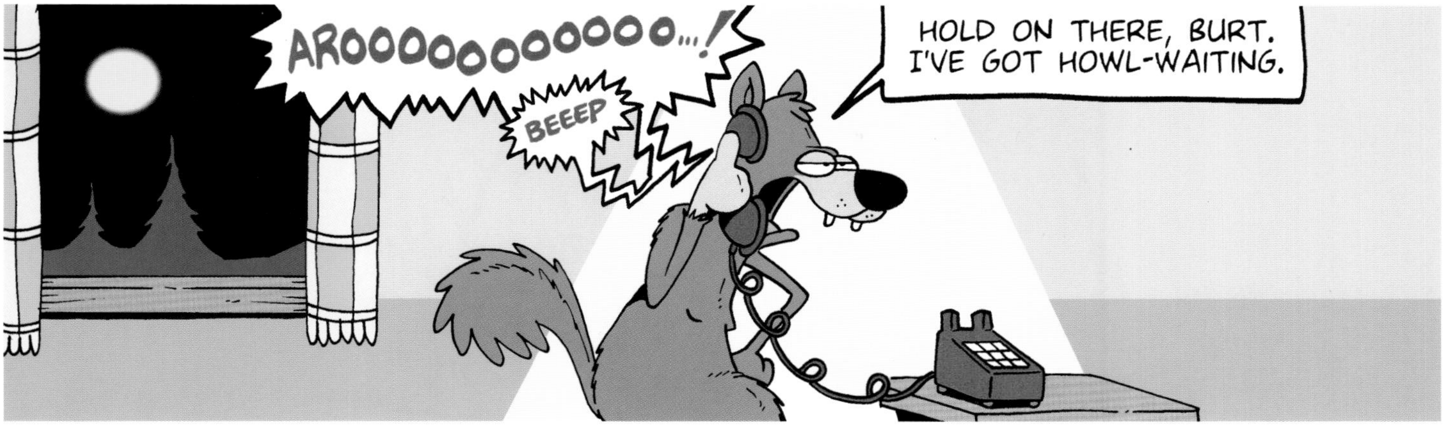
AROOOOOOOOOOOO...!
BEEEP
HOLD ON THERE, BURT. I'VE GOT HOWL-WAITING.

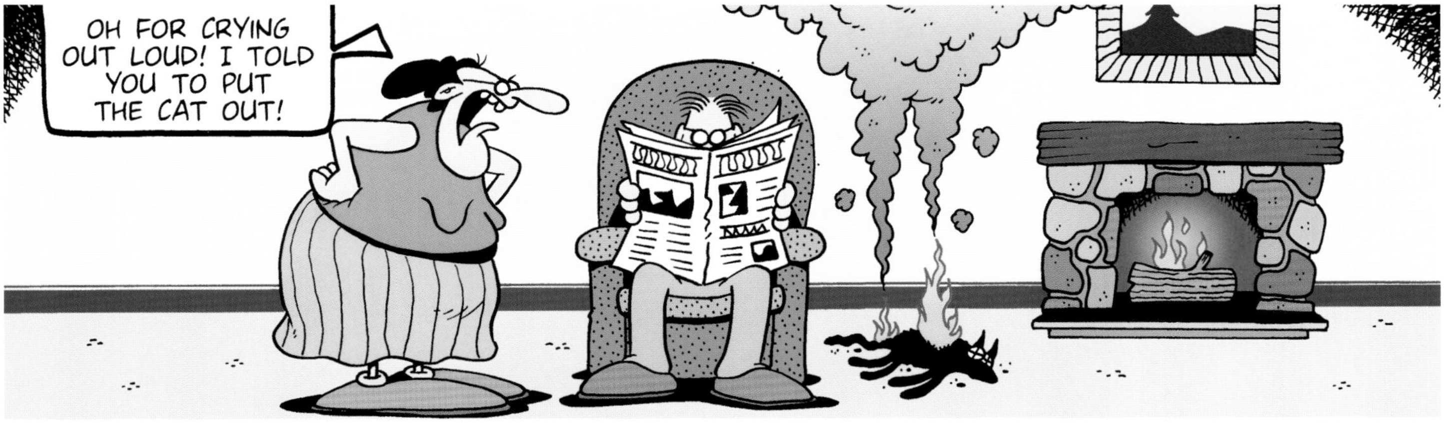
OH FOR CRYING OUT LOUD! I TOLD YOU TO PUT THE CAT OUT!

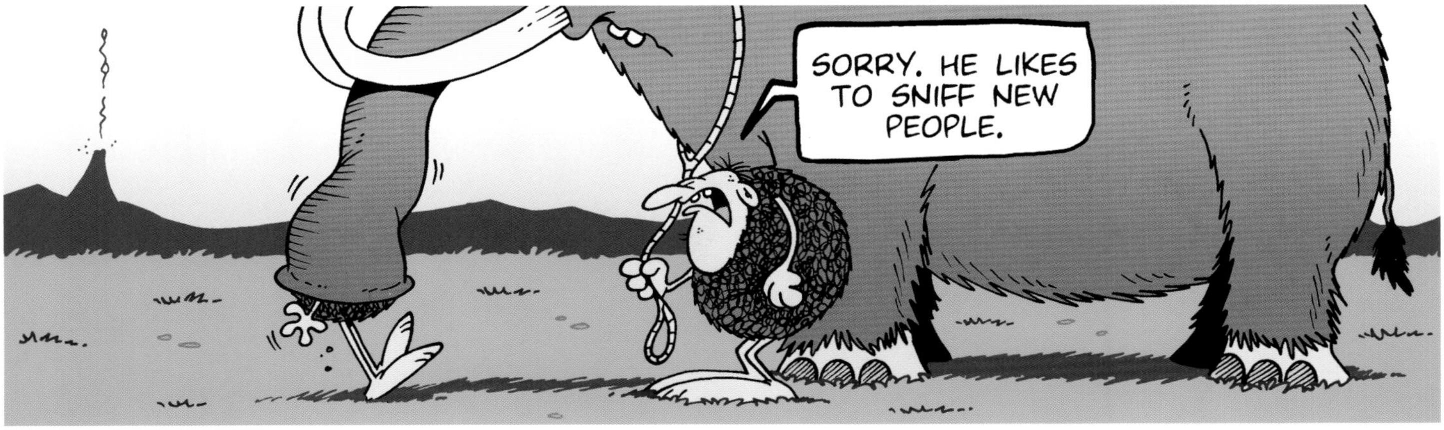
SORRY. HE LIKES TO SNIFF NEW PEOPLE.

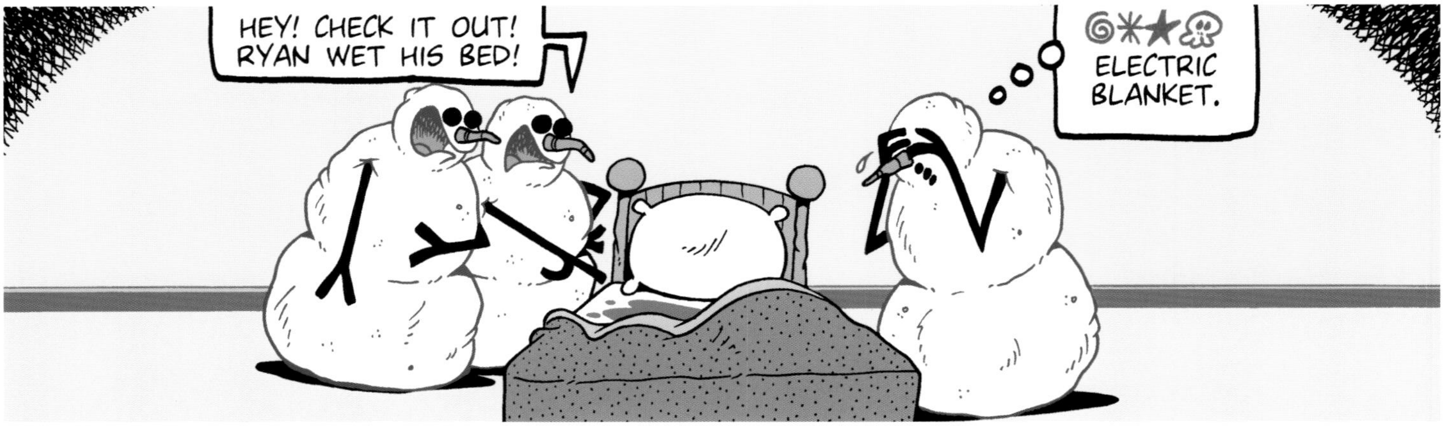
HEY! CHECK IT OUT! RYAN WET HIS BED!
ELECTRIC BLANKET.

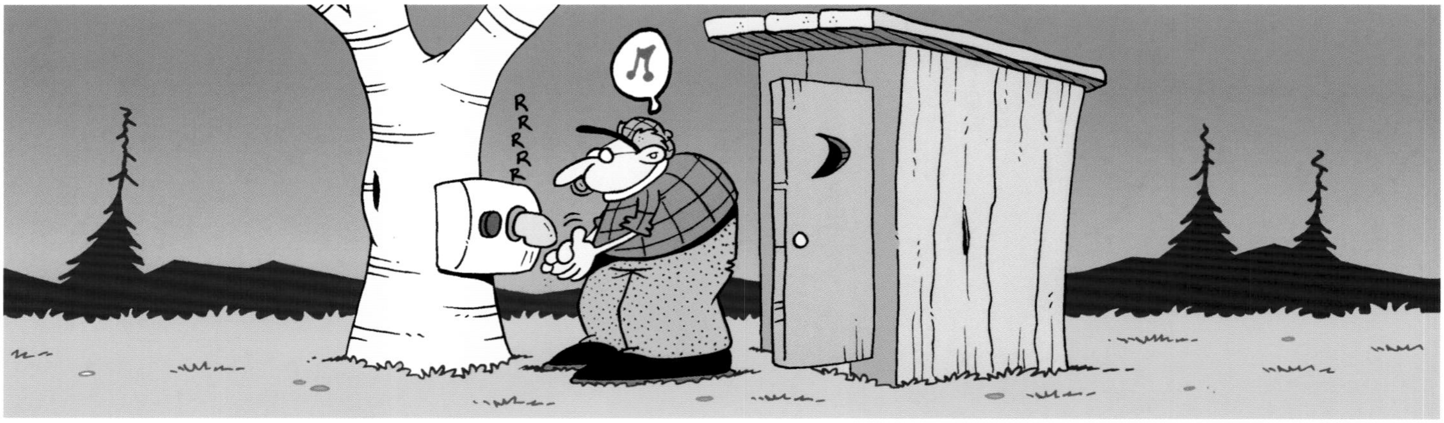
RRRRR

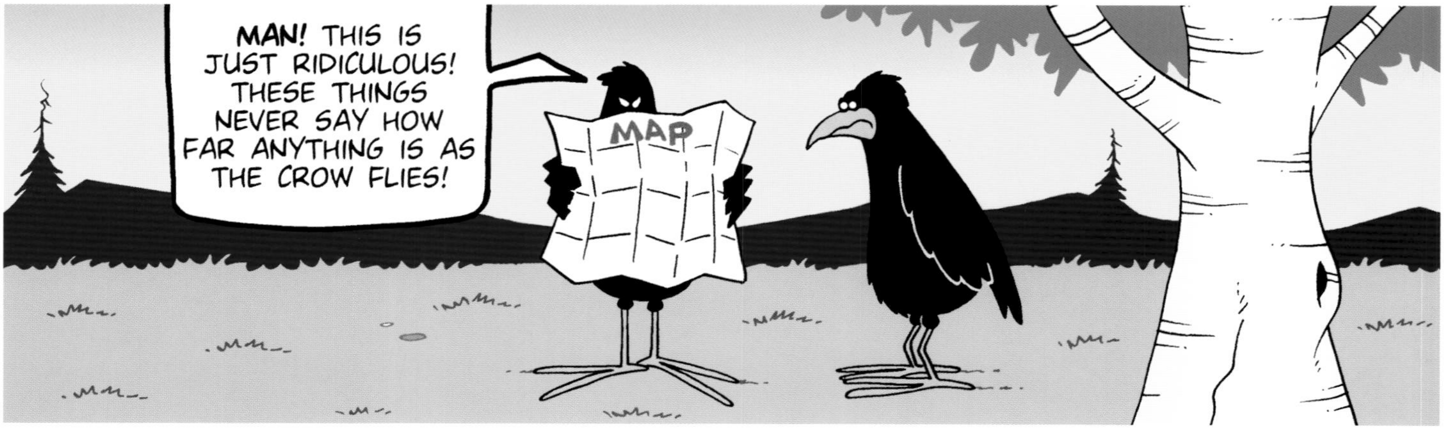
MAN! THIS IS JUST RIDICULOUS! THESE THINGS NEVER SAY HOW FAR ANYTHING IS AS THE CROW FLIES!
MAP

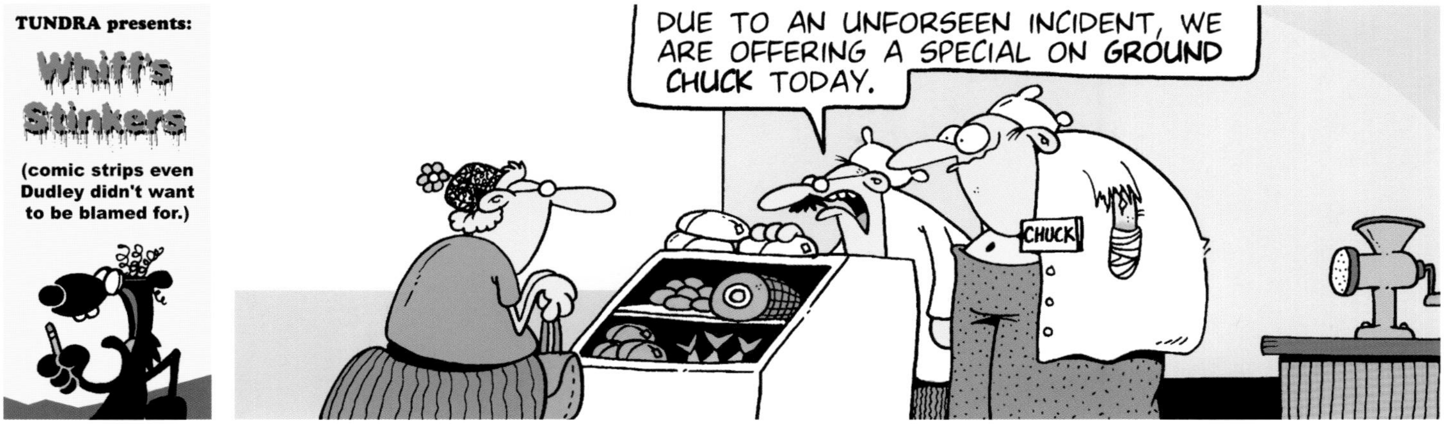
TUNDRA presents:
Whiff's Stinkers
(comic strips even Dudley didn't want to be blamed for.)
DUE TO AN UNFORSEEN INCIDENT, WE ARE OFFERING A SPECIAL ON **GROUND CHUCK** TODAY.
CHUCK

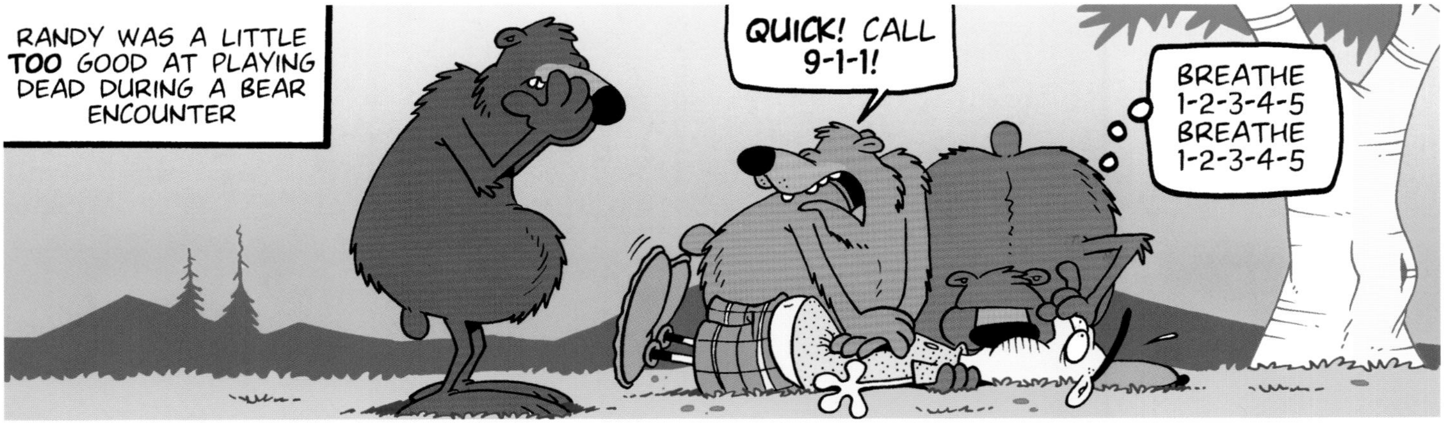
RANDY WAS A LITTLE **TOO** GOOD AT PLAYING DEAD DURING A BEAR ENCOUNTER
QUICK! CALL 9-1-1!
BREATHE 1-2-3-4-5 BREATHE 1-2-3-4-5

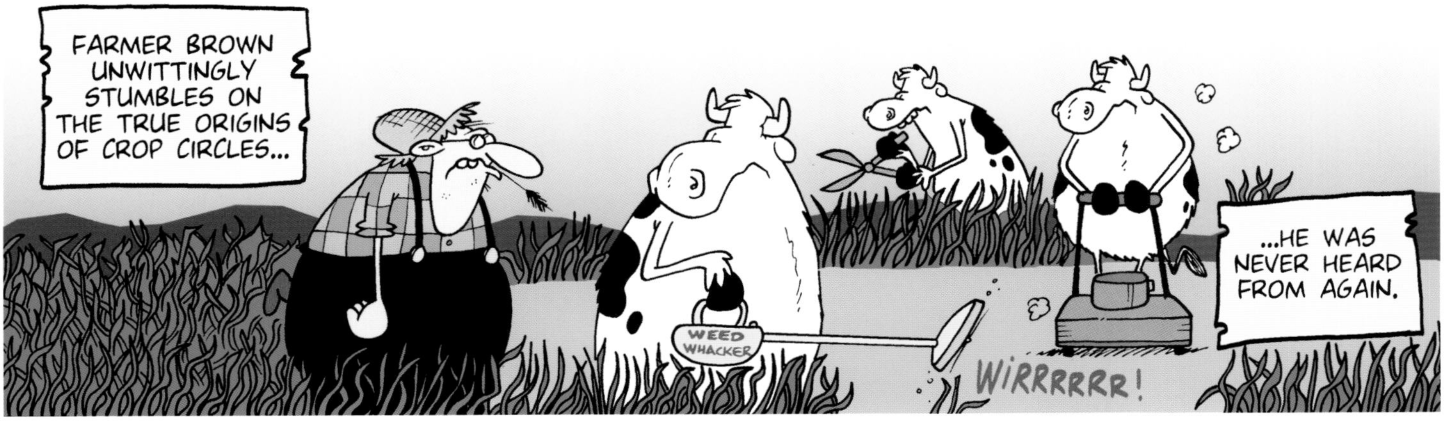
FARMER BROWN UNWITTINGLY STUMBLES ON THE TRUE ORIGINS OF CROP CIRCLES...
WEED WHACKER
WiRRRRRR!
...HE WAS NEVER HEARD FROM AGAIN.

Chad Carpenter's
TUNDRA
TUNDRA SEAL of APPROVAL
OKEY-DOKE!
www.tundracomics.com
WOW. THAT WAS QUITE AN EARTHQUAKE! I WONDER WHAT IT MEASURED ON THE RICHTER SCALE?
I DON'T GO BY THE RICHTER SCALE.
© TUNDRA 2006
WHAT DO YOU MEAN?
I GO BY THE DUDLEY FAT SCALE.
IF HE'S STILL JIGGLING AFTER 10 MINUTES IT'S AT LEAST A 6.0
H-H-HARD T-T-TO E-E-EAT J-J-J-JELLO...

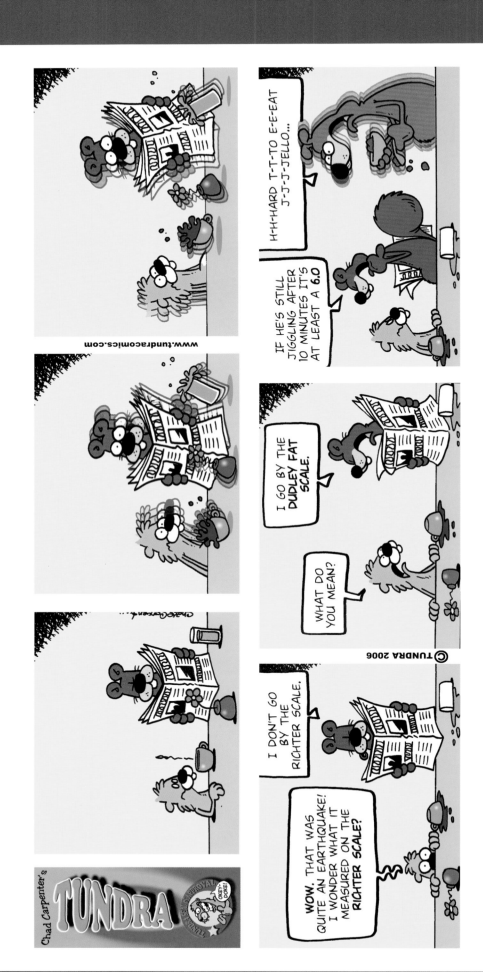

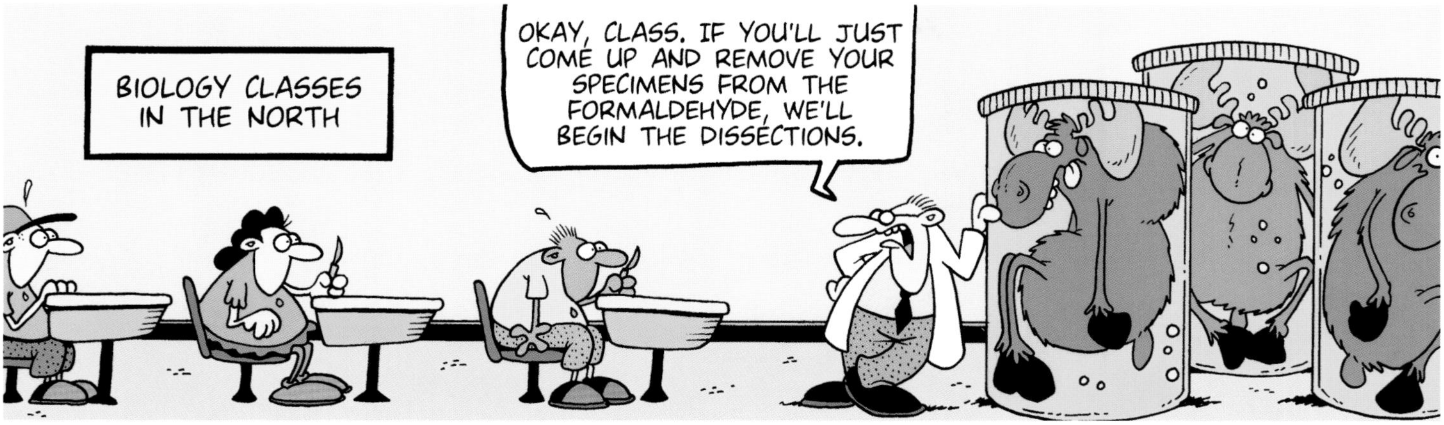
BIOLOGY CLASSES
IN THE NORTH
OKAY, CLASS. IF YOU'LL JUST COME UP AND REMOVE YOUR SPECIMENS FROM THE FORMALDEHYDE, WE'LL BEGIN THE DISSECTIONS.

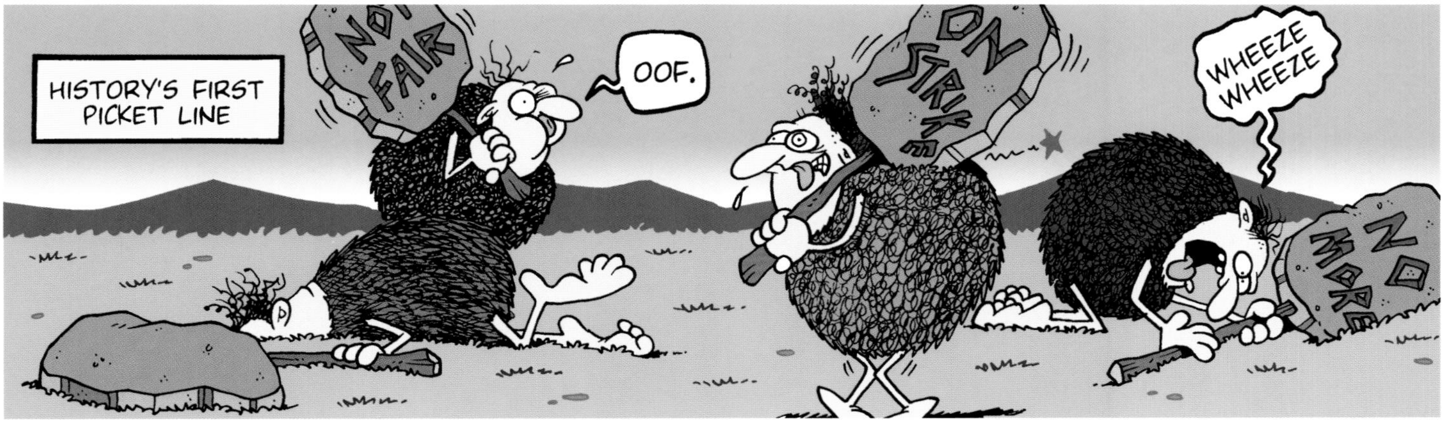
HISTORY'S FIRST
PICKET LINE
NOT FAIR
OOF.
ON STRIKE
WHEEZE WHEEZE
NO MORE

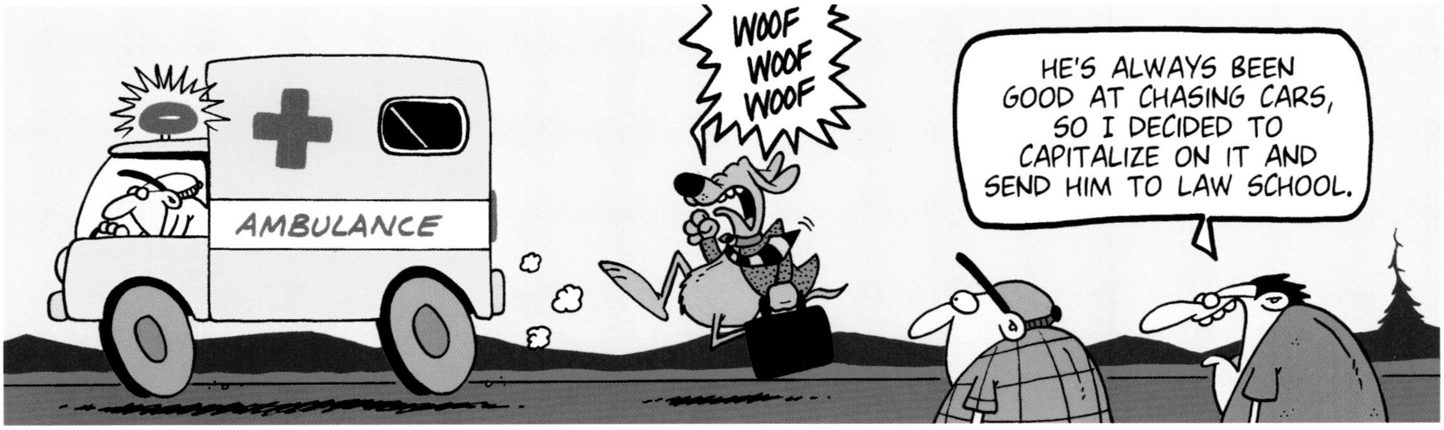
AMBULANCE
WOOF WOOF WOOF
HE'S ALWAYS BEEN GOOD AT CHASING CARS, SO I DECIDED TO CAPITALIZE ON IT AND SEND HIM TO LAW SCHOOL.

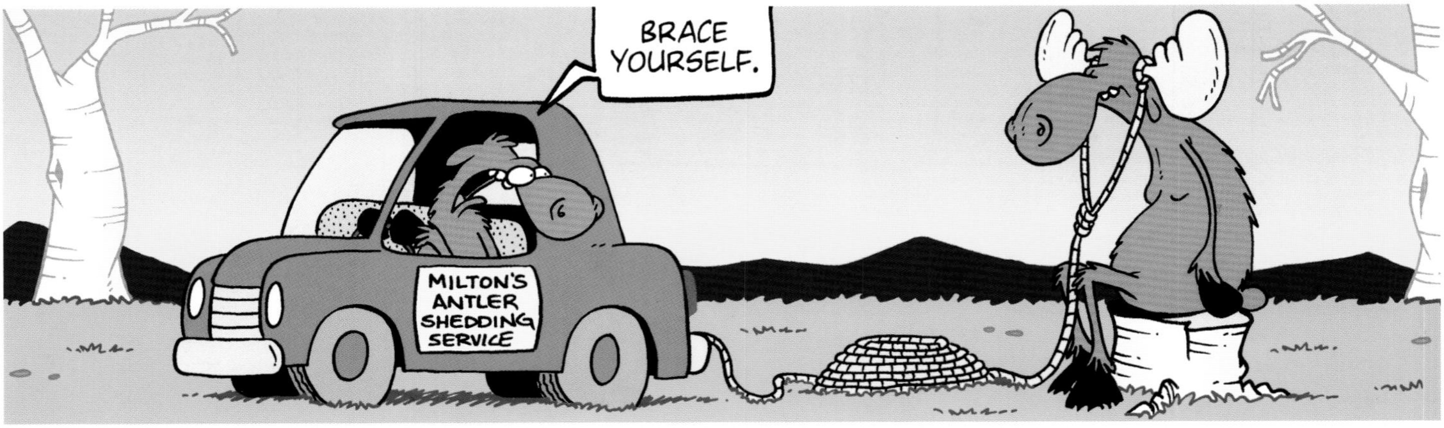
BRACE YOURSELF.
MILTON'S ANTLER SHEDDING SERVICE

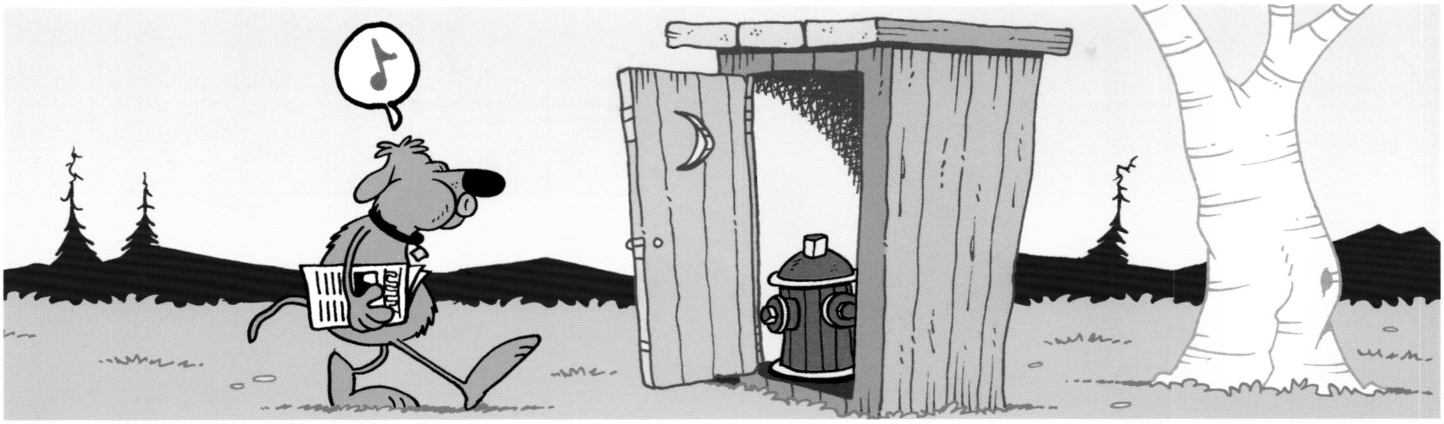

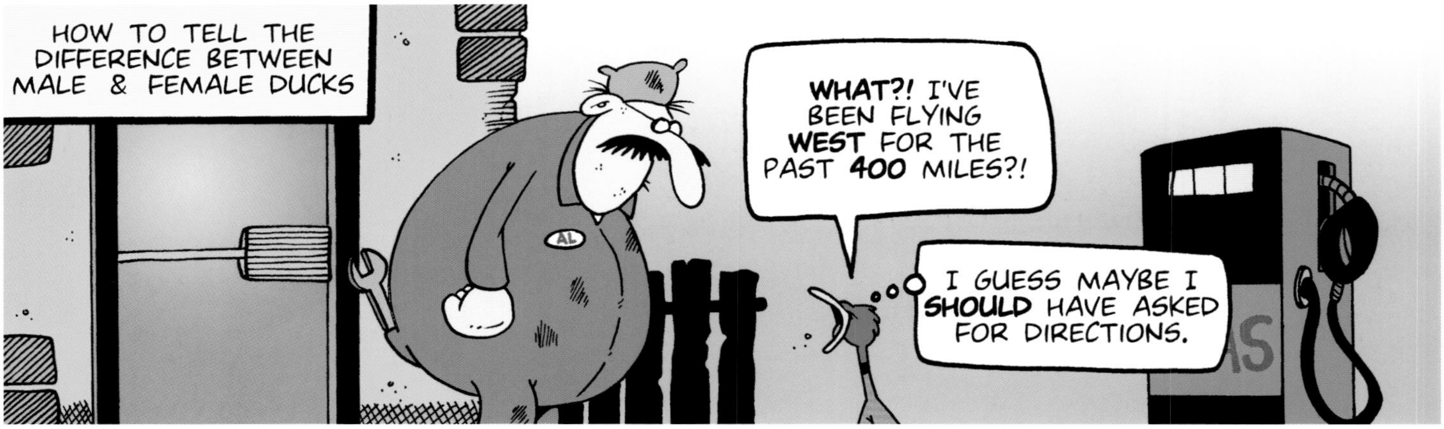
HOW TO TELL THE DIFFERENCE BETWEEN MALE & FEMALE DUCKS
WHAT?! I'VE BEEN FLYING WEST FOR THE PAST 400 MILES?!
I GUESS MAYBE I SHOULD HAVE ASKED FOR DIRECTIONS.
AL

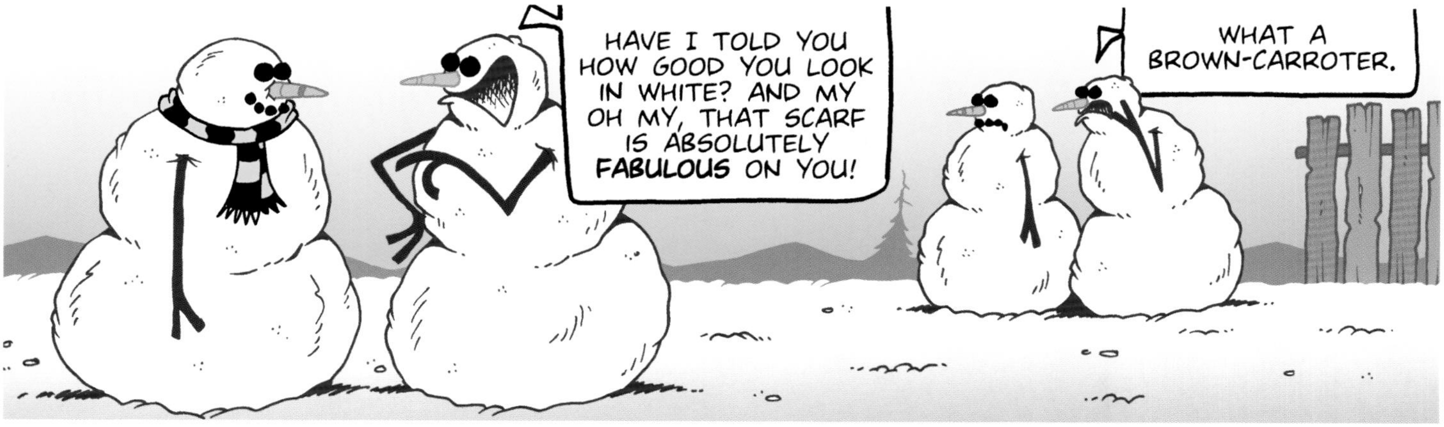
HAVE I TOLD YOU HOW GOOD YOU LOOK IN WHITE? AND MY OH MY, THAT SCARF IS ABSOLUTELY **FABULOUS** ON YOU!
WHAT A BROWN-CARROTER.

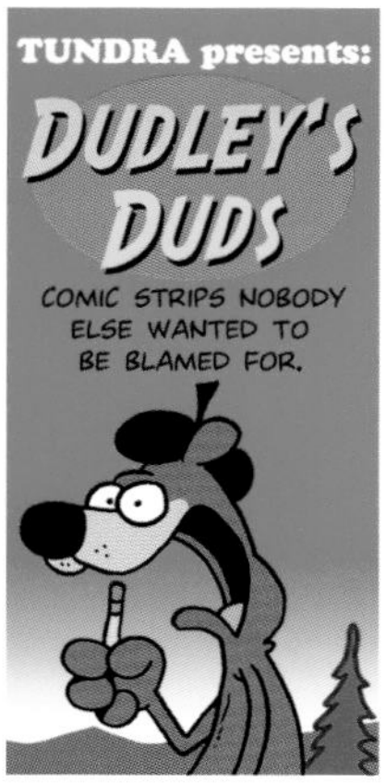
TUNDRA presents:
DUDLEY'S DUDS
COMIC STRIPS NOBODY ELSE WANTED TO BE BLAMED FOR.

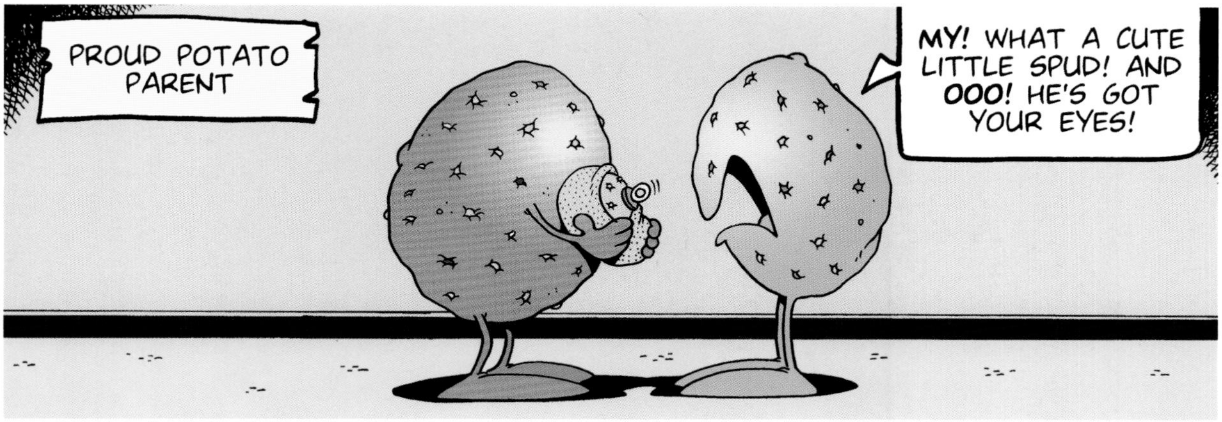
PROUD POTATO PARENT
MY! WHAT A CUTE LITTLE SPUD! AND **OOO!** HE'S GOT YOUR EYES!

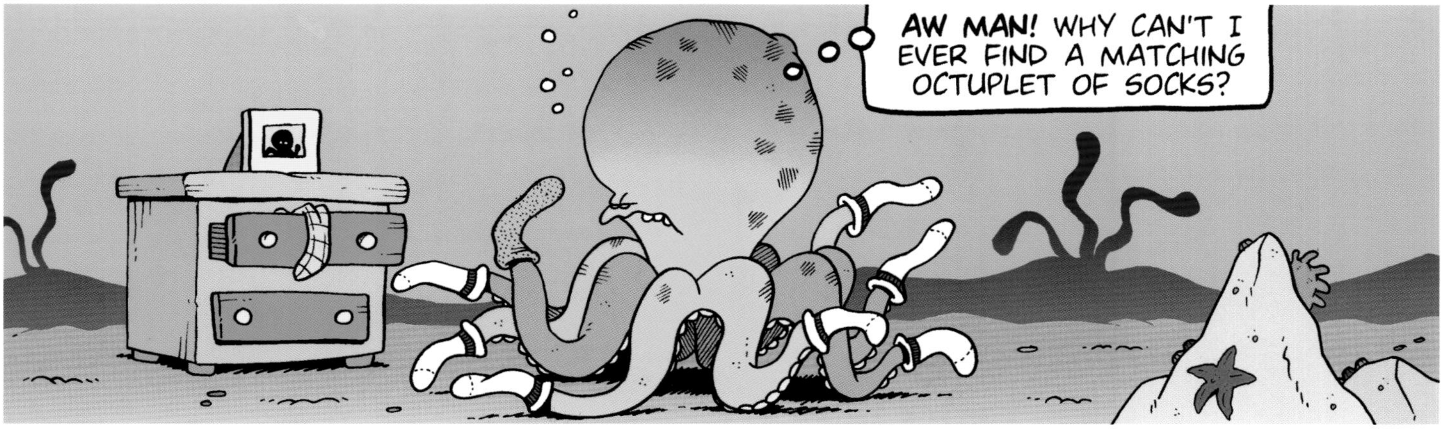
AW MAN! WHY CAN'T I EVER FIND A MATCHING OCTUPLET OF SOCKS?

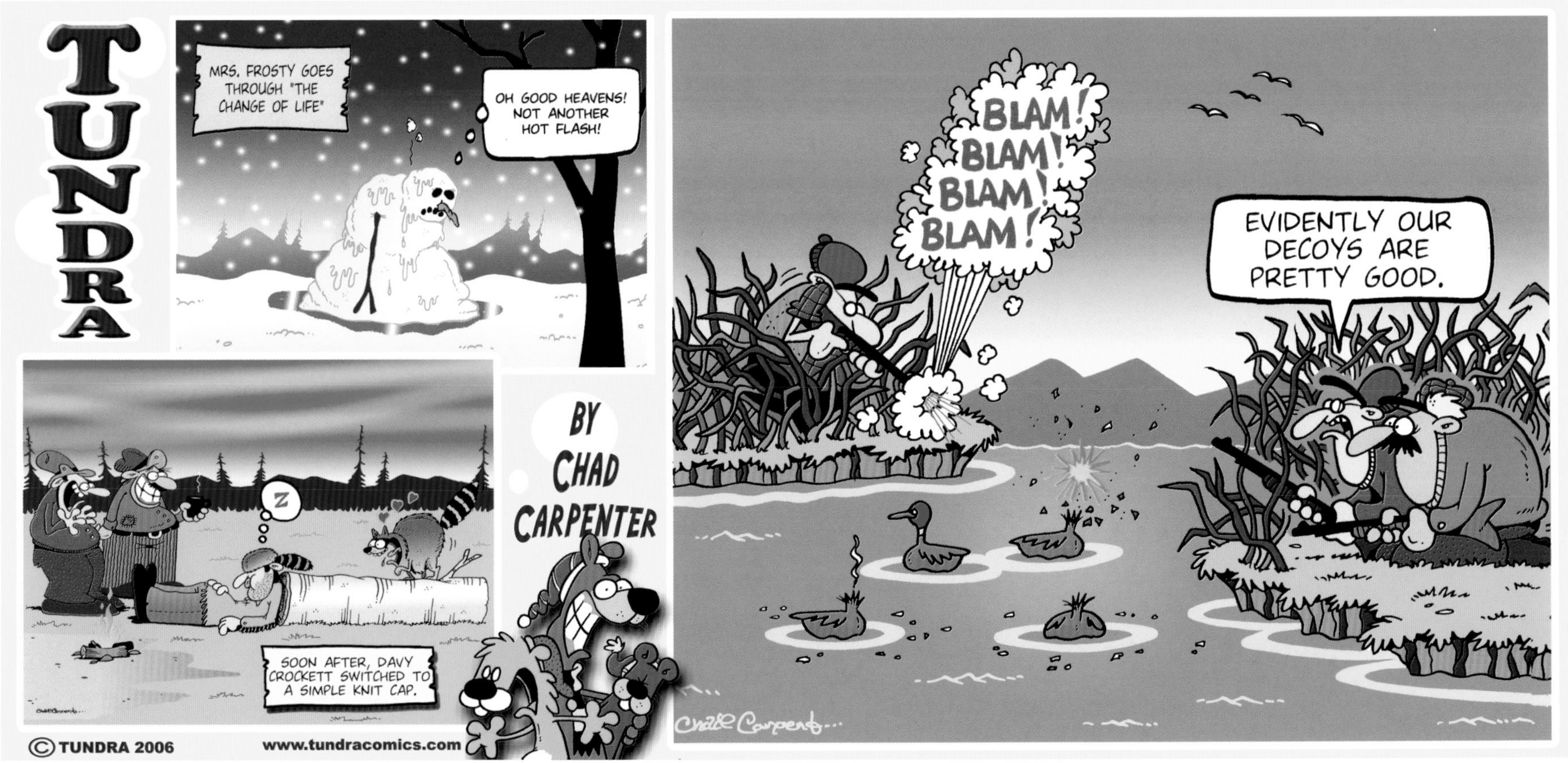
TUNDRA
MRS. FROSTY GOES THROUGH "THE CHANGE OF LIFE"
OH GOOD HEAVENS! NOT ANOTHER HOT FLASH!
Z
SOON AFTER, DAVY CROCKETT SWITCHED TO A SIMPLE KNIT CAP.
BY CHAD CARPENTER
BLAM! BLAM! BLAM! BLAM!
EVIDENTLY OUR DECOYS ARE PRETTY GOOD.
©TUNDRA 2006
www.tundracomics.com

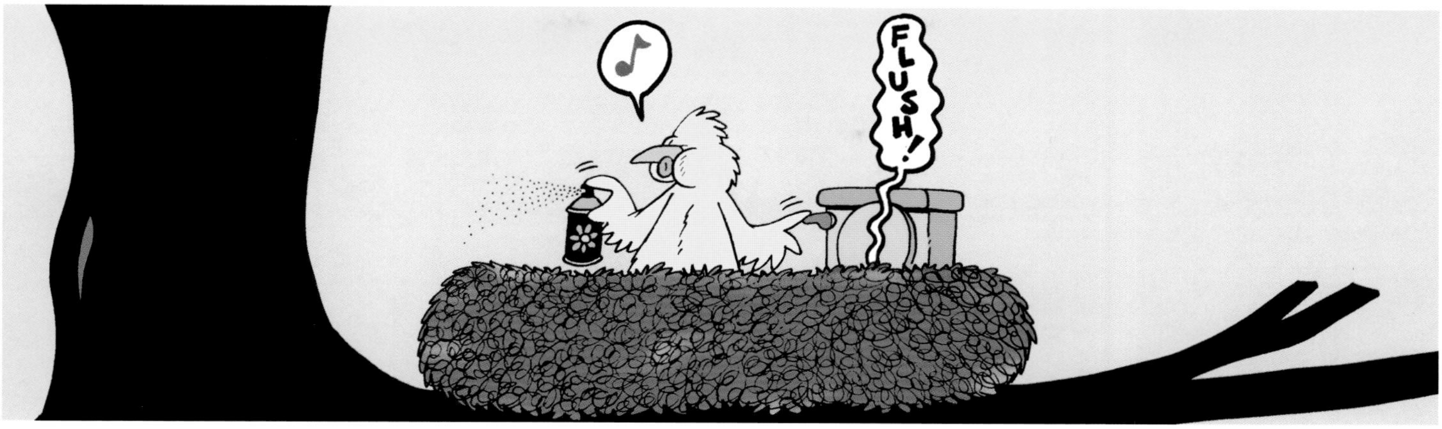
FLUSH!

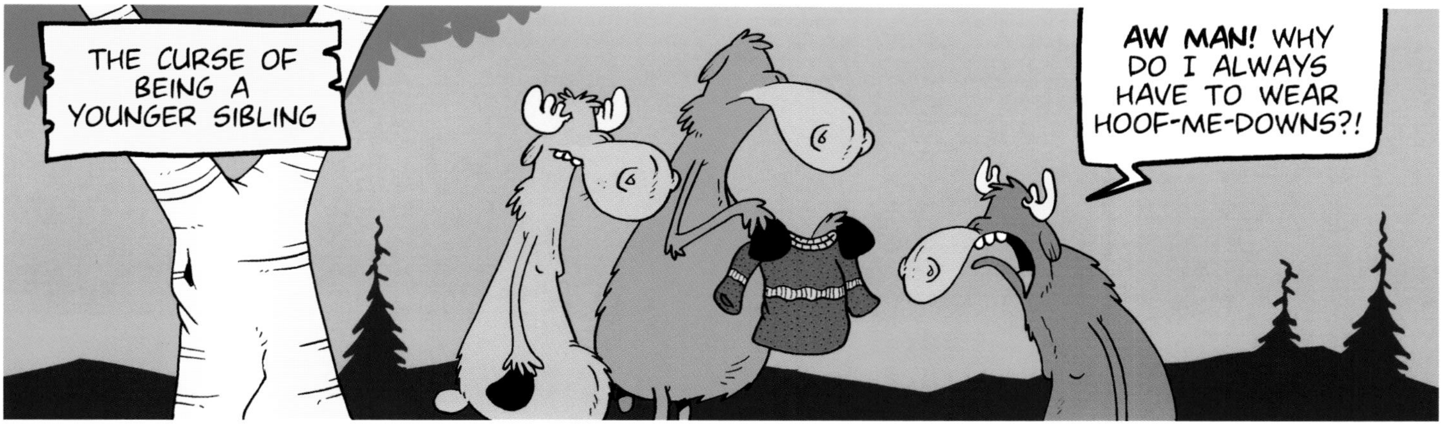
THE CURSE OF BEING A YOUNGER SIBLING
AW MAN! WHY DO I ALWAYS HAVE TO WEAR HOOF-ME-DOWNS?!

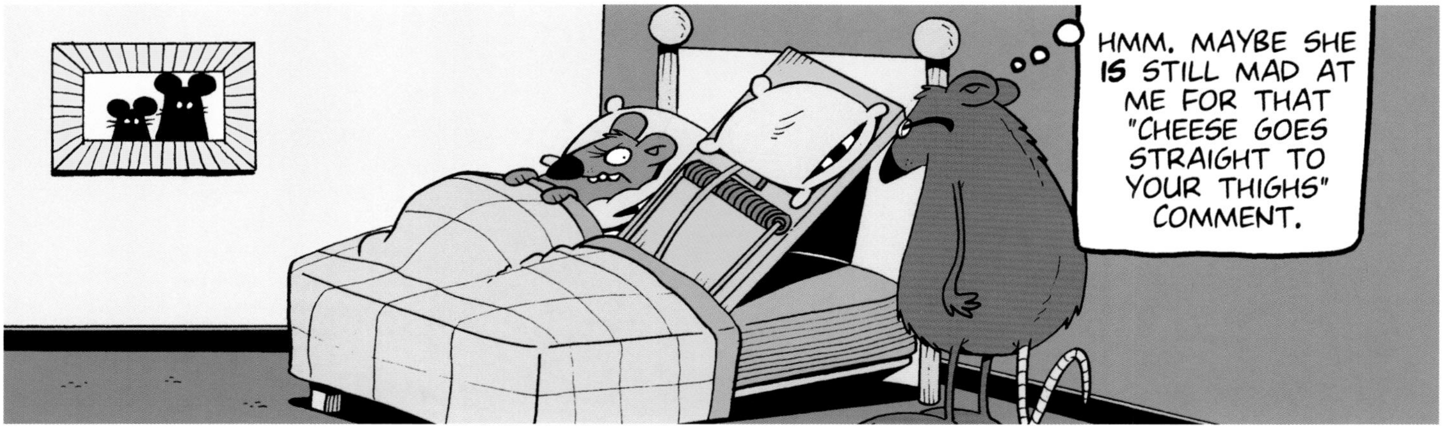
HMM. MAYBE SHE IS STILL MAD AT ME FOR THAT "CHEESE GOES STRAIGHT TO YOUR THIGHS" COMMENT.

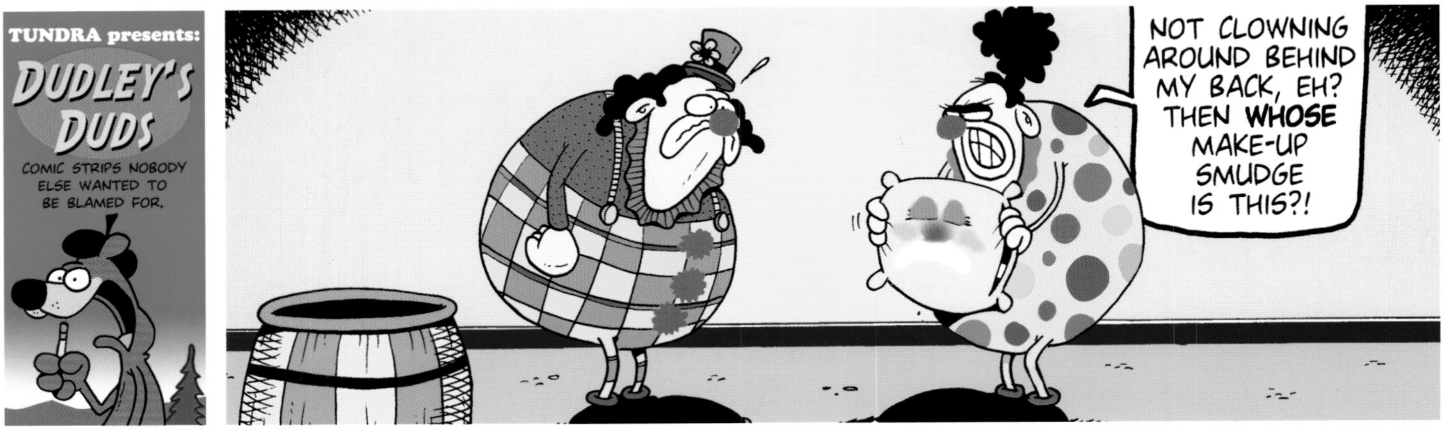
TUNDRA presents:
DUDLEY'S DUDS
COMIC STRIPS NOBODY ELSE WANTED TO BE BLAMED FOR.
NOT CLOWNING AROUND BEHIND MY BACK, EH? THEN **WHOSE** MAKE-UP SMUDGE IS THIS?!

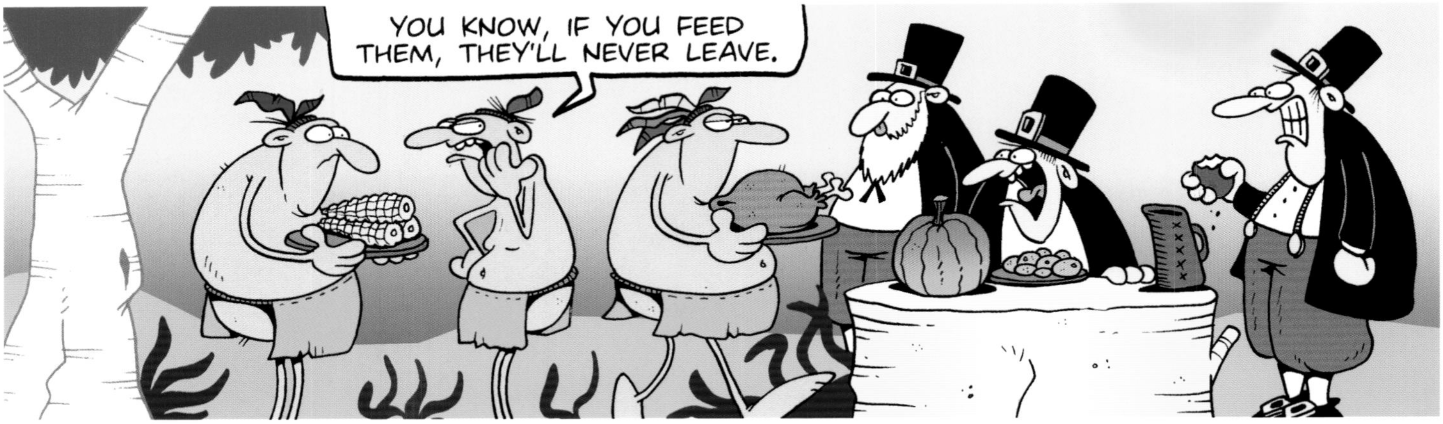
YOU KNOW, IF YOU FEED THEM, THEY'LL NEVER LEAVE.

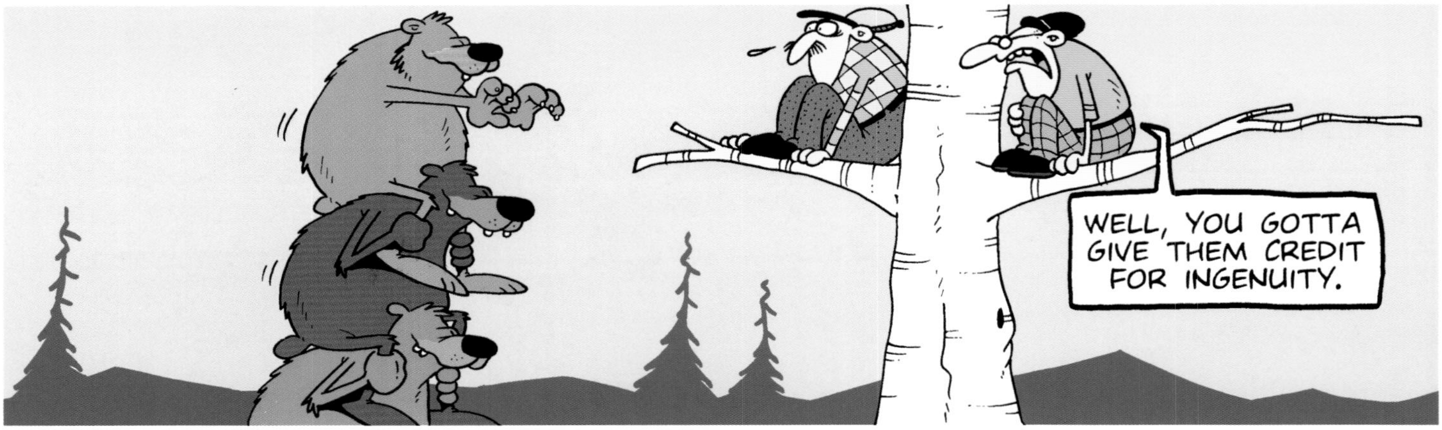
WELL, YOU GOTTA GIVE THEM CREDIT FOR INGENUITY.

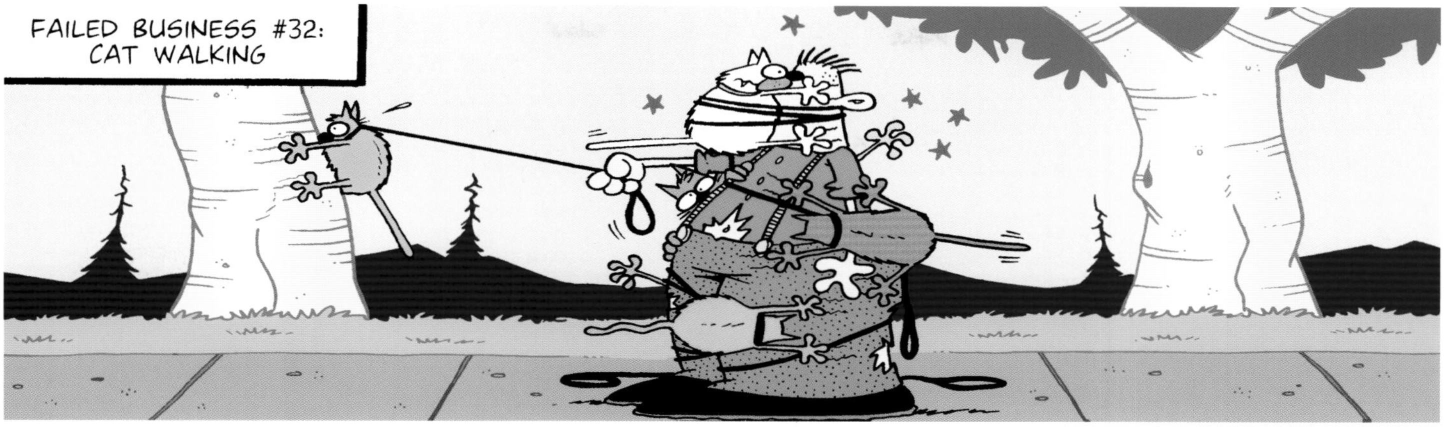
FAILED BUSINESS #32: CAT WALKING

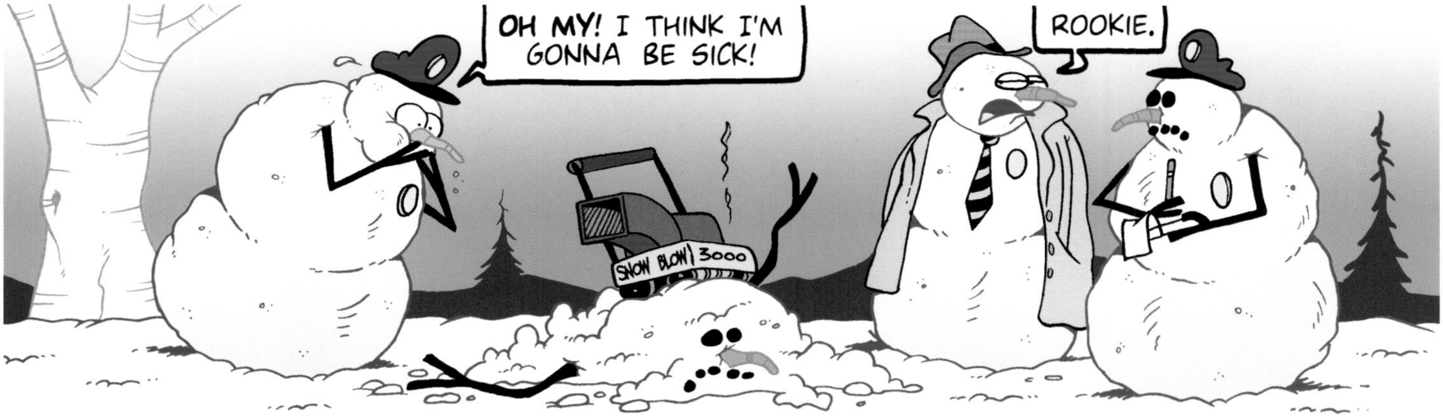
OH MY! I THINK I'M GONNA BE SICK!
ROOKIE.
SNOW BLOW! 3000

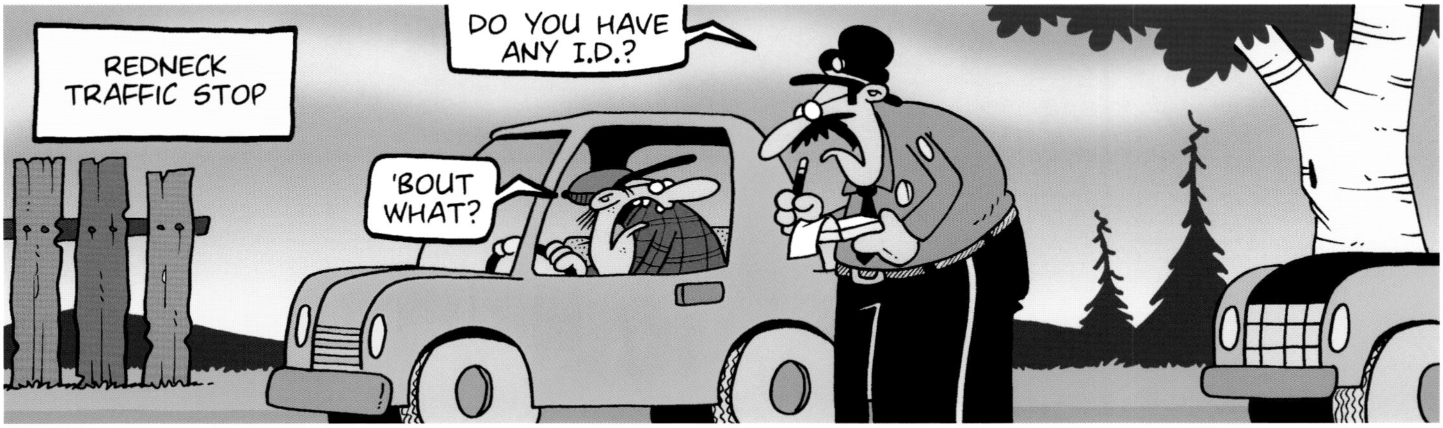
REDNECK TRAFFIC STOP
DO YOU HAVE ANY I.D.?
'BOUT WHAT?

CHAD CARPENTER'S
TUNDRA
SNAP!
I GUESS I SHOULDA WARNED YA NOT TO SIT DOWN TOO HARD. SEEMS WE GOT A FEW SINK-HOLES 'ROUND THESE PARTS.
©TUNDRA 2005
www.tundracomics.com
DON'T YOU WORRY MA'AM. WE'LL HAVE YOUR PRECIOUS LITTLE KITTY OUT OF THAT TREE IN NO TIME.
MEW.

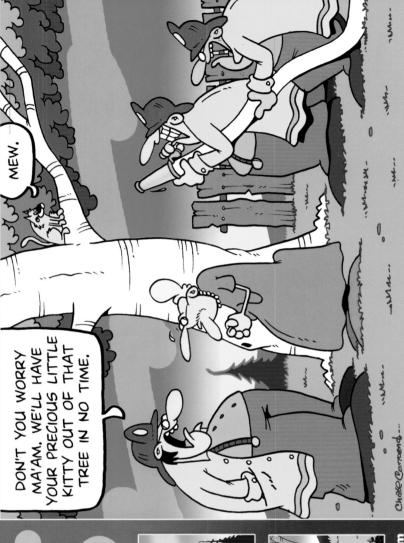

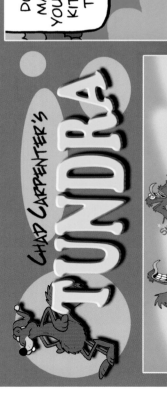

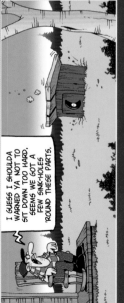

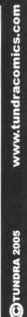

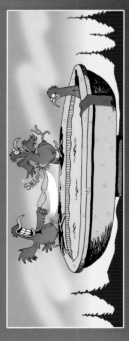

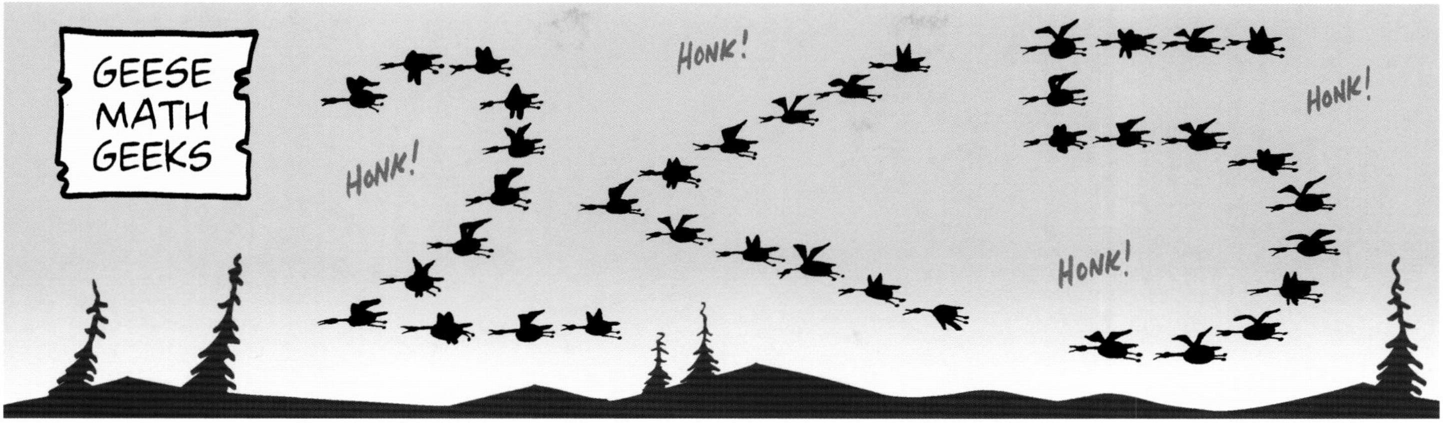
GEESE MATH GEEKS
HONK!
HONK!
HONK!
HONK!

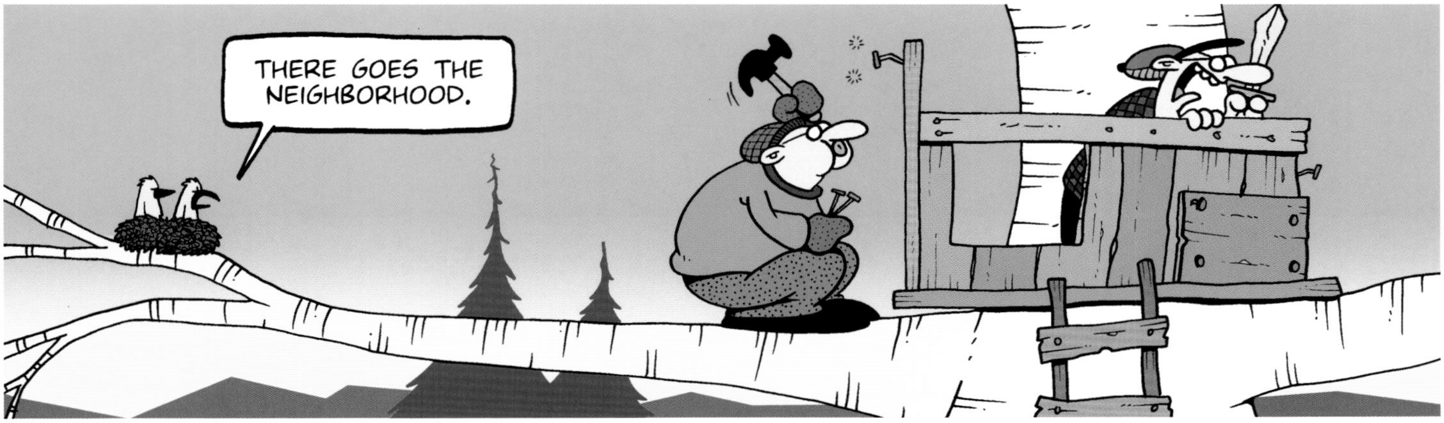
THERE GOES THE NEIGHBORHOOD.

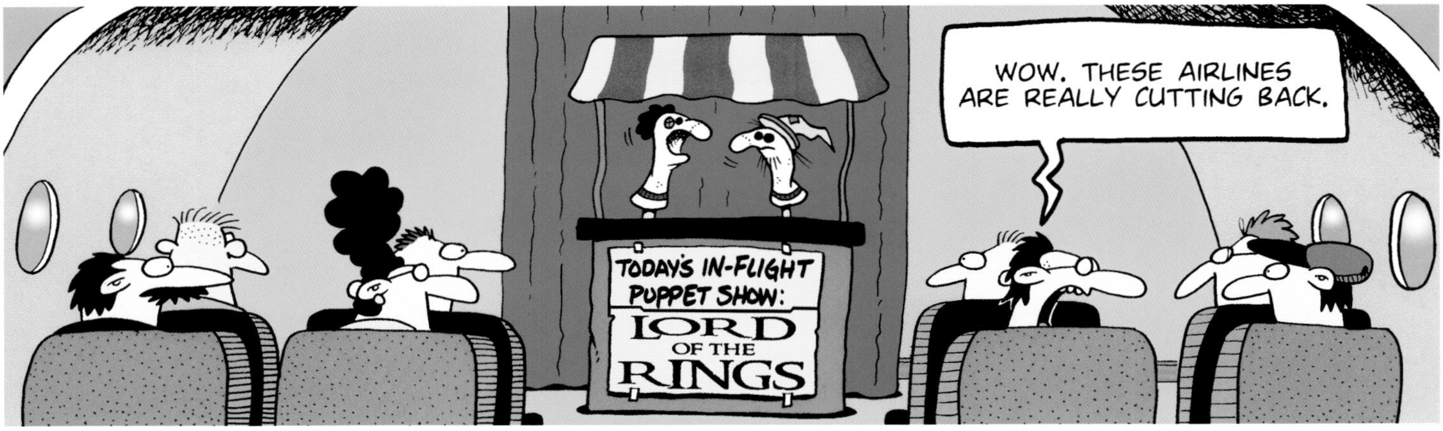
TODAY'S IN-FLIGHT PUPPET SHOW: LORD OF THE RINGS
WOW. THESE AIRLINES ARE REALLY CUTTING BACK.

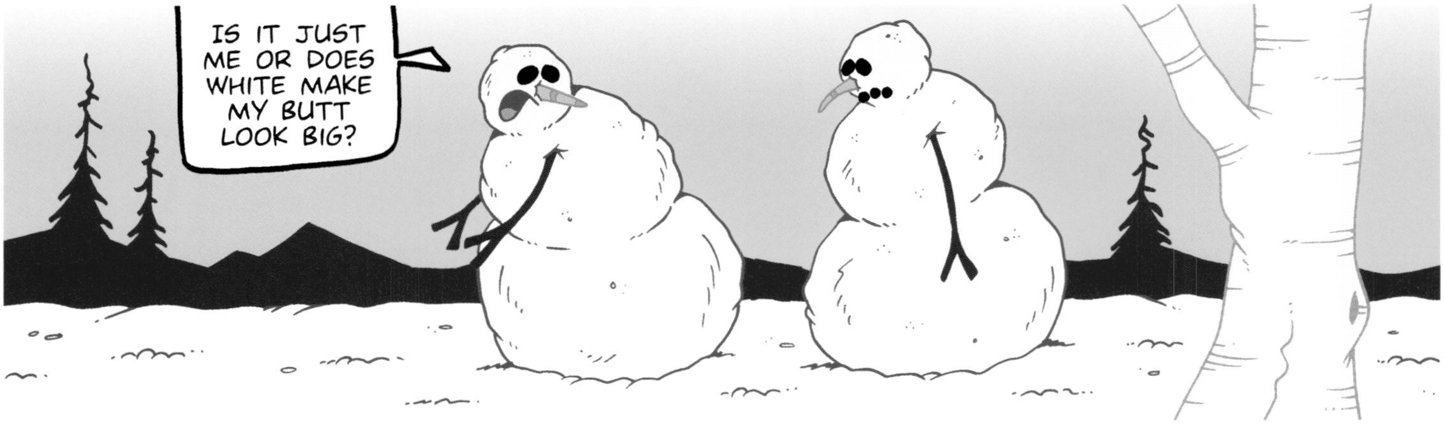
IS IT JUST ME OR DOES WHITE MAKE MY BUTT LOOK BIG?

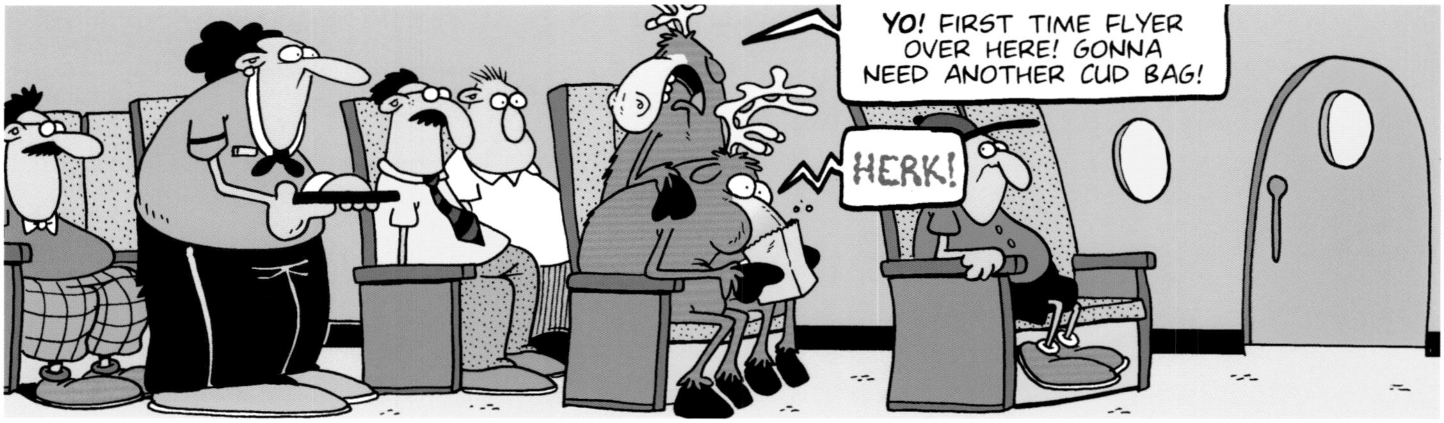
YO! FIRST TIME FLYER OVER HERE! GONNA NEED ANOTHER CUD BAG!
HERK!

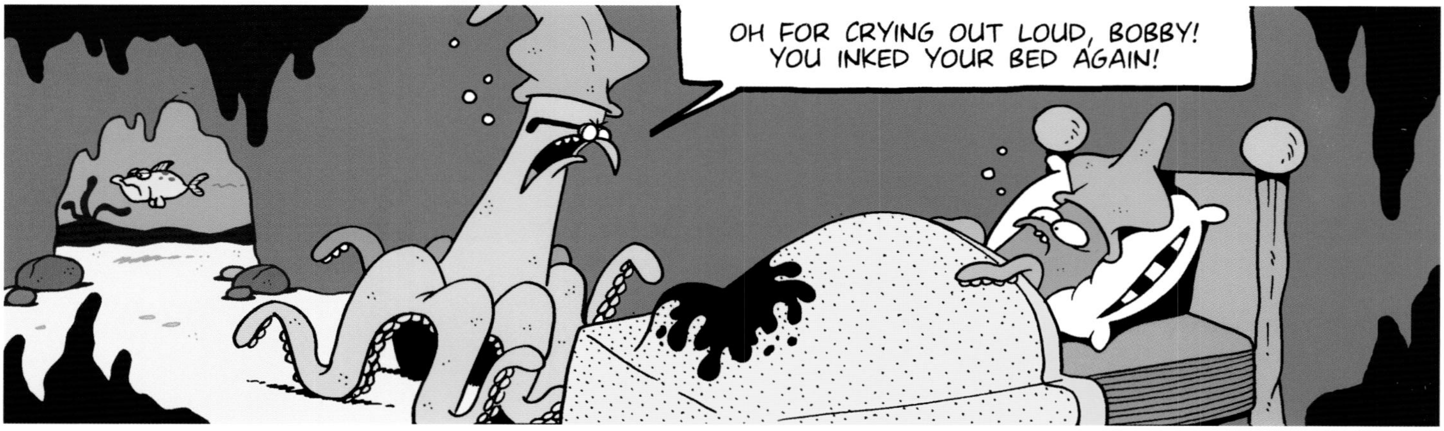
OH FOR CRYING OUT LOUD, BOBBY! YOU INKED YOUR BED AGAIN!

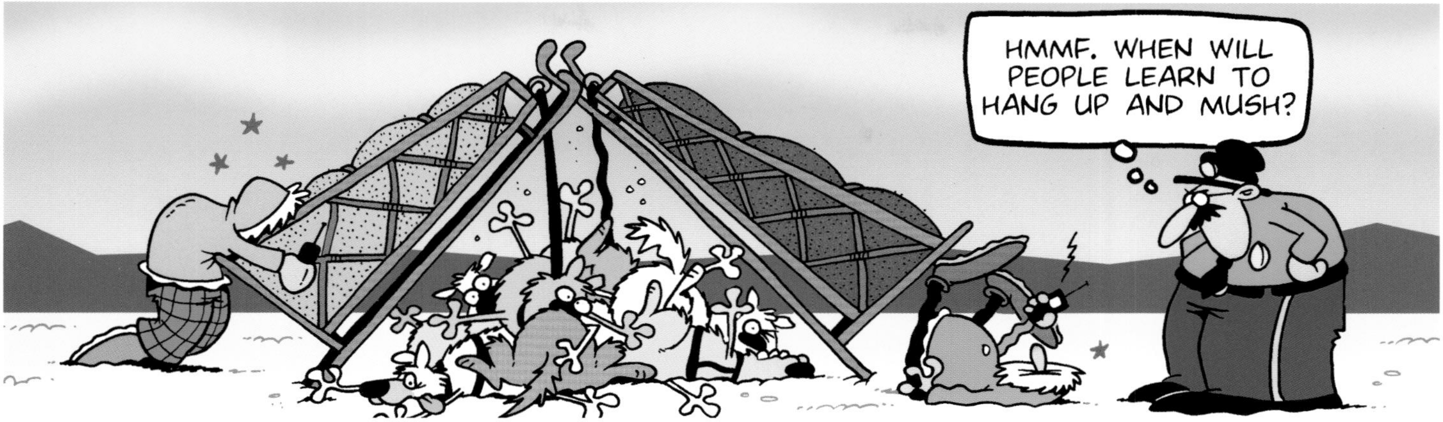
HMMF. WHEN WILL PEOPLE LEARN TO HANG UP AND MUSH?

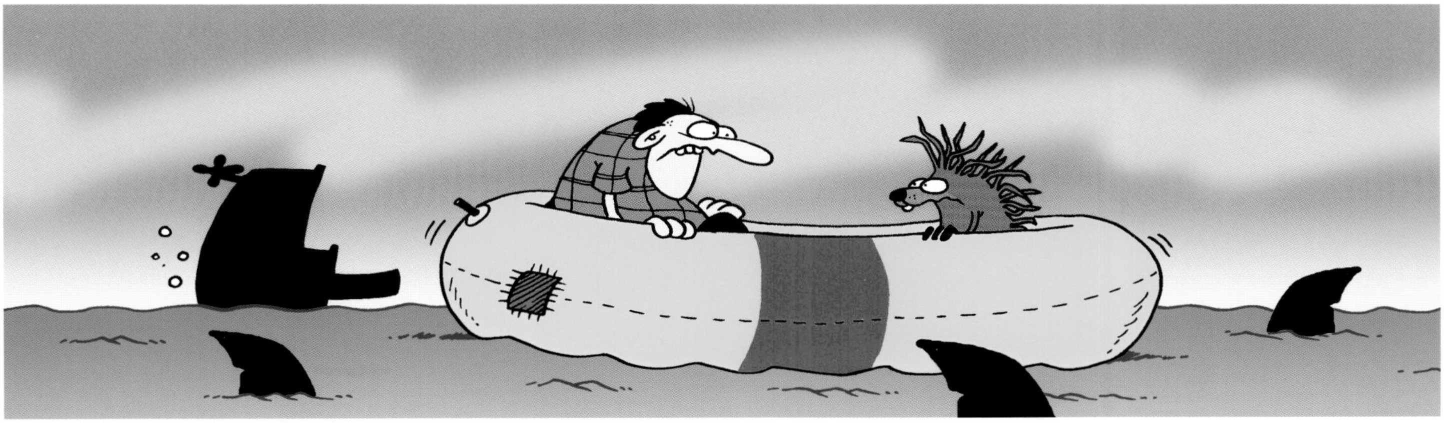

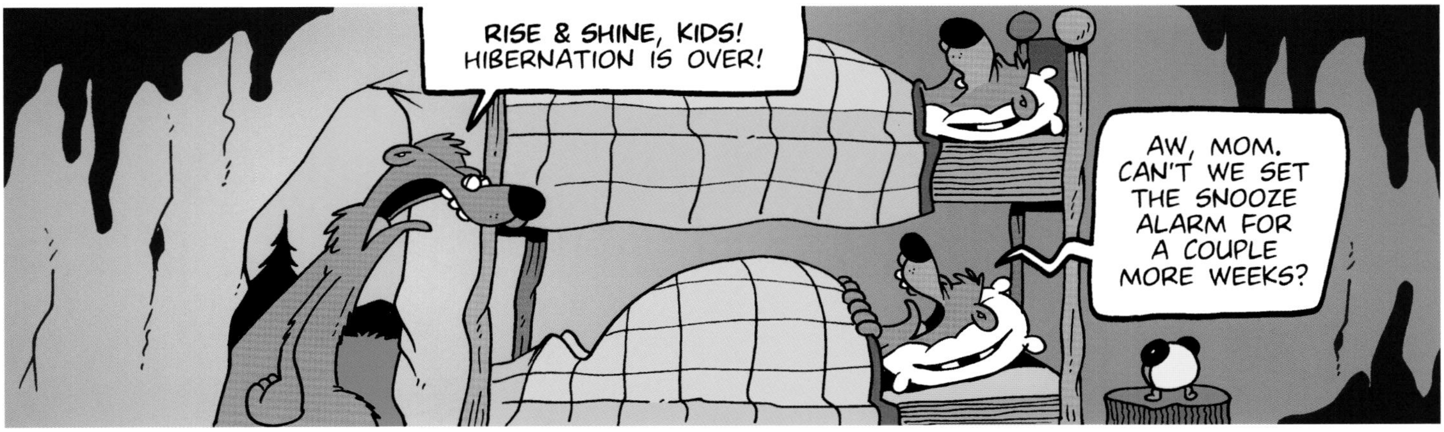
RISE & SHINE, KIDS! HIBERNATION IS OVER!
AW, MOM. CAN'T WE SET THE SNOOZE ALARM FOR A COUPLE MORE WEEKS?

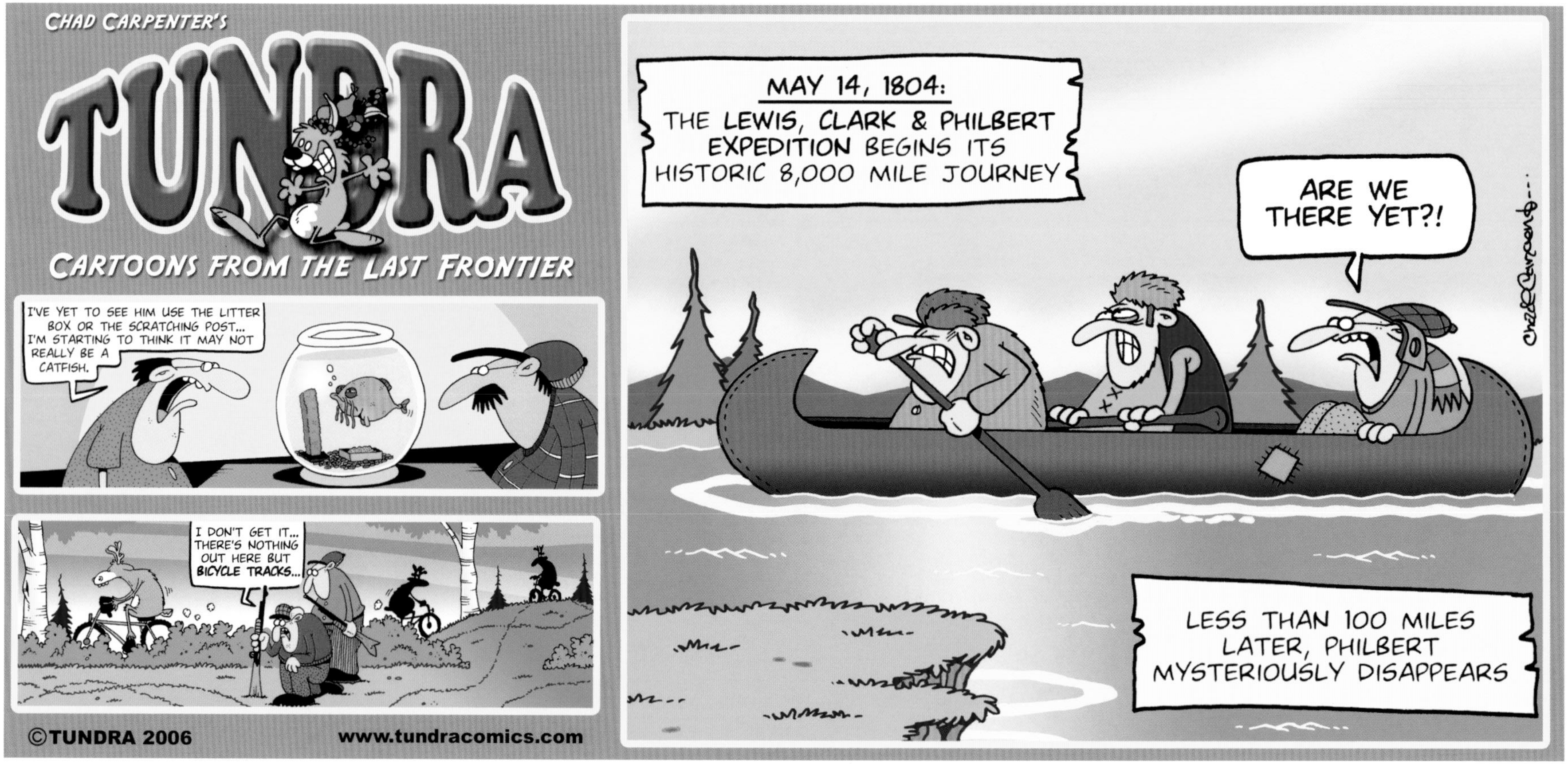
CHAD CARPENTER'S
TUNDRA
CARTOONS FROM THE LAST FRONTIER
I'VE YET TO SEE HIM USE THE LITTER BOX OR THE SCRATCHING POST... I'M STARTING TO THINK IT MAY NOT REALLY BE A CATFISH.
I DON'T GET IT... THERE'S NOTHING OUT HERE BUT BICYCLE TRACKS...
©TUNDRA 2006
www.tundracomics.com
MAY 14, 1804:
THE LEWIS, CLARK & PHILBERT EXPEDITION BEGINS ITS HISTORIC 8,000 MILE JOURNEY
ARE WE THERE YET?!
LESS THAN 100 MILES LATER, PHILBERT MYSTERIOUSLY DISAPPEARS

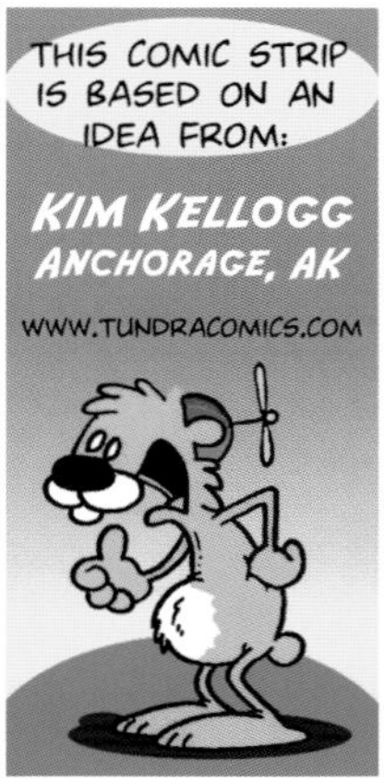
THIS COMIC STRIP IS BASED ON AN IDEA FROM:
KIM KELLOGG
ANCHORAGE, AK
WWW.TUNDRACOMICS.COM

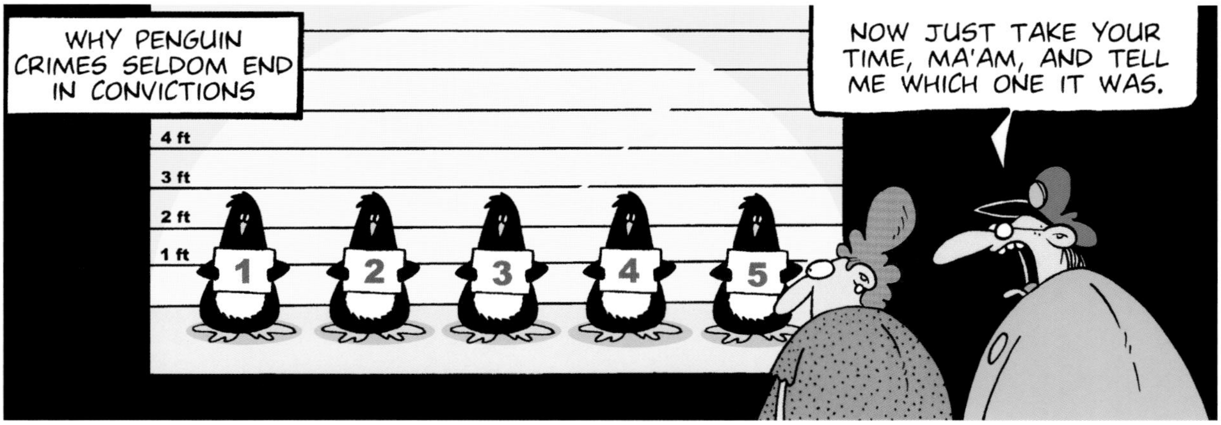
WHY PENGUIN CRIMES SELDOM END IN CONVICTIONS
4 ft
3 ft
2 ft
1 ft
1
2
3
4
5
NOW JUST TAKE YOUR TIME, MA'AM, AND TELL ME WHICH ONE IT WAS.

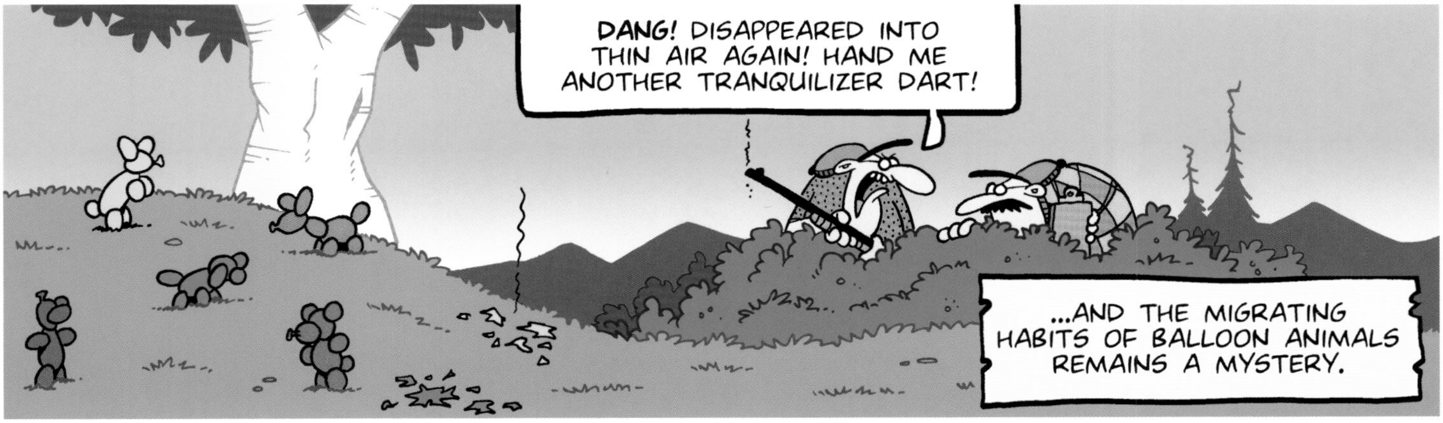
DANG! DISAPPEARED INTO THIN AIR AGAIN! HAND ME ANOTHER TRANQUILIZER DART!
...AND THE MIGRATING HABITS OF BALLOON ANIMALS REMAINS A MYSTERY.

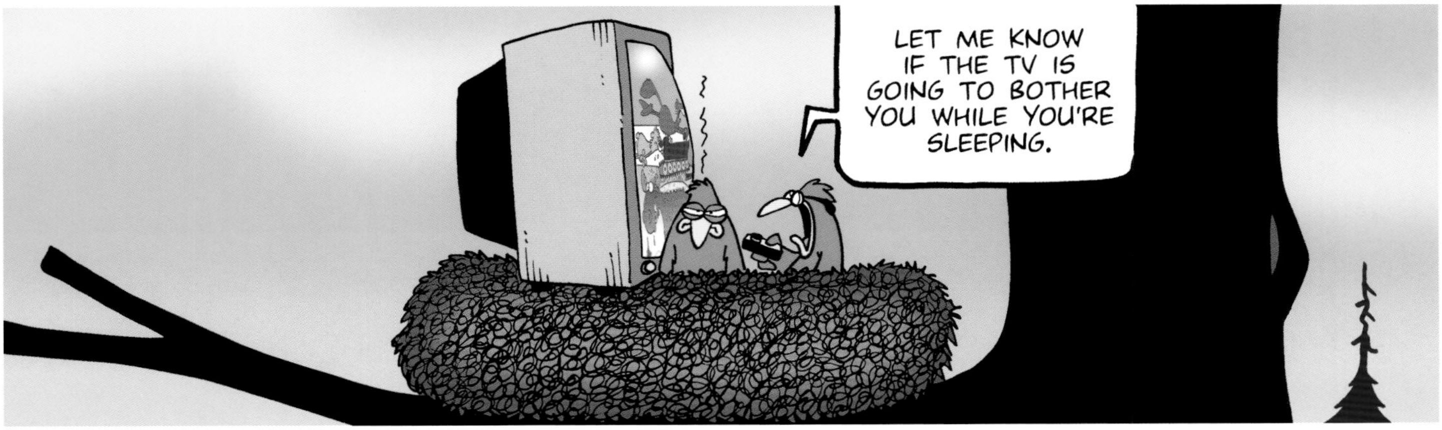
LET ME KNOW IF THE TV IS GOING TO BOTHER YOU WHILE YOU'RE SLEEPING.

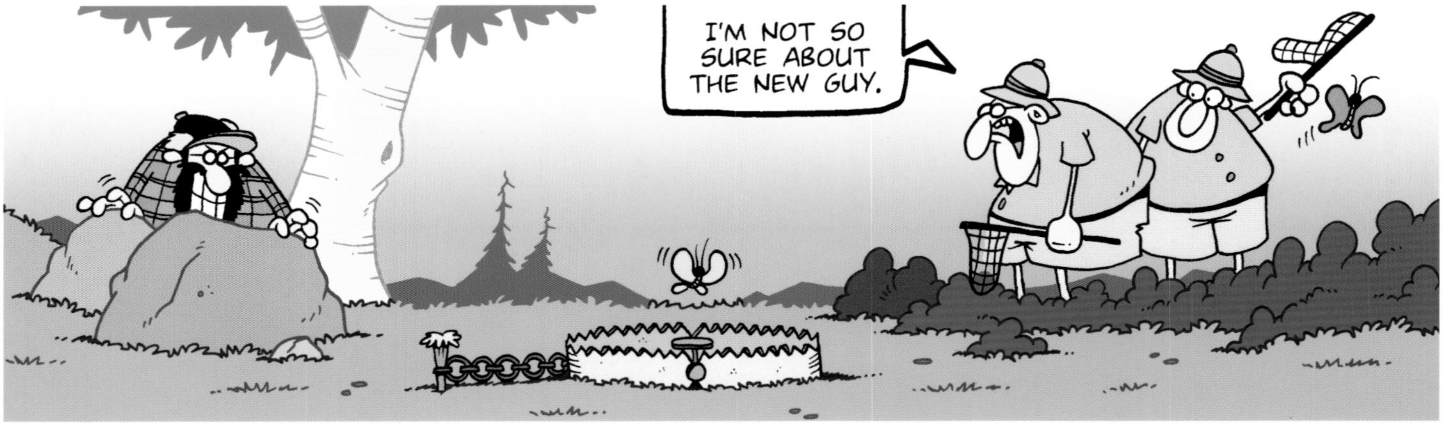
I'M NOT SO SURE ABOUT THE NEW GUY.

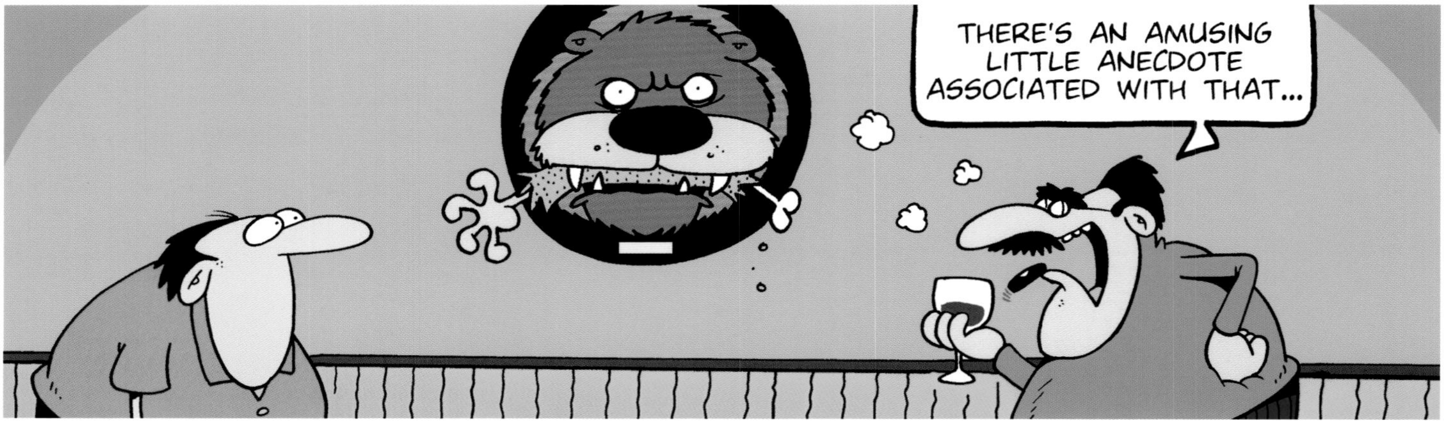
THERE'S AN AMUSING LITTLE ANECDOTE ASSOCIATED WITH THAT...

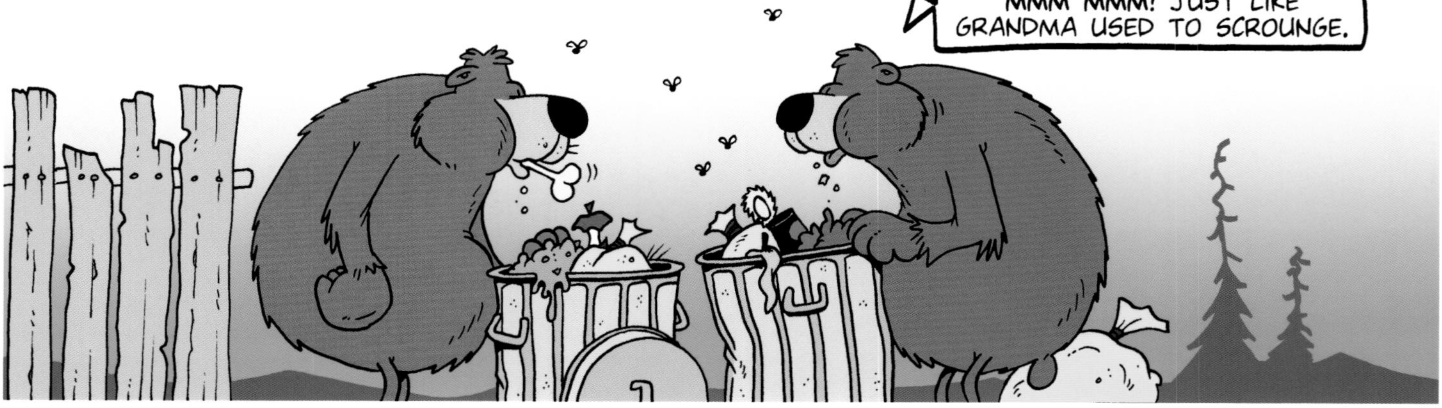
MMM MMM! JUST LIKE GRANDMA USED TO SCROUNGE.

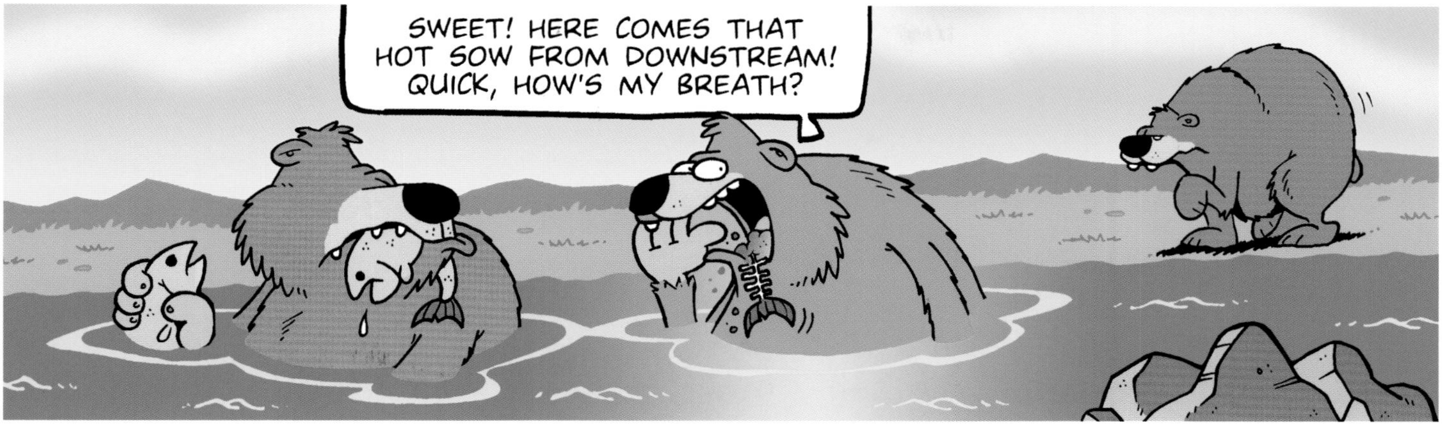
SWEET! HERE COMES THAT HOT SOW FROM DOWNSTREAM! QUICK, HOW'S MY BREATH?

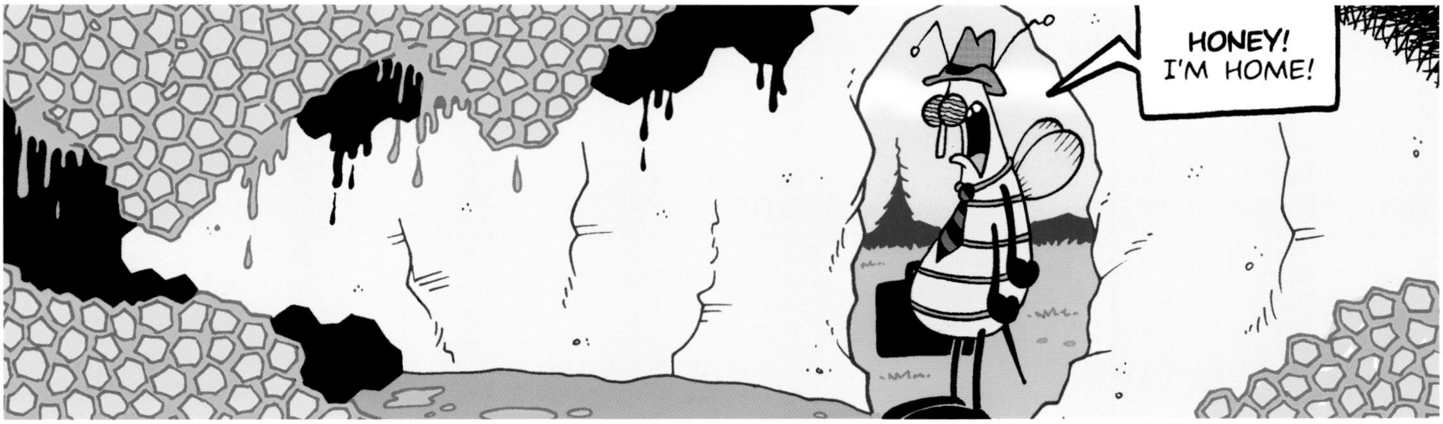
HONEY! I'M HOME!

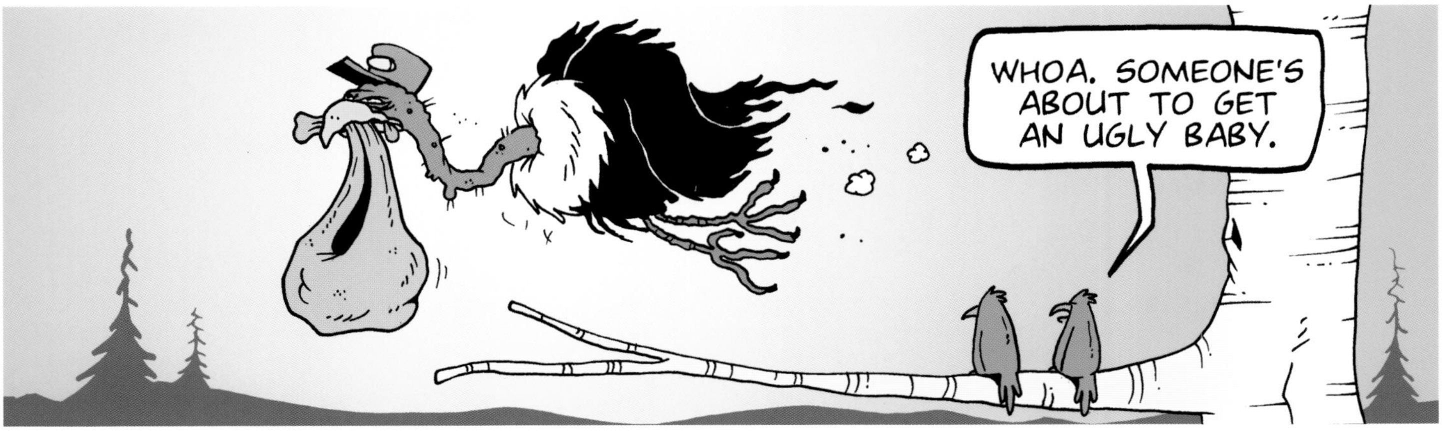
WHOA. SOMEONE'S ABOUT TO GET AN UGLY BABY.

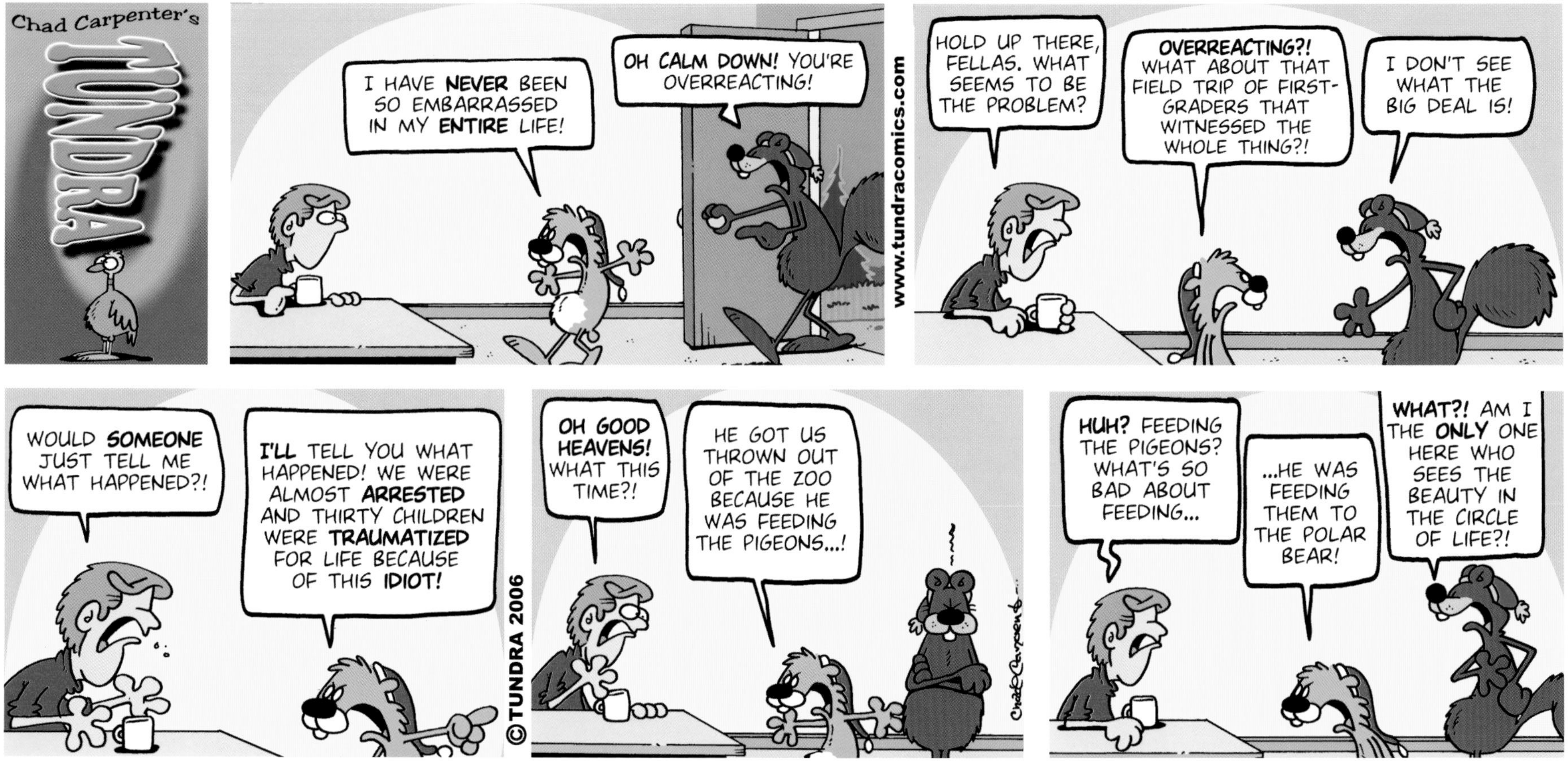
Chad Carpenter's
TUNDRA
I HAVE NEVER BEEN SO EMBARRASSED IN MY ENTIRE LIFE!
OH CALM DOWN! YOU'RE OVERREACTING!
www.tundracomics.com
HOLD UP THERE, FELLAS. WHAT SEEMS TO BE THE PROBLEM?
OVERREACTING?! WHAT ABOUT THAT FIELD TRIP OF FIRST-GRADERS THAT WITNESSED THE WHOLE THING?!
I DON'T SEE WHAT THE BIG DEAL IS!
WOULD SOMEONE JUST TELL ME WHAT HAPPENED?!
I'LL TELL YOU WHAT HAPPENED! WE WERE ALMOST ARRESTED AND THIRTY CHILDREN WERE TRAUMATIZED FOR LIFE BECAUSE OF THIS IDIOT!
©TUNDRA 2006
OH GOOD HEAVENS! WHAT THIS TIME?!
HE GOT US THROWN OUT OF THE ZOO BECAUSE HE WAS FEEDING THE PIGEONS...!
HUH? FEEDING THE PIGEONS? WHAT'S SO BAD ABOUT FEEDING...
...HE WAS FEEDING THEM TO THE POLAR BEAR!
WHAT?! AM I THE ONLY ONE HERE WHO SEES THE BEAUTY IN THE CIRCLE OF LIFE?!

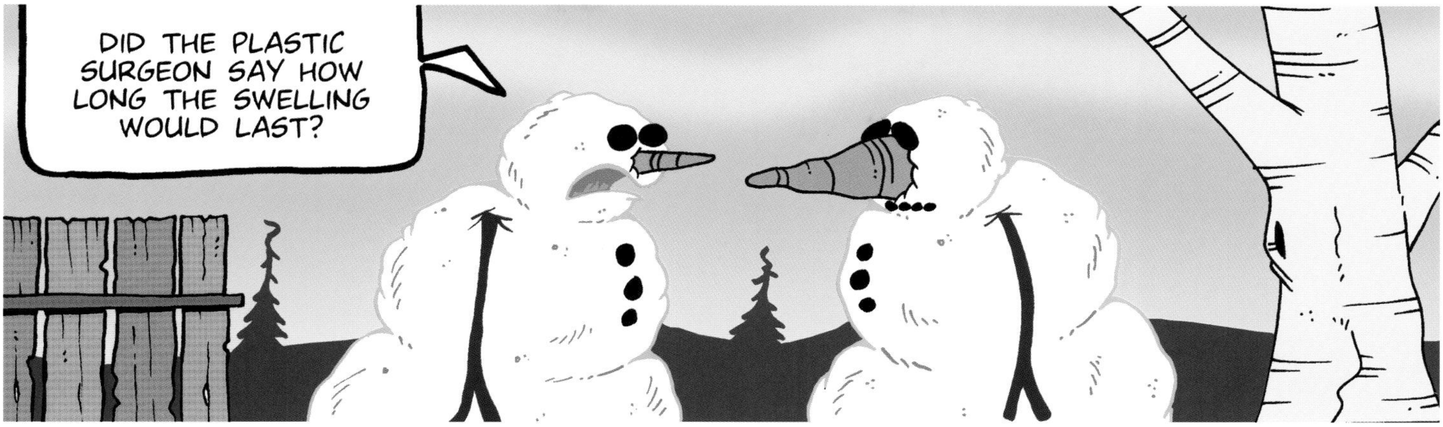
DID THE PLASTIC SURGEON SAY HOW LONG THE SWELLING WOULD LAST?

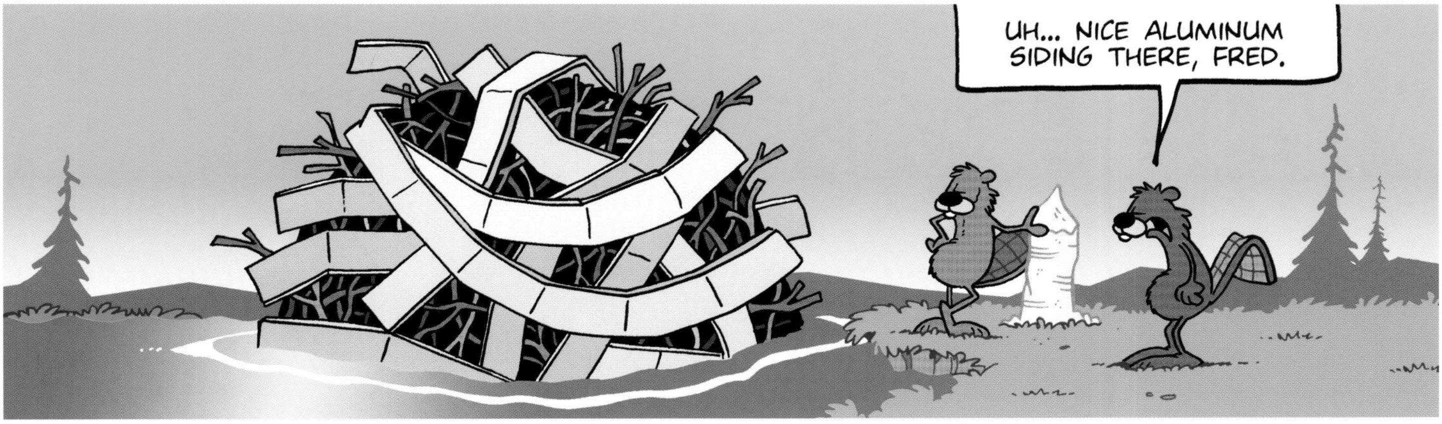
UH... NICE ALUMINUM SIDING THERE, FRED.

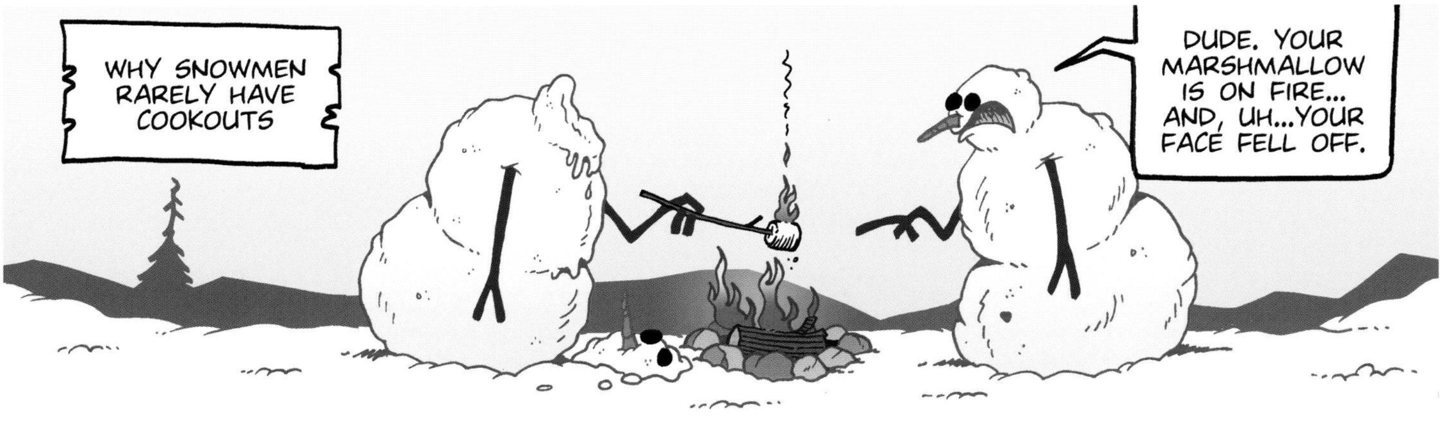
WHY SNOWMEN RARELY HAVE COOKOUTS
DUDE. YOUR MARSHMALLOW IS ON FIRE... AND, UH...YOUR FACE FELL OFF.

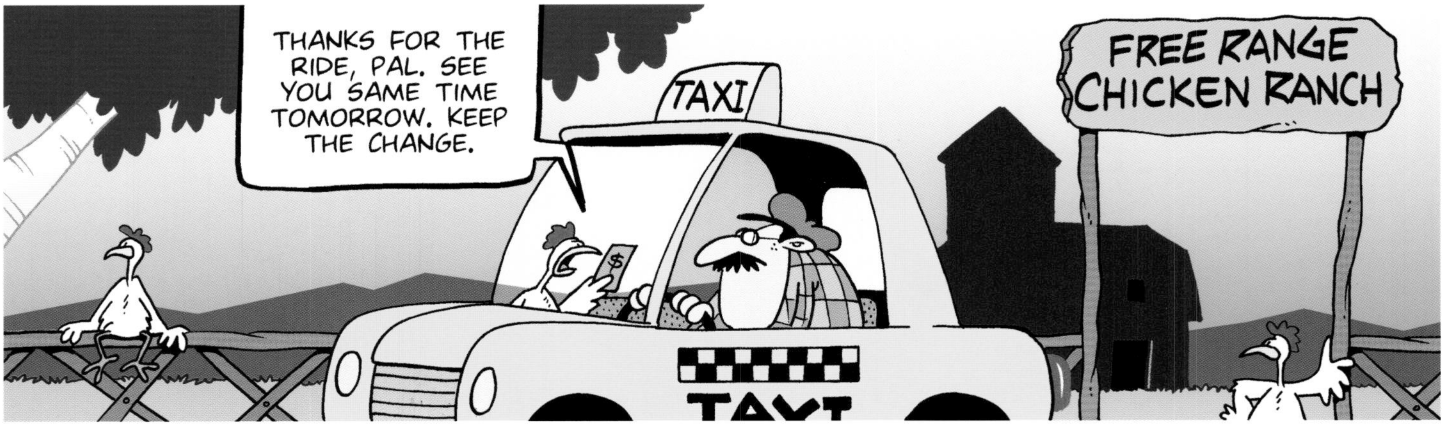
THANKS FOR THE RIDE, PAL. SEE YOU SAME TIME TOMORROW. KEEP THE CHANGE.
TAXI
FREE RANGE CHICKEN RANCH

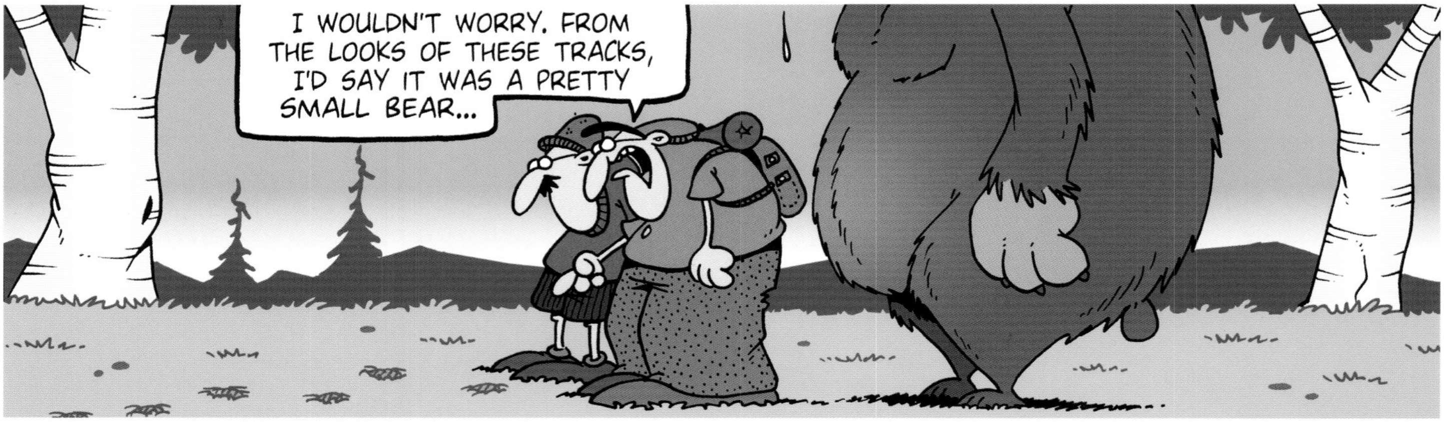
I WOULDN'T WORRY. FROM THE LOOKS OF THESE TRACKS, I'D SAY IT WAS A PRETTY SMALL BEAR...

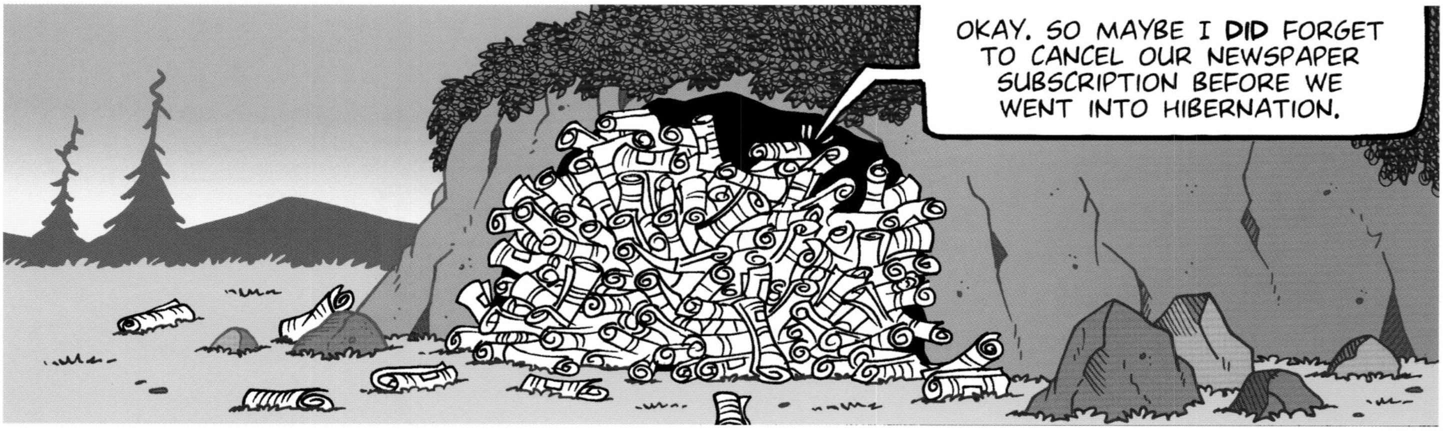
OKAY. SO MAYBE I **DID** FORGET TO CANCEL OUR NEWSPAPER SUBSCRIPTION BEFORE WE WENT INTO HIBERNATION.

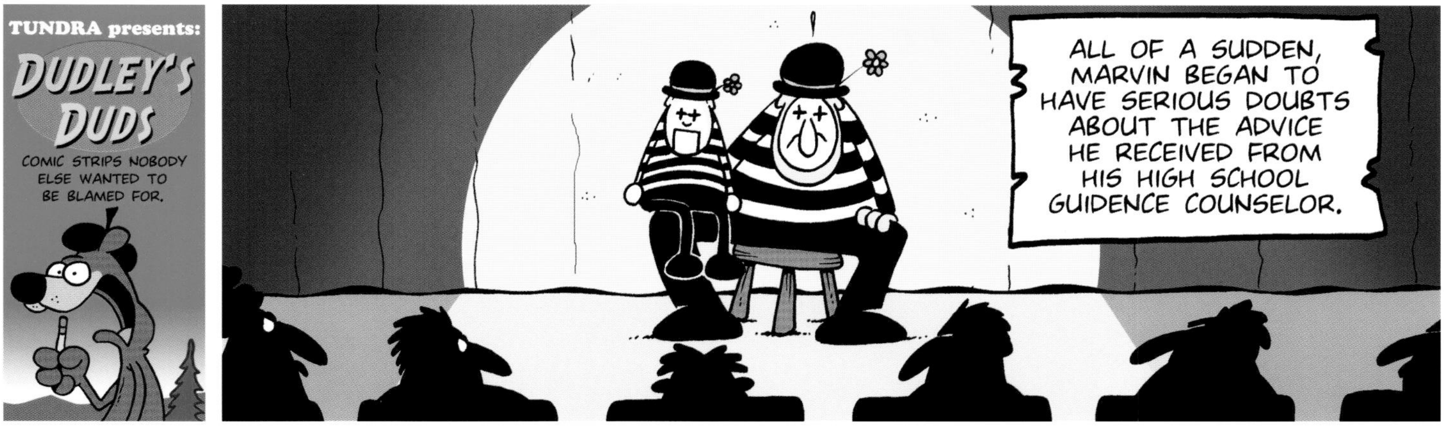
TUNDRA presents:
DUDLEY'S DUDS
COMIC STRIPS NOBODY ELSE WANTED TO BE BLAMED FOR.
ALL OF A SUDDEN, MARVIN BEGAN TO HAVE SERIOUS DOUBTS ABOUT THE ADVICE HE RECEIVED FROM HIS HIGH SCHOOL GUIDENCE COUNSELOR.

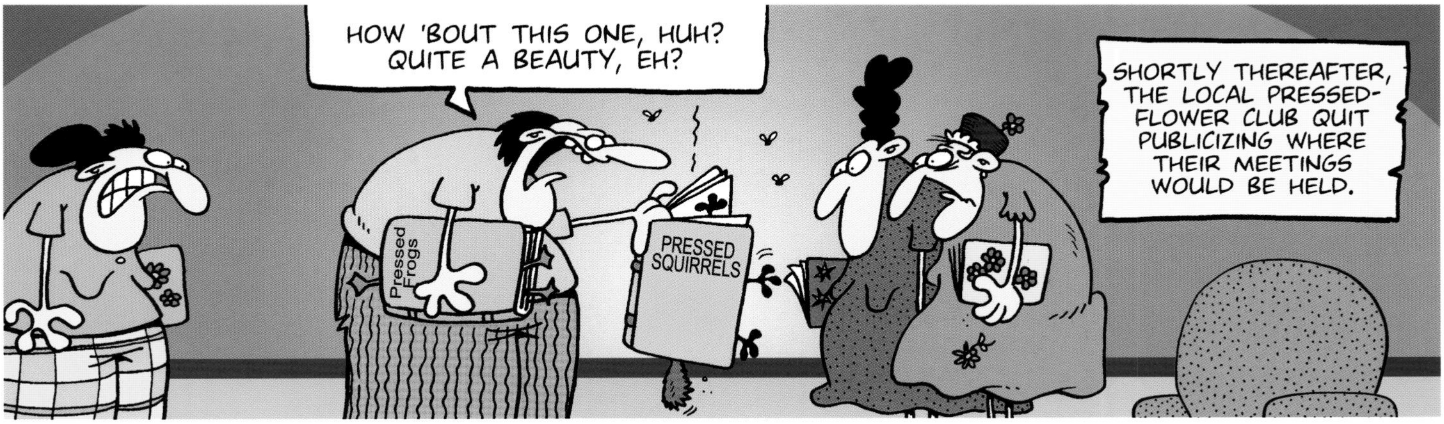
HOW 'BOUT THIS ONE, HUH? QUITE A BEAUTY, EH?
Pressed Frogs
PRESSED SQUIRRELS
SHORTLY THEREAFTER, THE LOCAL PRESSED-FLOWER CLUB QUIT PUBLICIZING WHERE THEIR MEETINGS WOULD BE HELD.

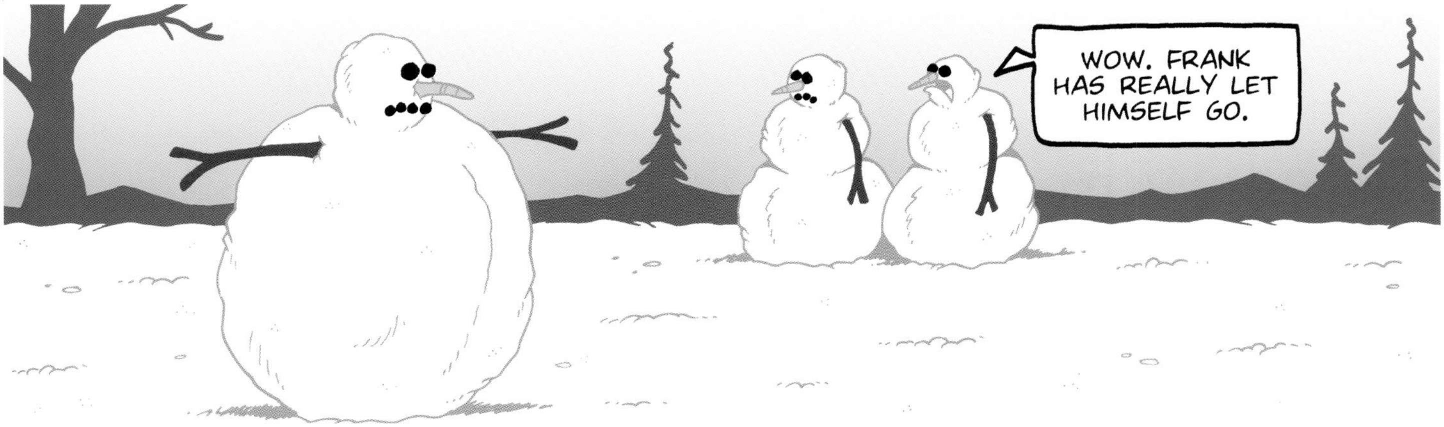
WOW. FRANK HAS REALLY LET HIMSELF GO.

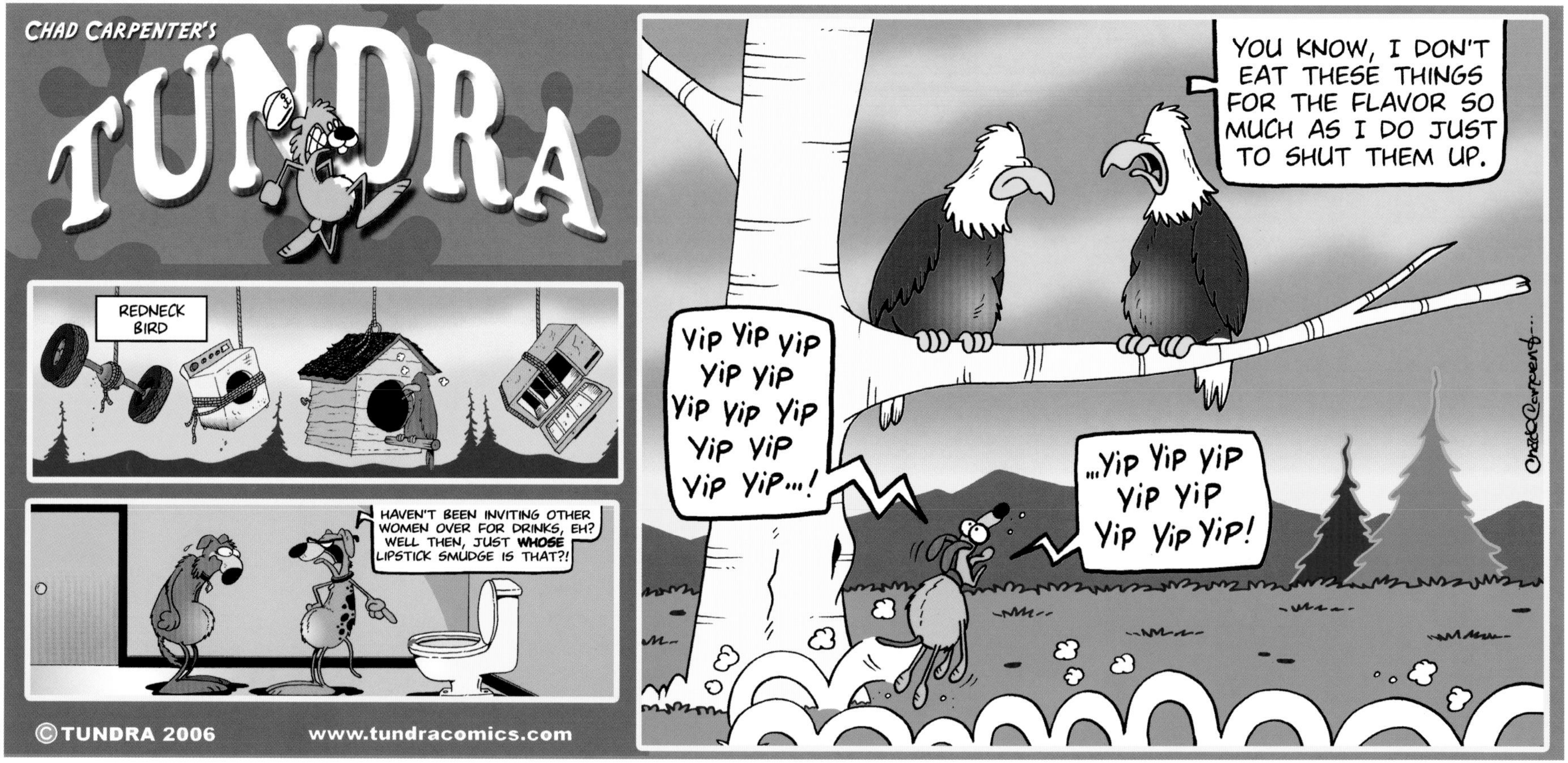
CHAD CARPENTER'S
TUNDRA
REDNECK BIRD
HAVEN'T BEEN INVITING OTHER WOMEN OVER FOR DRINKS, EH? WELL THEN, JUST **WHOSE** LIPSTICK SMUDGE IS THAT?!
©TUNDRA 2006
www.tundracomics.com
YOU KNOW, I DON'T EAT THESE THINGS FOR THE FLAVOR SO MUCH AS I DO JUST TO SHUT THEM UP.
YIP YIP YIP YIP YIP YIP YIP YIP YIP YIP YIP YIP YIP...!
...YIP YIP YIP YIP YIP YIP YIP YIP!

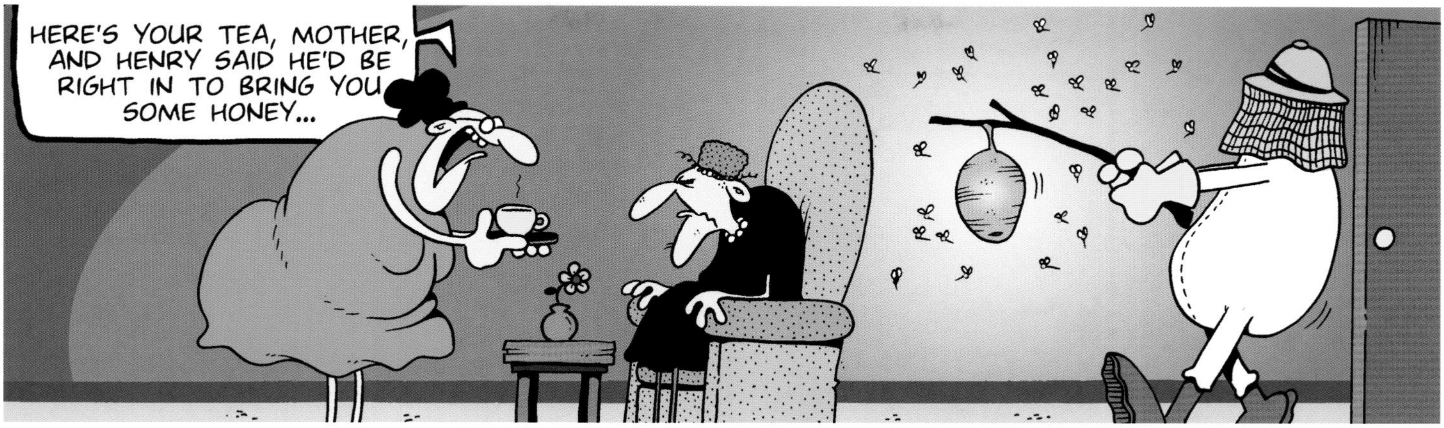
HERE'S YOUR TEA, MOTHER, AND HENRY SAID HE'D BE RIGHT IN TO BRING YOU SOME HONEY...

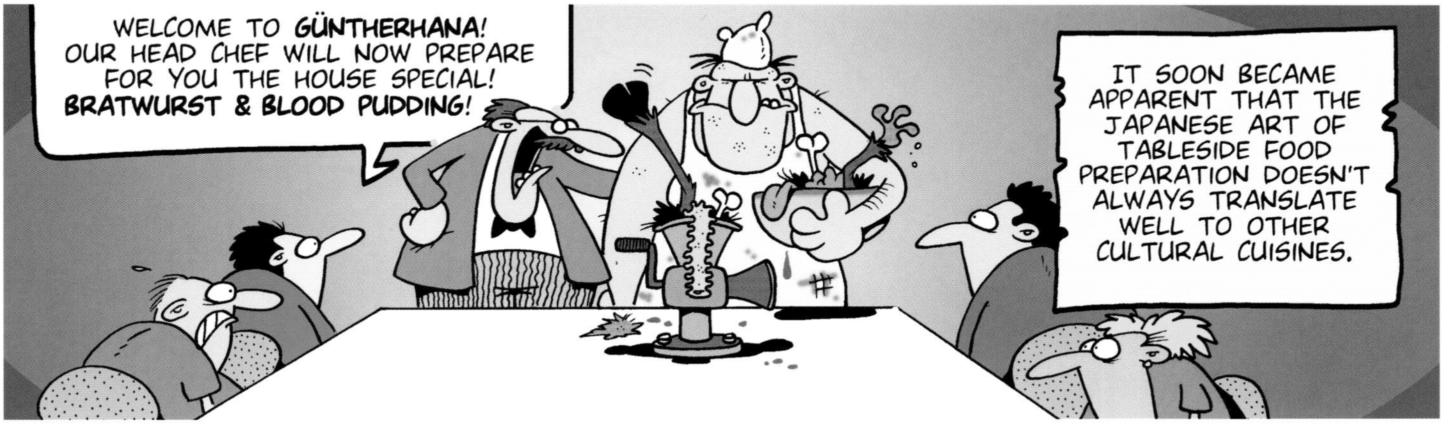
WELCOME TO **GÜNTHERHANA!** OUR HEAD CHEF WILL NOW PREPARE FOR YOU THE HOUSE SPECIAL! **BRATWURST & BLOOD PUDDING!**
IT SOON BECAME APPARENT THAT THE JAPANESE ART OF TABLESIDE FOOD PREPARATION DOESN'T ALWAYS TRANSLATE WELL TO OTHER CULTURAL CUISINES.

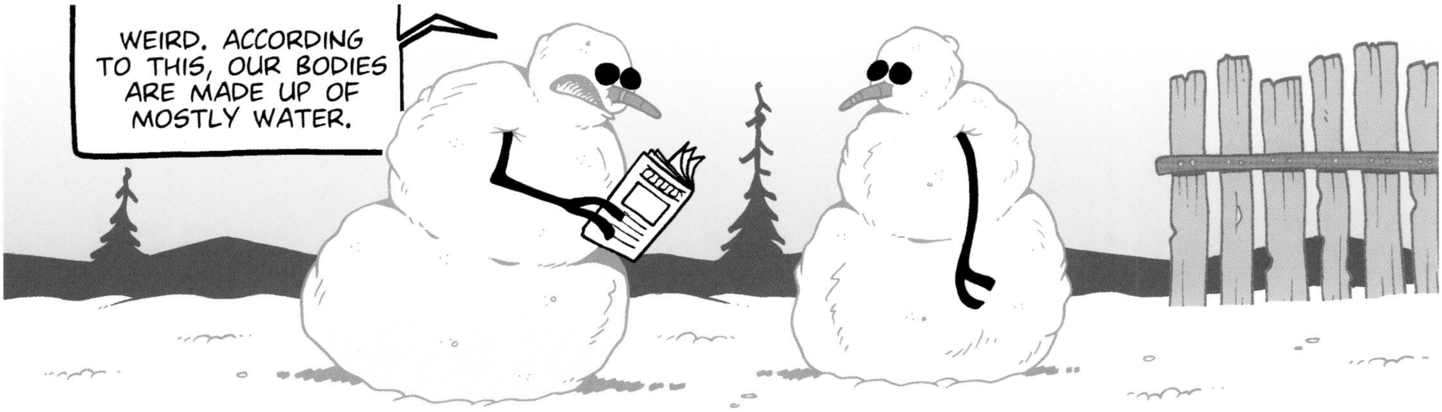
WEIRD. ACCORDING TO THIS, OUR BODIES ARE MADE UP OF MOSTLY WATER.

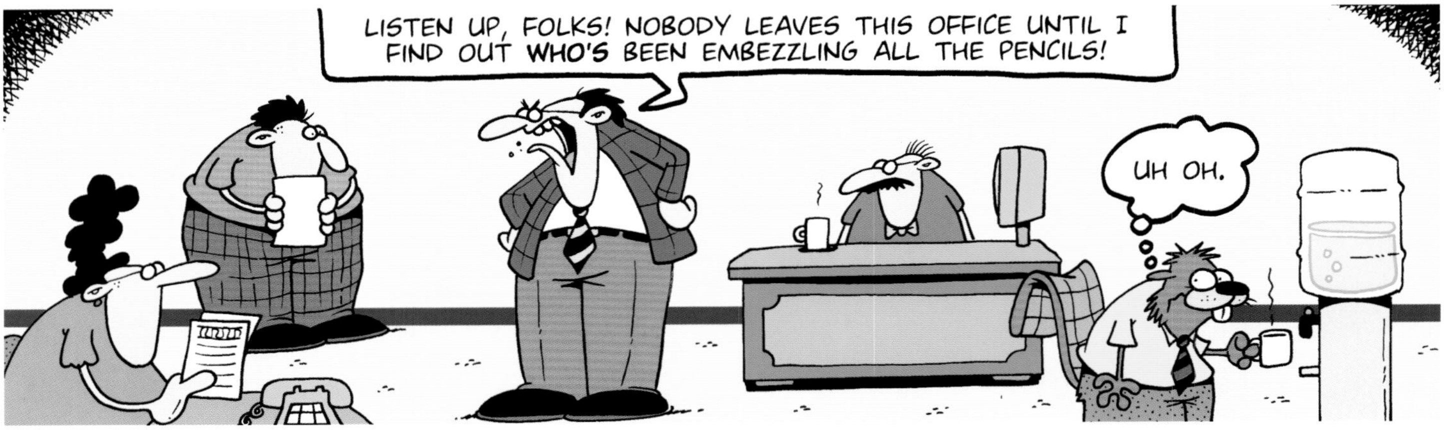
LISTEN UP, FOLKS! NOBODY LEAVES THIS OFFICE UNTIL I FIND OUT **WHO'S** BEEN EMBEZZLING ALL THE PENCILS!
UH OH.

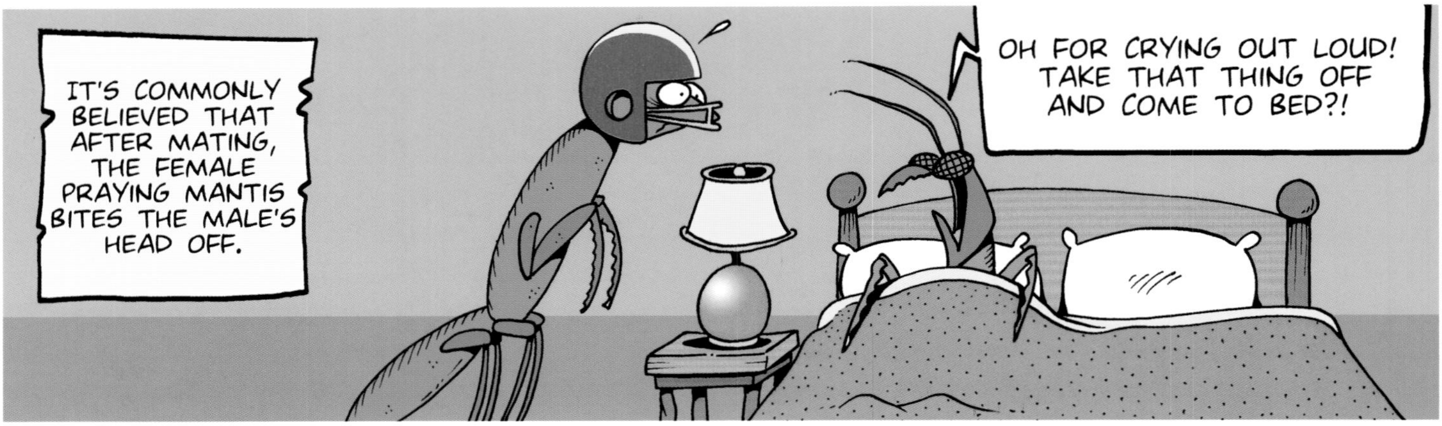
IT'S COMMONLY BELIEVED THAT AFTER MATING, THE FEMALE PRAYING MANTIS BITES THE MALE'S HEAD OFF.
OH FOR CRYING OUT LOUD! TAKE THAT THING OFF AND COME TO BED?!

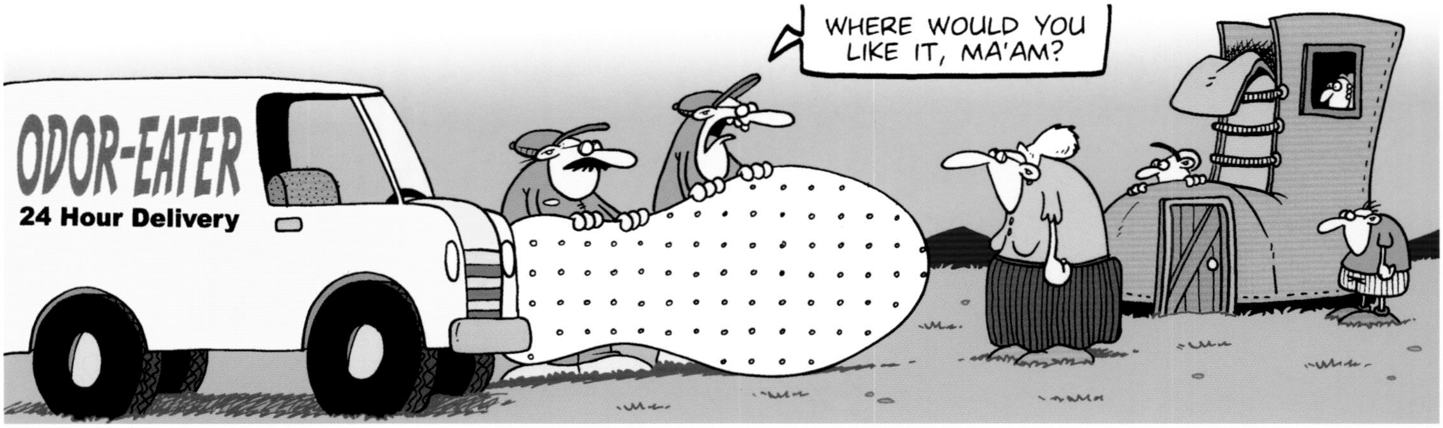
WHERE WOULD YOU LIKE IT, MA'AM?
ODOR-EATER
24 Hour Delivery

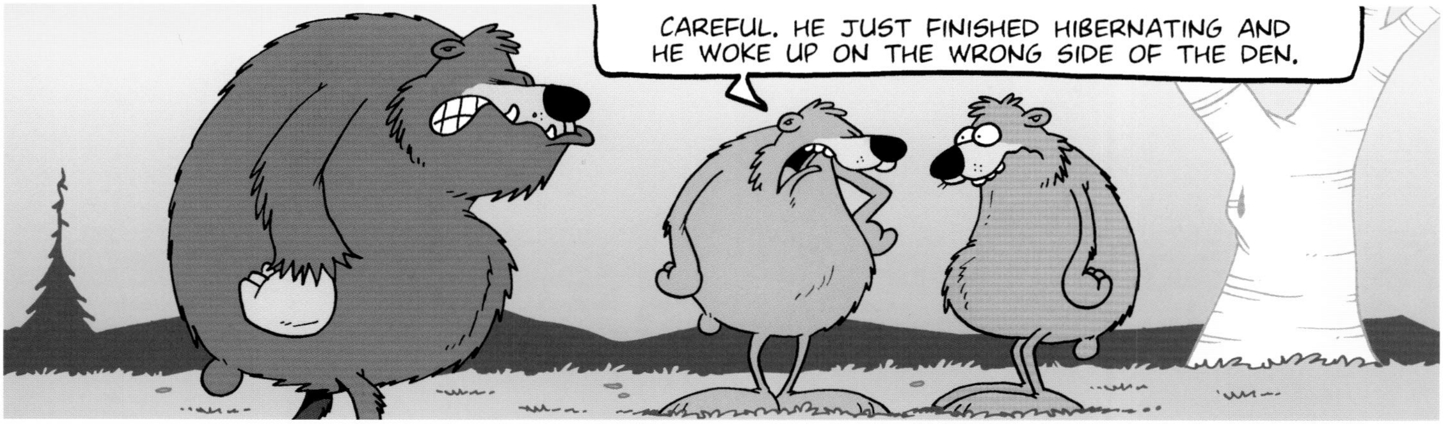
CAREFUL. HE JUST FINISHED HIBERNATING AND HE WOKE UP ON THE WRONG SIDE OF THE DEN.

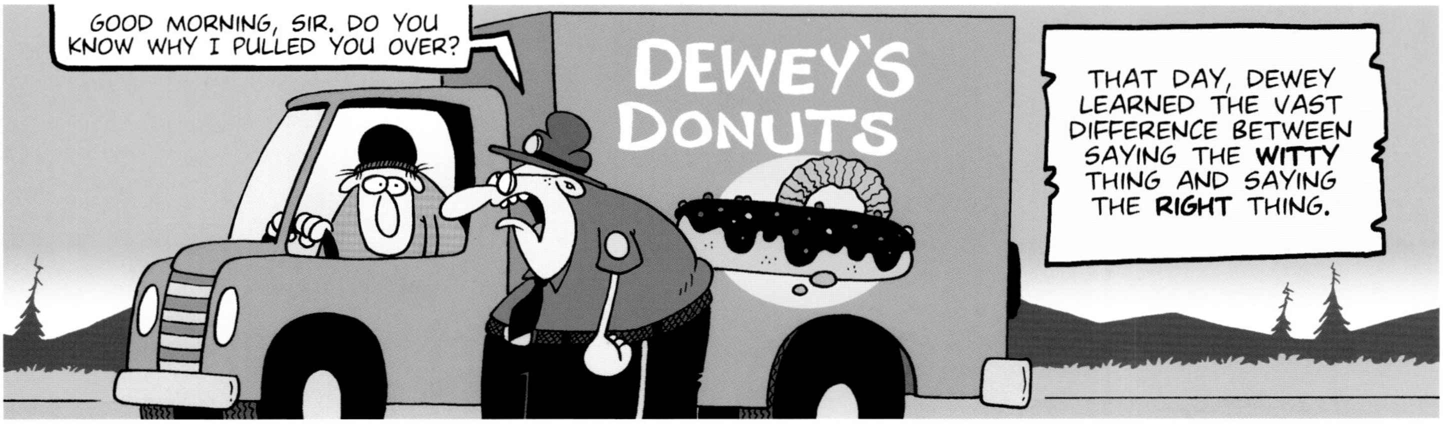
GOOD MORNING, SIR. DO YOU KNOW WHY I PULLED YOU OVER?
DEWEY'S DONUTS
THAT DAY, DEWEY LEARNED THE VAST DIFFERENCE BETWEEN SAYING THE **WITTY** THING AND SAYING THE **RIGHT** THING.

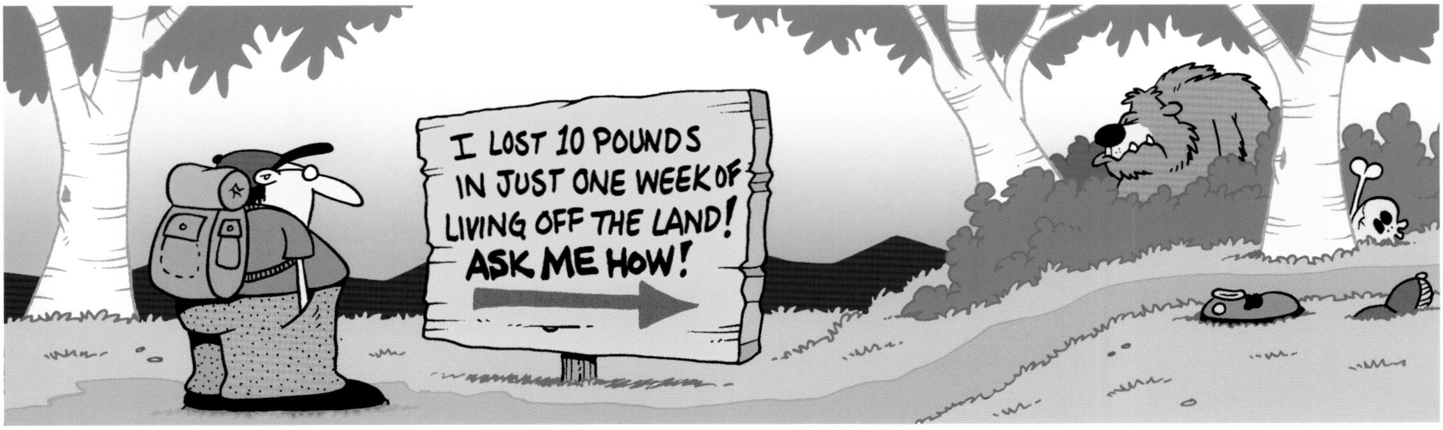
I LOST 10 POUNDS IN JUST ONE WEEK OF LIVING OFF THE LAND! ASK ME HOW!

Chad Carpenter's
TUNDRA
TSK TSK. WHAT IS THIS CRAZY WORLD COMING TO?
WHY? WHAT'S UP?
www.tundracomics.com
IT SEEMS THERE WAS THIS DOCTOR WHO LOST HIS MEDICAL LICENSE BECAUSE HE FELL MADLY IN LOVE WITH ONE OF HIS PATIENTS AND THEY RAN AWAY TOGETHER.
WHAT?! LOST HIS LICENSE?!
THAT'S RIDICULOUS! WHO HAS THE RIGHT TO TRY AND SEPARATE TWO LONELY SOULS WHO ARE PASSIONATELY IN LOVE JUST BECAUSE OF SOME LUDICROUS RULE?!
©TUNDRA 2006
YOU'RE ABSOLUTELY RIGHT, SHERM! WHAT IS THIS WORLD COMING TO?!
HE WAS A VETERINARIAN.

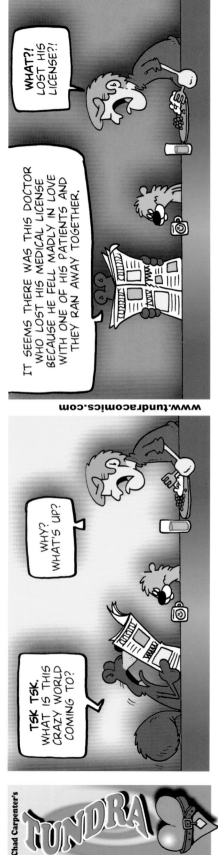

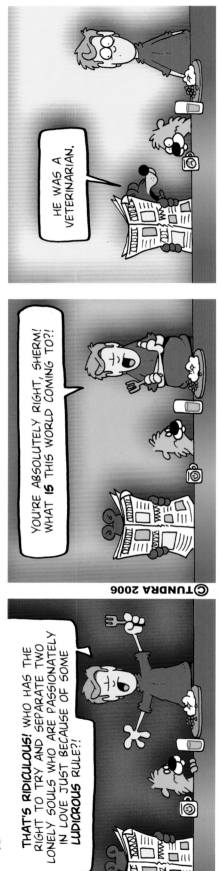

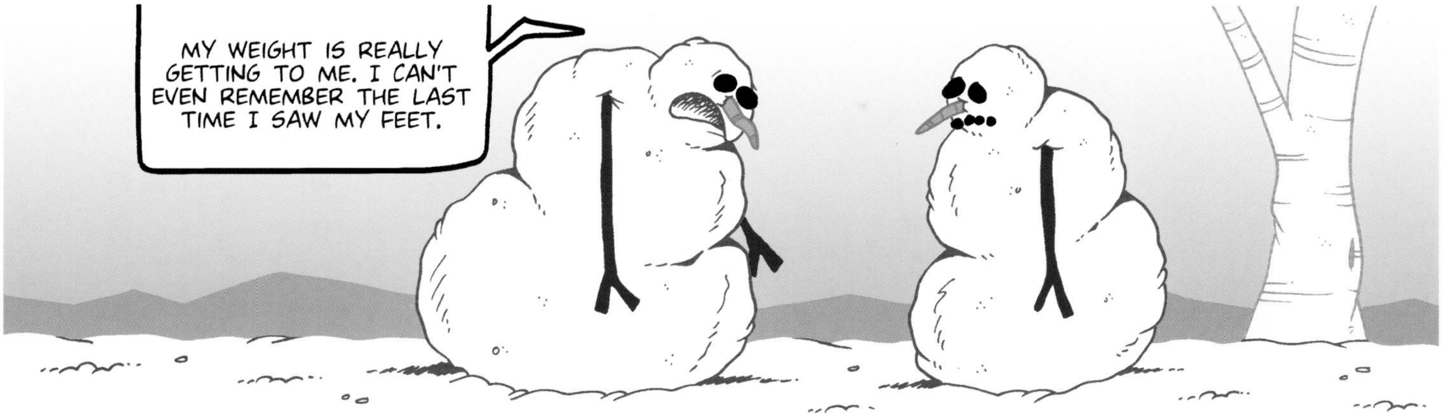
MY WEIGHT IS REALLY GETTING TO ME. I CAN'T EVEN REMEMBER THE LAST TIME I SAW MY FEET.

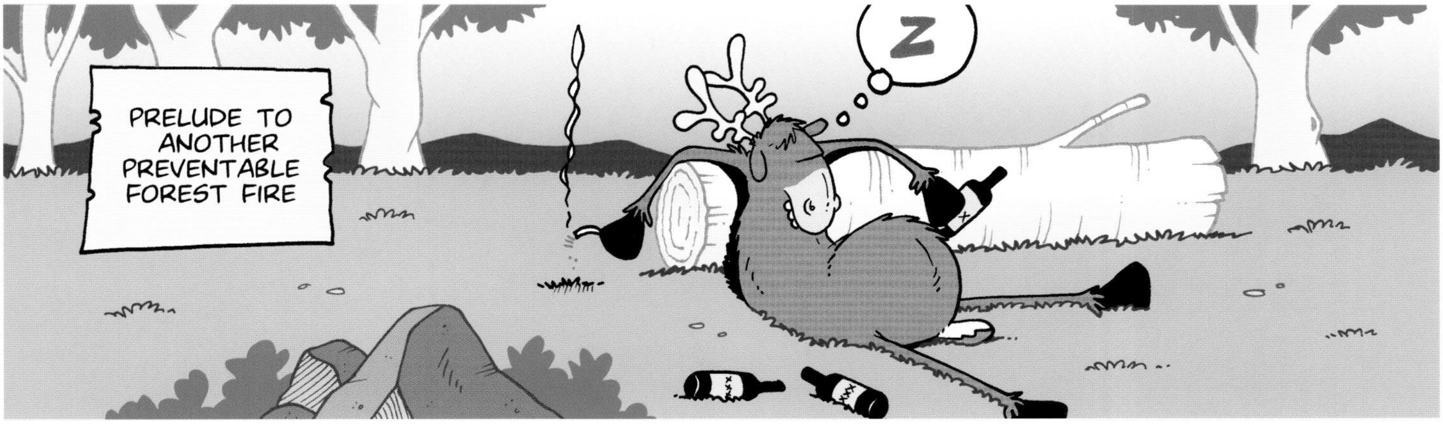
Z
PRELUDE TO ANOTHER PREVENTABLE FOREST FIRE

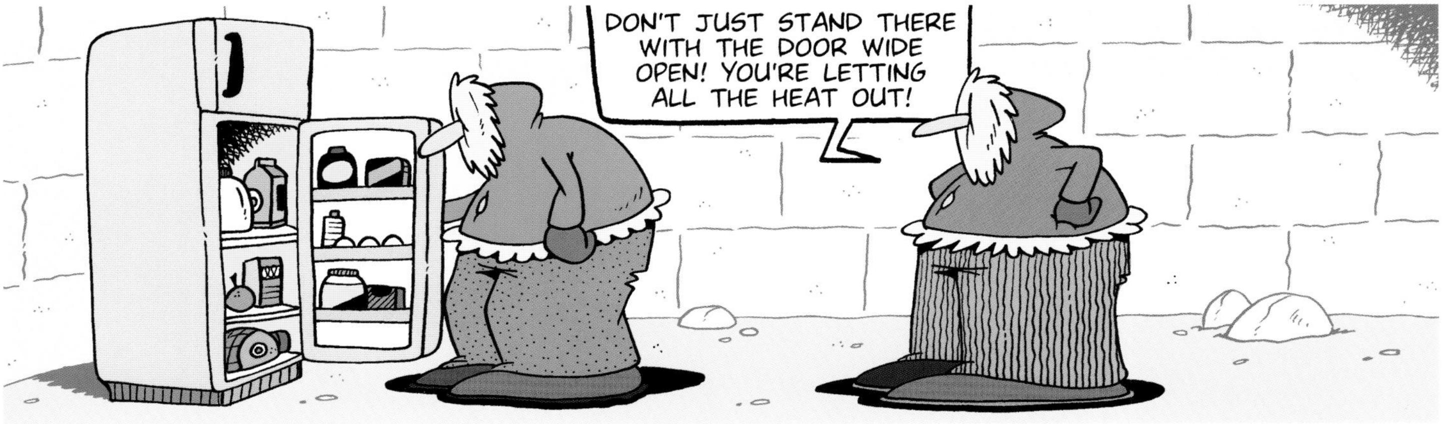
DON'T JUST STAND THERE WITH THE DOOR WIDE OPEN! YOU'RE LETTING ALL THE HEAT OUT!

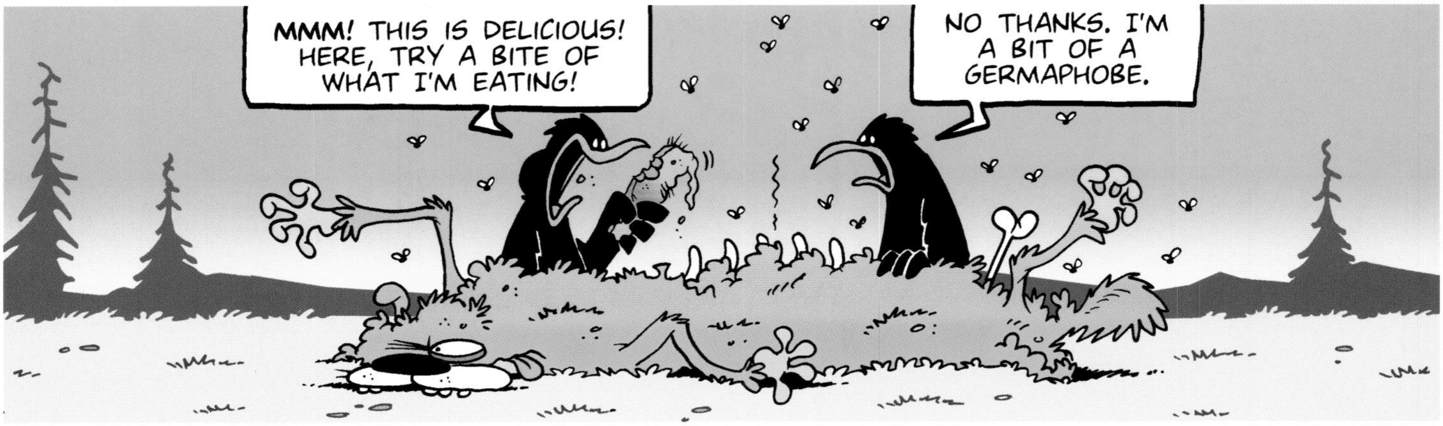
MMM! THIS IS DELICIOUS! HERE, TRY A BITE OF WHAT I'M EATING!
NO THANKS. I'M A BIT OF A GERMAPHOBE.

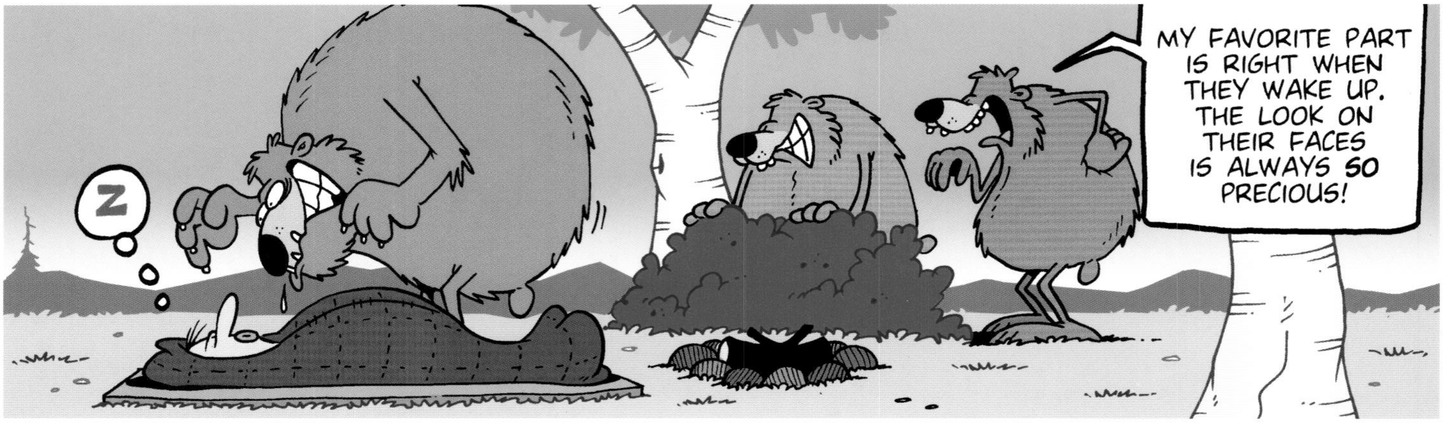
Z
MY FAVORITE PART IS RIGHT WHEN THEY WAKE UP. THE LOOK ON THEIR FACES IS ALWAYS SO PRECIOUS!

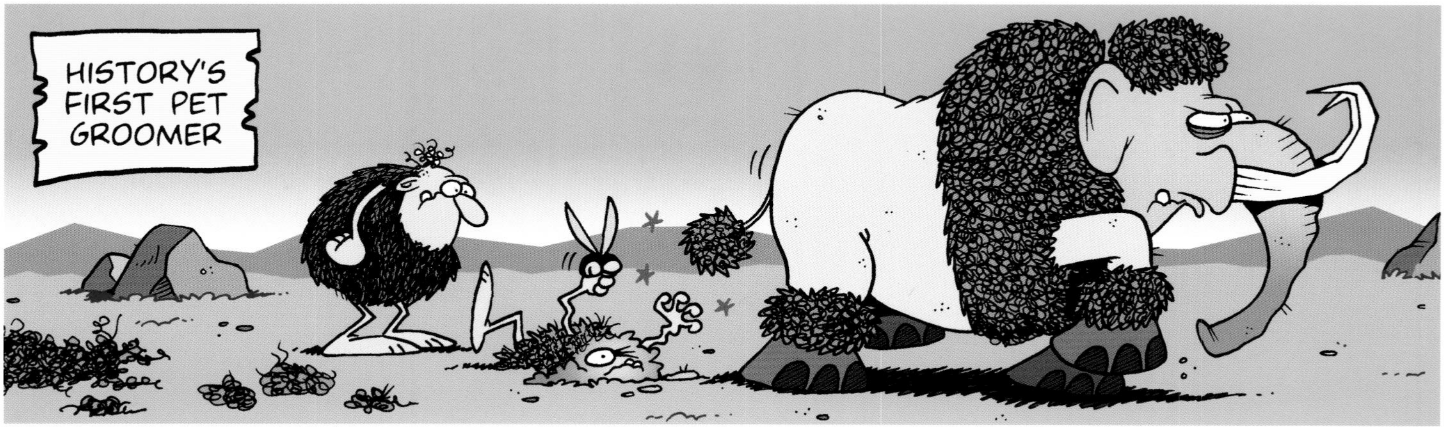
HISTORY'S FIRST PET GROOMER

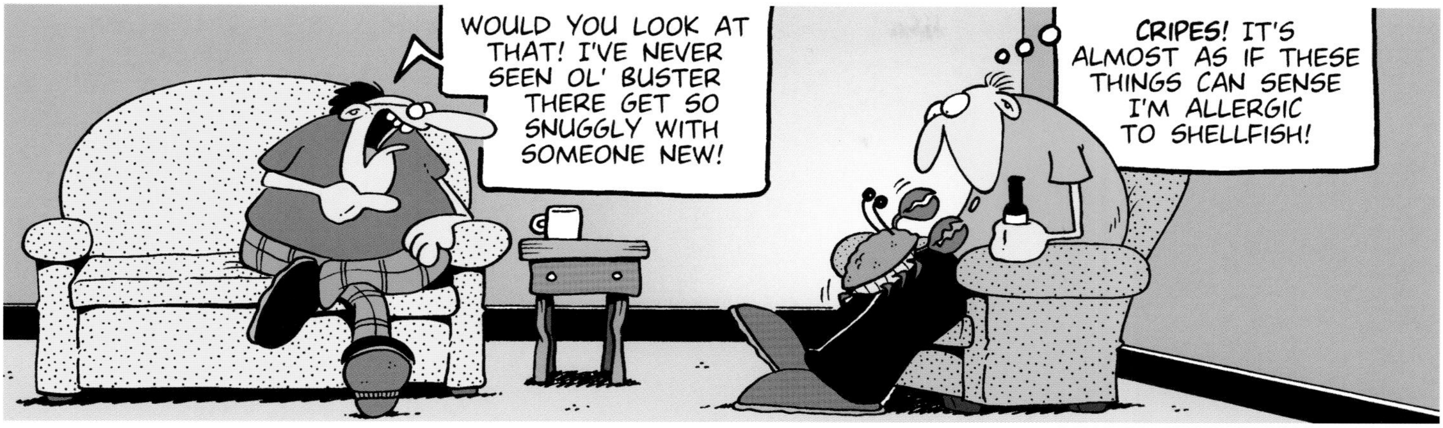
WOULD YOU LOOK AT THAT! I'VE NEVER SEEN OL' BUSTER THERE GET SO SNUGGLY WITH SOMEONE NEW!
CRIPES! IT'S ALMOST AS IF THESE THINGS CAN SENSE I'M ALLERGIC TO SHELLFISH!

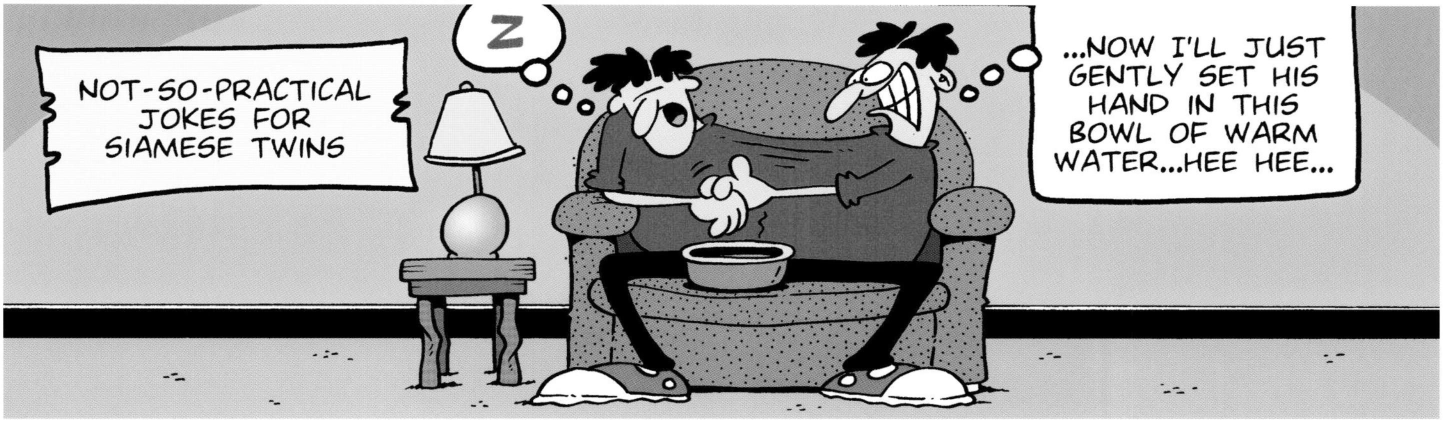
NOT-SO-PRACTICAL JOKES FOR SIAMESE TWINS
Z
...NOW I'LL JUST GENTLY SET HIS HAND IN THIS BOWL OF WARM WATER...HEE HEE...

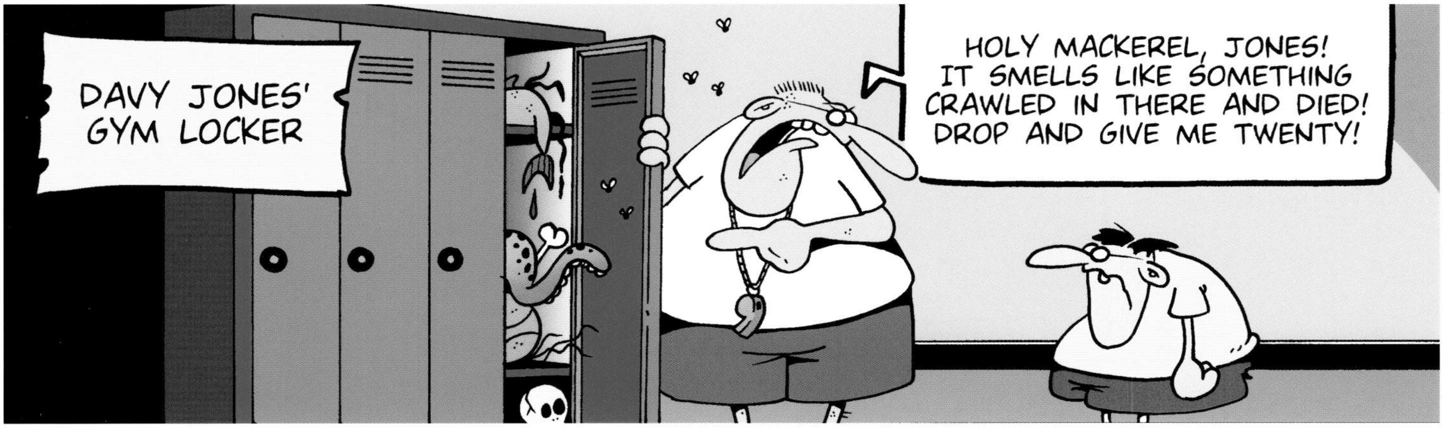
DAVY JONES' GYM LOCKER
HOLY MACKEREL, JONES! IT SMELLS LIKE SOMETHING CRAWLED IN THERE AND DIED! DROP AND GIVE ME TWENTY!

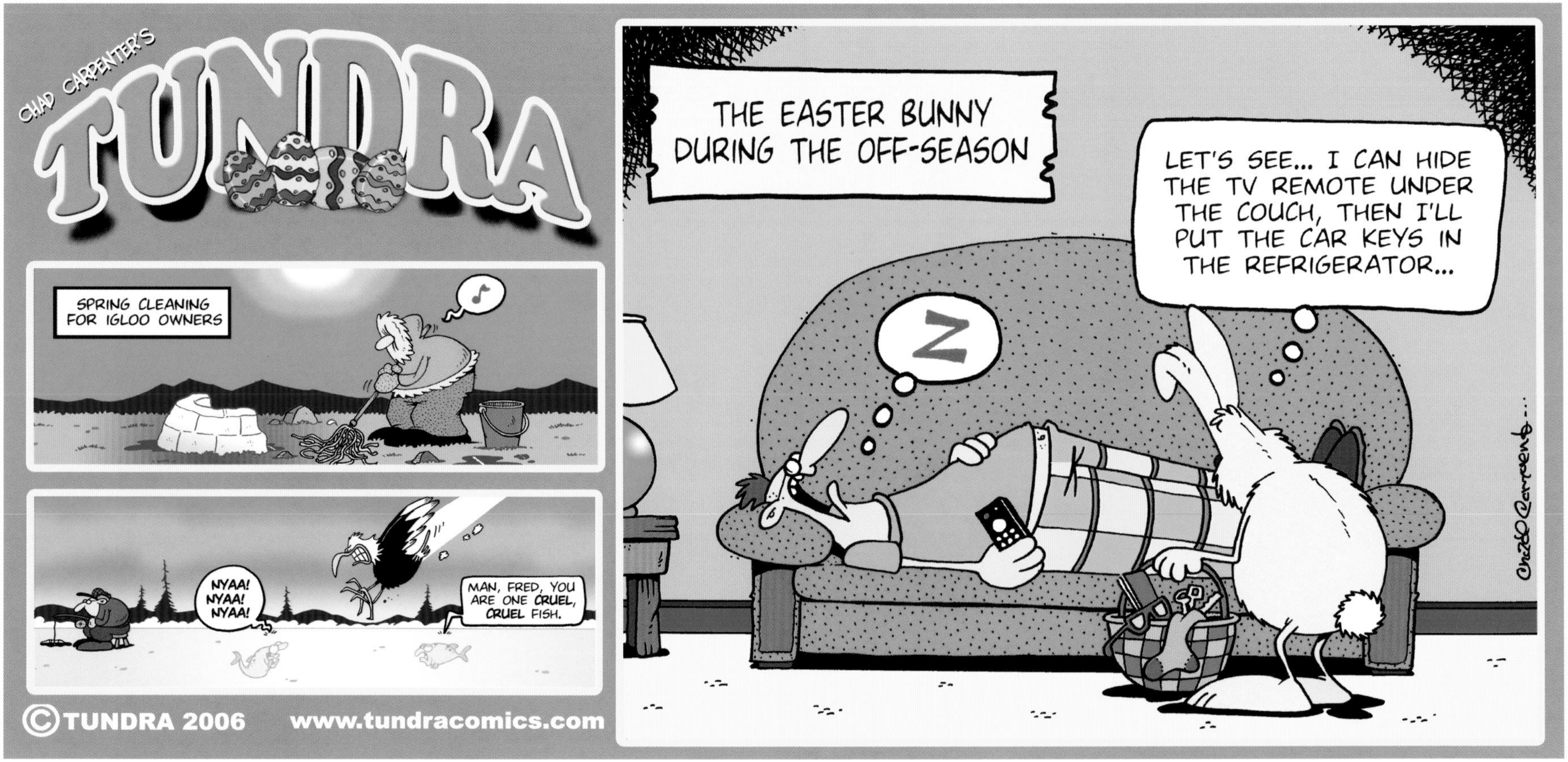
CHAD CARPENTER'S
TUNDRA
SPRING CLEANING FOR IGLOO OWNERS
NYAA! NYAA! NYAA!
MAN, FRED, YOU ARE ONE CRUEL, CRUEL FISH.
THE EASTER BUNNY DURING THE OFF-SEASON
Z
LET'S SEE... I CAN HIDE THE TV REMOTE UNDER THE COUCH, THEN I'LL PUT THE CAR KEYS IN THE REFRIGERATOR...
©TUNDRA 2006
www.tundracomics.com

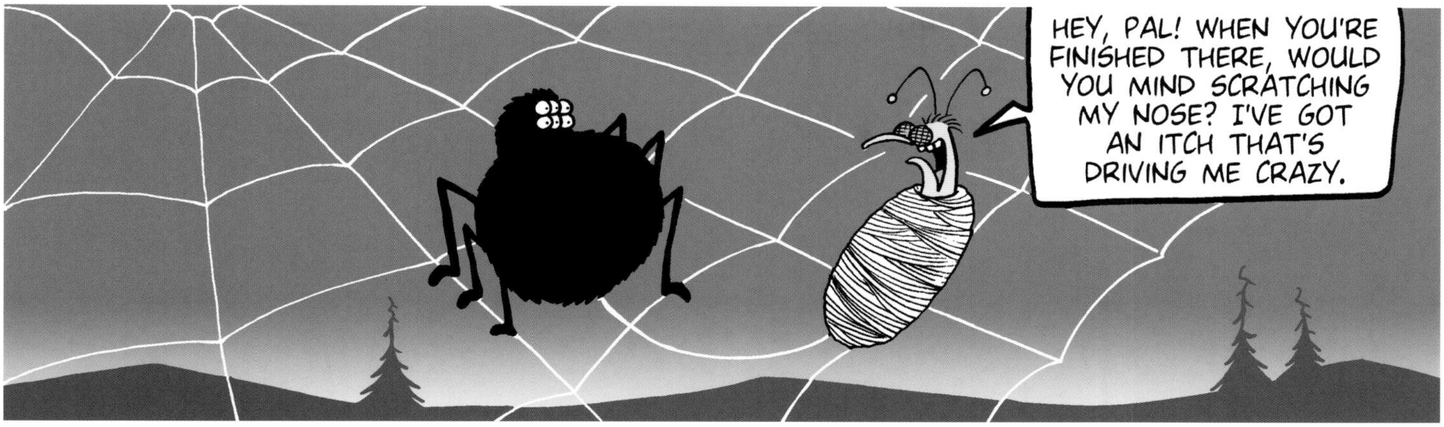
HEY, PAL! WHEN YOU'RE FINISHED THERE, WOULD YOU MIND SCRATCHING MY NOSE? I'VE GOT AN ITCH THAT'S DRIVING ME CRAZY.

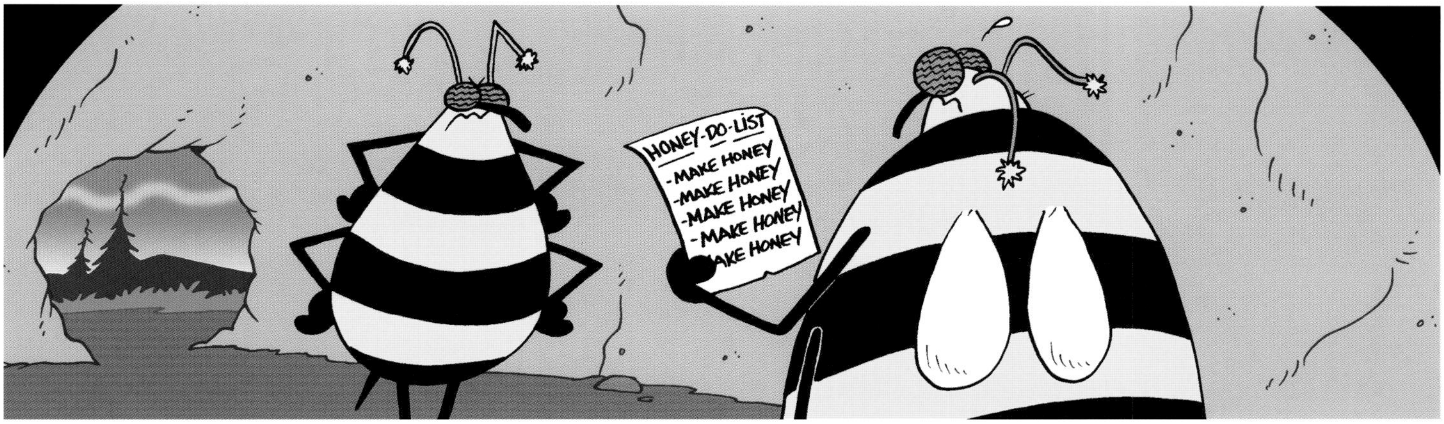
HONEY-DO-LIST
-MAKE HONEY
-MAKE HONEY
-MAKE HONEY
-MAKE HONEY

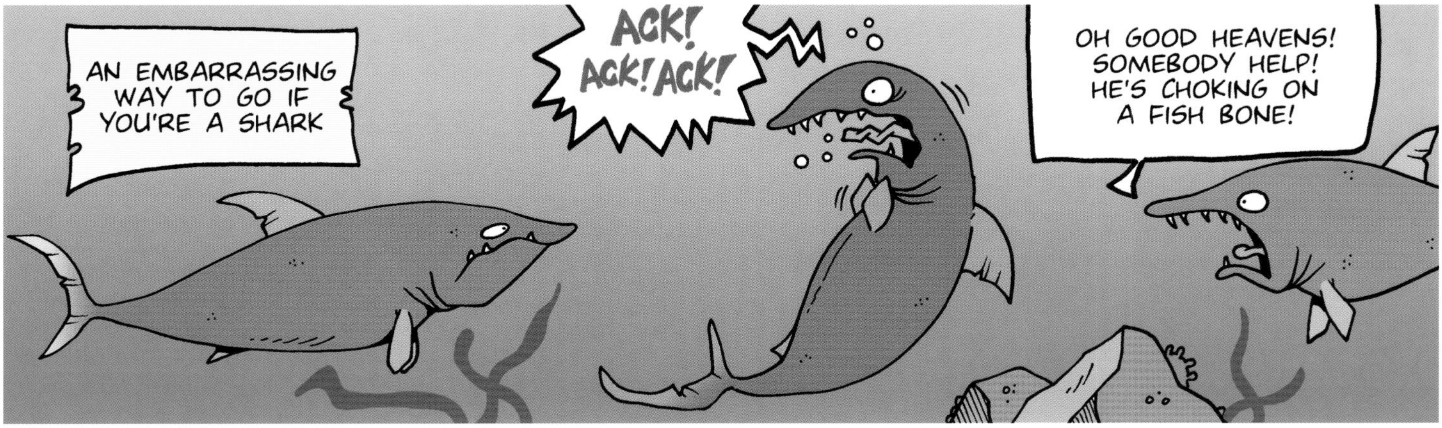
AN EMBARRASSING WAY TO GO IF YOU'RE A SHARK
ACK! ACK! ACK!
OH GOOD HEAVENS! SOMEBODY HELP! HE'S CHOKING ON A FISH BONE!

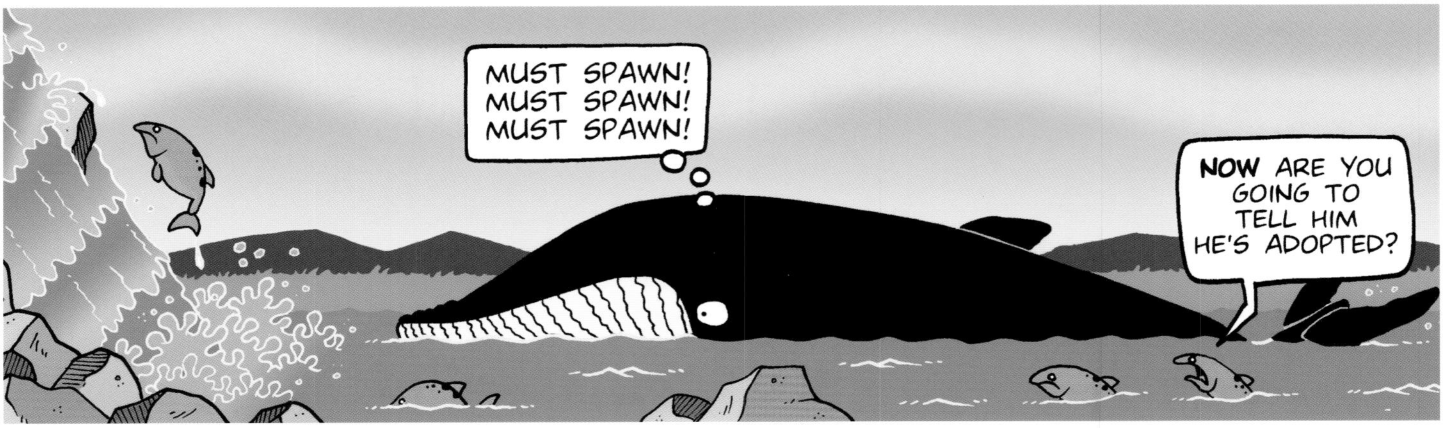
MUST SPAWN! MUST SPAWN! MUST SPAWN!
NOW ARE YOU GOING TO TELL HIM HE'S ADOPTED?

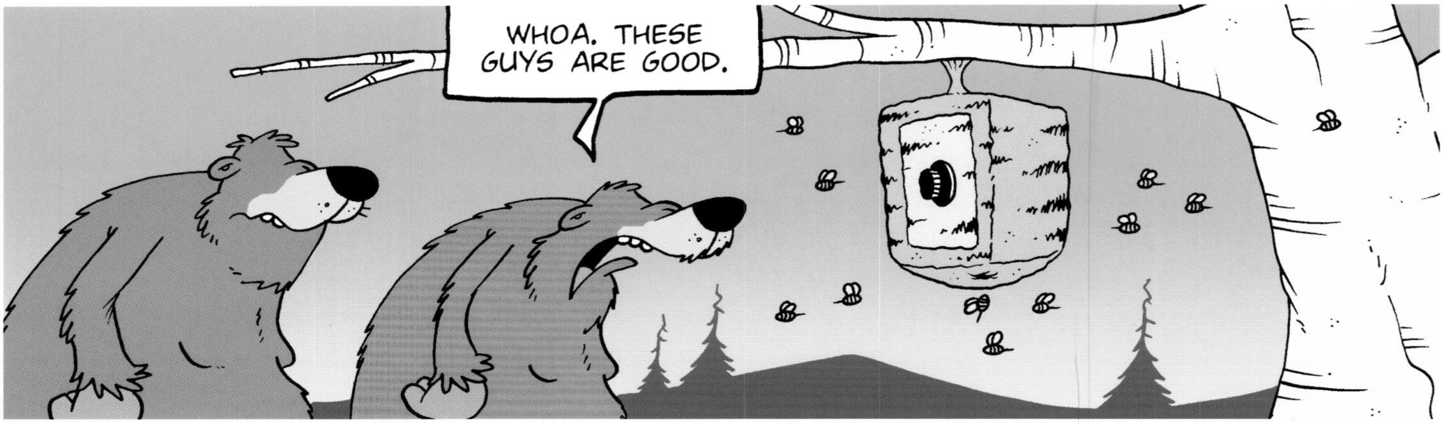
WHOA. THESE GUYS ARE GOOD.

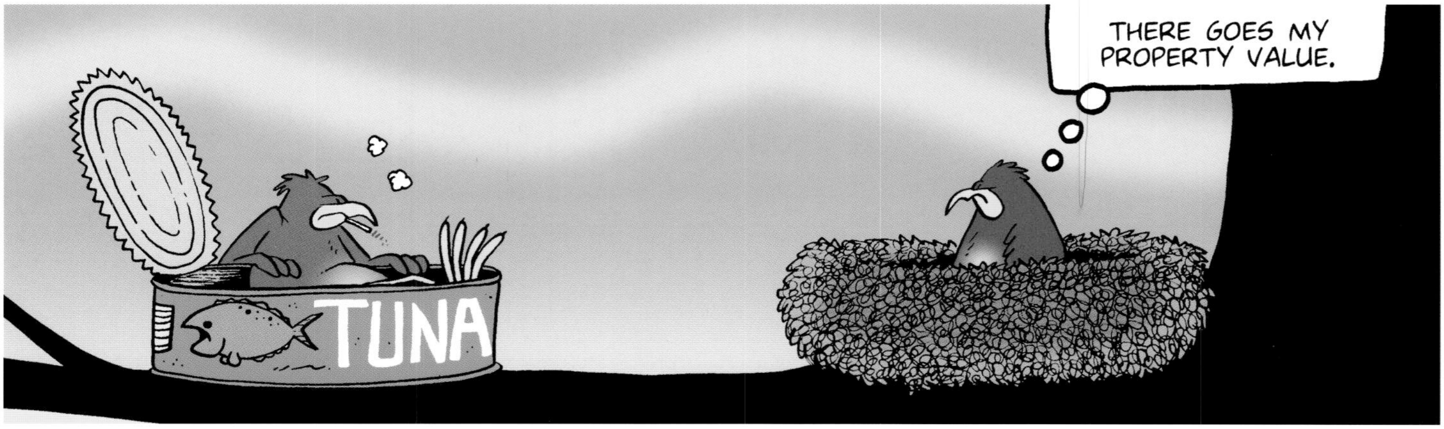
TUNA
THERE GOES MY PROPERTY VALUE.

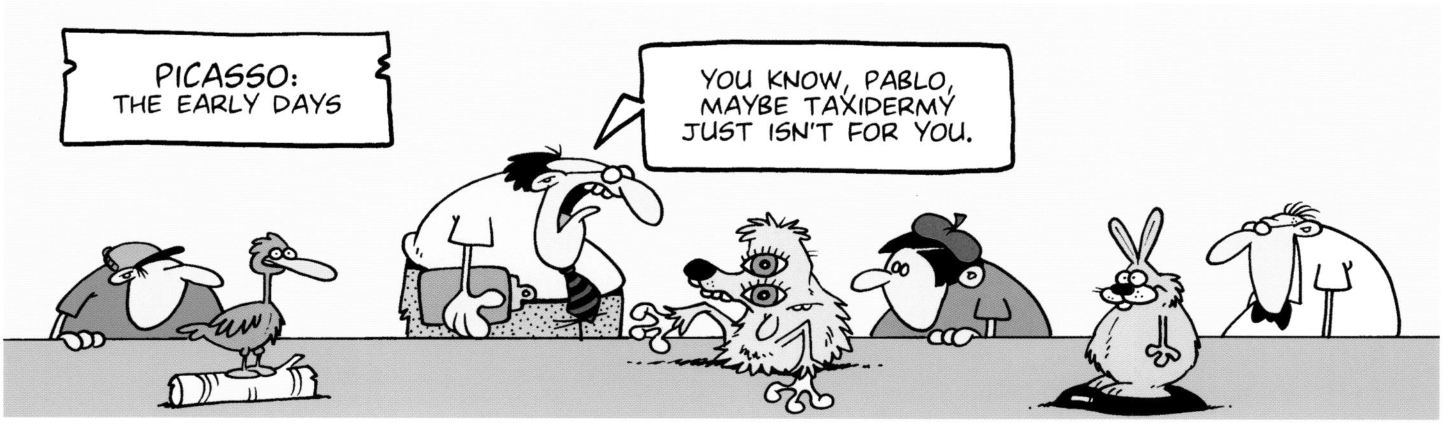
PICASSO:
THE EARLY DAYS
YOU KNOW, PABLO,
MAYBE TAXIDERMY
JUST ISN'T FOR YOU.

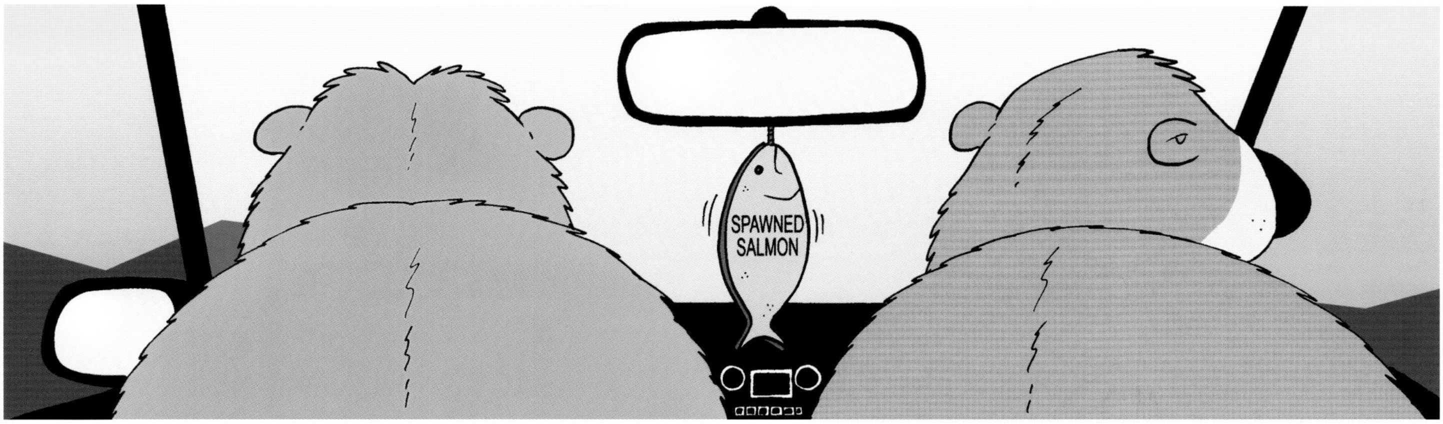
SPAWNED
SALMON

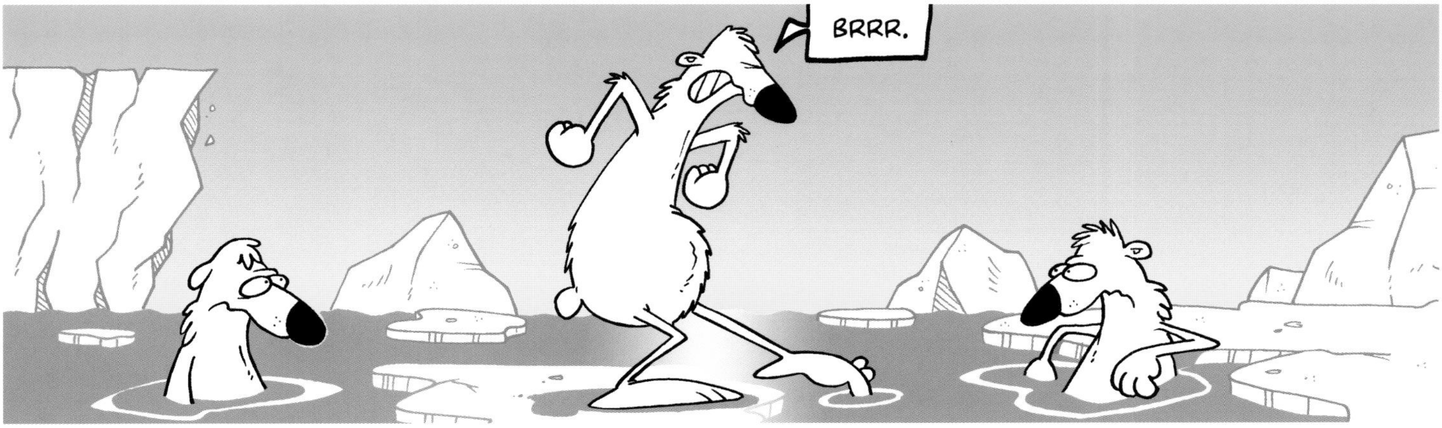
BRRR.

Chad Carpenter's
TUNDRA
I WONDER WHAT SNOWMEN WOULD SAY IF THEY COULD TALK? WHAT WISDOM THEY MIGHT IMPART?
WOULD THEY TELL US OF THE FLEETING FRAGILITY OF EXISTENCE? THE IMPORTANCE OF NOT SQUANDERING THE LIMITED TIME WE HAVE UPON THIS MORTAL COIL...
...OR SIMPLY SHARE WITH US THE GRACE WITH WHICH ONE SHOULD ACCEPT ONE'S OWN IMMINENT DEPARTURE FROM THIS DIMENSION?
ONE CAN ONLY IMAGINE.
HELP ME! I'M MELTING! AAAAIEEEE!
IT BURNS! IT BURNS!
AAAAURRRG! THE AGONY! THE HUMANITY!
© TUNDRA 2006
POOF!
www.tundracomics.com
MAYBE THERE'S SOMETHING TO THE WHOLE IGNORANCE IS BLISS THING...
IT'S GOTTEN ME THROUGH LIFE.

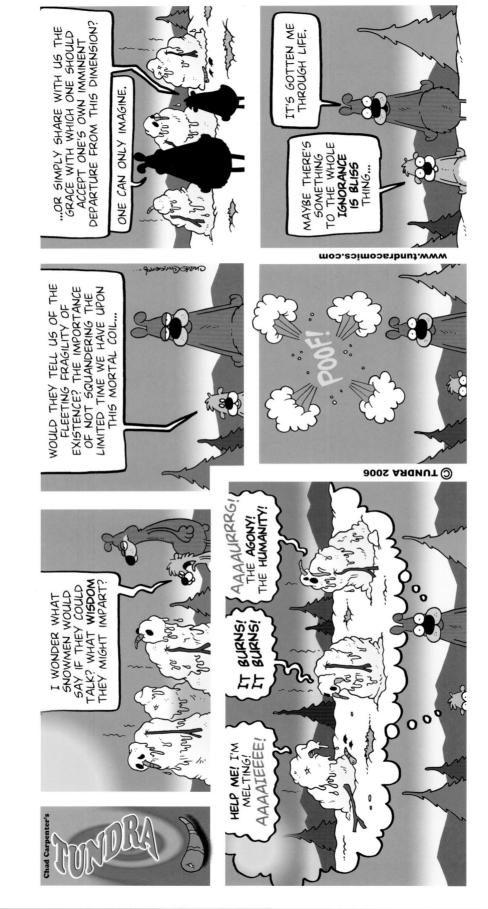

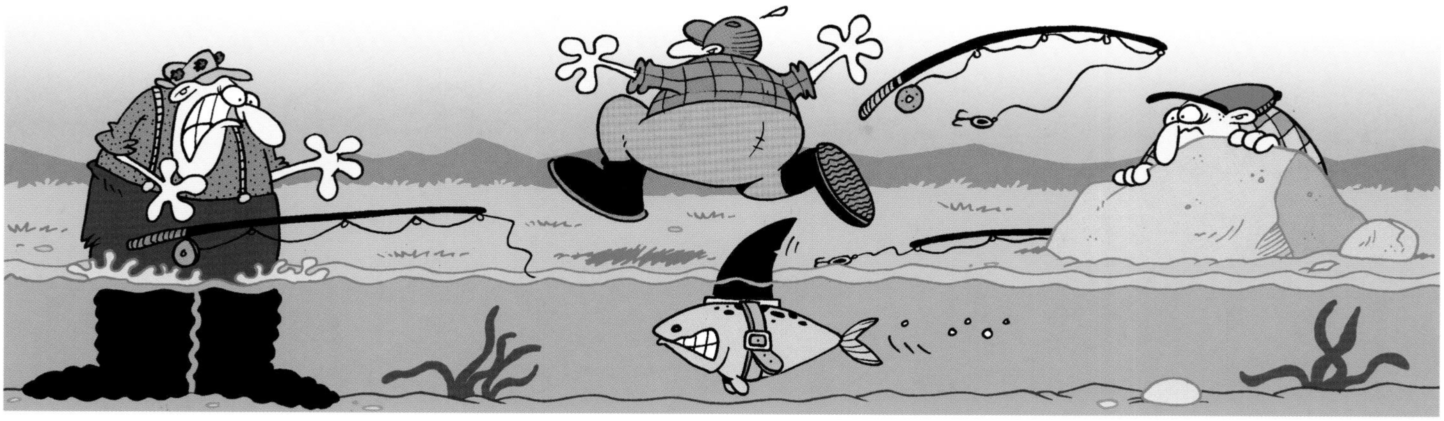

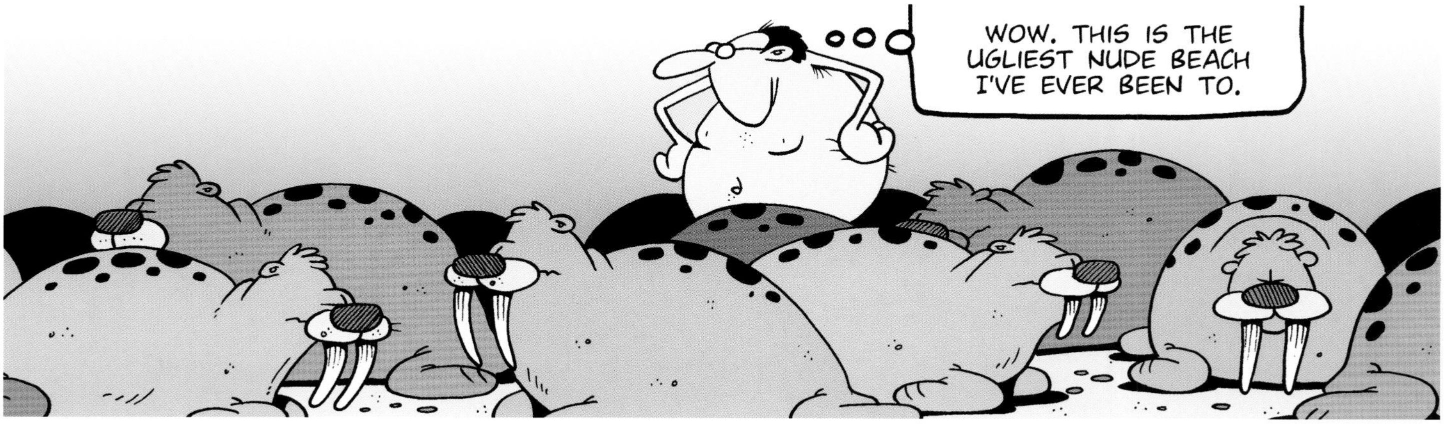
WOW. THIS IS THE UGLIEST NUDE BEACH I'VE EVER BEEN TO.

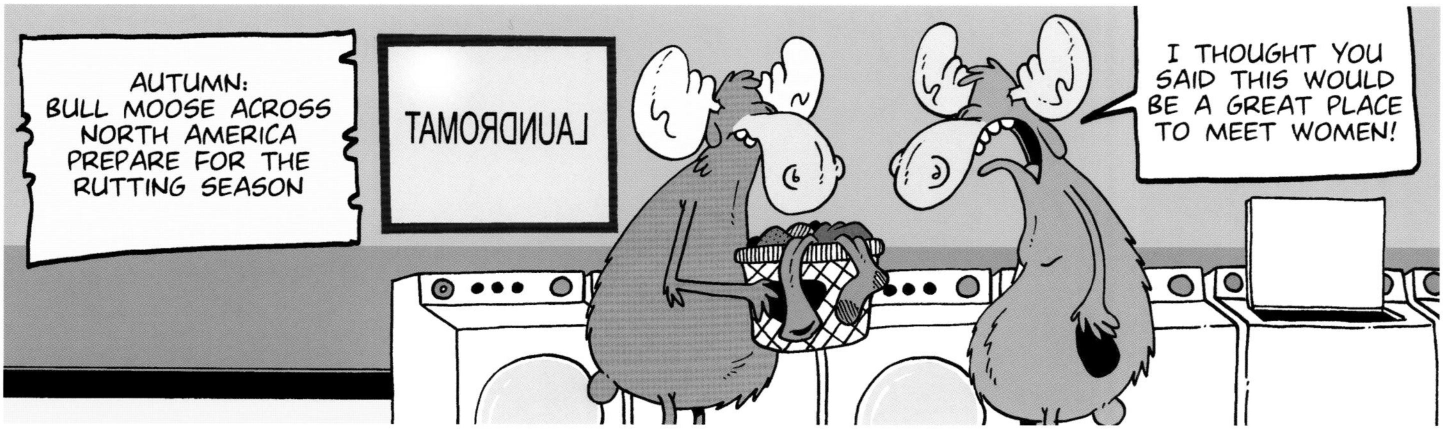
AUTUMN: BULL MOOSE ACROSS NORTH AMERICA PREPARE FOR THE RUTTING SEASON
LAUNDROMAT
I THOUGHT YOU SAID THIS WOULD BE A GREAT PLACE TO MEET WOMEN!

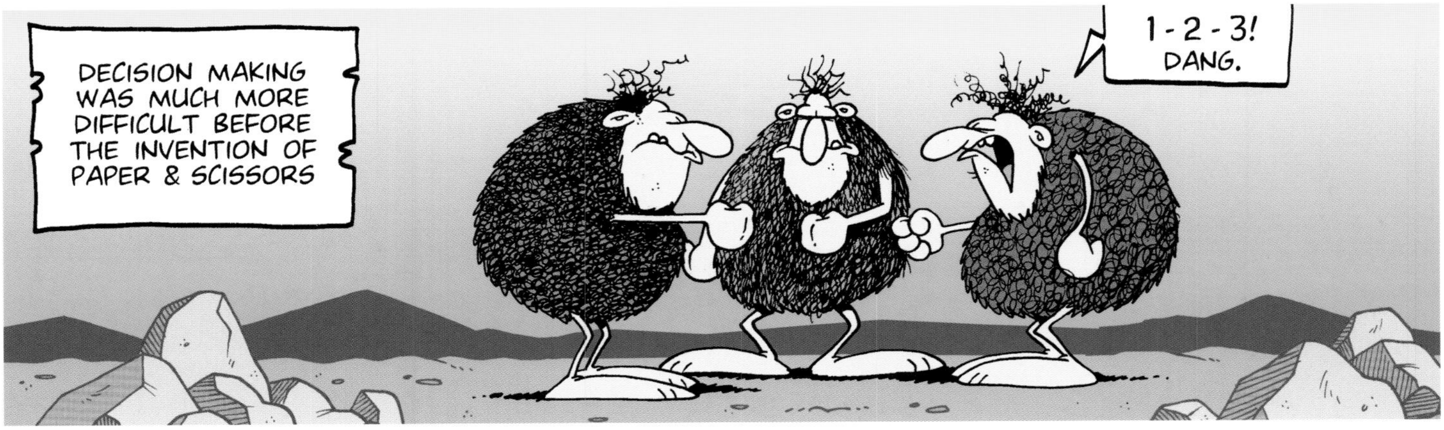
DECISION MAKING WAS MUCH MORE DIFFICULT BEFORE THE INVENTION OF PAPER & SCISSORS
1-2-3!
DANG.

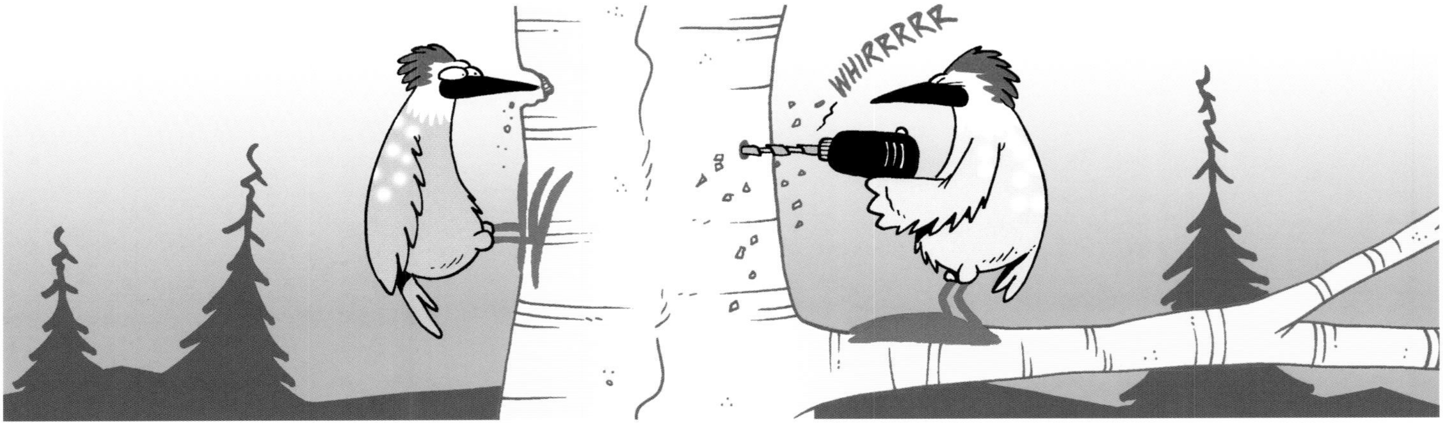
WHIRRRRR

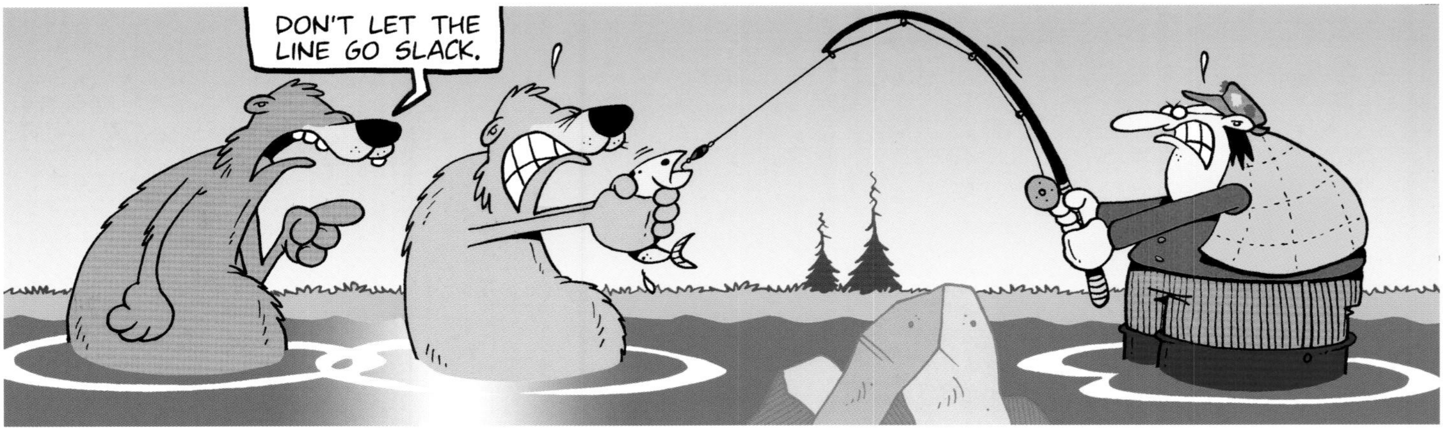
DON'T LET THE LINE GO SLACK.

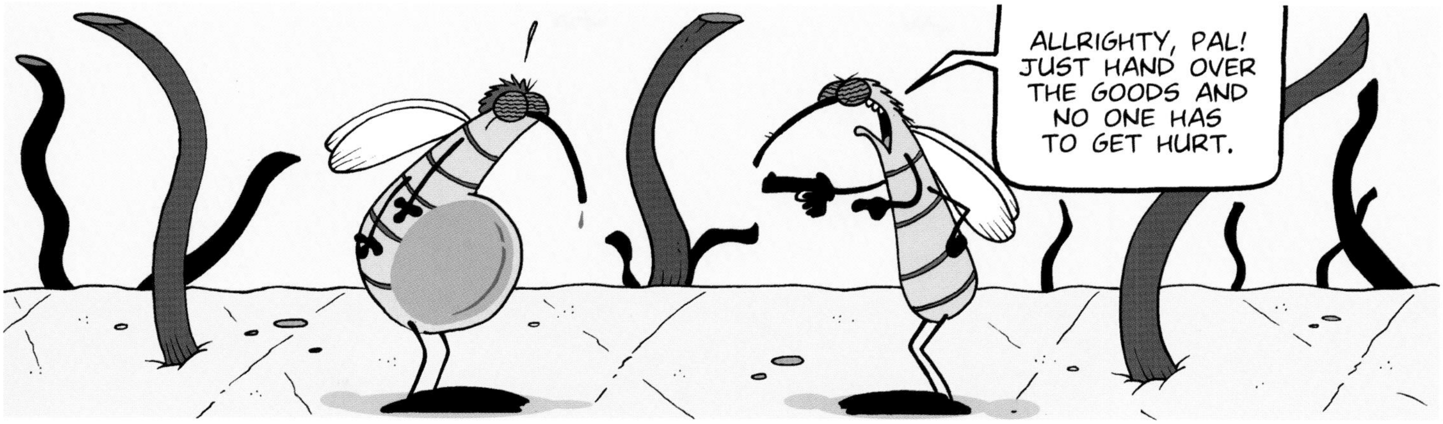
ALLRIGHTY, PAL! JUST HAND OVER THE GOODS AND NO ONE HAS TO GET HURT.

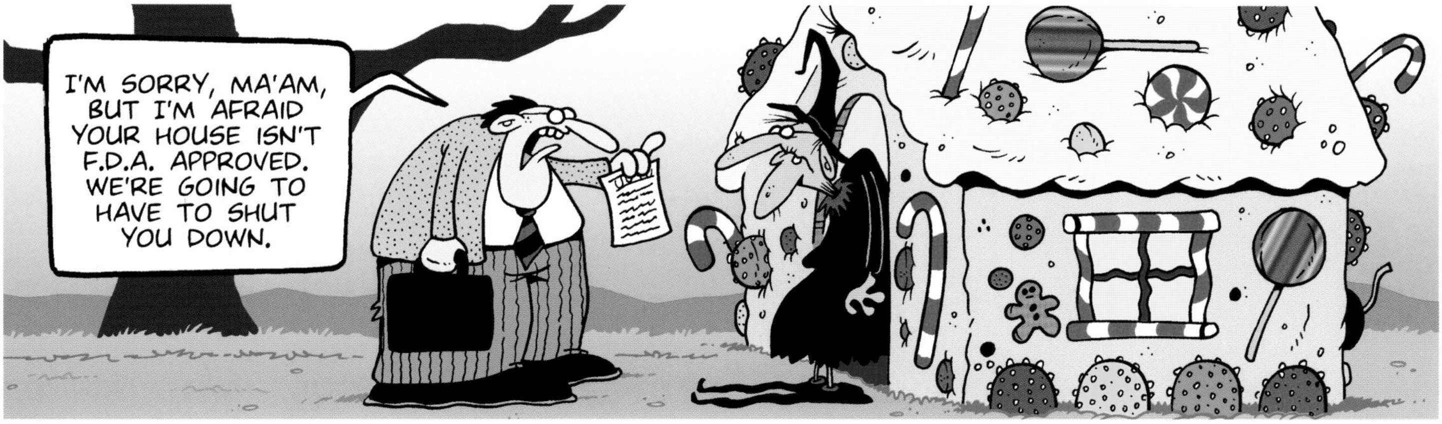
I'M SORRY, MA'AM, BUT I'M AFRAID YOUR HOUSE ISN'T F.D.A. APPROVED. WE'RE GOING TO HAVE TO SHUT YOU DOWN.

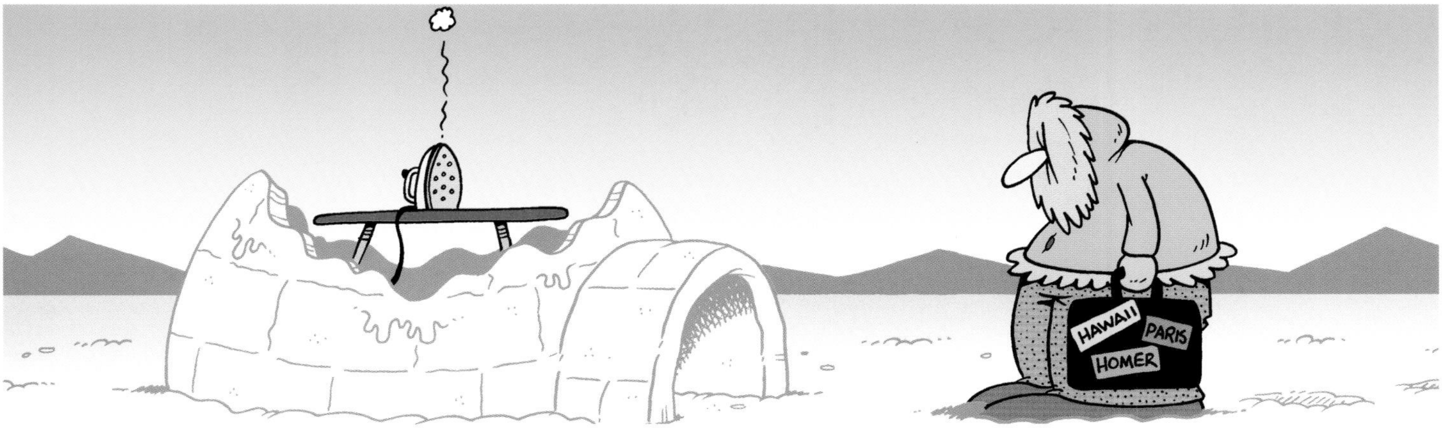
HAWAII
PARIS
HOMER

Chad Carpenter's
TUNDRA
ALASKA
SHERMAN T SKWERL
PO BOX 14
GANGRENE GULCH
MAY I HELP YOU, SIR?
YES. I NEED TO GET A NEW DRIVER'S LICENSE. IT SEEMS YOU SPELLED MY NAME WRONG ON THIS ONE.
GANGRENE GULCH
DMV
CERTAINLY, SIR. THERE WILL, OF COURSE, BE A $5 RESTOCKING FEE.
RESTOCKING FEE?! RESTOCKING WHAT?! I JUST NEED MY NAME SPELLED RIGHT!
GANGRENE GULCH
www.tundracomics.com
SIR, I HAVE TO RESTOCK THE INFORMATION BACK INTO THE COMPUTER. OH, AND OF COURSE THE $4 DISPOSAL FEE FOR YOUR OLD LICENSE.
WHAT?! DISPOSAL FEE?! JUST THROW IT IN THE GARBAGE CAN!
THAT BRINGS UP THE $11 LITTER RECEPTACLE USAGE FEE...
YOU HAVE GOT TO BE KIDDING! YOU KNOW, THIS IS WHAT'S WRONG WITH THIS COUNTRY! OUR ENTIRE ECONOMY IS FEE-BASED!
THIS NATION NO LONGER MANUFACTURES ANY TANGIBLE GOODS! ALL OF OUR FACTORIES HAVE GONE OVERSEAS! SO INSTEAD, OUR CHIEF PRODUCT HAS BECOME IMAGINARY FEES THAT OVER-BLOATED UTILITY COMPANIES, BANKING INSTITUTIONS AND GOVERNMENT AGENCIES SUCH AS YOURSELF MANUFACTURE OUT OF THIN AIR!
© TUNDRA 2006
WELL, FINE! HERE'S YOUR LOUSY MONEY! NOW JUST GIVE ME MY NEW LICENSE!
I'M SORRY, SIR, THAT'S NOT ENOUGH TO COVER OUR CASH ACCEPTANCE FEE AS WELL AS THE RANTING & SNIVELING FEE.

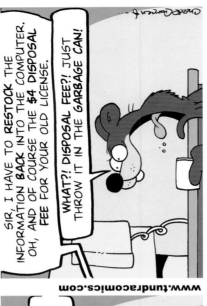

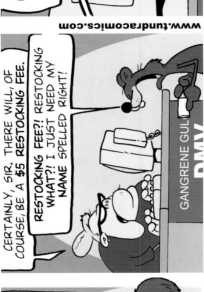

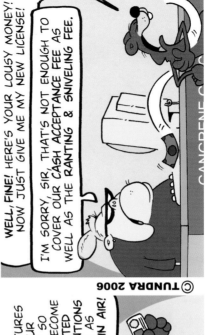

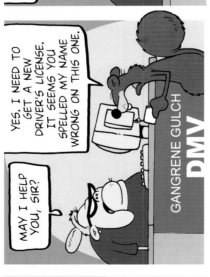

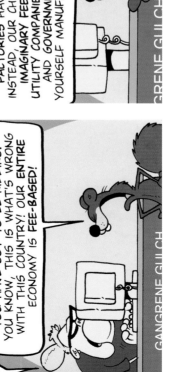

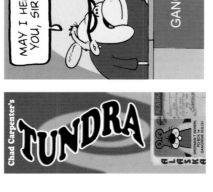

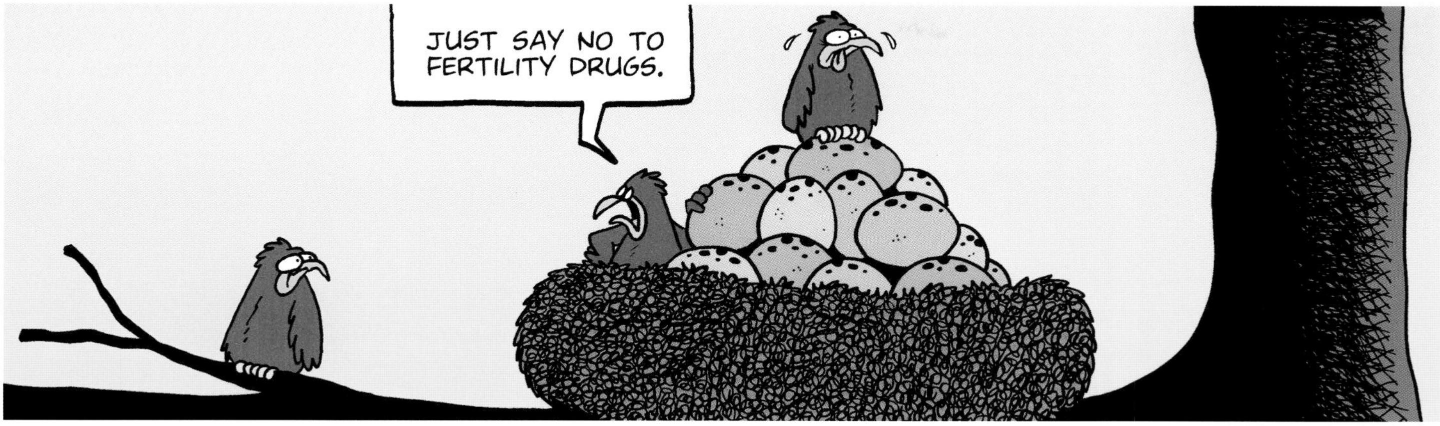
JUST SAY NO TO FERTILITY DRUGS.

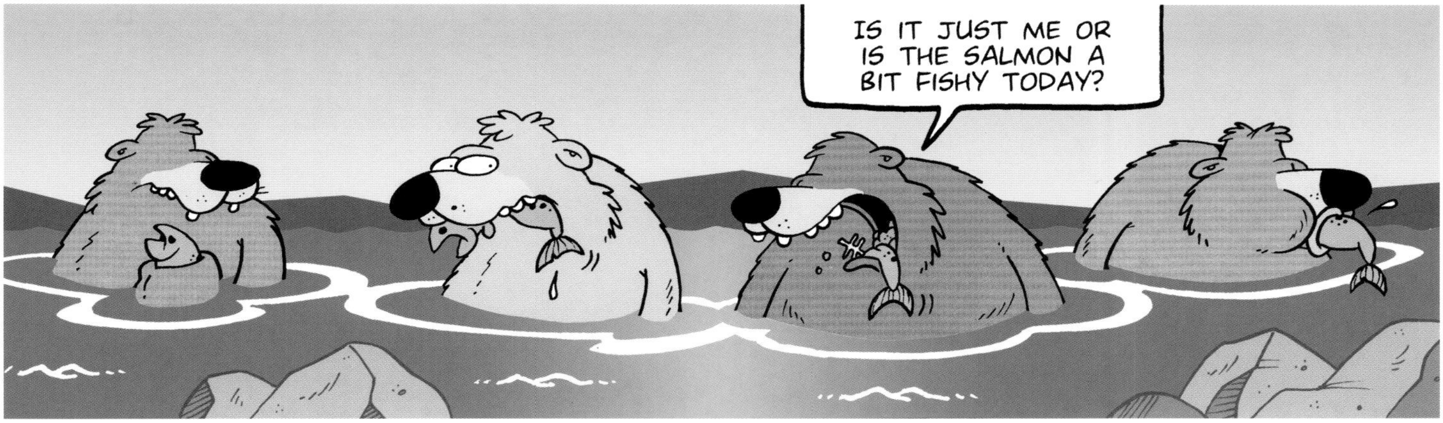
IS IT JUST ME OR IS THE SALMON A BIT FISHY TODAY?

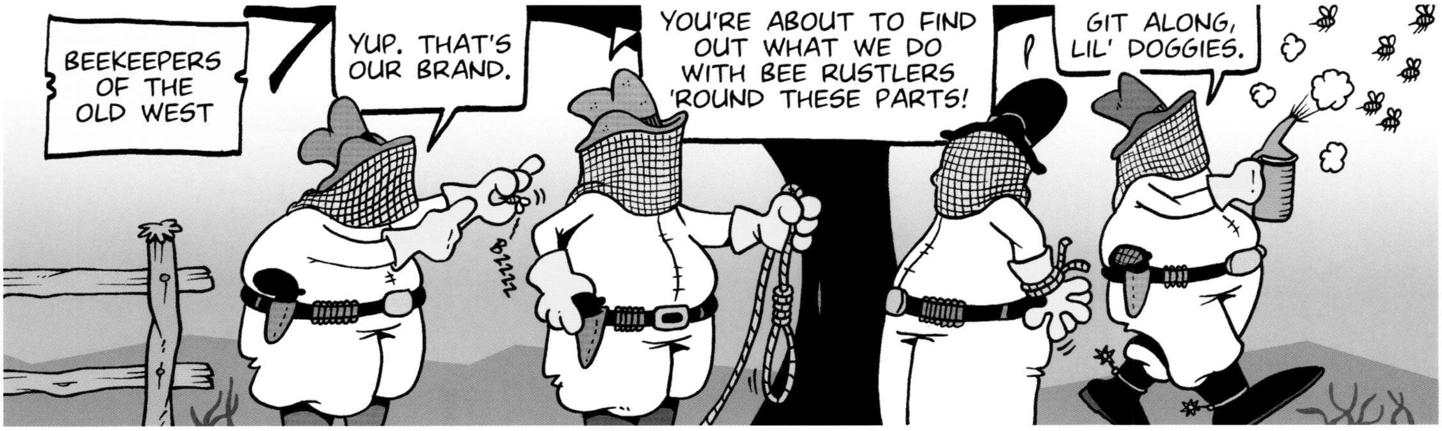
BEEKEEPERS OF THE OLD WEST
YUP. THAT'S OUR BRAND.
BZZZZ
YOU'RE ABOUT TO FIND OUT WHAT WE DO WITH BEE RUSTLERS 'ROUND THESE PARTS!
GIT ALONG, LIL' DOGGIES.

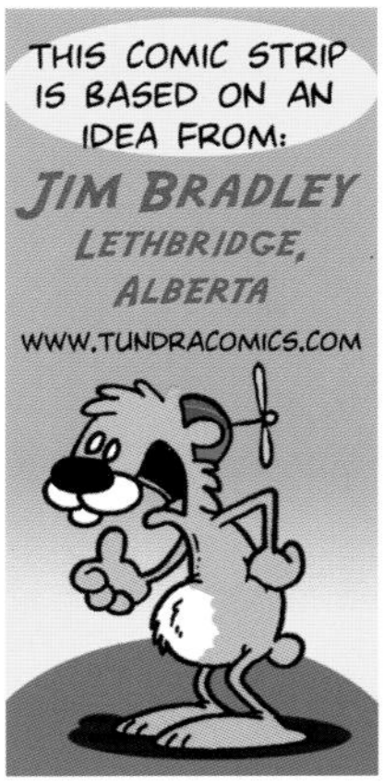
THIS COMIC STRIP IS BASED ON AN IDEA FROM:
JIM BRADLEY
LETHBRIDGE, ALBERTA
WWW.TUNDRACOMICS.COM

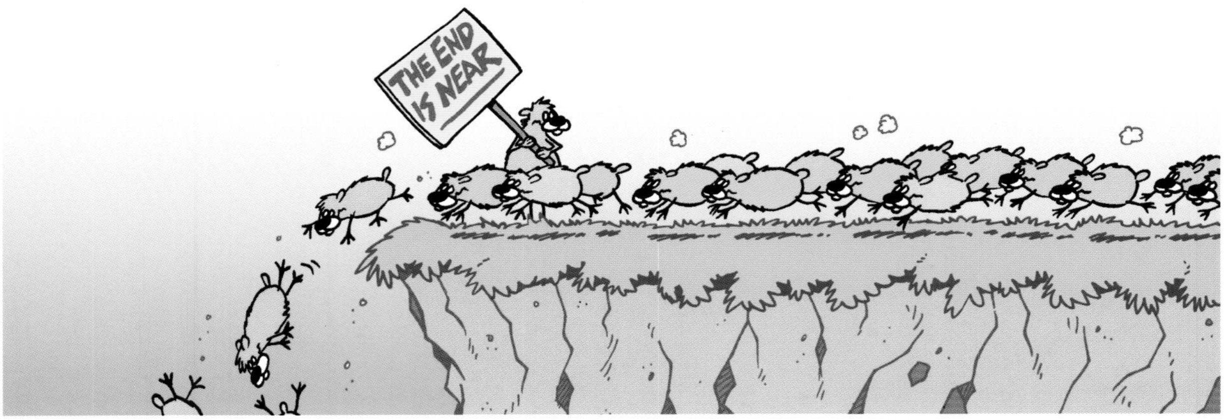
THE END IS NEAR

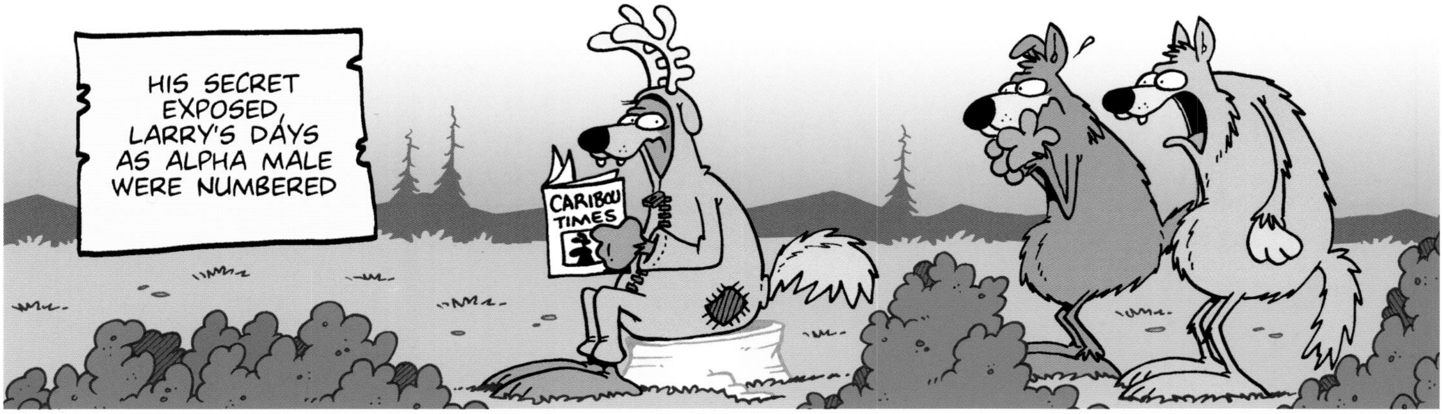
HIS SECRET EXPOSED, LARRY'S DAYS AS ALPHA MALE WERE NUMBERED
CARIBOU TIMES

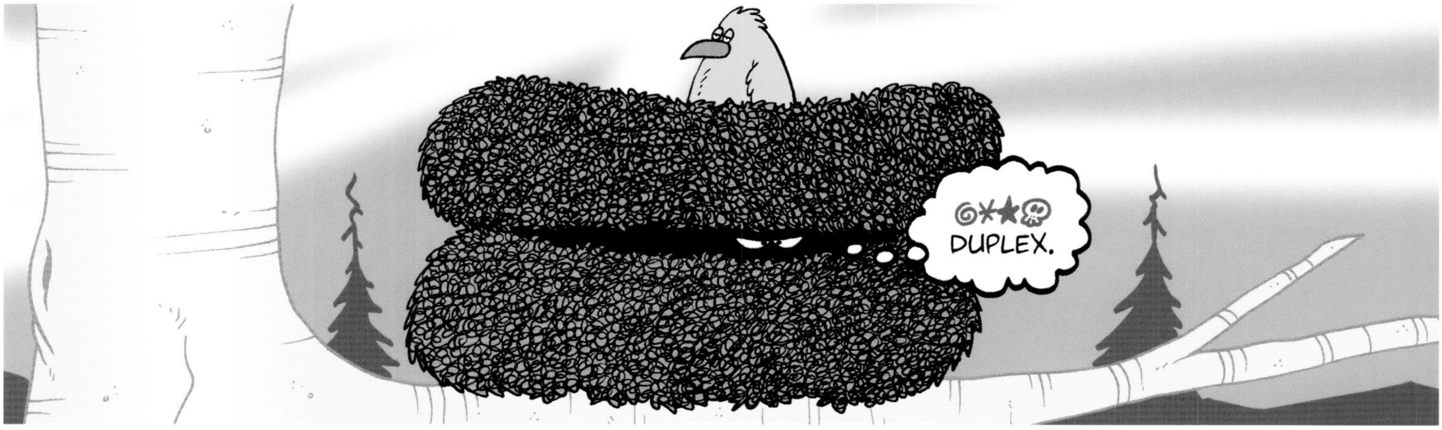
DUPLEX.

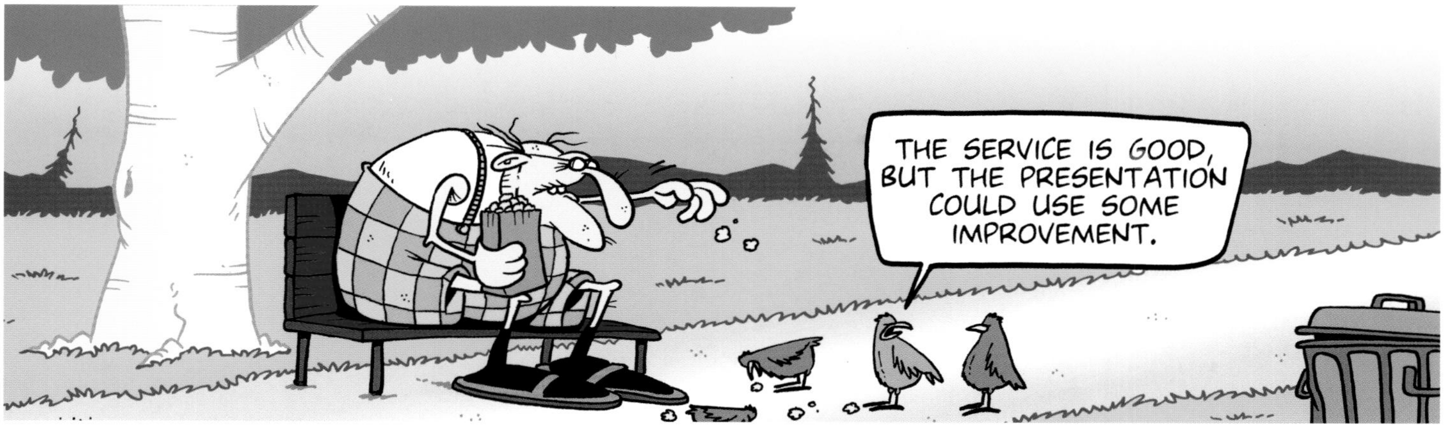
THE SERVICE IS GOOD, BUT THE PRESENTATION COULD USE SOME IMPROVEMENT.

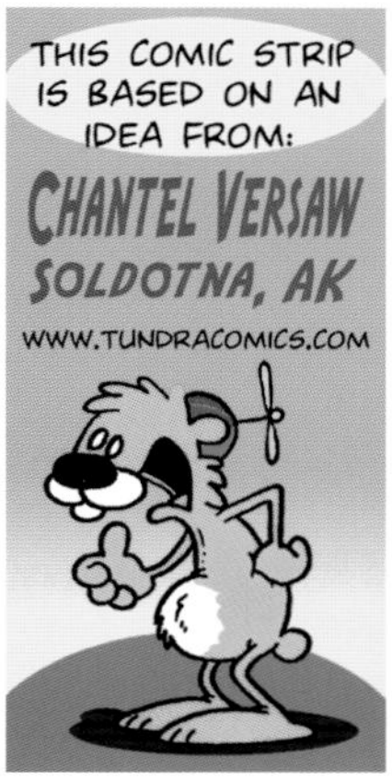
THIS COMIC STRIP IS BASED ON AN IDEA FROM:
CHANTEL VERSAW
SOLDOTNA, AK
WWW.TUNDRACOMICS.COM

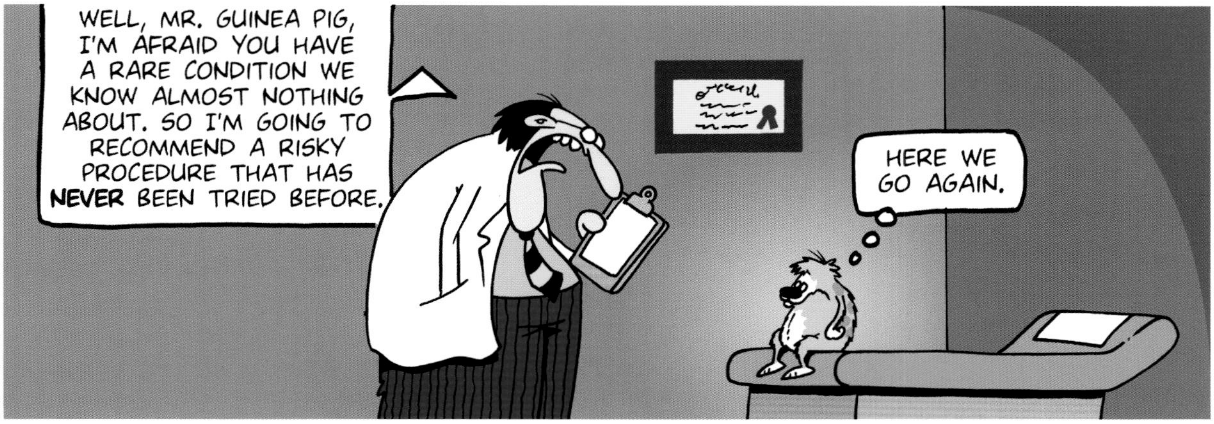
WELL, MR. GUINEA PIG, I'M AFRAID YOU HAVE A RARE CONDITION WE KNOW ALMOST NOTHING ABOUT. SO I'M GOING TO RECOMMEND A RISKY PROCEDURE THAT HAS **NEVER** BEEN TRIED BEFORE.
HERE WE GO AGAIN.

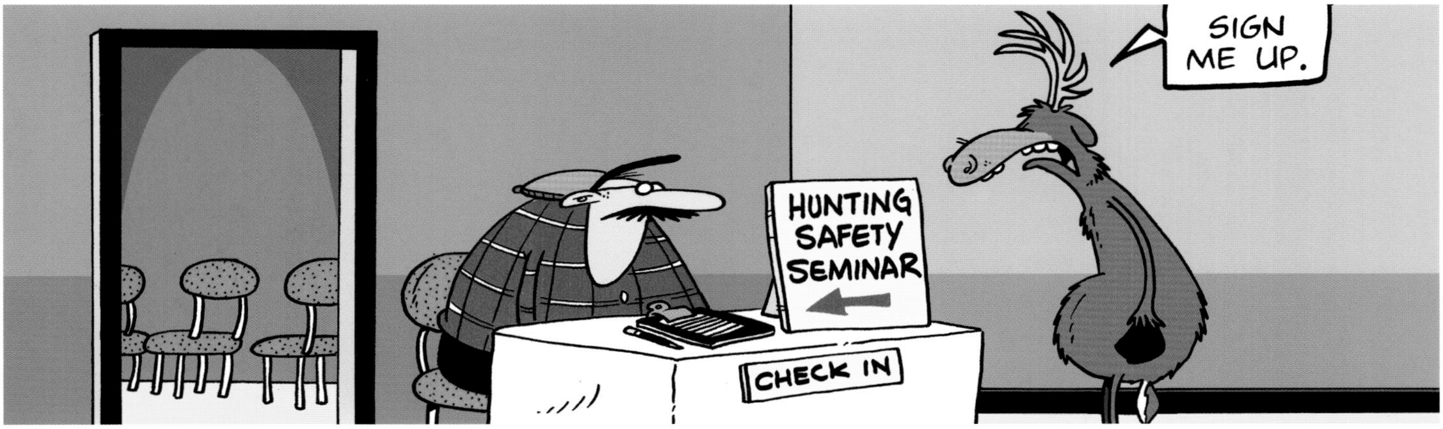
SIGN ME UP.
HUNTING SAFETY SEMINAR
CHECK IN

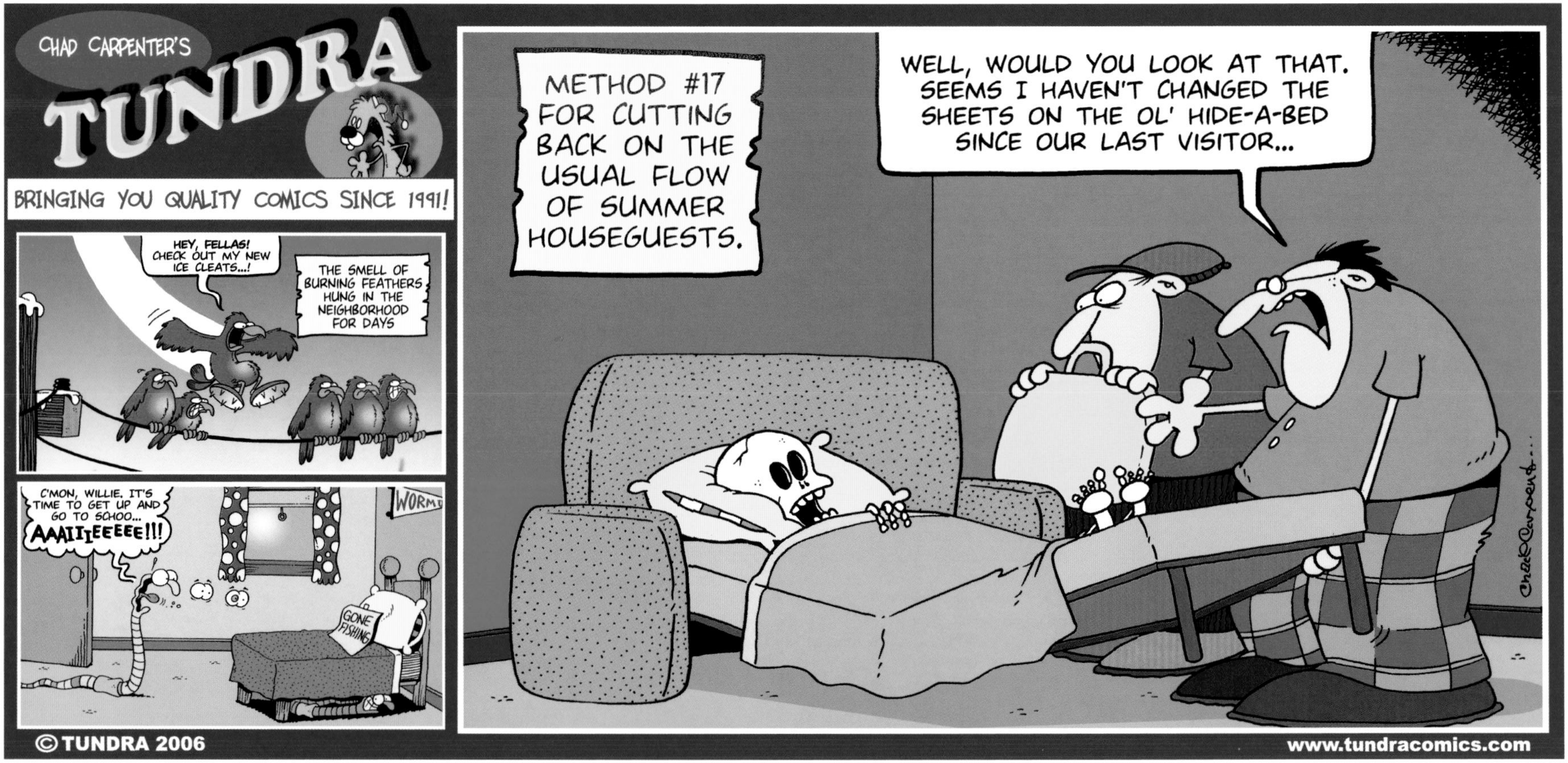
CHAD CARPENTER'S
TUNDRA
BRINGING YOU QUALITY COMICS SINCE 1991!
HEY, FELLAS! CHECK OUT MY NEW ICE CLEATS...!
THE SMELL OF BURNING FEATHERS HUNG IN THE NEIGHBORHOOD FOR DAYS
C'MON, WILLIE. IT'S TIME TO GET UP AND GO TO SCHOO...
AAAIIIEEEEE!!!
GONE FISHING
METHOD #17 FOR CUTTING BACK ON THE USUAL FLOW OF SUMMER HOUSEGUESTS.
WELL, WOULD YOU LOOK AT THAT. SEEMS I HAVEN'T CHANGED THE SHEETS ON THE OL' HIDE-A-BED SINCE OUR LAST VISITOR...
©TUNDRA 2006
www.tundracomics.com

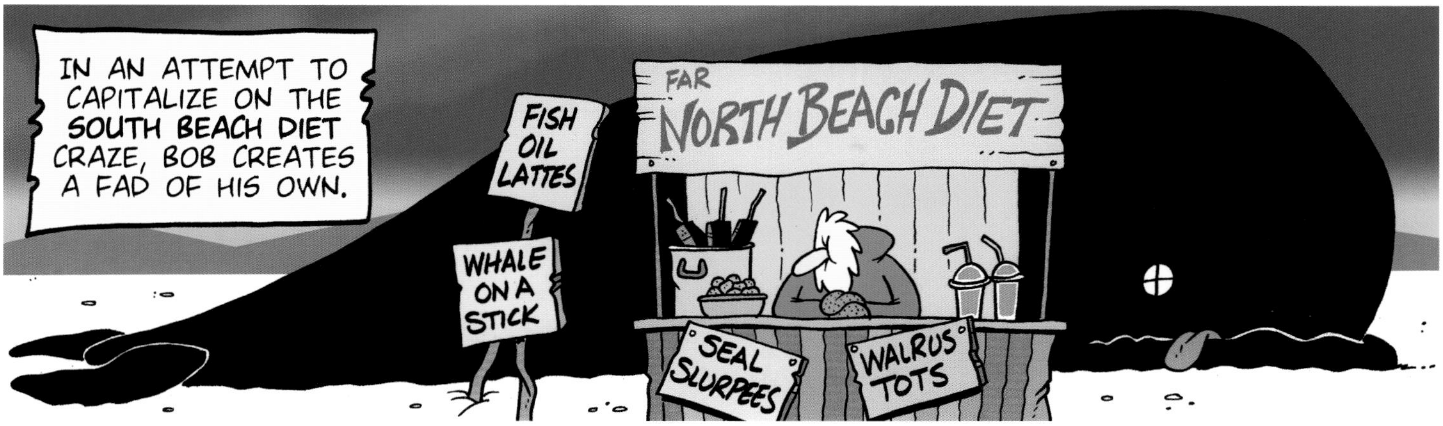
IN AN ATTEMPT TO CAPITALIZE ON THE SOUTH BEACH DIET CRAZE, BOB CREATES A FAD OF HIS OWN.
FAR NORTH BEACH DIET
FISH OIL LATTES
WHALE ON A STICK
SEAL SLURPEES
WALRUS TOTS

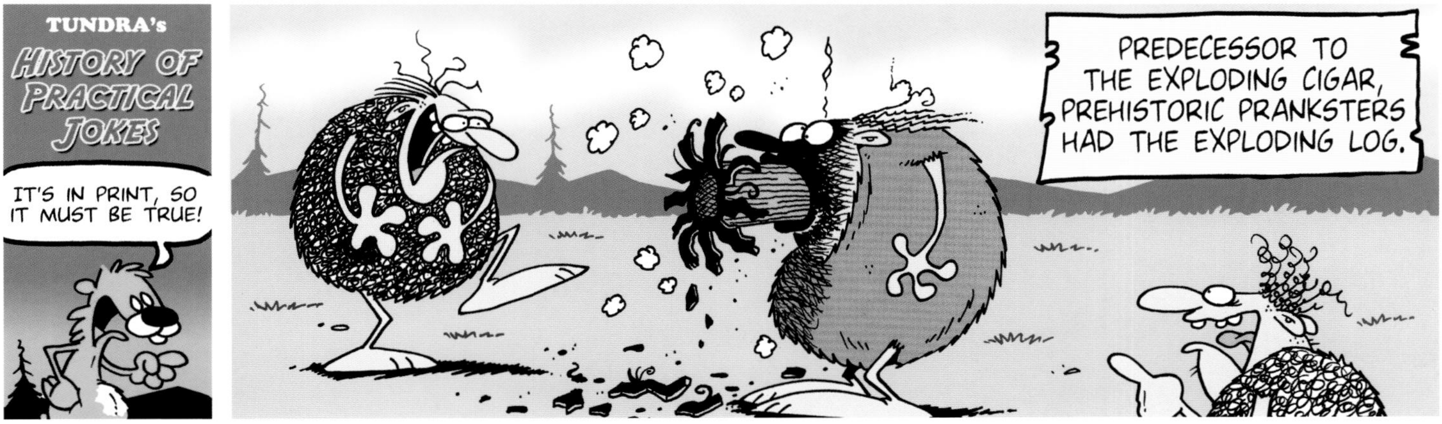
TUNDRA's
HISTORY OF PRACTICAL JOKES
IT'S IN PRINT, SO IT MUST BE TRUE!
PREDECESSOR TO THE EXPLODING CIGAR, PREHISTORIC PRANKSTERS HAD THE EXPLODING LOG.

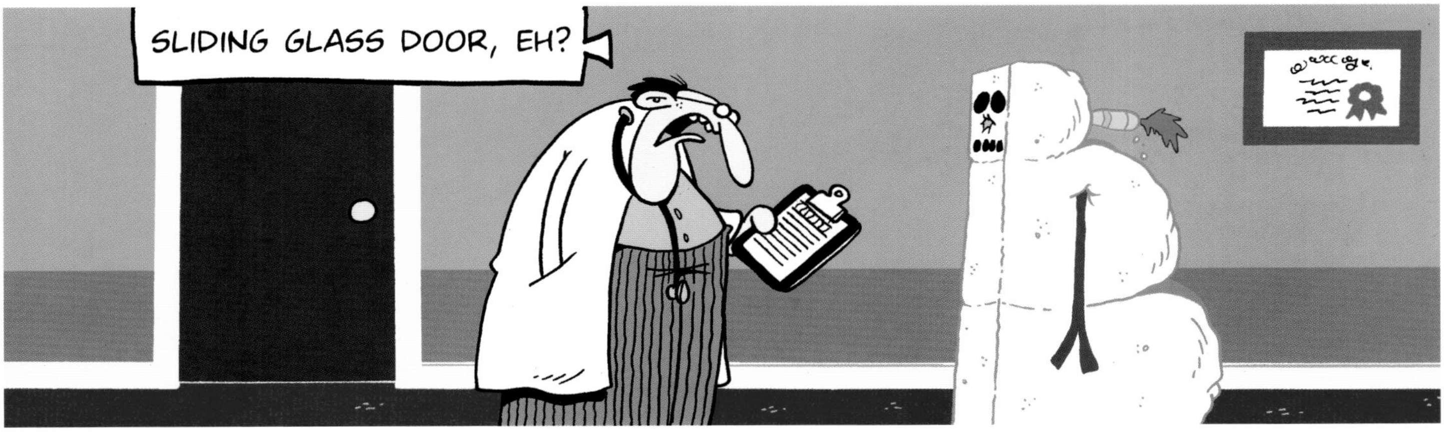
SLIDING GLASS DOOR, EH?

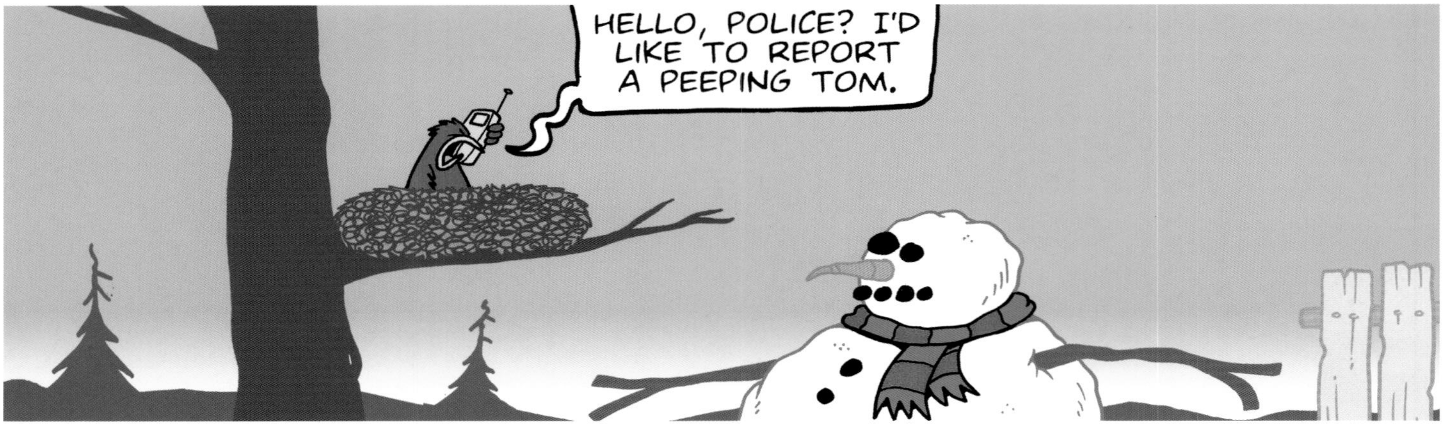
HELLO, POLICE? I'D LIKE TO REPORT A PEEPING TOM.

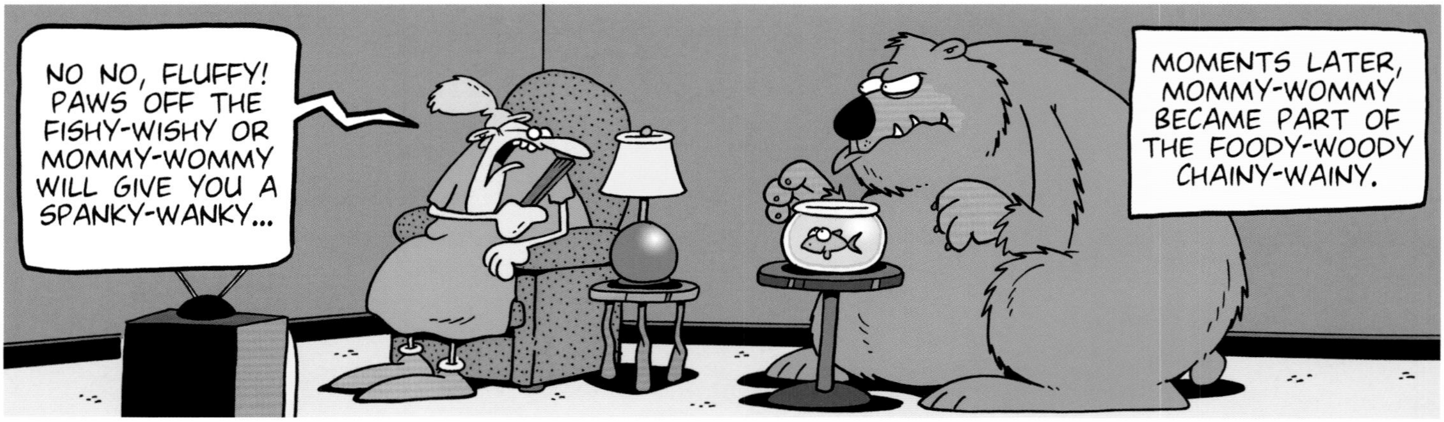
NO NO, FLUFFY! PAWS OFF THE FISHY-WISHY OR MOMMY-WOMMY WILL GIVE YOU A SPANKY-WANKY...
MOMENTS LATER, MOMMY-WOMMY BECAME PART OF THE FOODY-WOODY CHAINY-WAINY.

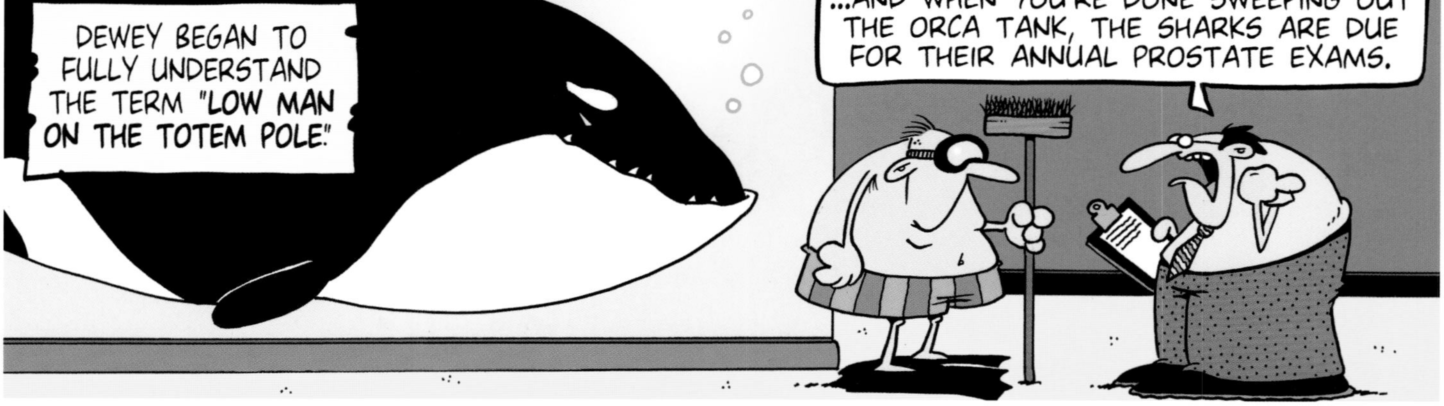
DEWEY BEGAN TO FULLY UNDERSTAND THE TERM "LOW MAN ON THE TOTEM POLE."
...AND WHEN YOU'RE DONE SWEEPING OUT THE ORCA TANK, THE SHARKS ARE DUE FOR THEIR ANNUAL PROSTATE EXAMS.

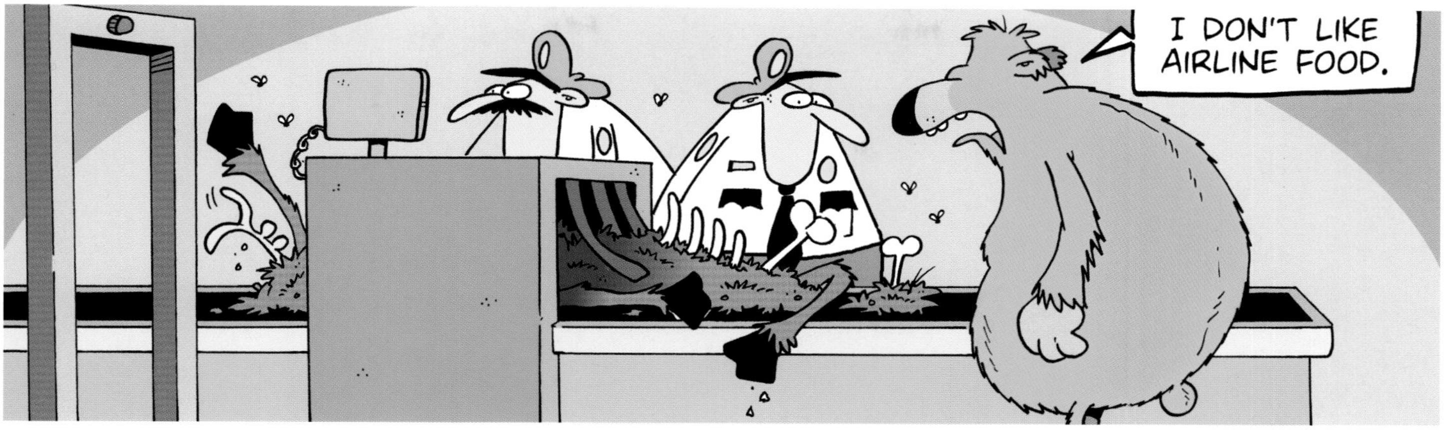
I DON'T LIKE AIRLINE FOOD.

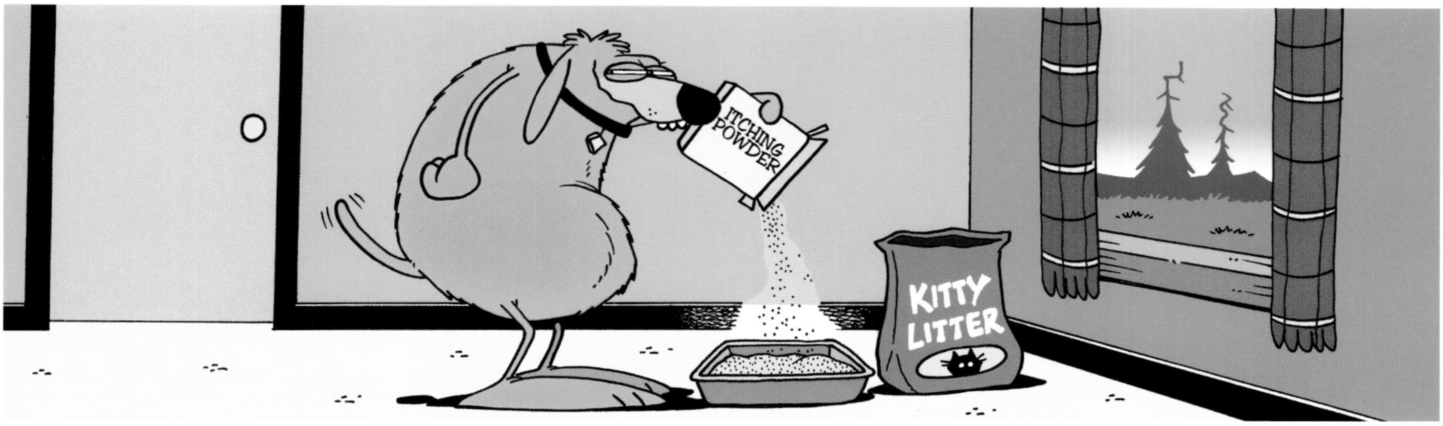
ITCHING POWDER
KITTY LITTER

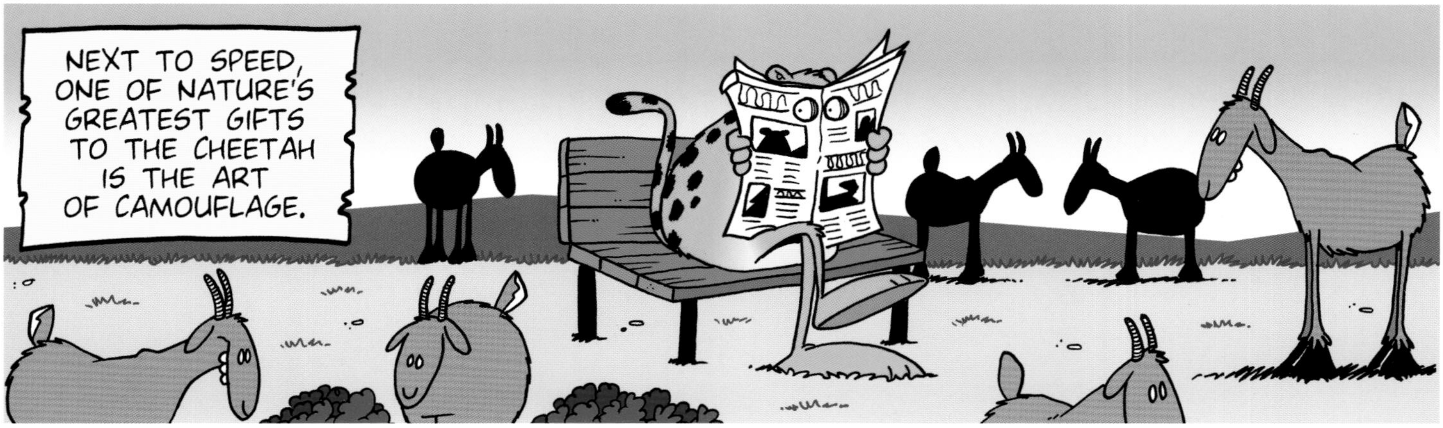
NEXT TO SPEED, ONE OF NATURE'S GREATEST GIFTS TO THE CHEETAH IS THE ART OF CAMOUFLAGE.

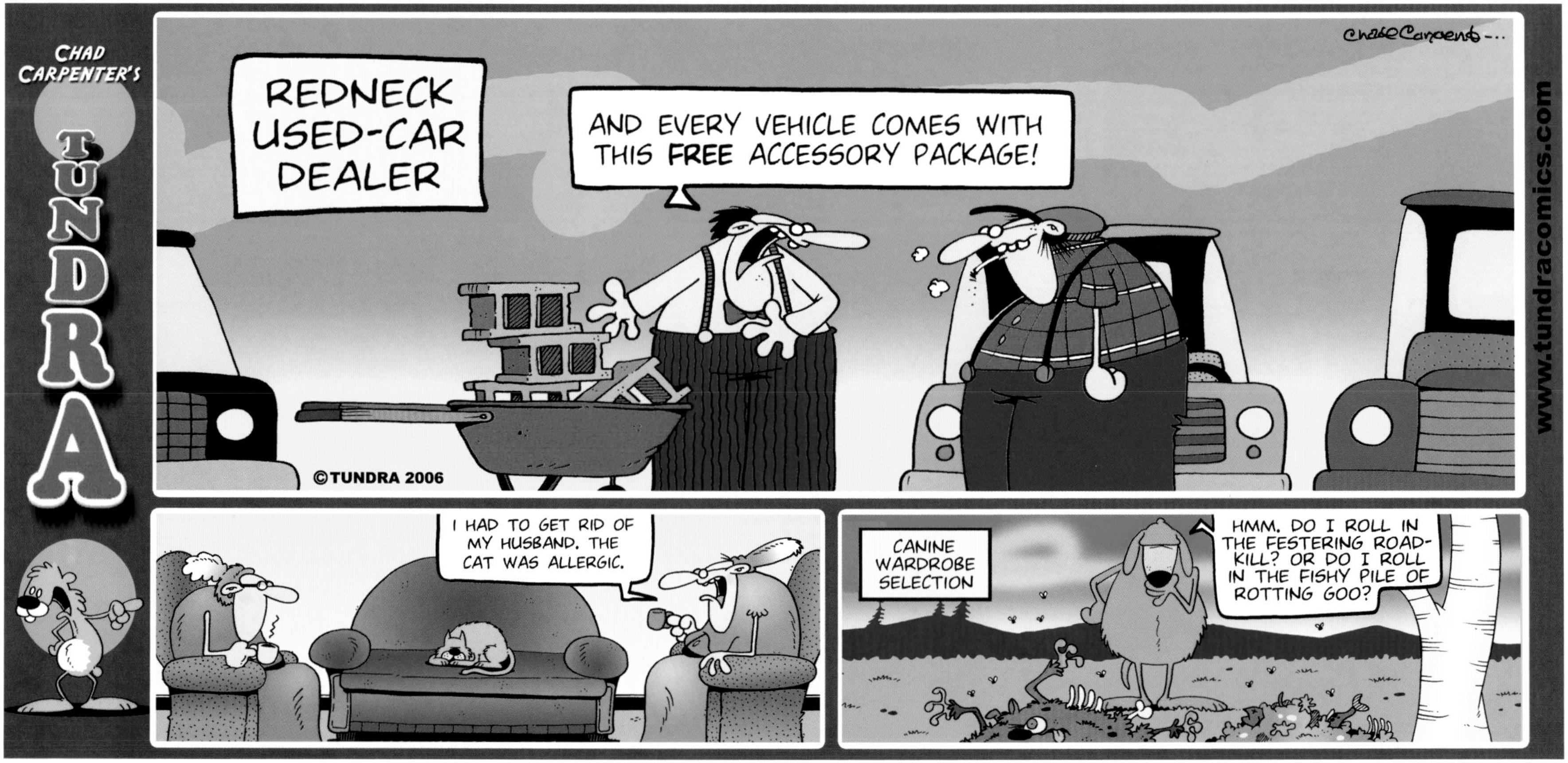
CHAD CARPENTER'S
TUNDRA
REDNECK USED-CAR DEALER
AND EVERY VEHICLE COMES WITH THIS **FREE** ACCESSORY PACKAGE!
©TUNDRA 2006
www.tundracomics.com
I HAD TO GET RID OF MY HUSBAND. THE CAT WAS ALLERGIC.
CANINE WARDROBE SELECTION
HMM. DO I ROLL IN THE FESTERING ROAD-KILL? OR DO I ROLL IN THE FISHY PILE OF ROTTING GOO?

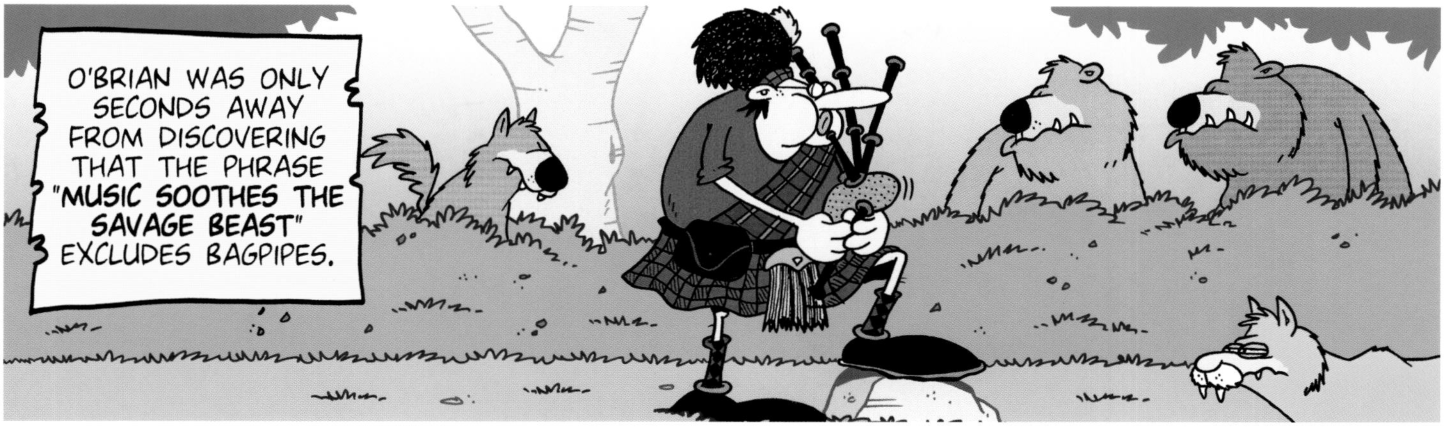
O'BRIAN WAS ONLY SECONDS AWAY FROM DISCOVERING THAT THE PHRASE "MUSIC SOOTHES THE SAVAGE BEAST" EXCLUDES BAGPIPES.

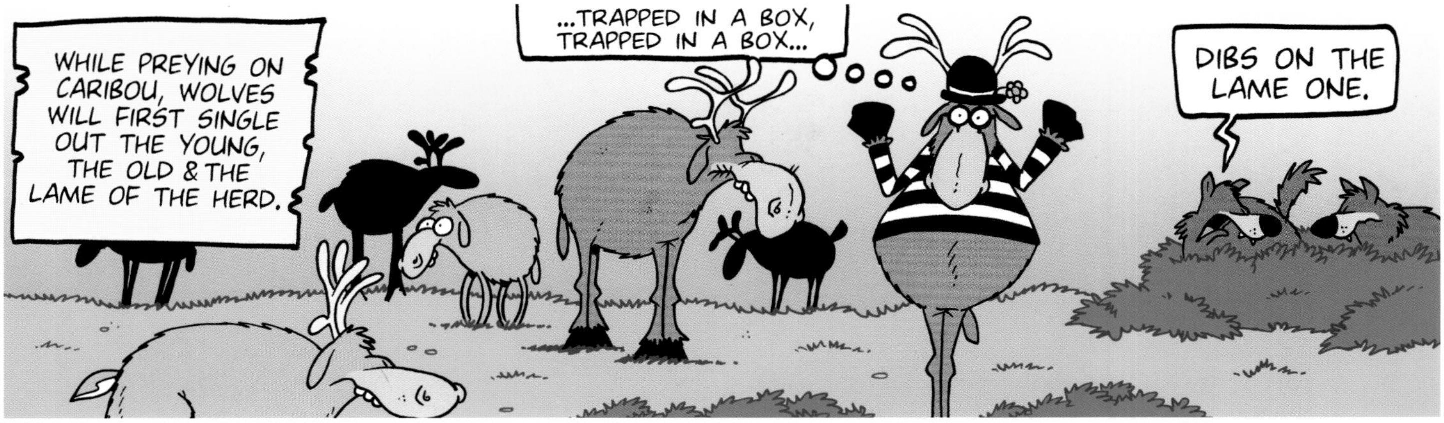
WHILE PREYING ON CARIBOU, WOLVES WILL FIRST SINGLE OUT THE YOUNG, THE OLD & THE LAME OF THE HERD.
...TRAPPED IN A BOX, TRAPPED IN A BOX...
DIBS ON THE LAME ONE.

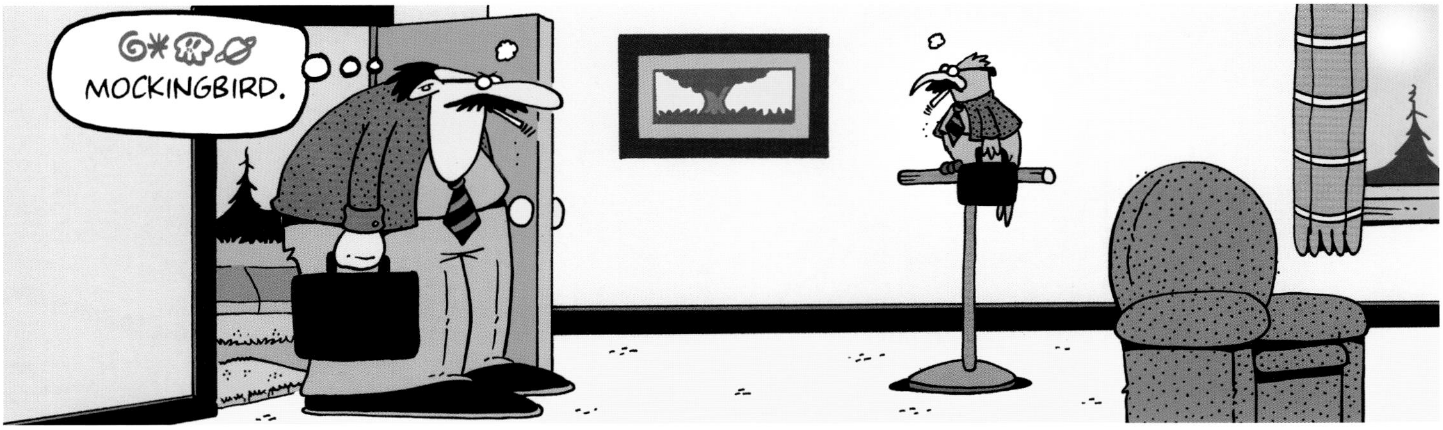
MOCKINGBIRD.

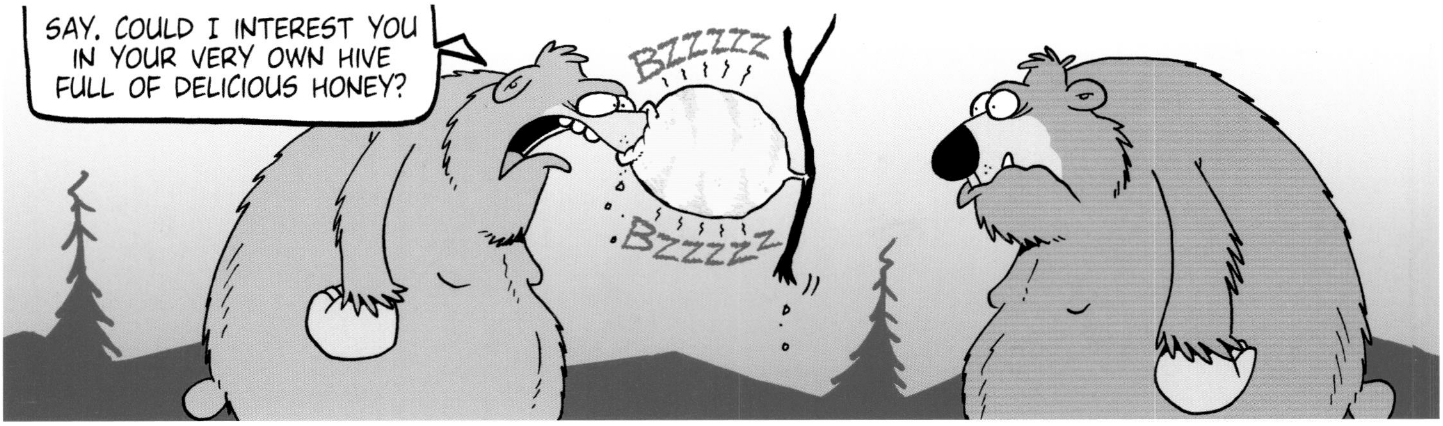
SAY. COULD I INTEREST YOU IN YOUR VERY OWN HIVE FULL OF DELICIOUS HONEY?
BZZZZZ
BZZZZZ

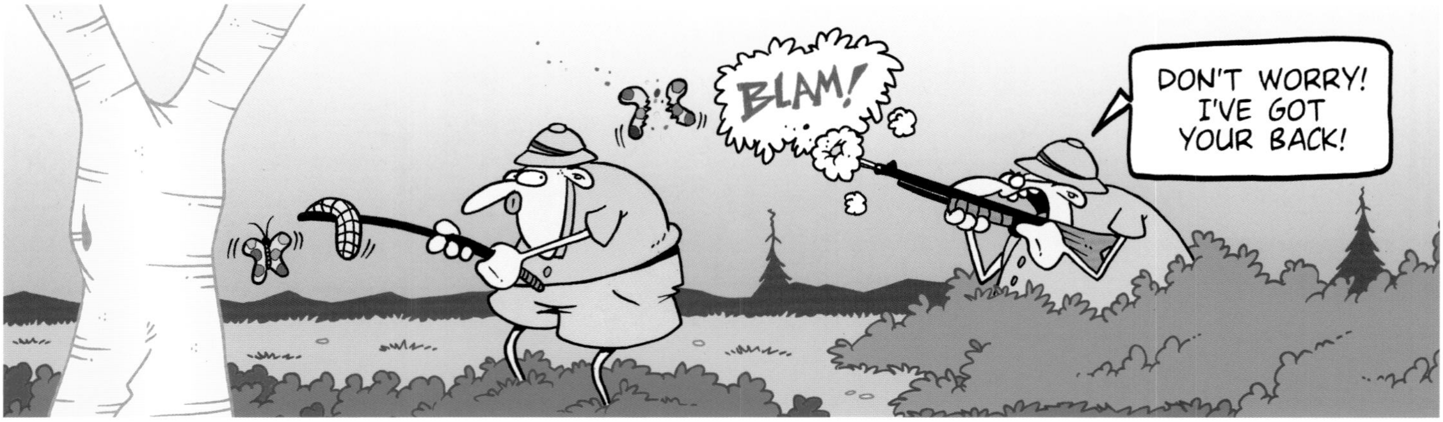
BLAM!
DON'T WORRY! I'VE GOT YOUR BACK!

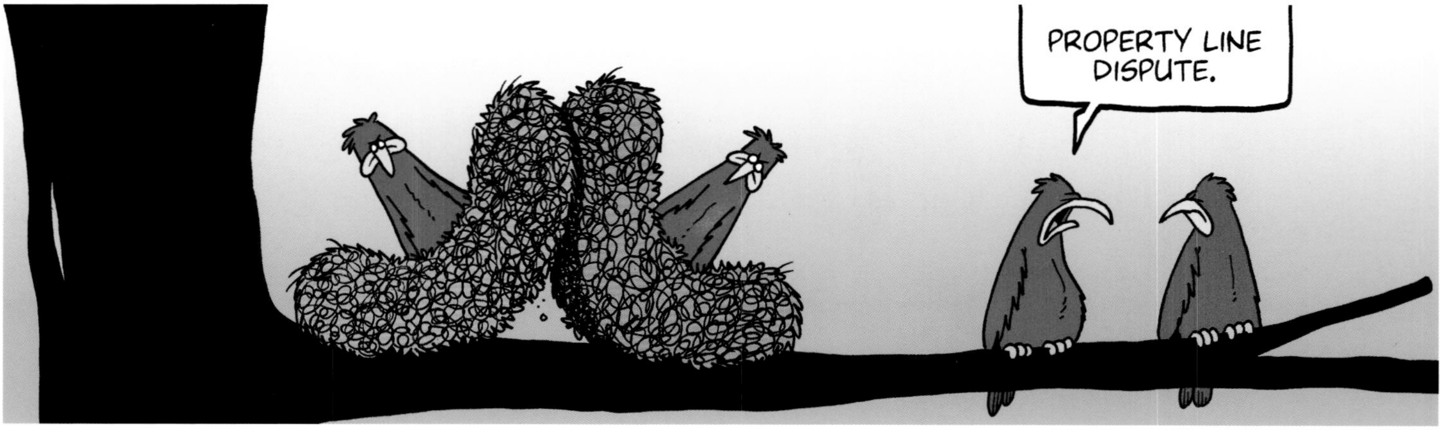
PROPERTY LINE DISPUTE.